Around The Way Girls 3

Also in Stores

Around the way Girls

Around the way Girls 2

Around The Way Girls 3

Alisha Yvonne
Thomas Long
Pat Tucker

URBAN BOOKS

Urban Books LLC
10 Brennan Place
Deer Park, NY 11729

ISBN: 978-0-7394-7100-5
Printed in the United States of America

Alisha Yvonne

Sugar & Candy Cane

Special thanks to:

My mother and father, Rhonda and Charles Brown, for your love and support.

My sister, Donna Smith, for loving me and being a fan.

Maria Delongloria for excellent editorial consultation. Great feedback, Maria! Thanks for all your input and expertise.

My friend and fellow author, Shelia Lipsey, for her editorial assistance with this story. What would I have done without you, Shelia? Thanks for being there!

Lanisha Johnson for her feedback and input on the Cane twins. Thanks for taking an interest in me and my work although some others turned away.

All book clubs and avid readers for your support. You make me shine, and I thank you.

Carl Weber and the entire staff at Urban Books, LLC for believing in me. Thanks for the opportunity to show diversity in my work.

Classy Ladies
1

SMACK!

"Ouch! What the fuck did you hit me for?" Candy asked her twin sister, Sugar, upon the sudden attack.

"Because! The muthafucker you sent to buy my package today just held me up at gunpoint! He hit me up for a kilo of my dope. You knew that muthafucker was shady, didn't you?"

"What? Oh, c'mon! Why were you trying to be Ms. Bad-Ass by doing the sell alone? I told you one day some shit could go down, but you wouldn't listen. Even though you're a hustler, you're still a woman. Men in the game will always push you over because they figure you don't know more than them. Even I know that, and I don't sell drugs." Candy caressed the side of her face because it stung like hell.

"I still don't understand why you set me up with 'im. You knew what he'd do!"

"Yeah, right. Like I'm gonna set up my only sister, my twin sister at that, to be held at gunpoint and possibly get hurt. Now I know we don't get along, but I would never set you up."

"Oh yeah? Then why did that dude press me up against the wall in the hotel room—gun aimed at my head, mind you—telling me how you hate me and how you're fucking my man behind my back? He knew Damon's name and everything! Explain it, if you can," Sugar exclaimed. She stood in Candy's face, heaving with anger.

"I don't know what that dude is talking about. Like I said, we *don't* get along, but I wouldn't exactly call it hate. Hate is such a strong word."

"Well, forget about that part. Tell me right now if you're fucking Damon. And don't you dare lie to me!"

"Hell naw. That nigga ain't my type. That's your piece of shit," Candy said, rolling her eyes.

SMACK!

"Ouch!" Candy grabbed her face again.

"You're fucking lying, you slut," Sugar yelled.

"I ain't lying about shit . . . and I'ma get yo' ass for slapping me like that," Candy stated just before launching at Sugar.

The twenty-eight-year-old identical twins tussled around on the living room floor of Sugar's house like mad women in a wrestling match. They'd always fought, even in high school.

Though to many people the girls' attitudes seemed to be jacked up, the one thing everyone had to give credit for was the fact that the girls were extremely smart. Sugar graduated valedictorian, and Candy was salutatorian of their high school. The twins were members of a prominent family in Nesbit, Mississippi who had a known history for getting their way around town. After high school, they relocated to Memphis with their mother to begin new lives.

Sugar and Candy Cane never even cut their closest friends any slack, and the same treatment went to each other. Today was no different.

"Stop pulling my braids, *bitch*!" Candy yelled.

"Well then, admit the fucking truth, *bitch*!" Sugar yelled back, still gripping a fistful of braids as she held Candy in the headlock.

"I ain't got to admit shit! I didn't do anything. Now let me go!" Candy screamed just before elbowing Sugar in the stomach.

Sugar gasped then was forced to release Candy as she doubled over. Candy straightened out her denim mini-skirt, pulled down her blouse, and then examined the scratch her sister left on her arm.

"I should kill yo' ass just for acting stupid! Look at my arm. All this over some damn he-say-she-say. You need to get your facts straight before the next time you think about coming to me with some bullshit!"

Sugar huffed as she straightened her back to look Candy in the eye. "Candy, if I find out you're lying to me, I'm going to break your fuckin' neck. And you don't need to take that as a threat. I mean what I say as a promise."

Candy turned and walked over to the door. "Bye, trick."

"Bye, whore." Sugar retorted.

Candy opened the door and bumped chest to chest with her mother as she attempted to exit. "Oh, excuse me, Mom. I didn't know you were outside."

Sugar was surprised to see her mother also. She tried to act as normal as possible. "Hi, Mom. What brings you by?"

"I was in the area, so I thought I'd look to see if your car was in the driveway. Why? Do I need a reason to come see you?" their mother said as she brushed past Candy.

"Uhmm, no. It's just that I could've had company over and been in the middle of something—if you know what I mean, Mom," Sugar said, trying to make an awkward situation light.

"Well, first off, let me say that when I noticed your sister's car outside, I figured you couldn't have been too busy, but I discovered I was wrong as I approached the door." The twins looked at each other then back at their mom. "What in the world was all that screaming and yelling I heard?"

Candy intervened. "Nothing, Mother. Right, sis? Tell Mom it was nothing at all."

"Oh yeah. Right, Mom. We're fine. It was nothing at all," Sugar seconded.

"Well, good. Now, the two of you come here and give me some love."

Sugar gritted her teeth, and Candy bit her pride as they all met in the middle of the living room to participate in a group hug. Their mother knew about the love-hate relationship between the twins, but the girls knew that Momma Cane didn't play when it came to sibling rivalry. Besides, she and her new husband were the only means for any type of support if they needed it. Their father had run out on them when the girls were only eight years old. He left them brokenhearted, but with enough financial means to carry them over into adulthood.

Candy was the first to break the hug. "Alrighty now. I've got to be getting out of here."

"Do you have to work at that old freight company tonight, baby?" her mother asked.

"No, ma'am, we don't work on Sunday nights, remember? But I do have to be in class in the morning. This graduate school is kicking my butt."

"Oh, keep it up, baby. The hard work will soon pay off."

"I know, Mom. See ya later. Bye, sis. I'll be giving you a call in a little while," Candy stated, smirking while her mother wasn't looking.

"Yeah. Why don't you do that, sis?" Sugar responded sarcastically.

Candy couldn't wait to get home to call Sugar. As she drove, she thought of some choice words she could say to her.

I shoulda busted her damn head. I don't appreciate her scratching me like a little-ass girl! Not to mention that bitch slapped me not once, but twice. She stepped to me all wrong from the beginning. If she would've came at any other woman like that, she would've gotten the ultimate beat down. She better be glad I decided to leave when I did.

Candy almost broke the door off the hinges after slamming it shut as she entered her townhouse. She went straight to the phone and dialed up Sugar.

"Yeah," Sugar answered.

"Yeah is right. It's me, and I'm still pissed off. Is Mom still there?"

"No."

"Good, because I'm about to tell you the fuck off about this ugly scratch you put on my arm."

"Put some Neosporin on it and get over it, bitch! You know how many scratches and scars you've put on me in the past. The way I see it, I still owe you," Sugar responded.

"You know what?"

"No. Tell me."

"I've got a good mind to tell Momma about yo' dope dealing ass. She thinks you're Ms. Can't-do-nothing-wrong, but I'm about ready to set the record straight."

"Oh yeah? Well, while you're spilling the beans about my business, be sure to mention why you never have a man to bring home . . . because you're a lesbian!"

"I'm not a lesbian. I'm bi-sexual, if you must know."

"I don't need to know all about your dyke tendencies, but if you're going to be spreading shit on me, tell your own bad-girl side of the story too. So, I'm a dope dealer, but you help me get away with the shit from time to time. What's the difference? Are you not a pusher too?"

"Hell naw!" Candy responded. "I only help because I don't want to see you get into trouble. I don't think Mom could handle reading about you in the newspapers or seeing you locked up in jail."

"Then why are you being contradictory with saying you're going to tell her what I do? Try using your head to make some sense with it instead of puttin' it between those stupid-ass chicks' legs you be messin' with. Ugh! I don't know how you can do that anyway."

Candy snickered at her sister's low blow. "Ha! Don't knock it until you try it, and besides, aren't you the one who's worried about me sleeping with a man—*your* man in particular?" Candy left Sugar speechless with her comment.

Candy laughed some more then hung up the phone in Sugar's face. Still fuming from the fight between the two of them, Candy decided to take off her shoes and listen to *The Best of Chuck Brown* CD. She set the player on track number three and started dancing around as soon as the intro to

"Bustin' Loose" began. The song lasted seven minutes and thirty eight seconds, just enough time for Candy to work up a sweat and relieve her frustration.

Candy adjusted the air conditioning thermostat so that she could simmer down before heading to take a hot shower. She sat listening to more Chuck Brown songs and thinking about her plans for the night. After "We Need Some Money" finished playing, Candy headed for the master bath to really unwind.

Candy Cane 2

Warm water jolted between Candy's legs as she lay horny and spread-eagle on the shower floor. The large bathing space was the thing that sold Candy on the townhouse apartment in the first place. Since this wasn't her first time, Candy knew exactly what to do when turning the faucet on full-blast, aiming it toward her midsection for erotic pleasure. Candy let her imagination run wild with a long-time fantasy while enjoying the shower's vibrations. Only moments had passed at the point of reaching her climax. She lay shaking, gasping and moaning. The dense steam in the bathroom did nothing to enable her to catch a decent breath. This time, Candy was weaker than ever before. She felt she could lie there, allowing the water to lick her for eternity.

Candy finally stepped out of the shower, clean-shaven and soaking wet. Her waist-length extended braids dripped down her back, running a seemingly nonstop stream between her butt cheeks. The A/C was on auto when it suddenly caught her by surprise, turning the once sensual water on her skin into what felt like ice. Candy shivered as she struggled with opening the bathroom closet to grab a towel. She quickly walked into the living room patting, squeezing, and massaging her scalp. She couldn't believe she'd forgotten to turn the thermostat to the off position before taking her bath.

Relaxed but chilled, goosebumps layered Candy's body as she walked nude back to the bedroom. Her clothes were already ironed and stretched across the bed for tonight's partying. *I wish Nikki would hurry up and call me*, she thought as she stood looking into the floor-length mirror attached to the wall. Candy was excited about going out with her friend of two years.

They'd met at an All-Star Monster Rap concert on Mud Island after sitting next to each other and then soon discovering they'd each come alone. Though Candy was twenty-six and Nikki was only nineteen years old at the time, they decided to keep in touch after learning more of each other's common musical interests.

Still primping, Candy began to admire her own nakedness as she posed seductively over and over again in front of the mirror. Tilting her head back, allowing her braids to fall off her shoulders, Candy ran her fingertips over her dark, hardened nipples. She often took advantage of caressing herself in the mirror while alone, so this moment was nothing new. Heated by the sight of her recently shaved vagina, Candy used one hand to make gentle sliding strokes between her legs while continuing to press on her tits in circular motions. Moistness now consumed her hand, enticing Candy to pleasure herself more.

Riiing. Candy's concentration was ruined by the sound of the phone.

"Hello," Candy answered.

"What's up? You waiting on me?" Nikki asked on the other end of the phone.

"Aaah, yeah, I am. Where are you?"

"Stop lying! Your ass probably just got out of the shower from masturbating—the shit you do best," Nikki mocked. "Anyway, I'm with some friends. We decided to crash a block party in North Memphis. Wanna come?"

"Bitch, I just did. Ain't that what yo' psychic ass just predicted?" Candy mocked in return.

"What?"

"Never mind. Just tell me what you want me to do. I've been waiting on you to call to say when you'll be ready, but I see you had other things on your agenda. Forget it. I can go out by myself," Candy pouted.

"Unh-uh. Don't you go acting that way. I told you we're going to hang out tonight, and we will. Why don't you drive to where I am, then we'll leave from here?"

"Okay, but where's your car?"

"I left it at home. Does it really matter?" Nikki asked sarcastically.

"I know you ain't getting smart!"

Nikki laughed heartily. "Look, just do what you gotta do then come and get me. That includes getting your ass back into the shower, but only this time, bathe for real."

"A'ight," Candy stated before hanging up in her friend's face.

Candy stared at the phone then realized she'd been careful not to use it with her sticky hand. *Good thing I didn't forget,* she thought, looking at her fingers. She looked across the room, spying herself in the mirror once more, but her sexual urge was lost. There was no sense in continuing. Besides, her friend was now waiting.

Candy quickly showered again. This time, she ran more cold water to help further simmer her mood. Upon drying off, it didn't take long to jump into her drop-waist jeans and off-the-shoulder fitted top. Candy stood before the mirror admiring how the fuchsia and dark denim ensemble highlighted her caramel skin and accentuated her figure. She loved showing off her slim waistline, her abs of steel, and her perfectly rounded ass. The only thing she had trouble deciding was whether to wear heels. She already stood five-nine, but at times, Candy found the attention from wearing stilettos exciting. She loved it when all eyes were on her. After finally making up her mind to throw on her fuchsia-colored, three-inch sandals, Candy knew her looks would knock 'em dead.

After perusing an unfamiliar neighborhood, Candy finally found her destination. There were people standing outside as far as she could see. It was tough finding a parking spot, but she managed. She got out of the car to locate Nikki. As she passed a crowd of men standing in the street, they whistled and called out sexy names to her. It was just the attention Candy expected, but she made no eye contact. She continued to look ahead as she swayed her hips more invitingly for the men.

Nikki was sitting on some steps leading to one of the residences when Candy found her. She spied Candy and beckoned her over. Everyone began to make talk of who Candy could be, pointing and even walking closer to eye her better. Candy made no commotion or sound, only placed her hand on her hip and swung her braids around to the side. Nikki motioned Candy again then stood to greet her.

"It's about time you made it, slut!"

Candy frowned. "Excuse me?"

"You know you need to lighten up. I'm only teasing," Nikki responded.

"Umph! I just got into an argument with somebody who called me a slut. I don't feel like hearing that shit again."

"Umph, my ass. How am I supposed to know when you done pissed people off? I told you I was only teasing, now quit actin' stanka-dank so I can introduce you to some folks."

"I don't wanna meet nobody. Let's go." Candy pouted.

"Okay. In a minute. I don't just wanna up and leave. My friend who I told you about last week brought me here. I don't want him to think I only came to eat and run. As a matter of fact, why don't you have something to eat? There's plenty on the grill," Nikki said, pointing.

Candy huffed then glanced at her cell for the time. "You know we gotta make the liquor store before eleven, right?"

"Yes, and we've got plenty of time. Don't sweat it. Go get a steak or something. You need some food on your stomach before drinking anyway."

"I'm not hungry. I've already eaten." Candy folded her arms.

"Ugh! I can't believe you're being so difficult."

"Okaayyy," Candy stressed. "I'm heading over to the grill. Get all your socializing done before I get back. Once I'm done eating, I'm leaving with or without you."

The two young ladies stared at each other in silence then Candy walked away. She found there was so much food, she couldn't make up her mind what she wanted. Everything smelled great. The cook returned to notice Candy's indecisiveness.

"Hey there. Who are you?" the man asked.

"Candy," she responded in short, frowning at the man as if he had no right to question her.

"Ms. Candy, you have a last name?" the cook inquired.

"Yes."

He shrugged. A raised eyebrow confirmed he was perplexed. "Well, you gonna tell me what it is?"

"Cane. Candy Cane."

"Oh, shit! Are you serious? Your momma named you Candy Cane? Are you one of those stripper type girls?" the man asked, shocked.

"Hell naw! And what you try'na say? That ain't the way my momma raised me, and don't even be insulting my momma like that, 'cause you don't know me or my momma." Candy was agitated. She shook her finger, popped her neck, and rolled her eyes at the man as she spoke.

"I'm sorry. I didn't mean to insult you, Ms. Candy Cane. Really, I wasn't trying to offend you. Strippers are beautiful women, too, you know?" He fought hard to wiggle his way out of the uncomfortable situation that arose. "So, tell me how you fit in on this block."

Candy admired how the man's neatly trimmed mustache framed his lips as he smiled. "I'm not sure if I fit in at all," she answered, looking around.

He laughed. “Well, let me ask the question a different way. Who do you know in this neighborhood?”

“Oh, I don’t know the residents. My friend, Nikki, invited me. I’m not sure who she knows either. I’m just here to pick her up.”

A few people stepped in between the two to get food off the grill. The gentleman carried on a conversation as if he and Candy were all that mattered.

“And . . . to crop a plate before you leave, huh?” The man squinted and shook his head.

Candy jumped from the grill, throwing her hands in the air. “I’m sorry. Nikki said it would be okay.”

“It is. I’m only pulling your leg.” The man held his stomach as he laughed.

Candy wasn’t in the mood for joking, but she managed to mask her impatience. After laughing, the man stood silently with a smile that Candy could read very well. They were on the same page and could answer each other’s thoughts without having said a word.

“So, what’s your name?” Candy asked him.

The man opened his mouth to speak, but was interrupted.

“Jay Hunt, but everybody calls him D-Jay,” a female voice answered from behind them.

Candy turned to notice Nikki. “Oh, so you know him,” she commented, looking back and forth at the two of them.

“Not really, but we’ve made a little small talk before you got here. This is Reno’s friend.”

Candy seemed confused. “Huh? Reno? Who’s Reno?”

“You know, girl. Dude I told you about last week. The one who brought me here to this party.”

“Oh yeah, right. I remember you telling me about homey now.”

D-Jay interrupted the ladies. “So, what y’all ’bout to kick up in Memphis tonight?”

Nikki was about to speak, but Candy cut in first. “Funny you should ask. We haven’t exactly made up our minds yet, have we, Nikki? Got any suggestions?” Candy asked D-Jay.

"Yeah, just one. Let me come along," D-Jay offered.

Nikki gave Candy an evil eye. This wasn't how she'd intended for the night to go. She just met that nigga, Reno, a week before, and she really didn't know his friend, D-Jay, at all.

Candy was just about to respond, but then another male walked up and joined their conversation.

"We having a meeting I don't know anything about?" Reno asked, grabbing Nikki around the waist.

"Oh, hi, Reno. This is my friend, Candy, the one I've been telling you about.

"It's nice to finally meet you. Don't worry, Candy. I got your girl's back. She's straight with me. I can tell she's a down chick and she's all right with me. I'm gon' wife her up real quick-like before some other nigga gets the chance," Reno said confidently.

Nikki looked stunned. She and Reno hadn't spoken of anything serious before. "Is that right? Hmph. I've never heard this before. I don't know you like that, and I see we've got some talking to do."

"I guess we do," Reno replied.

"So, how about it? Y'all gon' let some ballerz kick it with you or what?" D-Jay asked.

Nikki looked at Candy, hoping she'd decline. Candy did just the opposite. "Fo' sho'! In that case, we ain't driving, and we ain't buying shit. We don't eat fast food, and the only thing we're drinking is Moët."

D-Jay spoke out. "Moët? You can have Moët, Cristal and then some if you want to. What you think, we ain't got it like that?"

"I don't know. That's why I'm laying down all the ground rules for the privilege of hanging with my girl and me." Candy's ego was well out of hand.

Nikki's fair skin flushed. She stood raking her nails through her short, bobbed haircut without disturbing its style. Reno stared, admiring Nikki's sex appeal as she stood with her head back and one hand on her hip, exposing her silver belly ring as her crop-top rose above her navel.

Nikki wasn't at all thrilled about hanging out with the two men. It took her several phone conversations to finally feel comfortable going out with Reno alone. She didn't know these niggas, and she'd never been the one to readily hang out with people from around the way.

Nikki wasn't surprised at Candy's actions, though. Candy was just who she was—attention-thriving, money-hungry, and at times self-centered. At least Candy could've consulted with her first before making the final decision to go out with the men, but since they'd all be together, surely nothing could go wrong.

Sugar Cane 3

Sugar was ready to close the deal, but she couldn't afford to seem anxious. The hustlers cutting the deal with her were known for shooting people first and asking questions later. Sugar knew it was imperative to remain calm.

She headed to meet them once again without her boyfriend by her side, a circumstance beyond her control, but five years of pushing cocaine had made her tough, and now was the time to be braver than ever. The head man in charge requested she meet him and his crew in an abandoned downtown building to conduct the transaction. She knew going alone would be like pulling a rookie move, but since she'd dealt with these men before, Sugar decided to concur. She strapped up and went on her way.

After pulling up to the back of the building, she spotted a large door rising slowly to let her in. Sugar paused to think about what she was doing. She looked around and noticed the sun was going down, then suddenly became antsy about her decision to meet the men in a secluded place. She psyched herself into the hustler mode then drove into the old warehouse. Sugar got out of her car to face four husky-looking dealers in unfamiliar territory.

"You got all my shit in that little ol' bag, Sugar?" one of the men asked, pointing at the satchel in Sugar's hand.

"Yeah. Check it," she responded, extending the bag to the man. "What, you don't trust me no more, Gee? I thought we were better than that by now."

"We are, but business is never personal. Besides, you know I like you, but I'm about to break you off with a large sum of my loot. You don't blame me for being too careful, do you?"

"Naw. Check it then, Gee. I won't take it personal."

Gee moved forward to take the bag from Sugar. His three-man clique put their hands on their waists to clutch their glocks simultaneously. Sugar stood firm and mirrored them. She lifted her blouse to expose the gun at her side also.

Gee found that all the dope was present, so he handed Sugar a gym bag filled with money.

"You sure you got all my money in this little ol' bag, Gee?"

"Funny, Sugar. Real funny. Yeah, it's all there. What, you don't trust me no more? I thought we were better than that, Sugar."

"We are, but like you said, this is business. You can't blame me for being too careful, now, can you?"

The two stared at each other for a moment then Gee beckoned for his men to pull the money out of the bag and count it. It took quite a bit of time to count $150,000, but Sugar planted her eyes on the men's hands while they moved to stack and count the money. Gee seemed to be trying to distract Sugar with a conversation.

"So, where's your boy, Damon?" Gee asked.

"He's on his way here now," she lied without looking at him. She kept up with the men as they counted.

"Well, what time was he planning on getting here? My boys are almost finished."

"I imagine he'll be pulling up by the time I finish my sentence."

Gee looked at the closed door and wondered what Sugar was saying.

Once Sugar was satisfied the money was all there, she asked the men to re-bag it. They did, and she grabbed the bag. She became nervous that she wasn't going to make it out of the old warehouse, but she remained calm. She tried to think of a quick move that would get her out.

She walked to her car as fast as she could without showing signs of sweat. Her heart pounded rapidly, but the hustlers would never know it because her rap had been tight, and she knew exactly what to talk about. In fact, she appeared quite confident about her game—something she'd been working on ever since she began dealing cocaine on the streets of Memphis.

After making it to her car, she had a sickening hunch she needed to take precaution. She looked back and noticed Gee and his men standing firm with their guns next to their sides and fingers on the triggers. The looks on their faces were stern and spelled danger. Sugar studied their eyes as she opened the latch on her car door. She knew she wouldn't get out of there if she didn't come up with something quick.

The opportune moment came for her to scheme when her cell began to ring. She answered it, hoping it was Damon.

"Hello," she said.

"I'm gon' need to borrow your Chanel purse tomorrow," Candy said.

Sugar pretended Damon was on the other end. "What, baby? You outside? Okay. Naw, everything's fine. Just let me tell them to let you in, okay?" Sugar closed the flip on her phone then turned to Gee.

"Hey, Gee. Damon's outside. He says he got something for you, so let him in."

Gee looked at his boys then motioned for them to open the large door. One of them stepped forward then used a remote to lift the door. Sugar stood patiently beside her open car door. Once she felt the coast was clear, she jumped into her car, cranked it at the speed of lightning then burned rubber as she sped to beat the closing warehouse door.

When Gee realized she might make it out, he began shooting at her car. His boys followed suit.

Sugar heard her back window shatter after one of the bullets hit it. She damn near pissed on herself. She was still shaken by the earlier stick-up, and getting shot at in the evening was enough to make her quit the game for good . . . but business had to go on.

Sugar owned a $450,000 two-story, five-bedroom, three-car garage home in Collierville, a Memphis suburb, that her salary as a medical technician would not pay for alone. And that didn't even include the $4000-a-month clothing allowance she maintained along with the payments she made on four vehicles, a Lexus truck, a Corvette, one snow-white Mercedes Benz and another silver drop-top Benz belonging to her mother.

Sugar had opened a beauty salon to help cover the tracks of her extra income for Uncle Sam, but the salon was still too new and hadn't recouped enough expenses to carry all of her financial obligations. Business had to go on at all costs.

Sugar was skilled with driving at high speeds, so once in her car, she wasn't worried about the dealers keeping up with her. She was relieved when she finally shook them off her tail. Although she was a long way from the scene, she began to tremble like crazy.

I'm getting soft, she thought. *I can't keep up the game much longer. Having to be in this game alone is starting to spook me.* Thoughts came to mind of the gun at her head earlier, and she wondered where in the hell was her boyfriend. He promised to show for at least one of her transactions, but he was absent from both—something that was starting to happen more frequently.

She calmed down and smiled inside, knowing the mission of making $150,000 in one night was accomplished. After circling the streets, taking the long way home, Sugar pulled into her garage for the night. She entered the house through the kitchen and stopped to fix herself a glass of water. Her nerves were much better, and she replayed the whole trade in her mind. Proud of her accomplishment, she looked into the gym bag one more time.

She went up the winding staircase to her bedroom, where she tossed the bag of money into her walk-in closet. *I'll put it in the safe later,* she thought as she plopped down on her bed to call Damon.

Where the hell is he? I'm sick of his ass being a no-show. I've been trying to call him all damn day.

Damon's cell rang four times before Sugar got the voicemail again. She didn't bother to leave a message this time because she had already left several throughout the day. Sugar threw her hands up in the air then headed for the shower, thinking of Damon, angry as hell.

Candy is right. Damon's sorry ass could at least be there with me when the deal goes down. He introduced me to this way of life, and now he doesn't provide the backup I need.

Sugar reminisced on how shortly after high school she met Damon Williams, Jr., a college sophomore at the University of Memphis and a self-proclaimed roughneck. Damon had a winning smile and the right mack to go along with it. The two hit it off from the very beginning, considering Sugar had always been attracted to bad boys. Damon was perfect because not only did he have the looks and the attitude she liked, but she could also take him home to meet her mother since he was a schoolboy.

The fact that Damon was in college scored him higher than any other dude Sugar had brought home before. All Momma Cane wanted was for her girls to meet someone with dreams and a drive to make them happen. Little did she know that Damon was a wanna-be thug and his main goal was to live the fast life. College was his parents' dream for him, so he obliged.

Once in the shower, Sugar tried thinking pleasant thoughts to cool her temper. Although she was mad, she also knew she would never leave Damon. He was her man, and she got into the relationship playing for keeps from the beginning.

She got out of the shower and threw on a sexy silk negligee. Damon was certain to come over soon because she knew his routine. He'd come in, apologizing and making excuses. She'd cuss him out and threaten to call their relationship quits. He'd begin to beg and offer sweet kisses, then she'd purposely give in so she could fuck the shit out of him before forcing his ass to roll over and go to sleep with no further intimacy. If he even thought about touching her once the sex was over, he'd be thinking wrong. Sugar didn't plat that. If he couldn't touch her afterwards, he'd get the hint he was only a piece of dick to her. Nothing more.

Candy Cane
4

D-Jay and Reno took Nikki and Candy to The Martini Room in the Hickory Hill area of Memphis, for dancing and drinks. This place was ideal for the crew to all get to know each other better. The booth they sat in was in perfect view of one the many plasma screen TVs, and near one of the main bars. They talked and watched the latest videos while chilling.

Though Candy demanded they only drink Moët, what they all ended up with were several glasses of Hypnotiq. Candy could be classy on her own accord, but tonight she felt like a walk on the wild side.

D-Jay had driven the crew in his drop-top BMW. They all decided to ride the streets again just after midnight. D-Jay passed Reno a joint to the back of the car.

Candy turned to watch Nikki's reaction as the men swapped the weed. Though Nikki wasn't pleased, she kept silent. Reefa-smoking niggas were not her speed, and seeing Reno fire a joint to his lips had just cost him a chance to call her his lady.

An old school favorite, "I Love You" by Lenny Williams, began to blare through the radio. Still buzzed by all the alcohol, everyone in the vehicle sang the song as loudly as they could.

Reno's words slurred worse than any of them. He sat with his arm wrapped tightly around Nikki, howling like an animal in pain as he tortured the famous tune.

Without realizing it, D-Jay picked up speed. His passion for the Lenny Williams song made him lose touch with reality, causing his foot to become a little heavy on the gas pedal. Before long, blue lights and a long siren warned them to pull over.

Oh shit! D-Jay kept driving, trying to decide if pulling over would be the best decision.

"D-Jay, pull over," Candy yelled.

"Hell naw. Speed up. We can lose that cop, man!" Reno yelled.

Nikki's nerves had taken over. "No! D-Jay, pull this muthafucker over! I ain't trying to be killed tonight in a high-speed chase. Pull over, damnit!"

Candy seconded Nikki's comments. "She's right, D-Jay. This shit ain't worth dying over. Pull over. I don't see but one cop in the car back there. Let me do all the talking."

D-Jay finally slowed down then pulled into a closed gas station. The lot had very little lighting, which made Nikki nervous.

The policeman took a great deal of time getting out of the car. In the meantime, Nikki's mind began to race a million miles a minute. She envisioned being beaten by the policeman, and that no one would ever find their bodies.

The officer finally spoke through a loudspeaker, asking them to get out of the car, one at a time, very slowly, then to drop to the ground. With his gun drawn in one hand, he used the other hand to pat them all down as they lay flat. Confident no one was armed and after searching the BMW, the officer allowed them each to stand.

"Get up, each of you, and sit in the car until my backup comes," he said.

Candy was pissed about having dusted up her fuchsia top, but against her normal nature, she kept silent about it. She did, however, question what would happen to all of them. "What? Why, sir? What did we do?"

The policeman headed back to his car. "Lady, I'm calling the dogs. I'm no fool. I smell marijuana, and all of you are drunk."

"No, sir—" D-Jay began.

Candy shook her head, shushing him. She ran to catch up. "Officer, please, let me talk with you over here for just a minute."

She walked seductively, swinging her braids while strutting with him back to his car. Once they stopped at the police cruiser, she looked up into his eyes. Candy admired his soft-looking honey-bronzed skin tone and his dark, droopy eyes. He stood about six feet, two inches tall, another sexy aspect aiding her mind to go through with the rash decision she was about to make.

"Is calling the dogs really necessary?" she asked then looked behind her at the flashing lights. "Boy, are these lights bright. Why don't you turn them off?" she said, winking at the officer.

Candy knew from past experience dealing with a policeman that once the flashing lights were on, so was the video recorder and sound system. She was about to proposition the man, but she didn't want to be seen or heard on tape. And if the officer declined, being recorded could definitely be bad.

The policeman looked at Candy strangely then obliged. Once the lights were off, she continued with her routine to seduce him.

"You know . . . and I know . . . and we all know we're high. But, sir, all of that reefer is gone. We were just trying to have a good time, but we're on our way into the house now. I swear. Can't you just let us off on a warning or something?" Candy stood looking down at the officer's crotch, licking her lips as if she spied something luscious.

The officer responded. "Are you trying to tell me something's in it for me?"

"You're a smart man. That's exactly what I'm saying to you." She flicked her tongue seductively over her lips again.

"Get into the car," he said. Candy headed for the backseat. "No, get into the front."

They both got into the police cruiser. For the officer, Candy was undeniably sexy and damn hard to turn away. Oral sex was something he couldn't get at home. His wife had only tried it a couple of times with him, and she despised doing it. The officer wanted to drop his pants, but since his gear made it difficult, he unzipped his trousers then pulled his dick out. As Candy began to lean forward, he gripped a handful of braids then shoved her face into his lap.

As Candy went down on the officer, he dropped his head to watch. He couldn't believe how multi-talented she was when it came to pleasing him orally, especially since she didn't even know him. Relaxing her throat, she took all of his eight inches into her mouth, holding down on it for long periods of time without needing a breath. He couldn't believe how multi-talented she was when it came to pleasing him orally, especially since she didn't even know him. The officer moaned each time she'd lift off the head of his dick, flicking her tongue over it rapidly, then sliding her mouth down slowly, taking all of him again. Her tongue was wet and warm, and her lips felt like satin, a heavenly combination for the officer.

"You like that?" Candy asked.

"Oh G-G-God, *don't* stop!" The officer heaved.

Candy slid her mouth down over his shaft again, cupping her teeth with her lips and slurping in the process. The sounds drove him crazier every time. Thanks to Candy's generosity, the crew was going to be let off the hook for sure.

D-Jay, Nikki, and Reno didn't see Candy get into the police car. They all started to question her whereabouts.

"What's going on back there? It's hard to see. Ain't enough damn lights," Reno fussed.

"Man, I can't see shit either. Where the fuck did they go?" D-Jay pondered.

Nikki gasped. "I can see something. I don't see Candy, though. The policeman is in his car. Seems like he's looking down, writing something, perhaps. Maybe he's gonna let us off with a ticket."

"Damn, I sure hope so." D-Jay was hopeful.

D-Jay's cell began ringing, but he elected not to answer it once he glanced at the caller ID. He was already tense about what the police officer would do, and the last thing he needed was an argument with his lady to further put him over the edge.

I'll deal with her shit later, he thought. *It'll be just my luck that Nikki will say something just as I answer the phone. Another female's voice will cause an argument for sure.*

Candy was truly having a good time. When the officer was at the point of reaching his climax, she licked, slurped harder, and she even swallowed, leaving a lasting impression on the man. He wanted her phone number, but was too weak to talk. She left him speechless.

Candy was satisfied after having given the officer the blowjob of his life! Of course, she got some enjoyment out of it as well. Hearing the man's moans got her panties wet enough to stick to her. The officer wondered what she was doing as she pushed her pants down to her ankles. He speculated Candy would let him hit it since she was getting undressed. He watched Candy untie a bow on each side of her panties then pull them from underneath her bottom. She held them in the officer's face.

"You can have these as a keepsake if you want," she offered.

Still, the man couldn't talk. He just looked at her. She dropped the panties into his lap then pulled her pants back up.

Candy returned to D-Jay's BMW approximately fifteen minutes later as if nothing happened. One thing Candy never had a problem with was pretending. She was relaxed, so putting on an act was super easy.

"What y'all doing?" she asked, plopping down in the car.

Nikki questioned her whereabouts. "Candy, where did you go? What happened to you?"

"Nothing. I was right there." She pointed aimlessly. "Y'all couldn't see me?"

The policeman walked up to the car on the front passenger side, where Candy sat. "Sorry to have disturbed you good folks. This is a fine car. Slow it down a bit and take it on in for the night. Wouldn't wanna hear about you all being involved in any accidents. Now go on and be careful." The policeman handed Candy a business card then walked back to his cruiser.

Candy smiled, turning to yell to the officer. "Thanks, sir. We *will* be careful. We're going straight home." She reached for her purse to place the card inside and to retrieve her lip-gloss.

D-Jay turned back to look at Reno. Reno nodded his head, smiled and shrugged. The men could read each other's minds and all between the lines. Seeing how Candy had to refresh her lip-gloss, they knew exactly what had transpired between her and the officer and why they were off the hook.

Candy paused, glancing around at everyone in the car. "What? I know y'all heard the man say we could go," she stated, smoothing the applicator over her lips.

D-Jay stared at Candy, shaking his head. He cranked the car then drove off.

Nikki had had enough excitement for one night. "Can we go chill at somebody's house or something? We're lucky not to be going to jail after leading that cop on a chase, and not to mention the weed. Either take me home or let's find somewhere to park."

"Nikki, calm your li'l twenty-one-year-old nerves," Candy teased. "We messed up, but thanks to me, we're straight now. And you're welcome. Now let's go party some more."

Nikki felt a little strange about how Candy had just spoken to her. Candy was too relaxed. Nikki wondered if she was the only one who was still rattled by the fact that they almost went to jail. Maybe she should just forget it, too, as it seemed the others had. *It was over now, and everyone was okay.* She thought to herself.

"A'ight. Where to, guys?" Nikki asked.

D-Jay had a thought. "How about to my uncle's place? He asked me to house-sit this weekend. We could all chill over there for a while. I'll take you ladies back home when you're ready."

"That's cool with me. What about you, Nikki?"

"Well, okay. That'll work," she responded.

D-Jay headed for his uncle's house, driving more cautiously as the officer had suggested. Though it was after 1:00 AM, the next several hours promised many more challenges for the newly tagged crew.

Candy Cane
5

The drive was taking far longer than the women expected. Memphis was a pretty big town, but D-Jay had been driving for fifteen minutes, and Nikki wasn't familiar with the scenery.

"Excuse me, but where is your uncle's place?" Nikki asked.

"Hang tight, ladies. We're almost there," D-Jay responded, looking through the rearview mirror.

The ride took another twenty minutes. Nikki slid down in the seat and propped her head against the door, then fell asleep. Reno pulled her closer to him. At first Nikki wasn't sure she should lay on Reno. This was their first real date, and she didn't want to give mixed signals, but she leaned on him anyway.

Candy sat quietly, playing with her braids and daydreaming about calling the officer to do him again. He could come in handy for her at some point later. It would be nice knowing if she ever got into trouble or harm's way, she would have a police friend who could help her out.

The ride proved long for Candy, too. She fell asleep before reaching their destination. She awakened just as D-Jay pulled the car into the parking garage. She called for Nikki to get up.

"Nikki, you still knocked out? D-Jay done took us to the other side of the world, but at least we're finally here," Candy teased.

Nikki was groggy. "Damn. I was having a good nap. Shit, D-Jay, you should've just kept driving."

"Come on here, woman," Reno said, pulling her back over on him. "You must've forgotten who you're with. I can make sure you stay up."

Candy looked over her shoulder, frowning. "Ugh, I don't think so. Unless she's been lying to me, Nikki doesn't know you like that."

Nikki responded. "Naw. You heard me right, Candy. Reno, I like you and all, but me and you ain't getting down like that."

"No. Right now we aren't, but you'll be chasin' a brotha real soon. Wait and see," Reno said confidently.

The two women laughed. "You got jokes, Reno. I like you. You're super funny," Candy stated.

D-Jay was fed up with the small talk. "Okay, so what's up? Y'all gon' chat out here in the garage all night or what? I could just go on in the house and leave you muthafuckers out here to play the dozens or some shit like that. In the meanwhile, I'm going in." D-Jay got out of the car.

Everyone followed suit. They entered the house through the kitchen door, which could be accessed from the garage. It was a beautiful four-bedroom, ranch style home. Candy was shocked someone had actually entrusted such a lovely place to D-Jay.

"If this was my house, I would never leave, let alone leave it in the care of someone else," Candy stated. "I'd call in for groceries and movies and everything. This house is all that and a bag of chips."

D-Jay smiled. "Well, relax. Take your shoes off if you like. I'm gonna head into the back to get some music. Get cozy. I'll be right back."

Reno pulled Nikki to him just as she was about to take a seat. "You scared to sit closer?" he asked.

"Naw, but I do believe it's my free choice to sit next to you or not. I elect not." Nikki moved down a few spaces.

"A'ight. Be like that," Reno said, clearly aggravated.

Candy walked about the living room, admiring the extravagant furniture and delicate artifacts. The couches were huge, soft-plush and of a light beige color. The carpet felt like pillows with every step. Candy was truly impressed.

D-Jay returned with a case of CDs. "They don't call me D-Jay for nothing. I can cook, but my real love is being a deejay. Any requests?"

"Naw, man. Just do what you do," Reno replied.

"Cool. While I'm setting up the music, Nikki, you and ya girl can go behind that bar over there to fix yourselves something to drink."

"Oh, I'd like that, D-Jay. C'mon, Candy."

The four-foot-long bar was stacked with everything, including Moët. Candy walked over to the small refrigerator behind the bar. She opened it to discover a shelf of clear bottles with a blue, neon-like liquid in them. Nikki noticed Candy grinning.

"Yo, what's in there?" Nikki inquired.

"It's the Hypnotiq, baby, baaabay." Candy grinned even harder.

Nikki nodded. "Well, pull the shit out. What you waiting on?"

The ladies poured the alcohol into wine glasses then headed over to the couch. D-Jay selected the music then he and Reno fixed themselves drinks. The group danced, sang, ate snacks, and drank heartily.

Just as Candy's song, "Move Ya Body" by Nina Sky, began to play, she jumped up, spilling half of her glass of Hypnotiq onto the couch. D-Jay was furious.

"Yo, look what the fuck you just did!" he yelled, pointing at the sofa. "Sit yo' drunk ass down somewhere. No, better yet, hold on. I'm gonna get a blanket. We're all gonna sit on the fucking floor!"

D-Jay stormed to the back, angry as hell. Reno looked at both ladies, shaking his head. Candy shrugged.

When D-Jay returned, he continued his fussing fit. "Mutha-fucking niggas don't know how to act around nice shit. I'm starting to think we shoulda went over to that piece of an apartment you think is all that, so you could act ignorant over there," D-Jay stated, looking at Candy.

Everyone was quiet. Candy was too buzzed to be fazed by Jay's comments.

Nikki spoke on her friend's behalf. "Damn, D-Jay, it was an accident. I'll help you clean the spill up. All that shit-talking ain't necessary, though." Nikki headed in the kitchen, looking for something to wipe up the alcohol.

Candy seconded her friend's opinion. "I swear! But it's coo, though. You do have to admire the fact that I have my own place. Who'd you tell me you were staying with? Your moms, right?"

D-Jay snapped. "Mind yo' fuckin' business. And get yo' ass over here on this dark blanket with that food and drink before you waste something else."

Candy chuckled as she walked over to the navy-colored king-sized throw D-Jay had spread across the floor. Reno and D-Jay followed her, and so did Nikki after she managed to make the sofa look spotless once again.

Nikki's mind began to wander. D-Jay had just made mention of Candy's apartment. How would he know where Candy lived? Could she just be drunk and not hearing things clearly? Nikki questioned what she thought she heard.

"D-Jay, did I hear you say you know where Candy lives?" Nikki was perplexed.

D-Jay looked at Candy, whose face had become pale. "Naw. Hell naw. You didn't hear me say that," he replied, sipping his drink. "I was just talking smack. I just met this girl today. How could I know what kind of place she lives in?"

Candy rolled her eyes. "Oh, Nikki, I didn't let that shit D-Jay was talking get to me. I can see he's full of smack-talking."

Nikki still looked confused. "But, Candy, how did you know he lives with his moms?"

Candy laughed. “Dang, girl, what are you so paranoid about? You got a million and one questions.”

“No, I don't. I'm just a little confused, when I thought, for the most part, we all just met a few hours ago,” Nikki replied.

“We did. What, you think D-Jay and me didn't have some small talk when you were asleep on the way over here? And small it was. The nigga bored me to death. I fell asleep soon after you did.” Candy laughed.

D-Jay frowned, threw the last of his drink to the back of his throat then set his glass down. “And you muthafuckers ain't saying jack right now, so enough with the rambling and let's play a game of Spades. I got some cards over there.” D-Jay pointed to the mantel.

“Spades?” Candy asked. “What's up? You can't play a man's game of poker? If I play cards, I want to accomplish something out of it.”

Reno laughed. “Well, put your money where your mouth is. You ain't said nothing but a word. Show me the money and it's on.”

Candy shook her head, frowning as she replied. “Money? Whoa. I ain't said nothing about no money. My shit is too hard to come by. I work part-time for an international freight company, and I'm still in graduate school. I was thinking more along the lines of a little Strip Poker game. What y'all say? If you're scared, just say so. I can respect it.”

Reno seemed to like the thought of the ladies losing all of their clothing. “Hmmm. Interesting, but I ain't ever scared. I'm with it so long as you ladies don't bitch up when it's time to drop those panties,” Reno said with much attitude and confidence.

Nikki was stunned by all she was hearing. Could these grown people actually be considering taking their clothes off in front of each other after meeting for the first time? She became more inquisitive.

“Look, Candy. I don't know these men. You have got to be kidding me.” Nikki was obviously worried.

"Aw hell, Nikki. Now, what do you have to lose? You know I come from a card-playing family. We can team up on these guys. We got this! There's no way we'll lose. Think about how funny it's gonna be to have these fools sitting around in their birthday suits." Candy laughed.

Nikki thought for a second then burst into wild laughter. She was totally amused by the thought of the men losing as the outcome. Candy laughed even harder.

"Okaaay . . . and since seeing a naked man won't be something new for me, why don't we add an extra twist to the game?" Candy added.

"Like what?" Reno asked.

"Like how about the winners get to make the losers do something humiliating, like model in the buff, or dance with each other naked?" She laughed.

D-Jay responded. "You're sick, but since you seem to think you can't lose, I'm gon' take you up on your offer. I'd love to be the source of your amusement.

Nikki spoke up. "Wait a minute. I didn't say I agree to that extra stuff."

"Are you scared?" Candy asked. "Look at me. I'm your girl, and I'm telling you we can't lose."

D-Jay's cell began ringing. He looked at the caller ID then flipped the phone closed. Candy noticed his hesitation to answer the call.

"Do you need to check in before we begin, D-Jay?" she asked.

"What are you talking about?" D-Jay asked.

"Obviously that call is from your girl. We'll give you a few minutes to check in with her before we start the game. Be sure to tell her you'll be calling back real soon, because it's not going to take long for me and Nikki to strip you."

D-Jay replied to her snide remarks. "First of all, I'm a grown-ass man. I don't have to check in with anybody. Second of all, I'm glad you got all of this confidence about winning, but I'm telling you right now, if you bitch up when it's time to cash in the panties, you gon' see my smiling face turn into a frown."

Reno seconded D-Jay. "And trust me, you don't want to see D-Jay with a frown. This muthafucker can be a trip when he's *really* mad."

Nikki looked nervous. Candy attempted to comfort her. "Don't let 'em scare you, girl. They're full of shit. Like I said earlier, we got this!" She raised her hand to give Nikki a high five. Nikki obliged.

Reno and D-Jay looked at each other and smirked.

"Yo, I'll be back in a minute. I need to make sure I'm wearing the right briefs. I can't have y'all laughing at my Spider-man undies," D-Jay said.

"Yeah, yeah, yeah. Nigga, just take care of what you gotta do, and hurry up," Candy replied.

D-Jay went to the back of the house then returned. The guys suggested they all fix another drink before laying down the ground rules of a partnered game of Strip Poker. Most of the regulations were designed by the two teams, but since they were four consenting adults, the competition was about to be on.

Sugar Cane
6

Sugar went downstairs to her bar to fix a dirty martini. She sashayed around in her sexy nightie, wishing her man would call. She took a sip of her drink, then her cell rang. Excited that the caller could be Damon, she skipped to answer the phone. She picked it up without glancing at the identifier first.

"Where are you?" Sugar asked immediately upon picking up the phone.

"I'm at home, but I'd rather be with you, beautiful," a familiar baritone voice responded.

Sugar was surprised. "Oh, Blue? I thought you were someone else."

"Really? Sounds like somebody's man ain't in check. When are you gon' drop that loser and get with a real one like me? You've been making me beg for years, Sugar."

She laughed. "Blue, I got a real one. Besides, I just hung up the phone with him. I thought he was calling right back," Sugar lied. "I never would've guessed you or anyone else would be calling me at this ungodly hour."

"Well, you've got a point there, Sugar. Can't argue with you, because it's one o'clock in the morning. But after I tell you why I'm calling, you might decide to thank me."

"What? What's the deal, Blue?"

Blue was one of Sugar's cocaine suppliers and a partner as well. She'd dealt with him numerous times over the years, and she totally trusted him. She cared about Blue because he remained loyal to her and taught her more about the game than Damon did. Sugar never worried about Blue crossing her out, because he had just as much to lose as she. Sugar knew Blue had an eye for her ever since their introduction five years ago, but her heart was with Damon.

"My sources tell me the law has been watching us, Sugar."

"What?"

"Yeah. You heard me. Forget about me calling your house line anymore. And from now on, I think it would be wise if you carefully choose the words you speak over that line. You feel me?"

"Shit, this is bad news, Blue. I thought you had something good to tell me."

"I said you might decide to thank me for this call, Sugar. Hell, I'm trying to watch your back and look over my shoulder too."

"I know, but just call me human if I don't respond favorably to what you're telling me. I just ain't ready to shut down my business, Blue. How is our trail looking?"

"I hear the detectives are right on us. But I ain't talking about shutting down—at least not yet. We need to make as much money as we can before we get out. We're just gon' have to plan strategically, outsmart the smart."

"I hear ya. I thought we had all loose ends tied. Sounds like somebody in our clique is five-o."

"I don't doubt it, but hey, we're not running scared. You hear me?"

"Yeah. Gotcha. Give me a day or two to get back to you with a plan."

"I knew I could count on you to handle business, Sugar."

"Hey, my life is at stake here, and so is yours. I don't want to see either of us go down if we can help it," she responded softly.

Each held the phone, waiting for the other to say something. Blue was the first to speak. "So, do you suppose he's coming home tonight, Sugar?"

"Huh? Damon? Oh, yeah. I told you I just got off the phone with him. He should be walking through the door in a minute."

"I was gonna offer to come over to keep you company. Something tells me you're lonely."

"Well, your instincts are playing you. My man will be here shortly, so let me get off this phone. Hey, I do owe you a thank you. You could let me fall on my face in this business, but you keep holding me up. Thanks."

"No problem, Sugar. I'll always be here for you. Feel me?"

"Yeah. I feel ya. Rap with me later. A'ight?"

"Peace," Blue responded just before hanging up.

Her cell rang almost instantly upon closing her flip. She wondered what Blue had forgotten to tell her, but this time, she was careful to look at the identifier before answering. She was surprised to see that it was Damon calling.

"What?" Sugar answered.

"What you mean *what*?" he responded.

"Damon, it's late, and your raggedy ass still ain't here. What the fuck are you doing? And why didn't you meet me to do those transactions today? Do you know my ass almost got killed this morning because you weren't there?"

"Hold on, baby. You gon' let me answer, ain't cha?"

"This better be good or else your ass is out for real."

"Baby, you don't mean that. Stop talking negative about us. We gon' be fine. Just let me explain."

"I'm listening," Sugar responded, huffing into the phone.

"Baby, see, you be forgetting shit I tell you. You don't remember that I had told you I needed to do a very important favor for my cousin?"

"Naw. I don't remember you telling me no shit like that, but keep talking."

"See, that's what I'm talking about. You need to start listening to me, baby, 'cause I know I told you that this favor is gon' have us paid."

Sugar's patience was short. "Tell that to a bitch who cares, Damon. You got me fucked up, and you know it. Bring me my key tomorrow."

"Baby, ple—" Damon began.

Sugar hung up the phone before he could finish. She was overwhelmed with emotions. "Whyyyyy?" she yelled out loud. Tears began streaming down her face as she continued raving. "Why did I have to hook up with Damon before meeting Blue?" Sugar folded her arms across her chest and sulked some more. She loved when Blue flirted, letting her know what a good man he'd be to her. She could sense the realness in his language, but she wished his words were Damon's. By the time she'd had enough, Sugar ran upstairs to change.

This nigga thinks I'm stupid, she thought. *I heard music in the background, and I bet I know where he is.* She threw on a pair of jeans, a fitted short-sleeve top, and a pair of thong sandals. Sugar placed her driver's license in her back pocket along with a fifty-dollar bill in case of an emergency. She ran downstairs to the garage and jumped into her 'Vette, ready to ride down on a nigga.

Sugar happened to know where Damon liked to hang out. He didn't remember that she knew how to get to his relative's house, so it never crossed his mind that she could show up unannounced.

Sugar took the half-hour drive with her mind on a mission to set Damon straight. Once she arrived on the street of her destination, she turned off her headlights and cruised to the front of the house.

Sugar couldn't see Damon's car, but she figured it was in the garage. She could see the lights were on, but she couldn't see movement inside. After sitting in the dark for nearly an hour, Sugar got out of her car and stepped up to one of the front windows. Still, she couldn't see anything, but she could hear two male voices. She distinguished one of the voices to be Damon's. Although she couldn't determine what the men were saying, she could hear what seemed like loud, obnoxious but innocent laughter. This was a relief to Sugar. She figured

Damon just needed some time with his boys for a change. He just didn't know how to explain himself to her.

At least he's not cheating, she thought as she headed back to her car.

Sugar calmed down as she drove away, but she was still angry at Damon for not calling or showing up before her drug deals earlier. She almost hated Damon for not being there. She contemplated letting him go. She knew that Blue would always be there for her. Sugar couldn't explain it, but she felt she needed Damon. It almost felt like Voodoo or a curse of some kind. She just couldn't let go, and Damon knew it.

Sugar pulled down her street and noticed a black SUV parked on the curb just a few houses away. She thought of what Blue told her about the law being on their tails. She slowed just before entering her drive to see if she could spot someone sitting in the truck. After discovering there was a person in the SUV, she hurried inside her home and made sure everything was secured.

Sugar ran upstairs to her bedroom to check the loot she'd brought home earlier. She had taken it out of the closet to hide it before she left. She raised the throw-rug then lifted the floorboard. She glanced at the money then secured the floorboard again. Sugar was out of breath by the time she finished. She wanted to call Blue, but decided there was nothing he could do.

Sugar went downstairs to peep out of the living room window. The truck was still there. She suddenly had notions that someone could be trying to rob her. She set the alarm system then headed back upstairs.

Sugar took a deep breath, set her mind into hustler mode, then went to place all of her guns within reach. Instead of putting on the sexy lingerie she'd had on before, she put on a comfortable pair of sweats along with socks and gym shoes. She went through the house, stopping in every room to turn out all the lights. It was 3:30 in the morning, a time when all of Memphis would be asleep, but Sugar was up and ready for war.

Candy Cane 7

One hour after the card game began, Candy and Nikki sat nervously in their underwear while Reno and D-Jay were still wearing pants, socks, belts, and shoes. Nikki knew she had at least two more chances to win, considering she had on her bra and panties. Candy was down to only a bra since she'd given the officer her panties earlier, but she also convinced the guys to let her keep on one shoe in lieu of her panties.

Candy seemed extremely comfortable while Nikki's face was clearly distressed, filled with wrinkles. The men were hyped about how well the game was going. They didn't make the awkward situation any easier for Nikki as they taunted her.

"Yeah, y'all some tricks. Thought you was gon' have us down to our drawers, didn't you?" D-Jay asked. The women were silent. He continued. "I knew y'all didn't want this ass-kickin', but don't get quiet on me now."

The ladies maintained their silence. Once Nikki lost her bra, she began to feel a little solemn. The next hand could exploit all her private parts. Candy smiled lightly as she asked Nikki about her card hand.

"What's up, baby girl? You pretty quiet on me. Need to draw any more cards?" Candy questioned.

"Yeah. Actually, I do. Give me four," she replied, laying the unwanted stack face down.

D-Jay and Reno smirked then fell over with laughter. They could hardly catch their breath as they held their stomachs, beat on the carpet and slapped high-fives while showcasing their amusement. Candy attempted to calm them down.

"Wait a minute, damnit! This shit ain't over. The fat lady still has to sing," Candy mocked.

"Yeah, well, I guess your asses should still be worried considering I can hear her warming up her vocals," Reno said, falling over with more laughter. "C'mon! Show me what you got."

Candy spread her cards in the middle of the blanket. She had a pair of threes, a seven of hearts, a nine of spades, and a two of clubs. She was truly embarrassed by her hand. Nikki looked at her in dismay. The men laughed even more.

"Your turn, Nikki," Reno said. "Spread your cards."

Damn, Nikki thought just before laying her cards face up. She had five cards, but nothing matched. D-Jay and Reno rolled on the floor, laughing, holding their stomachs.

The men spread their cards face up, and each of them had a better hand than the two ladies. Candy tried desperately to hold back her own amusement. She was quite thrilled that she and Nikki would have to lose their clothing to the fellas.

"Sorry, baby girl. I tried," Candy said, shrugging.

Then it all came out. Candy joined the men in their glee. She laughed then took off her bra like it was no thing. Nikki couldn't move. Candy warned her to play fair.

"Nikki, you can't be a sour puss. Fair is fair, and we lost the game fair and square," Candy said.

"You said we wouldn't lose, Candy!"

"I know, and I really tried. I guess these guys are just better than we are at Poker."

D-Jay was fed up. "Enough with the chit-chat. Take off the drawers, sweet thang."

Nikki was disgusted, but she finally obliged. Now it was time for the dare part of the game. Reno made sure the women remembered the rules. "A'ight. Now the fun really begins. Right, D-Jay?" Reno asked.

"No doubt. Let me see. Since these ladies seemed so confident they would win, I hadn't given much thought to the cool part of the game. What you got in mind, Reno?"

"Damn. Umm, I don't know either. But I do know they're turning me on sitting here in these flawless birthday suits," Reno replied.

Nikki looked nervous. D-Jay scratched his head before responding. "You're right about that, dude. I think I have an idea. Wouldn't you like to see these two make out?"

"Damn, man, you mean a live VIP flick? Right here in front of us?"

"Yeah. Yeah. Something like that," D-Jay replied.

Nikki's heart sank into her stomach. "What? We didn't agree to no shit like that. What the hell are you talking about? I don't get down like that!"

D-Jay got up and stood over her. "You will tonight. I didn't make up the rules. Your girl did."

Candy spoke out. "Yeah, but D-Jay, you know I didn't mean for anything like sex to be a part of the humiliation. I wouldn't've asked you two guys to participate in anything that humiliating."

"You wouldn't've? Oh well. I guess we'll never know because me and Reno didn't fucking lose, did we?" Everyone remained quiet. "So, our decision has been made, and we're not going to keep discussing what we want out of the two of you."

"No!" Nikki screamed. "I'm not touching her. You can't make me do it."

D-Jay looked at Reno. "Man, do me a favor and pull out my glock from under that couch over there. I guess she thinks I'm playing with her."

"Naw, man. It doesn't have to come to that. Give Nikki a minute to think. She'll come around," Reno said.

"Fuck it. I'll get the gun myself," D-Jay responded.

Candy jumped. "Wait. Give us a minute to chat. Let us go in your bathroom. I'll talk to Nikki."

Tears began to form in Nikki's eyes. She'd basically figured there was no way out.

The ladies went inside the bathroom to talk. Nikki was so upset she was trembling. Candy tried to make the bad situation seem light. She placed her hands on Nikki's shoulders as she talked to her.

"Nikki, please calm yourself. I know things seem awful, but as soon as we do this, we can get out of here."

"Candy, that's easy for you to say. You're not the heterosexual female being forced to put your mouth between a woman's legs. I can't do this shit, Candy." Nikki's tears fell rapidly.

Candy reached to wipe away Nikki's tears, but Nikki slapped away Candy's hand before she could touch her. Candy watched Nikki sob. She didn't know what to say to put Nikki at ease. Nikki cried all she could then she toughened up. She even surprised Candy when she sucked up her tears.

"It's my fault that I'm in this messed up predicament. I shouldn't have listened to you about going out with these creeps when we really didn't know them," Nikki said as she dried her eyes. "I tell you what. If they don't murder us after we're done, I'm gon' kill yo' ass for being so trifling."

"What? What're you talking about? I can't help the way those guys are acting," Candy responded.

"Yeah, but you can help the way you're acting. If I didn't know any better, I'd say you're enjoying what's going on. You don't seem scared, and you aren't trying to take up for me."

"Nikki, do you want us to get killed? I'm trying to keep those guys calm out there. That's all."

"Whatever, Candy. Let's do this, so we can get the fuck out of here."

Nikki left Candy standing in the bathroom in awe. She walked back out to the living room, eyes tight and red, demanding they all get the game over with. D-Jay called to Candy, but she was already heading back into the room.

"Lay here and spread your legs," D-Jay said to Candy while pointing to the blanket with his gun.

The men stood over the women, drooling as Nikki went on to perform the humiliating sexual act. Nikki wanted to shed more tears, but her anger wouldn't let her. She kept her eyes closed and silently wished the men would call the game quits once they'd seen enough, but their amusement just wouldn't end. The men praised Nikki's performance and taunted her to keep going. Nikki's next hope for relief was that Candy would end the scene by faking an orgasm, but that didn't happen either. Nikki wondered if Candy was intentionally neglecting her feelings.

Candy knew Nikki wasn't enjoying herself, but despite the circumstance, Candy relaxed and relished the moment. Candy reached her climax, and it was even more intense than she'd experienced in the shower.

Nikki was pissed. She got up quickly, realizing she needed to spit. And what better place to spew out filth than on top of Candy? Candy screamed and blocked her face as she saw Nikki's spit coming.

"Heeeyyy! What the fuck—?"

"Shut up, bitch," Nikki screamed back. "Where's my clothes? I want to get the fuck out of here."

D-Jay and Reno no longer protested. They watched the women get dressed then took them back to Candy's car. D-Jay teasingly thanked the women for a good time then sped away. Had it not been a quarter to five in the morning, Nikki wouldn't have gotten in the car with Candy. She hated Candy, and she didn't want to have anything else to do with her. She had come to realize Candy wasn't a good friend after all. She'd known Candy to be freaky, but she never imagined there would come a day when she'd have to be the one to get kinky with Candy. Nikki sat quietly thinking on the ride home.

Just as Candy pulled up to Nikki's apartment, she tried to smooth things over. "Nikki, if it helps any, I'm sorry."

"Whatever, Candy. You never once really tried to stop what was going down. If the situation had been reversed, I would've taken a bullet for you rather than make you go through some grotesque shit."

"Yeah, right. How do I know you would've taken a bullet? So, you're saying I should've just put my life on the line, huh?"

"At least you could've been a little more sympathetic about everything. If I didn't know any better, I would say you were down with what those guys had me do to you."

"I was sympathetic, and I still am," Candy yelled.

"Oh, so that's why you pushed my face further into your stuff as you got ready to cum, huh? 'Cause you were sympathetic, right?" Nikki's anger was intensifying.

The ladies sat out in Candy's car, taking turns blasting each other out. Nikki was so angry she was on the verge of losing total control. Despite anything Nikki said, Candy continued to justify her selfish actions.

"Hey, there was no telling what those guys were gonna do. We weren't sure they were going to drive us away from there alive. I'm sorry I got a bit too caught up in the rapture, but there's no sense in crying about it now. We're both safe, alive, and well. Let's just put it behind us," Candy stated.

"What happened back there was rape as far as I'm concerned, and I think we need to report it."

"Look. You're only twenty-one years old, a very young age still. Shit happens. Keep living and some more shit is gonna happen to you. So you were forced to do something you didn't wanna do . . . you're still living . . . get over it."

POW!

Candy didn't even see Nikki's fist coming. Nikki hit her in the eye so hard, she went into a daze. But Nikki didn't just throw one punch> She kept the blows coming. Candy tried to swing back, but she couldn't see well out of one eye. Nikki grabbed Candy's head and repeatedly banged it into the steering wheel. The car horn blew in sync with the rapid pounding of Candy's head. Nikki's neighbors were awakened, and they began to come outside. One of the neighbors walked up to the passenger side of the car, beating on the glass.

"Nikki, what's going on?" the woman asked, dressed in her nightgown and robe.

Nikki let Candy's head go then got out of the car. She broke down with tears in the woman's arms. Candy got out of the car, staggering, apparently dazed from the blows to her head, screaming obscenities at Nikki. Nikki was still enraged. She let the woman go and met Candy before she could get around the car. The fight was on again.

The crowd of onlookers began to grow. No one would bother to get between the ladies, but the woman who knocked on the glass before tried to yell for the ladies to stop. The fight wasn't over until Nikki and Candy were both wobbling tired. They stood panting, waiting for the other to make a move.

Candy got her ass whupped, and she knew it. She tried to spread some of her embarrassment to Nikki by adding insult to injury. "That bitch is just mad because she ate my pussy and I didn't do her back," she yelled, pointing at Nikki.

The crowd gasped. Candy began to laugh as she headed to her car. Nikki gave Candy an evil eye then headed into her apartment.

This shit ain't over! She can bet her ass on that . . . it ain't over! Nikki thought.

Sugar Cane
8

Sugar lay asleep on top of her covers, fully dressed, with her hand underneath her pillow. Though she was sleeping lightly, she didn't hear the footsteps creeping up her stairs in the dark. Her bedroom door creaked as it slowly opened, making just enough noise to wake her. Sugar jumped up, drawing her gun from under the pillow. She pulled the trigger just as the person turned on the light.

Damon screamed, "Waaiiit! It's me."

Sugar missed Damon's head by a hair. She lowered her gun then plopped her bottom on her bed, panting, trying to catch her breath. Her heart was beating a mile per minute. "Shit, you scared me," she managed to say in a whisper.

Damon held his chest and leaned against the wall as he tried to shake off a feeling of faintness. He was close to hyperventilating. "Dayum, baby. You could've killed me. What's wrong with you?"

"Well, lucky you. I missed, but I probably should've killed you," Sugar stated, rolling her eyes.

Damon walked closer. "Baby, here you go again, talking more nonsense. I didn't mean to scare you, but you never acted like this when I came in late before."

"D-Jay, five o'clock in the morning isn't exactly what I call late. It's more like a new day. Another hour and I would be up making breakfast."

"I know your daily routine, baby. But why were you on the defense like that when I turned on the light?"

"I found out that I'm being followed. Blue thinks the law is after us, but I'm wondering if we're being set up to be robbed and killed."

"Baby, it's probably the law that's watching you. If someone in the game had wanted you dead, nothing would've stood in their way. You would've been dead by now."

"Well, thanks for the comforting speech, D-Jay," Sugar said matter-of-factly.

"That's my baby," Damon said as he went to sit next to Sugar. "You had me worried for a minute. I know you mainly call me Damon when you're pissed off."

"Yeah, but don't get too happy, because I'm still pissed. Where were you? What's going on? You aren't the man you used to be in this relationship. I need more from you."

"Like what, baby? What more do you need from me?"

"I need you to start showing up for my deals. The pushers don't take me seriously when you aren't around."

"Okay, baby. I can do that."

"And I need for you to start puttin' out some of your dough for our products. Lately I've been the only one coming out of pocket to fund our business. I'm tired, D-Jay. You have to be either with me or against me. No more half-steppin', D-Jay. If you gon' be with me, I don't want to hear any more excuses. And if you're against me, I need you to just back the hell on out of my life. I can do bad by myself."

Damon huffed loudly. "I'm with you, baby. That's why I told you I needed to do that favor for my folks. I was thinking of us. I completed the job, and I'll be collecting my cash real soon. It's just a little more than a few Gs, but a lot more than what I've given you lately. Okay?" Damon leaned closer to kiss Sugar.

Sugar pushed Damon's face away with an open palm. "Okay, but move. I don't want you near me."

"C'mon, baby. Don't play like that," Damon said, leaning to kiss Sugar again.

Sugar palmed him again. "I ain't playing, D-Jay. You've been out all night, and I don't know what you've been doing. Get away from me."

"I ain't been doing anything nasty, but I tell you what. I'm gon' take a shower. When I get back, it's on."

"Whatever," Sugar yelled, rolling her eyes.

Damon headed for the shower while Sugar took off her clothes and got into bed. She was exhausted because she'd only had a cat nap before Damon came in.

Damon spent fifteen minutes in the bathroom. Sugar had drifted off to sleep by the time he came out. He got into bed with her and pulled back the covers. Damon decided to wake her in an unexpected, sensual way.

Sugar hissed and moaned as Damon's warm, wet lips covered her vaginal opening while he fucked her with his tongue. She always loved the way Damon would make his tongue go deep into her canal as if he were on a scavenger hunt. Sugar began a slow grind as she placed a lock on Damon's head with her hands.

Damon wasn't going anywhere, even if she had wanted him to. He could never seem to get enough of her juices. He loved that she tasted just as sweet as her name insinuated.

After two orgasms, Sugar's vaginal walls were screaming to be tapped. Sugar pushed Damon's head up from between her legs. Damon knew the routine. It was his turn to enjoy a sexual favor. The favor would come in the form of a ride. Sugar could never imagine putting her mouth on a dick, especially Damon's. Just the thought of going down on a man made her sick, and besides, Damon hadn't proven he was worthy. She knew of his previous infidelity, and for all she knew he could still be cheating—perhaps even with her sister.

Sugar straddled Damon then rode him until he got ready to explode. She got off him, removed his condom, then massaged his dick between her breasts. She didn't stop until her 38-Ds were covered with heaps of cum.

Damon thanked her. "Damn, that felt good. Baby, one day you ought to just taste it," he said.

Sugar stared at him before she responded. "One day, huh? Are you crazy?"

"No, not crazy, just serious. You know I'm human too. You like to have your pussy ate, and I wanna get my dick sucked. What's wrong with me wantin' some oral pleasure?"

"Nothing, but what you want and what you gon' get are two different things. I might think about blowing my warm breath on it next time, but that's as close as I'm gon' get to puttin' my mouth on that thang."

"You put it between your breasts. That's close to your face."

"Nigga, my eyes were closed, and look how long it took me to decide to even try that."

"Well then close your eyes and open your mouth."

"You got me fu—" Sugar started then stopped herself. "You almost made me say something bad to you, D-Jay. Can we not discuss this anymore? I don't like arguing about sex because I give you plenty of it."

"Yeah, just not oral sex. But it's cool, though. We ain't got to talk about it no more. My lips are sealed."

"Good," Sugar added. "Hold on. Before you seal your lips, I need to ask you something."

"What?"

"Dude that robbed me told me that you fucking Candy. Are you?" Sugar's temper began to flare.

Damon was surprised by Sugar's question. "Hell, naw. What muthafucker told you that?"

"Some dude named Bo. I trusted Candy to set up the deal 'cause she said she knew him, but she obviously didn't know him well enough, 'cause he stuck a gun to my head. He also said that you've been screwing Candy."

"Baby, I don't know a Bo. You know how your sister is. She be pissing people off left and right. Sound like dude just wanted to cause bad blood between the two of you. He got me fucked up. I got the better of the Cane twins. I wouldn't have Candy come close to my dick. I can't believe you even sweatin' me on this tip."

"Well, believe it. And if I find out you fucking my sister, I'm gon' do a Loraina Bobbit and cut your dick off."

"Girl, go to bed and shut the hell up."

"No, you shut up."

The two lay quietly in the bed with their backs to each other. Even with the silence, the tension was thick. Damon thought hard about Sugar's earlier comment regarding his role in their relationship. He couldn't sleep until he made sure he understood Sugar.

"Hey, are you asleep?" he asked.

"No. What's up?" she answered dryly.

Damon turned to her. "Could you turn to face me for a minute?" Damon reached to pull Sugar close to him. She turned to listen. "You know I love you, right?"

"Why?"

"That's not how you should answer a question, Sugar."

"Well, I know you *say* you love me. Why?" she asked again with more attitude.

"Because I keep thinking you're trying to break up with me or something. You never pressed so hard on the money issue before. Now that you know I don't have much, you seem to be trying to make me squeeze blood out of a turnip, and we both know that's not gon' happen."

Sugar sat up in bed. "D-Jay, I think you've gotten too comfortable with me doing everything. You and me getting into the game was all your idea. Sure, I had the money to get us started in the beginning, but even when you didn't have anything, you used to give what you had. I saw that you were trying, so I stopped taking from you. Now you don't even try anymore, but you consider what I have in the bank *ours*. On top of that, all you do is ride the BMW I bought you and spend the money I hustle to make."

"I'ma do better from now on, baby. I promise," Damon responded.

"Mm-hmm," Sugar grunted while turning over.

"C'mon, baby. I promise."

"I hear you, D-Jay."

Damon reached over Sugar's hip and put his hand between her legs. He began sliding his index finger up and down her clit. Sugar didn't bother to stop him because his touch was like magic. He made her cream instantly. She throbbed to feel his finger inside of her.

"Give me two fingers, D-Jay," she pleaded.

"Naw, baby, you about to get the real deal."

Sugar reached over and felt his hardness. She was excited that he was ready for her so soon. She reached into the night-stand drawer for another condom. After placing it on Damon, she spread her legs and asked him to get on top. Damon did what was asked of him then took care of business. He thrust into her with long, hard strokes. She gripped his ass and pushed to help him repeatedly bang her. The heat of Sugar's pussy began to warm Damon's dick, causing his erection to become harder than before.

Sugar screamed. "Fuck me, D-Jay. Yes, fuck me!"

Finally she came, and the gripping of her pussy made him cum with her. Damon collapsed on top of Sugar. Neither of them had energy to move, and they were near asleep when Damon's cell began ringing.

"I'll get it," Sugar said, easing from under Damon.

"No! I'll get it," he yelled.

Candy Cane
9

Candy was fire-hot, steaming mad at Nikki. She couldn't believe how childish her now ex-best friend had acted. So what Nikki ate some pussy for the first time? It wasn't like it was the end of the world or anything.

And damn, who died and made Nikki queen anyway? Candy thought as she stood in the mirror, holding ice to her head. She checked out her eye as she held the phone, waiting for the party on the other end to answer. Her eye was a bit red, but there wasn't any swelling or bruises. *That bitch tryna act like she ain't ever fantasized about having sex with a woman before. Puhleeze! All women have thought about it at least once. I just taught her something she never knew about herself—she can eat pussy real good!*

"Hello," the male voice yelled into the phone, breaking Candy's daze.

"D-Jay, what's up?" Candy responded.

"Umm, whatcha need?" he answered rather shortly.

"Man, I just want to thank you. You came through for me, and I won't forget it."

"Well, remember me in the sum of those Gs we discussed for payment."

"I'm gon' take care of that. Don't you worry. After all, you deserve it. I mean, you and Reno had y'all acts together. You even had me scared for a minute." She laughed.

"Hmph. I hear ya. Look, man, I need to get off this phone. I'm at home with my baby, and I gotta show her some love right now."

"Oh, snap! I didn't know you went over to Sugar's house. Turn your volume down on your phone. She can't hear me, can she?"

"Naw. Everything's cool. But I'ma holla atcha later so we can settle my fee."

"A'ight. Holla," Candy said just before hanging up.

Candy began pacing the living room floor. Her mood had turned from upbeat to panic. "Damn," she exclaimed out loud. "Where in the hell am I gon' get five thousand dollars to pay D-Jay?"

Candy had solicited Damon to assist with making her long-time fantasy come true. She had dreamed for years of having Nikki perform oral sex on her, but despite how good she made having sex with a woman sound, Nikki wasn't biting the bait. So, Candy had to do what she had to do—offer Damon some money to help her.

Damon knew Sugar was at the end of her rope with him because he hadn't put money on the table in over a year. When Candy offered him $5000 to scheme on Nikki, he figured, what could it hurt? The whole plan was Candy's idea. Damon asked Reno to play along, and he told him he'd pay him a thousand dollars. Reno didn't hesitate to say yes.

Now Candy was up shit's creek because she never counted on things to happen so quickly. She had set Reno up to meet Nikki a couple of weeks before they all went out, and she figured it would take at least a month before the plot would go down. But when the opportunity to carry out their plans knocked sooner than Candy had expected, she jumped on it, even though she hadn't gotten the money to pay the men.

Candy damn near yanked a couple of braids out of her head as she tugged on them while pacing. She was extremely nervous about how she would get out of paying Damon. A thought came to her about asking Sugar for the dough, but then she realized she didn't have a valid excuse for needing such a large amount of cash. She stopped pacing long enough to get into the shower. She thought about masturbating, but the urge really wasn't there. Her mind was too filled with how to come up with Damon's money.

Candy got out of the shower then got in bed nude. She'd slept nude ever since she was a teenager and had her own room. It took Candy a long time to finally drift off to sleep.

After six hours of sleep, Candy was up and about, making phone calls. The activities of the night before and events of the early morning flashed in her mind. She still couldn't believe she had actually felt Nikki's tongue between her thighs. The experience was nice, but she knew the chance of Nikki performing oral sex on her again would not happen.

She tried several times to call Nikki, but Nikki kept hanging up in her face. Candy finally gave up trying to talk to her. Besides, she had more important things to take care of. Damon's money was one of them.

In thinking about the sequence of events that happened the night before, Candy remembered she had a new friend to call. She ran to her room to retrieve the number of the officer who had pulled them over.

"Hello," a male voice answered.

"Hi. May I speak to Officer Ricky Ware?"

"This is Officer Ware. Who's calling?"

"This is Candy. I met you last night. I was the lady in the drop top BMW you pulled over."

"Oh yeah. Hold on a minute, Candy." The officer clicked over then returned to the line. "Okay. I'm back."

"So, how are you?" Candy asked.

"I'm better now. I was hoping you'd call. I really had a great time last night. You're good at what you do. Do you know that?"

"Sure I do. There's more where that came from."

"Really?" Ricky Ware was getting aroused.

"Yeah. Need I prove it?"

Candy was teasing Ricky because she had begun to think he could be a source for getting the money she needed.

"Prove it how? You wanna hook up again?" he asked.

"Why not? Last night was just a sample of what I can do for you. Let me have a chance at making you scream."

"Well, um, let me see. I'm off duty tonight, but I gotta call home first. I need to make there aren't other plans made for me. If not, I'd love to meet with you this evening."

"Wait. I gotta be real with you. It's gonna cost you. The first time was a freebie because I needed you to let us off the hook for riding around high, smoking weed. I'm good at what I do, but I also think of it as a service. I'll need payment up front tonight."

"What? How much?"

"How much pleasure are you gonna need?"

"Candy, you were awesome. I know I'm gonna want more than last night."

"Oh yeah? You wanna hit it too?"

"That would be nice."

"Then I'll slob on your knob better than before, and I'll ride that dick until you scream for mercy."

"Yeah, but how much?"

"Five hundred dollars."

"Aw, c'mon now. I can go over on Brooks Road and get a trick way cheaper than that."

"First of all, I'm not your average trick. Not only do I have a deep throat, but I have class, too. You'll never have to worry about your business getting out on the streets. And once I find a guy I like, meaning you, you'll be the only man I'll turn sexual favors for."

"Give me a time and a place, and I'm there."

"I thought you had to call home first."

"Naw, fuck that. You've got me curious. Plus, ain't no need in me passing off a chance to get my dick sucked, especially when I can't get that kind of pleasure at home."

"How about if we meet around nine o'clock?"

"Fine. At least that'll give me time to get Mrs. Ware out of my hair."

"Good. I'll get to the hotel early to pay for the room, but you need to reimburse me. I'll call you with the location and room number. See ya tonight," Candy said just before hanging up.

Candy was so excited she started doing the Windmill dance. She knew with her skills she could easily get more than the five hundred she'd told him it was going to cost. After getting her dance on, Candy simmered down and went to find a sexy outfit in her closet for the night.

Candy placed three dresses on the bed. She figured a dress would be better for easy access. She decided on the dress with the tightest fit. It was black, long-sleeved, off the shoulder and made of see-through lace. Candy liked wearing this dress because it was practically transparent, creating the shock factor with most people and awarding her the attention she loved.

After several hours of lying around the house, the time had come for Candy to get ready for her date. She showered, made-up her face, pulled her braids around to one side with a ponytail holder, and put on a black thong that connected in the back with a rhinestone heart. Candy spun around in front of the full-length mirror on the wall, admiring her seductiveness. She wondered if not wearing a bra was a bit much, but then quickly decided her bare nipples looked fabulous through the lace.

Candy put on her black open-toe stilettos that laced around the ankles. Then her doorbell rang. Candy went to look through the peephole and couldn't believe her eyes. She opened the door to let the visitor in.

"D-Jay, what are you doing here? Why did you park your truck in my driveway? Are you trying to get us caught?"

"Relax. Your sister's at homc. I just called her house pretending to have the wrong number."

"Well, I was just on my way out, so you'll have to stop by tomorrow."

"Wait. Where's my money?" Damon asked, eying Candy from head to toe. "And what the hell are you wearing?"

Candy spun around. "You like?"

"Not particularly, but I guess it's you. I can't see Sugar in no shit like that, but you do you."

"Okay. Whatever. Anyway, I haven't been to the bank yet. You should've told me you would be over. I would've had the money."

"You ain't been to the bank yet?"

"What? You think I carry five Gs around with me daily?"

"No. Just when you owe somebody, Candy. I need that money like yesterday. Sugar ain't bullshittin' with me no more, and I promised her I'd help out on her next big deal."

"You got money in the bank, D-Jay. Why don't you just give it to her?"

"I can't do that. I got some other things I gotta take care of. Just pay up, so I can get yo' big sis off my back."

"Well, being only four minutes apart, I don't see how that makes her so much bigger than me, but give me until tomorrow evening. I'll have your dough."

Candy walked closer to D-Jay, slid her arms around his waist then mashed her breasts against his chest. Damon stood quietly, awaiting Candy's next move. She caressed his back then licked his earlobe. Damon closed his eyes and his dick got hard. Then he snapped back into reality. No matter how much Candy looked like Sugar, she was not Sugar. He pushed her off him.

"Have my money tomorrow, lady. No excuses," he said firmly before walking out on Candy.

Candy locked her door then finished preparing for her night. After putting on a pair of silver sequin earrings and grabbing a matching sequined clutch purse, Candy was on her way. She had her mind set to take Officer Ricky Ware on a sexual ride he'd never forget. Candy was indeed a treat for the man, but Officer Ware needed to beware the insatiable Candy Cane.

Nikki
10

Nikki drove to Walgreens to pick up some toothpaste. Her mind was heavy, and she felt she had no one to turn to. She listened to Hot 107.1, hoping to drown her blues with some upbeat music. Once she got to the store, she noticed that the parking lot was full, so she circled the block, waiting for an open space. Despite the radio playing, Nikki couldn't help thinking about how she'd been violated.

For years, Nikki had known what a skank Candy was, but she still figured Candy was a friend because they'd been there for each other during some rough times. Nikki didn't mind that Candy was bisexual and felt Candy respected her for being heterosexual. It wasn't until the night she was forced to perform oral sex on Candy that she realized how dirty Candy could be.

Nikki had thought Candy would help her by faking an orgasm early into the act so it would be over, but things didn't go down that way. Not only did the performance go on for longer than Nikki had hoped, but Candy had grinded and moaned until she had a massive orgasm. Nikki was disgusted then and sickened even more as time passed. She felt she would never get over what happened to her.

Nikki finally spotted a vacant parking space and pulled into it. She sighed as she got out of the car. After shutting the door, Nikki was startled by the sight of Reno standing on the passenger side.

"I need to talk to you," he said.

"You scared the hell out of me," she huffed, covering her heart. "Are you stalking me? What do you want?"

"I just want to talk," he said mildly.

"Are you crazy?"

"No. I'm serious, Nikki. We need to talk."

"If you don't get away from me, I'm going to start screaming for help."

"Please don't. I need to explain the events of the other night."

"Excuse me? You think I don't know what happened?" They were both silent, and then Nikki continued. "I know exactly what happened, and you aren't the one I need to be talking to about it. Instead, I think I'm going to call the police."

"What will you tell them?" Reno looked confused as he shrugged his shoulders.

"Your friend D-Jay had a gun."

"Did he use it?"

"I was threatened."

"Who'll side with you? Candy? Certainly not D-Jay, and I sure as hell won't, because telling the truth will get me jail time too." They stood silent before Reno continued. "Nikki, there's more to know about why that night happened if you let me explain. I want to get it all out in the open. You are a nice woman, and I've come to realize you didn't deserve to be treated that way."

"More to know? What are you talking about, Reno?"

"Nikki, Candy set you up. That whole night was planned. From you and me meeting to the conversation Candy had at the grill with D-Jay when you walked up. From the rigged card game to you having to do your girl—it was all planned."

Nikki looked as if she was about to faint. She leaned on the car for support. "The policeman who pulled us over was in on everything too?" she asked.

"No. That was about the only part of the night that wasn't meant to happen."

Nikki turned her back, using the car to hold herself up as she cried. Reno came around the car to face Nikki. She began yelling.

"You muthafuckers should go to jail! You can't get away with violating people that way. Why? Why did you do it?"

"Candy put up a price, but we haven't gotten paid yet."

"That stankin', tramp-ass bitch! I hate that ho. She's gon' get it one day."

"Why don't we be the ones to get her back?"

"What? We?" Nikki couldn't believe what Reno was saying.

"Yeah. I know just how to hurt her without ever laying hands on her," Reno said, watching Nikki shake her head. "No. Listen. I've got a feeling D-Jay isn't going to pay me my cut of the deal, so—"

"Was it really that much?"

"Not at first, but D-Jay has raised the interest, so now Candy owes him ten grand."

"How do you know all of this? What if she's already paid him?"

"He's been acting really strange lately. I've stood right outside his window and watched him look at my number on the caller ID then close his phone. He finally met with me to talk, but he told me Candy was broke, and he planned to get his money's worth by sleeping with her. He hasn't yet, and I know because I've been watching him like a hawk. Trust me. He doesn't have a dime of that money either. At least not yet."

"You tryna get paid. That's the only reason you decided to come clean, isn't it?"

"No, Nikki. I—"

Nikki opened her car door to leave. "Fuck you, Reno. I don't care if you ever get a penny of your money. You didn't have to help them treat me like that."

Reno gently grabbed Nikki's arm. "Nikki, I'm sorry. Please believe that. I've had a little time to think. Maybe I didn't understand it until after I realized I wasn't going to get paid, but now I know how fucked up it was to play a nasty game on you. I'm thirty years old, and I have a sister your age. When I thought of some niggas treating her the way D-Jay and I helped Candy treat you, it made me sick to my stomach. At this point, the money doesn't matter. I want to straighten up the principle of what happened. Candy and D-Jay are some tricks, and neither of them should be rewarded for being so cruel. Will you help me?"

Nikki stopped crying and shut the car door. "What do you have in mind?"

"Let's talk about it over dinner. My treat, of course. I wanna go somewhere secluded because I don't think we should be seen together if we're going to make this work."

"Whatever, Reno. I don't know why I'm trusting you, but I'll meet you, only if I can pick the place. Just don't think this is a date or something. I have no interest in you other than working together to hit Candy and D-Jay where it'll hurt."

"Cool. I tried calling you. Your number isn't the same, is it?"

"No. Candy kept calling me, so I changed it," she said, pulling out a pen and paper.

Nikki wrote her number down then passed it to Reno.

Later that night, Nikki and Reno met at Ron's Family Affair, across the bridge in West Memphis, Arkansas, to discuss details of their scheme. The restaurant was the only place Nikki could think of where she felt certain no one would know them, and besides, she'd been there before and knew the food was off the damn chain.

"How did you hear about this place? The food is great," Reno stated, shoving a piece of corn bread in his mouth.

"A member of my book club told me about it. I drive across the bridge at least two Saturdays a month to taste the greens," Nikki said.

"So, tell me. Now that you've heard what I think will work, are you confident we can pull off the plan?"

"Oh, no doubt. We can do this. You've just got to make sure to keep your ears open. We can't afford to miss our opportunity, and timing is everything. We've got to do this quickly and on the best day possible," Nikki responded.

"What's your idea of the best day possible?"

"A day when we know Candy and D-Jay will definitely be out of our hair, so we can get into her house, set up surveillance, then leave. Are you sure you can get the camera equipment from your friend?"

"Already done. Everything is in my truck, and I've taken care of the alarm code too," he said.

"How'd you manage that?"

"I found her home number on the Internet then gave her a call, pretending to be a representative of her alarm company. I told her I was phoning to make sure everything was okay because we'd received a message that her alarm was triggered. Of course she denied her system was malfunctioning, but I told her we were going to have to dispatch the police to her address if she couldn't verify her password and number code."

Nikki was shocked. "Oh, gosh. What did she say?"

"She cussed me out, saying she didn't want a fucking fine to pay because of my sorry-ass company's computers. She went on to say she'd had previous false alarms, and that she'd be looking for a new company soon. She gave me her password and number code, I thanked her, then she hung up in my face." Reno laughed.

"Oh, what an idiot." Nikki laughed. "What if they don't meet at Candy's to screw?"

"They will. I know their routine by now. It'll be after dark, and Reno will park a few streets over then walk to Candy's place."

"Reno, I'm still absorbing all you've told me. I believe you're telling the truth, but I can't understand how I've never met Candy's sister before."

"I've never met her either. I just know she's D-Jay's girlfriend, and I'm sure she'll shoot through the roof once she finds out about D-Jay and Candy."

"I'm sure she will," Nikki said, picking up her glass of soda. "I hate to break that woman's heart, but she needs to know what a creep her boyfriend is and what a ho her sister is."

Reno raised his glass for a toast. "Here's to a bitter but sweet revenge."

The two toasted then mentally rehearsed their plans once more. By the Fourth of July, the fireworks would be on in the Cane family home.

Sugar Cane
11

"C'mon . . . c'mon. Pick up the phone, Blue," Sugar said aloud as she listened to ringing on the other end of the line.

Sugar had just closed her living room curtain after peeping out the window at the black SUV parked a few houses away. She could see two men sitting in the truck, peering in her direction. She paced as she continued to redial Blue's number. "C'mon . . . c'mon!" she yelled.

"C'mon what?" Blue finally answered.

"Blue," Sugar said in amazement.

"Sugar," he said, mocking Sugar's tone.

"Blue."

"That's my name, Sugar. Now, do you have something to tell me?"

"The bug is back, Blue."

"Huh? Oh, you mean the folks."

"Yeah, and I've gotta make that run in a couple of nights. This is the biggest one yet. Gotta find some way to shake my folks. You know what I mean? I don't know about you, but I ain't willing to lose out."

"I can add, Sugar. I've been adding since the day we decided to take on the job. And no, I ain't willing to lose either. I've told you already. We gotta be smart. Are you on your cell?"

"Yeah. Why?"

"Let's plan, but let's keep it clean. You never can be too careful. Remember we need to make as much as possible out of this. I say we call up some of our loyal repeats for proposition. If we handle them all in one day, we're set and can be out for good."

"I'm down. Sounds like this is gon' take a huge investment, though."

"That's right. You know it takes green to make green in the world we live in. But don't worry, Sugar. I'm in this with you 50/50, as always."

"Cool. So, tell me about our folks."

"This is gon' sound weird, but since our folks love me, too, I'm gon' have to sit at home while you do the running," Blue said, talking in code about the narcotics unit.

Sugar couldn't believe her ears. "Blue, you sound like a damn fool. What the fu—" she said just before Blue stopped her.

"Hold on, Sugar. Let me finish."

Sugar and Blue discussed the do's and don'ts of their next dope deal for almost three hours. They continued to talk in codes just in case their cells and homes were tapped. By the time the two finished planning, they were fired up and ready to do the damn thang. Sugar couldn't thank Blue enough.

"Blue, it's been pretty cool working with you over the last five years."

"Same here. You were just a baby when you started, but now you're a grown woman. How do you feel about your accomplishments?"

"What? About stacking up a lot of cheese with a phat-ass house and bomb-ass cars to go with it?"

"Yeah. How do you feel?"

"Shitty. You're right about me being a grown woman now, and I've come to realize there's more to life than material things. I allowed a man to lead me into living in the fast lane, but the ride has not only destroyed others, but my sense of who I am is just about worthless too. I've been running scared, looking over my shoulders, praying every day I wake up that it's not the day somebody will decide to take me out. I didn't tell you before, but I came real close to losing my life twice in one day recently. I'm not enjoying life anymore. I've come to realize the game is for those without a conscience. Dreams of my mother looking down on me at my funeral are starting to wear on me, Blue. I'm still young, and I want to do something else with myself."

There was a long pause before Blue spoke. "You sure don't sound like the Sugar I spoke with last night. You said you weren't ready to shut down your business."

Sugar sighed. "I've wanted out many times before now, Blue. I've always felt the day I retire, my bank status should be swole. I gotta have means to keep up my house. I can't let five years of work go down the drain."

"I understand, Sugar. Believe me. You have my word that we're going to give up with style. I'm leaving the States, too."

Another long silence came between them before Sugar spoke. "Why do you have to leave?"

"I don't have to. Just something I've always wanted to do. Besides, it's not like I have a wife and kids, and if I did, I'd take them with me."

"Hmph. I hear you."

Sugar was sad to hear Blue say he'd leave the States, but she didn't know how to let him know her feelings. She wondered if she was being selfish by not wanting Blue to move on with his life. She couldn't be what he needed, because she loved Damon too much.

Blue and Sugar held the phone several minutes, then she heard Damon entering the house through the garage. "Blue, I gotta go. Damon's home."

"Umph. Well, don't forget to run our plans by him, so he can keep his eyes open for us."

"Oh, I'm going to tell him tonight."

"Alright, Sugar. Peace," Blue said before hanging up.

Damon began yelling. "Sugar, where are you? Sugar?"

"What?" Sugar said coldly, standing in the living room with her arms folded.

Damon entered the living room and headed toward her. "Baby, did you know that black truck is still parked down the street? Baby, they playing games with you. They don't want you to get by with shit."

"Shh." Sugar frowned and shook her head. "Be careful, D-Jay."

Damon cupped his mouth, realizing the house could be tapped and he'd already said too much. "Sorry, baby," he said.

"Me and Blue got something in the making."

"Well, what y'all gon' do?"

"Y'all? Don't you mean us, D-Jay? Didn't you just tell me that you were gon' try to do better in this relationship? Since you claim you can't be what you should be financially, the least you could do is watch my back."

"And I will, baby. I will. I'm down with whatever, and I'm gon' go with you."

"Good. Oh, and I'm gon' need that money you made."

"Huh?"

"Don't *huh* me, D-Jay. You know exactly what I'm talking about. Where's the money you got for doing that job for your cousin? The task you ain't told me much about. "

"Oh, um . . . um . . . It was more like a favor for 'im, baby. I haven't gone to get the money yet. Why?"

Damon put his hands around Sugar's waist then pulled her closer to him. He began kissing all over her face and neck, so she'd fall weak as usual. His plan worked and distracted Sugar from questioning him further, but then she pushed him away and looked at him from head to toe.

"What's wrong, baby?"

"Where have you been all day?"

"Damn, baby. Here we go again. Whatchu mean?"

"Damon D-Jay Williams, don't you play me stupid."

"I'm not, baby. I'm just saying I don't know why you questioning me like you think I've been up to something."

Sugar palmed Damon's forehead, almost knocking him into the wall. Damon caught his balance then held his head, trying to shake off a daze. Sugar was livid.

"I'm sick of you treating me like I'm some dumb chicken head you met on the street. I'm yo' woman. A good woman at that. I've put up with your shit for too long, and continue to take care of yo' ass. The least you could do is not come up in here late at night, smelling like some cheap-ass perfume."

Damon continued to cup his forehead. "That's not—" he started.

"Shut the fuck up," Sugar yelled as she walked closer to him, jabbing her finger into his chest. "Before you start trying to fuck up my mind with lies, just remember you have never known me to wear cheap perfume. So, I ain't smelling myself, and that's not an old scent left in your shirt from a hug I gave you long ago."

Damon turned red with anger. He grabbed Sugar's hand just before she poked his chest again then began speaking through clenched teeth. "Hold on, damn it. If you had let me finish, you would've learned I ain't been with nobody but my momma. She hugged me before I left her house."

Sugar snatched her hand from Damon. "So, you telling me you been at yo' momma's all evening?"

"Yeah. What? You wanna call her to ask her?"

Sugar stared at Damon, skeptical he was telling the truth, but she didn't want to phone his mother with questions making her sound as if she was keeping tabs on him. She stared at Damon until she couldn't stand to look at him anymore. "Get the fuck out of my face, Damon."

"Oh, now I'm Damon again. So, you still mad, huh?" he asked, opening his cell. "Here. Let me dial the number for you. You can ask Ma for yourself."

Sugar reached to close Damon's phone, knocking it out of his hand in the process. It split, sliding in two directions. He picked up the pieces then attempted to put it back together, but Sugar intercepted, knocking the phone out of his hand once again.

"Goddamnit, girl. Would you stop? You gon' help me tear this muthafucker up. Hell, I done dropped it enough already. You gon' be buying me another phone if I can't get it to work," Damon said as he snapped the battery back on.

"Nigga, did you forget I bought that one? Just like your truck, and your clothes, and your jewelry, and your bank account . . . I'm the reason your money is green."

"You know what?" Damon asked, pointing at Sugar. "You actin' real brand new right now. I don't know what's gotten into you, but I'm gon' walk away and let you slide this time."

Damon headed up the stairs. Sugar watched him in disgust. She wanted to ask him to leave, but her heart wouldn't let her. *That man has been bought and paid for over the years,* Sugar thought, shaking her head. *There's no way in hell I'm gon' let some other woman have him and enjoy the luxuries I've afforded him.* Sugar felt like crying, but she felt anger more than anything, so she couldn't seem to drop a tear.

Damon had disappeared from her eyesight, so she turned to peep out the window. The black truck was still sitting several houses down the street. More anger set in. Sugar hated being watched so closely. She had a mind to go face the men in the truck, but she kept her cool then headed upstairs to let Damon in on the plans she and Blue made earlier. Once she made it to the top step, she could hear Damon talking softly on his phone.

"You set me up, didn't you?" he said almost in a whisper. "I don't trust you for shit. You're always doing some sneaky, underhanded bullshit." There was a long pause then he continued. "Yeah, and now this woman is trippin' out on me. The whole scene is fucked up over here."

Sugar stepped into the room with Damon. She ogled him, making him uneasy to remain on the phone. He quickly changed his tone. "Yo, let me holla atcha later, man. My baby done came upstairs, ready for bed. You know how that is, right? A'ight. Peace," he said then closed the flip.

"Who was that?" Sugar asked.

"Um . . . um . . . what's-his-name, baby. We were talking business," Damon responded.

"What's-his-name, huh? When did he call? I didn't hear your cell ring."

"He didn't. I called him. I told you I needed to discuss some business with him."

"Well, tell What's-his-name that from now on when you're at my home, business is over."

Damon sucked his teeth and shook his head. "A'ight, baby. I'm tired of fightin'. Can we go to bed now?"

"Get yo' ass in the tub before getting into my bed," Sugar said, rolling her eyes.

Damon was agitated. "See . . . see . . . okay. Fine. Whatever makes you happy, baby. I'm not gon' argue," he said, annoyed that Sugar was insinuating he'd been messing around.

Damon undressed then got into the shower. Sugar waited until she'd heard the water running for five minutes then cracked the bathroom door to peep in. Damon was indeed in the shower. Sugar carefully closed the door then tipped over to the bed where Damon had placed his phone. She picked it up then hit the menu button. She found an option to scroll down to view the outgoing calls. Before she was finished, she heard Damon turn off the water. Determined, Sugar pressed the next button. She got a message that read: CALL LIST IS EMPTY. Damon had managed to erase the call history before getting into the shower. Sugar was boiling.

"Shit!" she yelled.

Sugar began pounding the phone on the bed. After finishing her tantrum, she looked up to notice Damon standing with a towel around his waist, staring at her as if he was confused.

"What the *fuck* are you looking at?" Sugar yelled.

She brushed past him, went into the bathroom, and slammed the door. Damon smirked as he went over to retrieve his phone.

"I *always* cover my tracks. She oughta know that by now," he said, laughing softly. "She'll learn," he said, nodding, looking at his cell. "Yep. She'll learn, and I'm just the one to teach her."

Candy Cane
12

Candy opened the door to her hotel room and stared into the eager eyes of Officer Ricky Ware. She recognized him immediately, although he was minus his uniform. He was just as sexy as she'd remembered the night before. Candy was ready to sop him up in one gulp as he stood staring at her.

"Wow. You look wonderful," Ricky said.

"Oh yeah. I kinda felt you'd think so. Come in," Candy responded, beckoning him.

Ricky entered the room, never taking his eyes off Candy. Flashes of what she'd done to him the night before came to mind. His dick got harder than ever before, causing him to want to rip Candy's garments to shreds in order to get down to business. Just looking at him, she could tell she had his mind, and she was ready to have some fun with him.

"I have a couple of bottles of Merlot, or shall we call for some drinks from the bar?"

"No. Merlot is fine. I'm amazed that you'd know what I like to drink," he responded, heading to sit on the bed.

"I've been told I know how to call 'em exactly like I see 'em. I knew what you needed last night, didn't I?"

"Yes," he said, nodding. "You sure did. You hit the nail right on the head, Ms.—Um . . . What did you say your name is again?"

"How about I refresh your memory?" Candy responded, walking over to him, circling her tongue around her lips.

Candy stood over him and began kissing his forehead with slow, short pecks. She left a wet trace down his nose as she guided her tongue to his mouth. She snaked her tongue in his mouth long and hard then pulled away slowly to drop to her knees. Ricky was excited. He damn near came before she ever placed her hand on his muscle.

Ricky sat helpless, like an infant, panting as Candy pulled down his pants. She took his dick out of his briefs then massaged it tenderly. Ricky heaved and moaned as he placed his hands on Candy's head to guide her downtown. She flicked her tongue all around his shaft then stood and walked away. Ricky screamed like a bitch.

"Candy, no! What are you doing?" he exclaimed.

She turned and smiled. "I see you remember my name," she said. "Let's take first things first."

"Excuse me?" he asked, squeezing himself to ease the throbbing.

Candy opened a bottle of Merlot then filled two glasses before answering Ricky. "We need to have a few drinks first. Plus, I already told you I need my money up front. Hotel fees, wine, and all."

"But you—"

"No buts. I need you to pay up before I change my mind. Make it quick," Candy demanded.

Ricky jumped up, switching with his pants scrunched at his feet. He picked up his windbreaker to retrieve his wallet. He pulled out several hundred-dollar bills then peeled off Candy's fee. She took notice as Ricky placed the rest of his money back into his jacket pocket. She smiled to herself as she thought of how she would milk him for the other big, green faces.

Ricky made it over to Candy without falling flat on his face. They made an exchange between the money and a glass of wine.

"Thank you," Candy said, smiling. "Now, drink up. We've got to get down to business."

Ricky gulped every drop without taking a breath then tossed the glass on the bed. He grabbed Candy's head with both hands, forcing her to her knees. She set her glass on the floor beside her as she attempted to swallow Ricky whole. She did what she had to do with one hand because she wasn't letting her money out of her sight—at least not until Ricky was drunk and couldn't move.

Candy let Ricky bust in her mouth, careful to let every drop slide down her throat. Ricky had pulled Candy's ponytail loose and gripped two fists full of braids as he shook, trying to keep his balance. Candy wasn't finished, and she let him know it.

"You're not done, are you, daddy?" she asked.

"No," he said, blowing. "No, I'm good for some more."

"Good, 'cause I'm ready for phase two. Go lie on the bed while I fix you another glass of wine," Candy said as she walked away.

Ricky hopped over to the bed, removed his shoes, and kicked off his pants. To his amazement, he already had another hard-on. He looked up and noticed Candy heading his way. She looked sexy as hell as she swayed toward him in her erotic ensemble. She handed him the wine then began taking off her shoes.

"What are you doing?" Ricky asked.

"I'm about to get in bed with you."

"No. Please. I mean yes," Ricky stuttered. "I mean I want you with the heels on. Please leave them on."

"Okay," she said, putting her sandals back on. Candy straddled Ricky as he sat on the bed. "Whatever you want, daddy. Tonight I'm yours. Drink up."

Ricky did as told. He tried to sip his wine, but Candy got impatient. As he put the glass to his lips, Candy lifted it, forcing him to take large, fast gulps. He finished the wine in no time. Candy smiled inside. She knew the sleeping pills she'd crushed in his drink would kick in soon.

She raised her dress over her head. Ricky assisted her with taking it off. Her breasts stood at attention, and her hazel-brown nipples seemed to be eyeing him. Ricky was about to lose his mind.

"Damn, baby. You one sexy-ass bitch," he said just before taking one of her breasts into his mouth.

Candy let out a series of exaggerated moans. "Aaahhh . . . Ooohhh . . . yeeesss. Don't stop," she said, stuffing her breast into Ricky's mouth.

"Mm-hmm. You like that, don't you?" Ricky mumbled as he flicked his tongue over Candy's breast.

"Yeah, daddy. Now, c'mon. Suck my clit like you're doing my nipple."

Ricky paused for a minute. He couldn't believe Candy had just asked him to go down on her. Who was the trick here? She should be doing everything he told her to do. After all, he was the one putting out the dough to bust a good nut. *She got this shit twisted*, he thought.

Candy stood on the bed in front of Ricky with her legs spread apart. She slid her thong to the side then spread her lips. She began stroking her clit with up and down motions. Ricky was turned on by the sight of her juicy pussy, but he hadn't performed oral sex in years. *I shouldn't be doing this,* he thought.

"Yo, I can't put my mouth on you. I'm a married man. I ain't ever tasted another woman's pussy before."

"Really?" Candy asked, surprised.

Candy began grinding as she continued to play with her clit. She stuck two fingers inside herself then placed them in her mouth and sucked them slow and hard. Ricky was turned on like a muthafucker. He panted as he watched her seductive show. Then suddenly, Candy caught him off guard as she squatted, dropping her wet pussy into his lap. She grabbed the back of his head then kissed the hell out of him. Her tongue was warm, and the heat between her legs seemed to be getting hotter by the second. She kissed Ricky like she didn't want to let go, and quite frankly, he was confused as to whether he wanted her to stop. Their lips and tongues were locked, coating Ricky's taste buds with all of Candy's savory juice. After about five minutes of nonstop grinding and kissing, Candy finally pulled away.

"Now . . . as you were saying?" she said with a raised eyebrow. Ricky sat silently in a daze. "Let me help you, daddy. You seem to be at a loss for words," Candy said, lifting her bottom to push two fingers deep inside her.

Once Candy pulled her fingers out, she squatted again then painted Ricky's lips with a high-gloss consisting of her moisture. He was stunned, but when she forced her fingers into his mouth, his dick got so hard it hurt. He began sucking her fingers then Candy exaggerated more moans.

She stood on the bed in front of him then spread her lips to enable him to better enjoy her nectar. Ricky loved tasting her. In fact, after she threw one of her legs over his shoulder, he gripped her ass and helped her grind into his face. She had a crippling hold on the back of his neck, damn near smothering him as she climaxed.

Candy stepped off the bed to retrieve a condom from her purse. She turned and noticed Ricky stroking himself. She shook her head.

"Unh-uh, daddy. Momma's gotcha," Candy said.

Candy walked over to the bed then gave Ricky more oral pleasure. Just before he was about to erupt, she pushed him down on the bed, slid the condom on him, then rode him with quick, intense strokes. Ricky exploded faster than he had intended, but it was definitely something he couldn't help.

He fought hard to catch his breath. Candy leaned forward to kiss his nose then rolled off him. Ricky couldn't believe how much satisfaction he'd just experienced. Candy had him wide open for her. He knew he would make her a regular pastime.

He felt himself getting weak and sleepy. He tried to shake the feeling, but he couldn't seem to move. *She'll laugh at me if I don't hang in,* he thought. *I can't fall asleep now.* Despite

Ricky's efforts to shake off his sleep, he drifted into a deep slumber, snoring like a bear in hibernation.

Candy called his name and pulled on his balls to test if he'd awaken. Nothing seemed to wake him. Candy eased out of bed, put on her clothes, and went through Ricky's pockets. She took three one hundred-dollar bills and a twenty, which was all the cash he had, and she also stole a credit card then disappeared.

When Ricky woke up, he didn't know what hit him. It was three o'clock in the morning, the contents of his pockets were missing, and so was Candy. Ricky scrambled to get his clothes on quickly. He feared the fight he'd possibly have once he got home.

"Shit!" he yelled aloud. "How could I be so fucking stupid?"

He started to phone Candy, but decided he'd wait until daylight. He needed to get home fast, before Mrs. Ware came looking for that ass.

Sugar Cane
13

It was eight o'clock in the morning before Sugar opened her eyes in bed. She couldn't remember the last time she'd slept so late. Except for weekends, her morning rituals began at 6:00 A.M., something her body was trained to do. After arguing with Damon half the night, Sugar felt drained. She could hardly turn over, but once she did, she discovered Damon was missing. She raised up to grab her cell.

"Yo. Whaddup, baby?" he asked just after answering the line.

"Don't baby me, Damon. Why didn't you wake me before you left the house this morning?"

"'Cause you looked tired. I was gonna check on you in a bit."

"Where are you?"

"Why?"

"'Cause I wanna know, and don't answer me with a question."

"I'm trying to see if my cousin gon' pay me today. There. Satisfied?"

"You get your ass back here quick with that money, Damon. I need to give Blue my share for the products, and you need to be here to go over tomorrow's scheme with us."

"A'ight. Cool. I'll be home in a bit. Just let me take care of this first."

Sugar hung up in his face. She called her shop to tell the girls she wouldn't be in then got out of bed to get dressed. After tidying up for the morning, Sugar dialed her twin.

"What," Candy answered with a groggy voice.

"What are you still doing in bed? I need you to get up and meet me for breakfast."

"For what?" Candy whined.

"I'll tell you all of that at breakfast. Just meet me at IHOP."

"Sounds like there's something in this for me," Candy said, sitting up in a hurry.

"Possibly."

"Possibly my ass. Something in this for me or not, Sugar? I got somebody on my ass about some money I owe. You never wanna meet with me unless you need help, and today just might be the day we could help each other. I need at least ten grand when we meet. Can you make that happen?"

"You ain't shit, Candy. You know that? I'm your sister, but you'll scheme on me too."

"Hey, you obviously want me to do a job. Sister or no sister, you gotta pay up. Ain't nobody else gonna run game for free. You might as well pay me too."

"You know what? On most occasions, I don't like you. Today is no different."

"Whatever, Sugar. You want me to meet you or what?"

"Yeah. I need you to be bag lady today like last time. I don't need the folks discovering us. Bring a large purse. I'll try to have your money, but in the meantime, I need you to write down the contact information for the lady who does your hair. I'm gonna need some braids."

"I've got her card. You just have my money."

Candy hung up on Sugar. Although Sugar had Damon thinking she was struggling with money, she actually had the means to carry the deal over, and she had the ten thousand dollars to give Candy, too, but she wouldn't readily admit it to her. Sugar meant what she said. At times, she really couldn't stand Candy. She sat daydreaming about the last fight she and her sister had. She wondered if Candy would really stoop as low as sleeping with Damon.

I love her, but I'd kill her, Sugar thought.

Sugar sipped a cup of coffee as she awaited Candy's arrival. She kept looking at her watch because she knew she needed to meet Blue, and she'd also promised her mother she'd stop over to see her for a bit.

Sugar looked out the window and noticed Candy heading inside the restaurant. Candy wore a gray, oversized sweat suit, with mahogany make-up to darken her skin, and an auburn-colored, shoulder-length wig. She had a large tote bag on her shoulder. She looked as if she were on her way to work out, but she also looked like she was going to sweat to death. It was the first of June, one of the hottest mornings all year.

Candy pranced in as if nothing was wrong. She slid into the booth behind Sugar with her back to her. She placed her phone up to her ear as if she was on a call as she attempted to speak with Sugar. "What's up, sis? Why are you sitting there looking like you lost your best friend? I lost mine, but you don't see me gloomy."

Sugar spoke softly, moving her lips as little as possible. "I ain't seen you look sad about much at all. You're a strange one, I must say," Sugar replied. "What the hell have you got on?"

"You said to disguise myself. I'm trying to disguise how fine I am, until the big day tomorrow."

Sugar rolled her eyes. "You mean how fine I am, 'cause you'll be me tomorrow."

"Anyway. Is this breakfast on you?"

"No. Dutch treat. You've got your own money—or at least you will in a minute. Give me a few minutes in the bathroom then I'm out. Look for the bag behind the door."

Sugar stalled for a minute then left a tip before heading to the restroom. She spent about three minutes in there then left the restaurant. The undercover cops were quick on her tail.

She noticed them following her, so she phoned Candy to make certain she got the money and headed out of there.

"Yeah," Candy answered.

"Did you go get the bag?" Sugar asked.

"Yeah," Candy answered. "I stuck it inside this big satchel you had me bring."

"Well, I was just checking 'cause now would be the perfect time to get the hell out of there. The folks are following me."

"Umph," Candy responded. "I'm eating. I didn't come all the way out here for nothing."

"Yeah. Well, hurry up. Momma is looking for you to stop by this morning anyway."

"For what?"

"Just because I told her you would. You ain't been over there in a minute."

"A'ight, but I'll have to stop by later this afternoon. I've gotta take care of something first."

Nikki
14

"Did you get the number, Reno?" Nikki asked as she and Reno stood outside a phone booth.

"Yeah. I got it right here," he responded.

"And are you sure Candy and D-Jay are going to be hooking up this evening?"

"I'm positive. I spoke with him this morning. He assured me that Candy didn't have his money, which I know is a lie, and that he'll be getting what he's owed in a sexual way."

"Cool. Then it's on. Since Candy wants to continue playing games, we got something for her ass."

Nikki began dialing the number listed on the piece of paper Reno handed her.

"Hello," a proper feminine voice answered.

"Hello. May I speak to Candy?" Nikki asked.

"Candy? I'm sorry, my dear. You have the wrong number."

"Oh." Candy looked at Reno. "I apologize."

"No problem," the woman responded before hanging up.

Reno looked confused. "What happened, Nikki?"

"You gave me the wrong number. That's what happened."

"Naw. Couldn't be. Let me dial the number. You must've hit a wrong button or something."

Reno dialed the number then held the phone to his ear, waiting for someone to answer.

"Hello," the feminine voice answered again.

"Hello, ma'am. How are you today?"

"I'm doing well," she said.

"I'd like to speak to Sugar if you don't mind."

"Sugar? Who is this? Are you some kind of pervert or something?"

"No, ma'am. I'm only trying to reach one of your daughters."

"Well, someone just called here asking to speak to Candy. Now you want to speak to Sugar. I don't take too kindly to harassing phone calls. You better not call here again. You hear me?"

"Ma'am, I'm truly sorry. I was only trying to reach your daughters, Candy and Sugar Cane. I was told they could be reached at this number. Do you not have two daughters?"

"Yes, I do. One of them just left here, and I'm expecting the other here soon. But my girls are Stephanie and Stacy Perry. Cane is my ex-husband's name. People still like to call me Momma Cane, but I've remarried. My girls were adopted by my current husband, John Perry."

"Which one is on her way? Would it be the one who dates Damon Williams?"

"No. That's Stacy. She just left, but I'd like to be able to tell her you called. To whom did you say I'm speaking?"

"I didn't say, but thank you very much. I've realized I do have the wrong number," Reno said before hanging up.

Nikki stared at Reno, waiting for his response. "So, what happened? What did she say?"

"Sugar and Candy are truly a couple of bad girls. They're using aliases. Can you believe that shit?"

"Huh? What are you talking about?"

"Their mother says Cane is their father's name. Their real first names are Stephanie and Stacy. They've got everybody fooled."

"Whoa," Nikki responded. "So, are they there or not?"

"Their mother says one of them just left and the other is on her way. Sugar, who is also known as Stacy just left, so Candy is the one on her way over.

"I don't know, Reno. Are you sure? This sounds risky. We could get caught."

"I say let's do this. Stacy is the one who dates Damon, and she's the one who just left."

"I still think it's risky, but I don't wanna back down now. Let's go."

Nikki and Reno split and headed to Candy's apartment. Reno packed all the necessary equipment in Nikki's handbag and showed her what to do with it. He circled the block while Nikki went inside the apartment.

Nikki had no trouble using the alarm code Reno gave her. Once inside, she reset the alarm on stay mode then freely moved about the apartment. She went inside Candy's bedroom to set up surveillance because she figured the bed was a sure spot to catch the two of them on tape.

As Nikki went over to Candy's dresser, she spotted a picture of Candy and a woman having an identical appearance to Candy with the exception of the hairstyle. Candy generally wore braids, whereas Sugar would wear her hair straight in a wrap. She was stunned. In the years she'd known Candy, she never knew she had a sister, let alone a twin.

Nikki set up the hidden camera. She grabbed her bag then headed toward the bedroom door. She stopped in her tracks when she heard Candy entering the apartment, laughing with someone as she turned off the alarm. Nikki's heart began to pound. She suddenly had a notion to get under the bed. It was a good thing Nikki was petite because there was very little room underneath the bed. She lay flat on her stomach with her arms at her side, clutching her bag.

Candy entered the bedroom first. "Hold on, D-Jay. Just give me a minute to tidy up my room," Candy said, opening the closet to toss in a large bag.

Nikki took notice. She wondered what could possibly be in the bag because it sounded heavy when Candy threw it in the closet. She knew to remain quiet until she could find the perfect opportunity to sneak out.

Nikki watched as Candy walked over to the bed. She saw Candy's clothes dropping to the floor, piece by piece. Then Candy began calling for Damon.

"Okay, D-Jay. You can come in now," Candy yelled.

Damon entered the room. "Damn, girl. You couldn't wait for me to take your clothes off, huh?"

"You ain't mad. I did you a favor. Now all you need to do is get naked and join me over here," she said, patting the bed.

"So, what about the money?" Damon asked.

"I told you. I don't have it right now," Candy said, pulling Damon close to kiss him. "But I promise I'll get it to you tomorrow."

"Tomorrow's a new day. I'm gonna have to add more interest on it."

"Unh-uh. Not after I'm through with you," Candy said, unfastening Damon's pants. "You're gonna forget all about interest when I'm done."

Nikki observed Candy on her knees beside the bed. All she could hear was a lot of smacking and Damon hissing and moaning. Nikki felt sick. She couldn't imagine being close to her own sister's man, let alone having sex with him. Nikki hated Candy. She wished she could come from under the bed and beat the shit out of her. She kept telling herself to remain calm.

"Oooohhh," Candy moaned as Reno entered her canal.

"Mm-hmm. You miss this dick, don't you?"

"Oh yeah, D-Jay. Beat this pussy up. Beat it up, baby. I love it when you throw that dick like that," Candy said through clenched teeth.

Nikki lay there wishing the two of them would hurry up. She'd had about all she could take of them moaning and pouncing over her head. Her phone began to vibrate. She knew it was Reno, wondering what was taking her so long, but she couldn't move. She only hoped Candy and Damon wouldn't hear or feel the vibrations. Her wish came true because the sex fanatics were at it strong, and they wouldn't have heard a trumpet even if it was blown right next to their ears.

The sex-capade between Candy and Damon lasted for about forty-five minutes. Nikki felt about as disgusted as she did the day Candy and the others ran game on her. She knew she had to make Candy pay.

Candy put Damon out of the apartment then went to the shower. Nikki wanted to come from under the bed, but she realized she needed to play things slow in order to retrieve the camera so she wouldn't have to come back. Though Candy and Damon's entrance was an unexpected one, it was also a welcomed one because they made Nikki's job easy. All she needed to do was to get the surveillance material then leave.

As Nikki predicted, it didn't take Candy long to shower. She got dressed, set her alarm then headed out the door. Just to be careful, Nikki waited another five minutes before crawling from under the bed. She stretched and shook her legs to revive the blood circulation. She claimed all of her equipment, stuffed it in her bag then headed for the front door. Suddenly, the alarm began blaring, and to make matters worse, Candy was putting the key in the lock to come inside.

Nikki ran back into the bedroom like a track star. She slid under the bed and dragged her bag with her. Candy punched the alarm code then began looking through her apartment. She wondered if someone was in there or if this occasion was just another false alarm. Candy hurried to her closet to check for the bag. After noticing it hadn't been moved, she closed the door then turned to leave the room. She was startled by her neighbor's Persian cat.

Candy held her chest. "Oh, Tinker, you scared me. I must've left the kitchen window open again, huh?" She picked up the cat then headed to the kitchen. "You're probably the reason for all of these false alarms, huh?" she asked, petting the cat.

Candy pushed the cat out of the window then closed it. She felt relieved that no one had broken into her apartment.

She went to get her ID out of the pants pocket she wore earlier, which is why she had to come back home. Then her cell rang. She recognized the caller then debated on whether to answer. Candy let out a loud laugh then clicked the talk button.

"Hello," she said then paused. "Officer Ware. How are you?"

He began spilling his guts about how he couldn't believe she'd ripped him off. She laughed and denied his allegations to the end.

"I'm telling you, daddy. I didn't take your credit card and your money. And I didn't use you. I took care of you."

Candy paused to listen some more then she promised Ricky she'd take care of him later. Candy continued to butter him up.

"Listen, daddy. I need a favor. I need you to help me and my sister do something," she said.

Ricky hung up on Candy before she could ask the favor. She laughed out load. "He'll need me sooner than he thinks," she said, laughing more as she set her alarm.

Candy left, but Nikki didn't budge. She waited about fifteen minutes before she got up. Once she was satisfied Candy wouldn't return, she went to the closet to see what was in the heavy-sounding bag. She couldn't believe she had forgotten to check it the first time. Nikki dragged out the bag so she could see in it clearly. She unzipped the bag and discovered a heap of money. Nikki felt like she'd hit the jackpot.

She ran to the alarm keypad to deactivate the system. She reset the alarm then wasted no time getting the hell out of there. She called Reno to meet her around the corner.

She couldn't believe she'd broken into Candy's home in broad daylight. On one hand she felt she'd done wrong, and on the other hand, she felt she only gave Candy what she deserved. Everything had worked itself out. Reno and Nikki had the money that Candy never intended to pay Damon and that Damon never intended to pay Reno.

Sugar Cane
15

All was set and ready for the next day's activities. Sugar had just made it home from visiting her mother, and she was confident that everything would go over well. Although Momma Cane was surprised to see her with braids she also felt it was a nice change.

Sugar went straight to the mirror after getting upstairs. She wasn't used to the braids yet, but she felt they were sexy.

She picked up her cell to call Blue.

"What's up, sweet thang? Tell me what you know," Blue asked just after answering the line.

"I know I'm ready. How about you?" Sugar asked.

"I stay ready."

"Is that right?"

"Exactly right."

"I wish there was some way for me to confirm that," Sugar responded, smiling and blushing.

"You can confirm it."

"I can? How can I do that?"

"Come see me, Sugar. I want you. After tomorrow, I'm out of here. I need to be with you at least one time before I go."

Sugar wanted to cry when she thought of possibly never seeing Blue again. She held her cell up to her chest as she fought back tears. Blue began yelling in the phone. He feared she had hung up.

"Sugar?" he called.

"Yes. I'm here."

"Did I scare you or something? You don't have to. I'm just finding it hard to hold back my feelings now."

"Where are you?"

"Downtown at The Peabody Hotel. Will you meet me?"

"What about the folks?"

"If they want a show, we can give 'em a show. How about in the lobby? Or even up on the roof with the ducks if you like. I don't care. I just want you tonight."

Sugar smiled. "You're funny, but convincing. I'm on my way."

Sugar ran upstairs to shower. She made sure to put on her favorite red satin-and-lace thong set then sprayed a dash of Very Sexy by Victoria's Secret on each side of her neck and wrists. She slipped on a sundress, grabbed her keys, and was out the door.

Sugar made it downtown in no time. She phoned Blue for the room number once she was in the hotel lobby. After stepping off the elevator, her heart began to pound. She barely had a chance to knock on the door before Blue opened it and pulled her in.

He tongued her with a passion she'd never known. Sugar didn't want the moment to end. She felt goosebumps up her spine when Blue slid his hand underneath her dress to caress her thigh. He never stopped kissing her. He backed her into the wall and began placing slow, luscious kisses down her chin then her neck. She rubbed his bald, chocolate head then guided his lips to meet her breasts. Blue pulled her dress off her shoulders then down her hips without ever looking up. He sucked and nibbled her breasts through the lace, but Sugar got impatient and began removing her bra.

Blue worked his tongue down her stomach. He held her ass as he blew into her navel. Sugar licked and massaged her breasts. Her soft moans turned Blue on. He longed to hear her moan louder, so he placed his mouth over her warm spot, attempting to make her hotter. He wiggled his tongue around her thong and into the crevice of her lips, teasing her clit with rapid, wet strokes.

Sugar could hardly stand. Blue loved tasting her, and despite her leaning over him, he wasn't about to stop—at least not until he extracted all of her sap.

A few minutes later, Sugar damn near collapsed. Blue picked her up to carry her to the bed. She lay there, unable to move. Blue spread her legs to taste more of her. Sugar screamed for mercy.

"Blue, please. Please, Blue. I can't take any more," she said.

She lay trembling as she begged him to be gentle. Blue pulled her thong off then went for a condom.

Sugar watched as he walked back toward her. Blue's dick seemed to be aimed straight for her tunnel. Sugar suddenly had a second wind. As Blue began to stick it to her, she threw her hips back at him. His moans escalated and their rhythm got faster. The two of them began to sweat, but neither seemed to notice. They continued to bang their bodies at a rapid, vigorous pace.

Sugar screamed as she climaxed for the second time. Blue couldn't hold back any longer. He erupted like a roaring volcano. The two of them were hot and limp. They couldn't move if they had wanted to. But they didn't want to, and so they lay meshed, trying to catch a cool breath.

Blue finally gathered the strength to roll over. He lay on his back, still out of breath, wondering what Sugar was thinking. After five long years of wanting her, he never figured the day would actually come when he'd get to lay her down. She was all he ever dreamed she'd be and more. He wished he didn't have to leave her, but his old way of life was behind him, and he felt Sugar should be too.

Blue lazily staggered to the bathroom. He threw the condom away then washed up. He went back into the room and stood over Sugar as she lay half asleep. He surprised her with a temperate, wet towel between her legs. Sugar sighed as Blue washed her gently. He set the towel on the floor then got back into bed.

Sugar turned on her side, eyeing Blue as he lay with his eyes closed, seemingly drained. The room was dreadfully silent, with the exception of the two of them breathing. Sugar traced Blue's six-pack with her eyes then down below his belt-line. The heat between her legs became warm all over again.

She began to have serious thoughts of doing things to him she'd never experienced before. She eased closer to him then licked his nipple. Salty sweat flavored her tongue, but she didn't mind. She rubbed between his legs, causing an immediate erection. Blue lay silent, never bothering to open his eyes. Sugar lapped more of his salty skin, making her way between his legs.

I can't believe I'm actually doing this, she thought.

She took one long look at Blue's dick then wrapped her lips around it. Blue's body jerked with pleasure. The sudden impact of Sugar's tongue was an astonishing surprise. Blue recalled Damon once telling him that Sugar would never perform oral sex on him, so he wasn't expecting this favor.

Though Sugar was surprised by her actions, she was even more shocked at how much she loved tasting Blue. She began mimicking what she'd seen on flicks and what her sister once told her to do.

Blue began to wonder if Damon had lied because Sugar's performance was more like one of a pro. He stroked her head as she took care of business.

Blue sat up in bed, but Sugar didn't stop. He reached to pull her body toward him. She looked up, confused, when he touched her waist.

"Bring your ass around here, baby. I wanna taste you too," Blue said. "C'mere. Let's get this sixty-nine thing going." Blue lay back with Sugar on top of him.

They gave each other oral pleasure for what seemed like forever. Sugar was strung out. Blue had her hooked from their first episode of sex. Damn whatever Damon would think. She wasn't going home 'til morning. She wanted as much of Blue as possible, and by the way things were going, she knew they'd pull an all-nighter.

During one of their breaks, Blue wondered what Damon would think of Sugar not coming home.

"So, how are you going to explain not going home?" he asked.

"I shouldn't have to. That's my house. That nigga lives with me," she responded, rubbing on Blue's chest.

"I know, baby. But what I'm saying is there's a thing called respect. You just admitted he does live there with you."

"Well, on most occasions he lives with me, but when it comes to speaking of respect, I'm not doing any more to him than he would do to me. You know better than anyone how many times I complained about him not coming home better than anyone. I think I vented to you just about every time."

"I hear ya, but I'm also worried he would be trouble when you get home."

"Damon doesn't want that. Trust me. I'll be fine."

"Okay. With that said, I'll leave the subject alone. Just let me know when you're ready for round six."

"Oh, you've lost count. But anyway, I'm ready," Sugar said seductively.

Blue smiled then turned her over. At the rate they were going, the two of them were bound to be sore the next morning—a pain sure to be well worth it.

Lady Canes
16

Candy desperately needed to ask Ricky for a favor, but she feared he wouldn't oblige. He'd been hanging up on her ever since she left him high and dry in the hotel. She desperately needed to ask him for a favor, but she feared he wouldn't oblige. She was depending on him since she'd promised Sugar she could get him to participate with fooling the cops.

I've got to keep trying, she thought as she dialed Ricky's number.

"Yeah, this is Ricky," he answered.

"Miss me, daddy?" Candy asked.

He immediately recognized her voice. "Hell naw, bitch. Why the fuck are you still calling me?"

"'Cause I miss you, daddy. Can you blame me after the way you made me cum the other night?"

"You got me in a world of trouble at home. Not to mention that you stole my fucking credit card along with a few hundred dollar bills."

"So whatchu saying, daddy?" Candy asked with a fake irritated tone.

"I'm saying that unless you ready to give me back my credit cards and my money, you need to lose my fucking number."

"Well, I ain't got yo' credit card or your money, but I got something else of yours deemed very priceless."

"What the fuck are you talking about?" Ricky was getting agitated.

"I'm talking about your pussy, daddy. I told you it's yours. What? You didn't believe me? Why don't you come and get some?"

Ricky began to have flashes of how Candy could please him. He softened up. "I want my belongings back, but I can't discuss anything further right now. I'm about to go on duty."

"Oh, good. 'Cause I need to ask for a favor then perhaps some time after you get off duty, we can hook up."

Candy explained the situation about what she and Sugar needed to accomplish. Ricky was surprised she would tell him such private information. She even offered to take care of Ricky's sexual needs free for six months if he'd help out with their plans. She also offered him ten thousand dollars, a lump sum she knew she couldn't afford, but she figured fucking his brains out regularly would get her out of ever having to pay him.

Ricky was a little reluctant at first. He knew helping the twins get away with a felony could not only get him fired, but it could land him jail time too. He listened to Candy beg some more then he gave the situation some more thought. After realizing he couldn't possibly be blamed for anything, he decided to assist the twins.

"Stop bullshitting me, Candy. I want my credit cards, the money you stole, and you better make good on the added incentives you promised me for helping."

"Okay. Okaaayyy."

"You think I could ever have a ménage trois with you and your sister at some point? I've always wondered what doing twins would be like," he stated.

"Are you sick?" Candy asked. "You're pushing your luck, and besides, we're freaky, but we don't get down like that."

Ricky laughed. "A'ight. Just thought I'd try. But if you ever change your—"

"I won't be changing my mind," she snapped.

Sugar left her house around three o'clock that afternoon, knowing full well she was being followed by the law. She pulled up to an Exxon Tiger Mart to get gas then went inside to use the restroom. At least that's what the detectives who followed her thought. What they didn't know was that the woman who exited the restroom with long, butt-length braids, wearing a red-fitted top, tight denim Capri-pants, Louis Vuitton sandals, and carrying a matching Louis Vuitton purse, was not the same woman who entered the restroom wearing that outfit.

Candy walked out to Sugar's red Corvette, removed the gas pump then replaced it on the handle. She grabbed the receipt then got into the car, heading for a little joy ride.

After ten minutes had passed, Sugar left the restroom dressed in one of Candy's favorite outfits. Heads turned as she walked out of the store to get into her sister's 2006 Infinity.

Sugar was pissed. She had cussed at Candy during the time they shared in the restroom while changing. Sugar couldn't believe that Candy had seen fit to wear a black lace spaghetti-strapped cat-suit and a pair of clear hooker-heeled slide-ins. And of all days, Sugar had decided to wear a thong. She contemplated going home to change, but she called Blue on the way.

"Blue, I've got to go back home," she said just after he answered.

"Why? What happened?"

"Can you believe my twin wore some stripper type shit to the gas station to meet me?" Sugar huffed.

Blue wanted to laugh, but he knew better than to test Sugar at that moment. She sounded ready to explode.

He tried to calm her down. "It can't be that bad, can it?"

"Oh, yes the hell it can. I'm driving around with my ass out. If I get pulled over, I'm going to jail for indecent exposure. Candy needs her ass kicked for this shit."

"Calm down, Sugar. You can't go back home. You could blow everything we're trying to do today. Now, while Candy's got the boys strung along, let's stick to the plan. All of our connections are going to meet you in the designated locations rather than the usual spots. Just go ahead and bust the moves. You'll be finished in no time."

"Oh, yeah? Well, that's easy for you to say. I'm the one who has to run around here looking like the Tramp of the South."

"I'm sure you make the most beautiful tramp of them all." Blue laughed.

"Don't aggravate me, Blue. Please don't do that. You just don't understand how upset I am right now. Damon's sorry ass is a no-show again. He won't even answer his phone. I did all that explaining about our scheme for nothing."

"Okay. I understand you're pissed, but we can't back down now. This isn't the first time Damon's failed us. I know you might be scared, but seriously, we need to keep things moving."

"Don't worry about it. I'm still moving."

The men in the narcotic vans and plain cars followed Candy closely, but far enough behind her so she wouldn't notice them. Too bad she already knew about them, and soon it would be too bad for them that she wasn't who they thought she was.

Candy led the men on a wild goose chase for most of the day. They parked and watched as she spent two and a half hours in the nail salon, then two more hours as she got a Brazilian wax job in a full service spa. Candy left the spa feeling great and ready to eat. She forced the detectives to drive around in circles for another hour before pulling into the parking lot of Applebee's on Union Avenue.

Candy sat and enjoyed dinner and a margarita. She waited around until near dark to leave the restaurant. She'd received the text message she was looking for, and it was time for the next phase of her plan to stall the police narcotics unit.

Candy drove out into oncoming traffic on Union Avenue, swerved then hit the brakes hard to keep from smashing into another car. It just so happens a police patrol car was near and witnessed the entire incident. Candy was immediately summoned to pull over.

The officer walked up to the car. “Do you have your driver’s license and registration?” he asked.

“Why? What did I do?” Candy asked, smirking at the man.

“Ma’am, just let me ask all the questions for now, if you don’t mind. I need your license and registration, please.”

Candy smiled then winked. “Sure,” she responded, extending her identification to the officer.

He gazed at the picture then the name on the ID. *Stephanie Perry,* he said to himself then gave Candy a puzzled look.

“Rick—I mean, sir, is there a problem?” Candy asked, a bit agitated that Ricky had discovered her real name.

“Uhm, no. Not a problem,” he responded as he shook off his trance. “But I do believe you’ve been drinking, so I need to ask you to step out of the car.”

“Aw, c’mon. I’m not drunk. I only had one margarita, and that was over an hour ago. I just wasn’t paying attention. I didn’t realize those cars were so close before I pulled out.”

“Exactly the reason I need to give you a breathalyzer test. I’m not sure how much you’ve had to drink. Now, step out of the car.”

Ricky made sure he took his time when performing the breath test on Candy. He also made her walk a straight line. After determining what he already knew, that she wasn’t drunk, he sat in his car and patiently ran her tag number and ID for warrants.

The Narcotics Unit couldn’t believe how things were going. An anonymous tip had told them Sugar would be making all of her buys and sells, but it appeared that they had been given the run around. The woman they had followed showed no signs or interest in making transactions.

Even though it was dark, they continued to follow the little red Corvette once she'd been cleared by Ricky to leave.

After getting the okay from Sugar, Candy headed to a local Wal-mart then filled a basket with feminine products, shampoo, tissue, and snacks. She noticed some men following her, but pretended to be shopping also. She parked her basket near the restroom then went inside where she had to continue the argument she'd had earlier with Sugar.

"You know, if we weren't in Wal-mart, and if I didn't need to get out of here fast, I'd fuck you up," Sugar stated through clenched teeth.

"Whatever, bitch. If you're really so mad that I forced you to look good for once in your life, then why don't you just hit me now and get it over with?" Candy taunted.

"Don't tempt me, bitch," Sugar replied while she and Candy swapped outfits. "And you better not had been somewhere stankin' up my clothes."

Candy sucked her teeth hard. "Well, bitch, if they're funky, what're you gonna do about it now? Not shit. You'll just be walking out of here with a sour ass," she said just before throwing Sugar's keys at her.

Sugar finished dressing. "Move," she said as she shoved Candy out of her way.

Sugar headed out of the restroom, located the basket Candy stored nearby then went to the checkout counter. Her next destination was home. She'd already secured the money made from her transactions, so she was finally feeling peaceful.

Candy waited until Sugar called her with a signal that it was okay to exit. Candy smiled inside as all eyes were on her while she walked to her Infinity. Since her day's work was done, she was ready to find Officer Ware, so she could personally thank him for his role in her scheme.

The Narcotics Unit was dumbfounded when the day was ended and no bust or arrest had been made. They had nothing on Sugar Cane aka Stacy Perry, and they weren't happy.

Sugar drove home to soak in a bubble bath. She couldn't believe how smoothly her plans had gone. She got into the tub with a glass of champagne and her cell phone to celebrate.

"What's up, Blue, baby?" Sugar sang into the phone just after he answered.

"You got it, Sugar."

"Talk to me. When are you leaving?"

"I'm packed up now."

Silence came over the two of them. Neither knew what to say to the other. Finally Sugar spoke up.

"Guess what I'm doing," she said.

"Uhm, I don't know. Why don't you tell me?"

"I'm in the bathtub, drinking champagne, talking to you, and playing with myself."

"Oooh . . . really?" Blue got an immediate erection.

"Yes, really."

"I would ask if I could join you, but I know Damon will be home shortly."

"And . . . so what? He couldn't get in if he tried."

"What happened to his key?" Blue asked, confused.

"Oh, he still has it, but I knew he'd stand me up today, so I arranged for the locks to be changed this morning."

"Hmm. He's gonna be one mad brotha when he tries to come over tonight."

"It doesn't matter. Why don't you catch a cab over here? I'll be in the tub until you let me know you're outside. Besides, it's time for him to eat a mile of my mess. Don't you think?"

"Well, if you say so, Sugar."

"Look, Blue, if you're scared, say you're scared. I can respect that. I just don't want you to vacate the States tomorrow, leaving me hanging. I need you right now."

"This very minute?"

Sugar smiled. "Yes. This very minute."

"Then I'm on my way."

Blue called a taxi and was over to Sugar's place in less than an hour. They made love practically non-stop. When Damon rang the doorbell and beat on the windows and doors because his key wouldn't work, Sugar and Blue didn't stop what they were doing. They attended to each other's needs as if nothing else mattered. This was the first time Damon had to leave Sugar's house steaming mad, but as far as Sugar was concerned, it wasn't going to be the last time.

Rude Awakening 17

A month had passed, and Sugar hadn't heard from or seen Blue. She let Damon back in two weeks after Blue was gone. Feeling sorry for herself, she felt the least she could do was give Damon another try. Although his ways hadn't changed, he became a source for getting over a feeling of loneliness.

It was the Fourth of July, and Momma Cane had planned a gathering at her house which included all kin. Her ex-in-laws came over, as well as nieces, nephews, cousins, and close friends. Momma Cane had a house full, and the backyard was swarming with people too. There was a card game going in the den, a Soul Train line kicking off in the backyard, and adults and young children popping fireworks around the side of the house.

Sugar had helped Momma Cane purchase most of the food and fireworks for the event. Candy didn't pitch in. As a matter of fact, she showed up at the gathering mad as hell because she'd been robbed of the money Sugar had given her. She had a look on her face which pretty much dared anyone to say the wrong the thing to her.

When Candy had returned home from carrying out her part of the drug scheme, she went straight to her closet to recover her funds. After discovering the bag of money was missing, the first person she called was Damon. He was the only one she could think of who might've known about the loot. She had no idea that Nikki and Reno were behind the robbery.

Two of Momma Cane's eight-year-old nieces came running into the house with a package. It was marked: FOR MRS. PERRY'S EYES ONLY . . . ENJOY! They handed it to her. She stared at the package in confusion.

"Where'd you kids get this envelope?" she asked.

"Some man dropped it off. He said to give it to you," one of the girls replied.

Momma Cane opened the package and discovered a DVD. "Aw . . . Lawd. I bet I know what this is. Henry must've dropped this off. He told me he would let me see the recording he made of last year's family reunion." She looked at her nieces. "Go get the rest of the family. I think everyone should see this."

Momma Cane headed to the den to start the DVD player. People began to crowd the den. Once the DVD began to play, everyone looked confused as they watched the introduction to *The Simpsons*. Momma Cane was mad.

"I'm sorry, y'all. I'm getting ready to call Henry up right now. He brought me the wrong show."

No one moved because they'd just gotten comfortable.

Damon didn't go into the den. He stood over in the corner of the living room, sipping spiked punch. Sugar walked around the house, ignoring him as she'd become comfortable doing. He was only good for night-time companionship, and he knew she felt that way.

Candy spotted Damon standing alone. She wondered if he had hidden her money in his truck. She wanted to convince him to leave the reunion with her, so she could get him drunk and search for her dough, so she went over to chat.

"I don't understand why you let her dis you like this, but suit yourself," Candy said.

"What do you mean?" he asked.

"As fine as you are, you don't need a woman who doesn't pay you any attention. You could be anywhere but here, doing whatever you want, with whoever you want."

"And let me guess. The whatever and whoever involves you. Am I right?"

"To some degree you're right. I can be the whatever and whoever. She's walking around here like you don't exist. I'm merely saying you don't have to put up with her."

"Well, thanks for pointing out an issue in my relationship. And thanks but no thanks for the offer to leave here with you. You've been around here frowning and cussing at people, but now you suddenly wanna be nice to me. I don't know what you've got up. I don't trust you."

"Excuse me? You should be happy I would want to be nice to you. And besides, you know what I have to offer. What do you mean you don't trust me?"

"Look what you did after luring your best friend away with you."

Candy was quiet for a minute. "So? You helped."

The two of them were silent again before Damon spoke. "So, whatever happened between the two of you? Did y'all ever make up?"

"Hell, naw. Fuck her. I'm moving on," she said as she took Damon's cup from his hand then took a sip.

"Ugh. I wasn't finished with that."

Candy took a large gulp then handed him the cup. "Oops. My bad. You're finished now."

Damon stared into the empty cup. Candy moved closer to him and began licking on his neck. She was already tipsy before gulping his drink, and she was feeling wild. She knew where she was and that there were other people in the house, but she just didn't give a fuck. She snapped out of it when Sugar's voice pierced her ears.

"What the fuck do you think you're doing?" Sugar yelled.

Candy backed away from Damon. "Uh . . . nothing," she said. "I was just—"

"You were just up on my man," Sugar said, interrupting Candy's excuse.

Sugar walked up to Candy's face and looked into her eyes. Just when she was about to raise her hand to slap Candy, Momma Cane intervened.

"Stacy!" Momma Cane yelled.

Sugar just knew she was in trouble, so she turned, ready to explain the situation to her mother. When she turned around, she got the surprise of her life. Standing next to her mother was Blue.

"Stacy, you've got company," Momma Cane said.

"Blue, what are you doing here?"

"I'm back for you," he said. Sugar's eyes became glassy as he continued. "One week was too long without you, so you can imagine what I'm feeling now that it's been one month."

Sugar was at a loss for words. "How long will you be staying?"

"Just long enough for you to pack your things." The whole room was silent. "I'm not leaving without you."

Damon turned red in the face. "Hol' up. Nigga, this is my woman," he said, grabbing Sugar around the waist.

Blue stepped closer to Sugar. "She *was* your woman. I'm back to claim her now." He took Sugar's palm into his then led her into his arms.

Damon was pissed, and he was about to show it. Before he could react, loud screaming and shouting came from the den.

"Stephanie Perry! I think you better get in here," one of Momma Cane's female cousins said.

Candy, Sugar, and everyone else in the living room ran into the den to see what was going on. Momma Cane's cousin was standing behind the big screen television yelling, "Hurry! Help me shut this thing off!"

Momma Cane, Sugar, Candy, Damon, and Blue were all frozen solid. Their mouths were dropped and none of them could blink if they wanted to. The vision that played across the TV screen was too shocking.

There before God and everybody was video porn of Candy and Damon as he had her in doggy-style, repeatedly spanking her ass while hittin' it. Momma Cane collapsed to the floor hard after fainting.

Damon finally collected himself. He darted across the room, stepping over little kids and old people, trying to stop the DVD. He managed to yank the plug out of the socket, and then the room went silent.

Everyone stared back and forth at Damon and Candy. Candy tried to express an apology as she walked toward Sugar. Sugar didn't want to hear it. She lunged at Candy, and once again, the fight was on between the Cane twins. People couldn't get out of the way fast enough.

Sugar got her hands around Candy's neck and wouldn't let go. When someone finally pried her hands, Sugar managed to grab a fistful of braids. She pulled on Candy's hair like she was trying to draw blood.

Sugar won when several braids broke at the root of Candy's head. Sugar fell to the floor. Blue tried to grab her, but she jumped up quick. She was back on Candy. They rolled around on the floor until Blue broke them up.

"Sugar, c'mon. Let's get out of here."

Sugar was fuming, but she didn't care about losing Damon. Every time someone snapped Momma Cane back into reality, she'd faint again. Sugar looked down at her then turned to Blue.

"I'm ready. Take me away from here. I'll be back to check on my momma soon, but right now, I just need you to get me out of here."

"You ain't said nothing but a word," he responded, leading Sugar out the door.

Two months later, Candy and Damon were still kicking it from time to time. Nikki found a new boyfriend and moved on with her life. Reno had let her keep all the money they stole from Candy. He knew it could never be repayment for the dirty trick played on her, but he didn't know how else to show he was truly sorry.

Sugar enjoyed living in Mexico with Blue, so she made arrangements with a real estate agent to sell her home. On her visit back to the States, she saw Candy at her mother's house, but they didn't have many words for each other. After signing all the necessary paperwork, Sugar was back off to Mexico.

Candy was sad in a way to see her sister go, but on the other hand, she had to go on with her life too. She decided she liked who she was and she would try to be nothing more than Candy Cane—an around the way girl.

One day, she lay across the sofa, looking at television when a knock came to her door. She pulled the curtains back and discovered the postman standing there. She opened the door.

"Yes, may I help you?" Candy asked.

"Ms. Perry? Are you Stephanie Perry?" the man asked.

"Yes, that's me. How may I help you?"

"Ms. Perry, you don't clean your mailbox often enough, and I've got several pieces of mail that won't fit. I was going to return it, but I figured I'd knock on the door first," he said, handing her the mail. "Clear your box, ma'am. It sure would make my job a lot easier."

"Thanks. I'll keep that in mind," she responded then closed the door in his face.

Candy scanned over her mail, piece by piece. She came across a letter stamped URGENT in bold, red letters. She started to throw it away rather than open it.

I wonder why people always sending junk to my place, trying to sell me something. Now this is supposed to be urgent. Whatever.

She tore open the letter then realized it was from the Memphis and Shelby County Health Department. Candy's eyes damned near bulged out of her head. She began skimming the letter, but then her phone rang.

"Hello," she answered in a panic.

"Did you get the letter?" Ricky asked.

"Huh?"

"They told me you'd get it by now. They said you need to report to them."

"What are you talking about, Ricky?"

"The Memphis and Shelby County Health Department. I'm bisexual. I married my lover, Vic, six years ago in San Francisco. After that condom broke on you and me last month, something told me to get checked out. It turns out I'm HIV positive, and that means you could very well be too, baby girl."

Fainting obviously came easy to the Cane women, because Candy hit the floor hard, like falling timber.

THOMAS LONG

BORN INTO THE GAME

Acknowledgements:

Thank you to all of the readers who have enjoyed my previous works. I hope you enjoy this one as well!

Peace & love,

Thomas Long

Tamara
1

Gettin' money was like second nature to me. If there was a dollar to be made out in the streets, you best believe that I was down to get it by any means necessary. Hook or crook, Tamara Barnes was one bitch that was all about the cheddar.

Unlike most girls my age in the hood, I didn't sell pussy to get what I wanted. The fact that I was fine enough to make you wanna leave the one you're with to come get a sniff of this good stuff over here didn't have shit to do with my game. I met niggas all the time that got all caught up when they saw my sinfully sexy smile, dark cocoa-colored thighs, and my juicy ass. I knew that they would spend that cheese on me if I would only give them a chance to hit this from the back. However, I was too smart to sell myself that cheap. That kinda trap was for them hoes that didn't have the ambition to make money any other way.

What those hookers made in a month sucking and fucking every Tom, Dick, and Harry, I made in a coupla hours out in the streets selling coke. I sold dreams to the poor and disadvantaged. I made them feel good when they wanted to escape the reality of being broke, black and just plain fucked up in this white man's world. Slingin' them thangs was my hustle, and I was the best that ever did it. Ain't no bitch out here that could do this gangsta shit like I did. Her ass ain't been born yet.

When you think of an independent woman, a picture of my pretty-ass face should appear in your mind. I believed in gettin' out on the grind and gettin' that cake for myself. I bought my own Gucci, Louis and Prada. When I wanted to cop something like a brand new Lexus or Benz, it felt good to know that I could get it with cash money right on the spot. I made my own money and didn't need a man to tell me how to spend it. Besides, I was allergic to dick, so a nigga served no purpose in my life unless he could put me up on to a lick so that I could make my bank account grow.

I knew since I was like twelve years old that I was attracted to females. I finally decided to act on it when I entered high school. My first time was with this bomb-ass chick named Peaches. We became cool because we were in some of the same classes. She started to hang out and party with me and my sister in our freshman year. When she felt comfortable, she let it be known to me that she was attracted to me physically. She told me she sensed that I was attracted to her as well. I couldn't lie about it because I caught myself more than a couple times checking out her phat ass and big titties on the sly when she would spend the night at our house.

When we finally hooked up, she did things to my body that let me know that I was gonna have to apply to the state of Maryland for my Lick-Her license because I was a bonafide lesbian, fa sho! I had slept with two dudes from around the way before I got with Peaches, but I wanted no parts of a man after I felt what another female could do for me.

Since Peaches turned me out, I became open to a new world. My girl, Latoya, and I had been a couple since my last year of high school. We had an open relationship, where it was no thing for her to bring home a new female friend as a treat for us to engage in a ménage á kinky.

I had an identical sister by the name of Tamia. I was the oldest by ten minutes. The only way you could tell us apart was by the birthmark she had on the right side of her neck. It was true what they said about twins in that when one of them felt pain, the other one felt it just as bad. I could remember every time that she went through relationship pains with one of them clown-ass niggas she fooled around with. I felt just as bad she did. It was the same for her whenever Latoya and I were on the outs. If something wasn't right with her, I sensed it even if we weren't around each other. We did everything together. She was my co-defendant anytime drama would pop off. We had to scrap back to back on many occasions.

Tamia and I had the hottest dope spot in East Baltimore. Barclay and 23rd Street was the strip that we called our money pit. We held that spot down for three prosperous years and planned to keep holding it down until we either got put six feet under or the Feds came and laid us down for a long bid. On a good day, we would split about 10 grand between us after we paid all of our workers.

We had a bunch of li'l niggas that shoulda been in school somewhere working for us. In our organization, they fit perfectly. They were old enough to count product and money, but too young to do any serious time if they got knocked off. We paid each of them $200 a week to do hand-to-hand sales.

Marky was our top lieutenant who oversaw the daily operation of business. He kept the rest of our workers in line, and for that we paid him three times as much as the others. He was sixteen years old, but very mature for his age.

Our workers were loyal to us because we always paid them on time and never came up short. They all came from poor, broken homes, and we gave them a chance to make some grip to be able to buy them new Jordans or the latest Rocawear and Sean John gear that their mothers couldn't afford. Not only were they loyal, they would kill on a dime for us if anybody dared to wanna go to war with us. All of them were quick to pop that steel to defend our strip.

We had a lotta haters out there that wanted our spot. A lot of these other niggas in the city wished they could keep the money pouring in like we did. They broke their mugs down at us when they would see me and my sister pull up at the club in one of the many flashy whips we both owned. They could ice-grill us all they wanted, but there wasn't a damn thing they could do to stop us from gettin' paper.

A dope strip is only as good as the product that is sold. We called our coke Prime Time because it was always right as rain. If our product wasn't top-notch, we knew that our customers would go elsewhere to get their daily fix. The only loyalty that a fiend had was to whoever had a good blast that could satisfy their jones when it kicked in. We made sure that we had them fat crack rocks getting pumped out on the block 24 hours, 7 days a week. A true hustler never slept because if she did, she was bound to miss out on a shitload of money. We wanted it all because being broke just wasn't in our nature.

It might seem kinda crazy to see two females stacking chips like we did when the drug game was supposed to be a male-dominated sport. However, when your pops was the infamous Timmy Barnes, anything was possible. My father was and still is the baddest motherfucker to ever walk the streets of B'more. His reputation preceded him everywhere he went. He was known as that nigga not to fuck with in the streets. He kept a loaded .38 with him that he had no problem using if someone was foolish enough to test his hand. He started hustling back in the late 70's and had the game on lock in no time at all. When the crack epidemic hit America in the mid 80's, his status as the King of the East Side elevated to a whole new level.

Timmy Barnes wasn't the typa hustla that didn't give back to the hood. He had a kind heart. I could recall on many occasions my dad pulling out a wad of cash to pay somebody's electricity bill or eviction notice to keep them from hitting rock bottom. He didn't look down on his customers and call them dope fiends. Instead, he considered them to be clients that purchased goods from his corner store. He looked at himself as a pharmacist who supplied his customers with medicine when they were sick. Only he could make selling dope sound like it was harmless and respectful. When Jay Z said that a true hustler could sell water to a whale, he was talking about my pops.

Timmy Barnes drove a big-boy Benz around town that made heads turn everywhere he went. He was flashy with all of his diamond rings, fur coats, and the slick tailor-made suits he was usually draped in when he hit the town to party with his crew. He got love from everybody from politicians to legitimate businessmen. He could have any woman he wanted because he was The Man. As smooth as he was, he was just as ruthless and not afraid to knock a motherfucker outta his shoes if you ever crossed him.

My mother, Priscilla Hampton, met my father when she was a nineteen-year-old college freshman at Coppin State. Her long, flowing hair and Pam Grier-like body reeled him in. She was ya typical girl from around the way with big dreams of getting a good job and hooking up with a cat that had money. She had a thing for bad boys that drove flashy whips. Her lucky number was called when Timmy Barnes walked into her life.

She got pregnant with me and my sister not long after they started messing around. After we were born, she became his main girl, even though he kept a slew of other bitches on the side. Keeping it real, I loved my dad to death, but he was just a straight playa. That's just the plain facts of the situation. I knew he loved my moms, but he just couldn't keep his dick in his pants. My mother was cool with their arrangement as long as he took care of home and never let his dirt find its way to our doorstep.

Timmy Barnes was the best father that anybody could ever have. He spoiled me and my sister to death. There was nothing in this world that was too good for his two little angels. He not only showered us with material things, he also spent as much quality time with us as his lifestyle would permit.

My moms told me that Daddy wanted badly to have a son that he could turn the family business over to when he was ready to retire from the game. They tried for many years to conceive another child, but it was to no avail. Daddy was informed by his doctor that he was sterile a few years after we were born so his plan to have a male heir to the throne wasn't gonna happen. Consequently, he turned to Plan D. He decided to teach the game to his twin terrors, which was what he called us. He knew that he couldn't run the streets forever without either death or the Feds knocking at his door eventually. My sister and I would be the bearers of his cross after his time was up in the game. We were only too eager to follow in his footsteps. Thanks to him, hustlin' was a part of our genetic makeup and the only lifestyle that we wanted to live.

We were about ten years old when he decided that we were old enough to understand his lessons on street life. He would pick us up after school take us around with him in his travels so that we could see the ins and outs of the business. He taught us how to hold and shoot a gun when we were twelve. When we were fourteen, he bought us our first pistols, a pair of shiny little .22 revolvers. We still carry them joints to this day because they're small enough to conceal in ya purse, yet potent enough to back a nigga off of you if ever a situation arose.

He broke down prices as far as how much we should pay for product. He showed us how to cook and bag coke. He made us sharp enough to know when a nigga was trying to run game on us. He taught us to always stand our ground and to never lay down for anybody. By the time we entered high school, Tamia and I had more game than any of the other chicks our age, as well as most dudes, and we were ready to conquer the world.

When the Feds came and arrested Daddy three years ago and sentenced him to twenty-five years for a kingpin charge, our world was turned upside down. The Feds seized all of my father's assets, including all of his jewelry, clothes, and cars. They took our home and we were forced to move in with my Mom's parents. They were even able to get access to his hidden stash as a result of his right hand man, Brit, making a deal with the Feds to get a reduced sentence. Brit led them right to the four million dollars that my father had stored away in foreign bank accounts.

After the Feds were done rearranging our lives, all we had left was the twenty-five grand that my mother had stashed at her best friend Melissa's house. That was more than enough dough to get us back into business. My mother had grown accustomed to her high-end lifestyle, so she didn't put up a fight when we told her about our plans to get in the drug game. She knew that my pops had well prepared us to do what needed to be done for us to get back on top. We had an image to uphold and we had every intention of doing just that.

When my pops went to jail, he divorced my mother about a year later. He knew that he would be gone for a long time and saw no need for her to hold up her life waiting around on him to come home. That was just the type of gangster nigga he was. The average hustler tried to carry on a relationship with his woman while he was locked down, as though things would still remain the same between them despite him being behind bars. Any nigga that thought his woman wouldn't give another man some pussy or even catch feelings for another man while he was locked down lived in a fantasy world. Women had physical and emotional needs to be fulfilled just like a man did and my mother was no different. Since my father caught his case, she had dated several dudes, but never anything too serious. Deep down inside of her, I think that the love she had for him just couldn't be replaced by any man. She was Timmy Barnes' ride or die chick for life. All of those other cats were just stand-ins until he came home.

At eighteen years old and fresh outta high school, Tamia and I had to represent our pedigree and stake our claim to a piece of this drug pie. When Daddy went to jail, most of his drug spots were taken over by niggas that lived in those particular areas. We knew that we didn't have a team strong enough to put up a fight for them, so we let that slide for now. However, my father's biggest money-making spot before he got knocked off was his 23rd and Barclay location, so we decided to set up shop there. That was one spot we had to get because it was too much money over there to let it slip through our hands. It was also the neighborhood that my Pops grew up in, and where he started his empire.

Most of the niggas around the way feared my Pops enough that they just fell in line once we let it be known that the Barnes family was still running things. A couple of local young niggas named Money Mike and Drew tried to bring us a power move, but we handled that shit quickly. We got in contact with some dudes from Jersey—we called them Uncles Tony and Frank—that my pops used to use for muscle in situations like this, and they made them motherfuckers disappear without a trace. We'd had little to no problems keeping things intact since then.

We were two boss bitches doing things that these other hoes only dreamed about doing. Our pimp hand was as respected, if not more, than any of these other male hustlers in the city. Everybody knew that we weren't afraid to put the murder game down if we were ever crossed.

Looking at how good the game had been to us, I marinated on our good fortune as I pushed my powder blue Jaguar down I-95 to pick up Tamia because we had business to handle. We had plans to put the whole city on lock. It was time for us to expand.

Tamia 2

I fumbled around with my hair as I tried to get my curls to bounce back into place. I just got my wig done two days ago by my girl Edy at Salon Plaza in Randallstown, and now my hair looked a mess. I planned to make another appointment with her for the next day to get my curls reset. It was so damn hard to stay looking fly as I did, but a true diva had to do what she had to do to maintain her image. When you had pockets as deep as mine, you could afford to get ya hair done two times in the same week. Living the good life—now that's what's up.

"I don't know why you up in that mirror acting like you ain't the most beautiful woman in the world. Baby, your hair looks fine," Devin said with a bright-eyed smile.

"Thanks for the compliment, boo. I know you mean well, but a sista like me gotta always be on point. I can't go out not looking my best," I replied, trying not to blush.

"T, I known you're gonna think I'm nagging you and all, but I really think you need to take my advice and get up outta the game now while you're on top. Let me show you how to invest your money legitimately like I did. Don't be like so many of them other fools that are greedy and don't know when to quit. When they finally decide to make that move, it's too late because the Feds are on their asses. The way they're giving out time today, making a million dollars ain't worth spending twenty plus years in the joint," Devin said with a sincere tone in his voice.

"I hear you, baby. I just need you to ride this thing out with me for a little while longer. I got something big about to go down. If this jumps off like I think it will, then I might just take you up on that offer," I said half-heartedly. I sensed from his facial expression that he knew I wasn't about to leave the streets alone anytime soon.

"Do ya thing, princess. I'm just telling how I feel about the situation. What you do is totally up to you. Just know that I got ya back no matter what. I'm about to get up and take a shower because I gotta go open up the barbershop," he said. He got out of the bed and made his way into the bathroom. He showered, got dressed, kissed me on my cheek with those deadly lips of his and was out the door.

I met Devin at Sista's Place four months ago. He was the man in my life at the moment. He owned a barbershop and a car wash that did pretty good business. He was outta the hustling mob and had made a name for himself in the game. After he served several small stints in jail, he realized that he had enough of the life.

Even though he was retired from the game, he still walked with a suave gangster swagger that attracted me to him. He was thugged-out, intelligent and made love to me like a man that knew he was supposed to give his woman multiple orgasms before he was allowed to go to sleep.

He was always on me about leaving the game behind, but I just wasn't hearing that right now. The game was in my blood and I had money to make. I had almost a cool $2 million saved up now, and I needed at least $2.5 million more before I would even consider getting outta the game.

Devin put something on me last night with his freaky Cancer behind. He was in his mid 30's, but he looked like he was twenty-one with his toned body and magical mouth. He had me digging my nails into the wall behind my bed with the way that he put his head game down. His long stroke wasn't no

slouch either. I ain't met a young dude yet that could work me like he did with his love tool.

I had a thing for older dudes because most cats my age were too immature to handle a woman on my level. They were too concerned with trying to get me in the sack as opposed to getting to know me as a woman. I wasn't a chicken head and refused to be treated like one. Guys my age didn't realize that a man had to feed my mind first with something that could hold my attention before he even had the slightest chance to get between my legs. It's true that I sold drugs and might've been a little young, but I also had substance to me.

Since I was a kid, I loved to read a variety of books. My favorite book of all time was Elaine Brown's *A Taste of Power.* She was one bad bitch that didn't take no shit and made power moves that most women would be scared to make. She made men respect her for her mind and her ability to lead. If they ever tried to disrespect her, she was down to get medieval on their asses and pop that steel. Even though she was a social activist and I was a drug dealer, we had a lot of ways in common. In the drug game, Tamara and I made niggas bow down and respect our gangsta. I was never afraid to roll up my sleeves and scrap with a motherfucker or draw that heat if the situation called for it.

I also read anything that I could from Donald Goines because his books were about street life and a reflection of what I saw every day out in the hood. Recently, I started to read a lot of the latest urban fictions books that came out, but most of them were kinda watered down and told a fantasy version of the game. The first book that I read outta these new age joints that was real was called *A Thug's Life* by Thomas Long. That was my shit right there. His book talked about my city and I could feel the grittiness of his writing style. He made the words jump off the page at me like I was in the movies. He gave his readers a picture of the hustling game that was hardcore thug shit without glamorizing the life.

The next joint that I copped that caught my interest was called *Street Life* by a brother named Jihad. I finished his book in a day. I respected the way that brother turned his life around and became a positive role model. It was after reading those two books that I was convinced that I wanted to be a writer. I also read several other books that were put out by Urban Books like *Dirty Money* and *Girls from Da Hood*. Urban Books was started by Carl Weber and I saw their ads in all of the magazines, like *Vibe* and *Sister 2 Sister*. They were doing it up big in the publishing game.

My life story was a novel in itself. I had been working on my book off and on for the last year and planned to self-publish once it was completed. I hoped to be finished with it by the end of the next month. When I heard about sistahs like Vickie Stringer and Teri Woods that owned their own publishing houses, I was sure that I could be just as successful with my writing thing. If there was one thing that was for sure, I knew how to package my product and market it so that it sold like crazy. At the very least the streets had taught me that much. I was an expert saleswoman with certifiable credentials. I planned to put Tamara down with my plans to start a publishing company in the future. For now, this was my little secret.

After I finished fixing my hair, I slid on my capris and a pair of sandals. As I was getting dressed, I felt a sharp pain in right temple that made me double over in agony. I felt nauseous and wanted to throw up. When I lifted my head, the room was spinning around and I was dizzy. I had a terrible headache that made me wanna cry.

I made my way back over to the bed so I could sit down and gather my senses. This was the second time this week that this happened to me. I brushed it off as being nothing after the first time, figuring that it must have been just another one of my migraine headaches. However, this time the pain was much more intense. This episode made me a little nervous because all of my life I'd been a healthy person. I planned to make an appointment with my doctor the following week for a check-up. For now, I popped one of my Imitrex pills and hoped that it kicked in soon enough to take my pain away.

Tamara happened to stop by my house when I went through my last episode. She walked in the room and saw me laid out across the bed in a catatonic state. She knew about my migraine headaches, but she sensed that this might have been a little more serious. She could see it in my eyes that something else was wrong, but I played stupid and told her that I was straight. On the real, I was in some serious pain. She accepted my answer for the moment, but I knew she would be on my case again very soon about it. Tamara always liked to play that big sista role with me like she was my second mother. Shit, she was only ten minutes older than me, but she acted like she was ten years my senior. For now, I wanted to keep this situation to myself until I knew for sure what was going on with me.

I finished getting dressed and made my way into the living room to wait for her slow behind to come and pick me up. I powered up my Dell laptop computer and started to put the final touches on my novel while I waited. No sooner than I sat down, my cell phone went off.

"Yeah, who dis?" I asked.

"It's me, Heavy, baby. Where the hell are y'all at? We was supposed to be meeting at three and it's three-thirty now. What the fuck is going on?" he asked.

"Be patient, nigga. Something came up that we had to handle. We're on our way. Stop acting like a bitch and just hold on," I replied. I had to cover for the fact that Tamara was late once again. She had no sense of time whatsoever.

"Yeah, whatever you say. I thought y'all was supposed to be some balla bitches. I'm trying ta get this money and y'all holding me up. Do I need to go elsewhere to find somebody that's on it like me?" he inquired.

"Stop talking shit, fool. You know damn well ain't nobody else over East that's getting dough like us. Who you gonna get to take our spot?" I shot back. He was silent for a moment. "Yeah, I thought so. We'll see you in a few. Hold tight, nigga," I said.

"Only because it's you do I have a little bit more patience. I'll see y'all when you get here," he said.

Heavy pushed weight on the West Side in the Fairmount Avenue area. His real name was Bernard, but everybody called him Heavy because he was just that—a short, fat motherfucker with nappy hair and rotten-ass teeth. He looked like a cross between the chubby kid from the movie *Juice* and the actor Forest Whitaker. He had four thick rolls of flab on the back of what was supposed to be his neck. His cheeks were so puffy that he looked like a blowfish.

As unpleasant as he was on the eyes, his hustle game made him look like a number one stunna to a lot of these girls. This cat was paid out the ass. What he lacked in looks, he made up for with the fat stack of cash he kept in his platinum, diamond-encrusted money clip. He had more hoes than a pimp. He was one of the few playas on the other side of town that was on our level as far as being a grinder.

As I sat on the couch, I tried to come up with a name for my book. I kicked around several titles before I came up with the name *Murder Mami's*. My book was about three Dominican broads that came to America and locked the drug game down in New York City. These bitches took no prisoners and caught mad bodies on their way to the top. Not only were they fine as hell, they were meaner than a motherfucker. They had the Feds, the DEA, and the Mexican Mafia on their asses. My joint was gonna be action packed with some drama shit poppin' off on every page. I could see my name now up on the top of the *Essence* bestsellers list. I jotted down my ideas on my laptop until I heard Tamia's key turn in the door.

"Yeah, yeah, before you even get started, I know I'm late, hooka. What the heck are you doing? What you writing, a love letter to Devin?" she asked.

"I wasn't gonna say nothing about you being late. Stop trying to read my mind. What I'm writing is none of ya business. You need to worry about getting to where you need to be on time when we've got business to handle. That nigga Heavy done already called me, bitchin' about us being late," I said with a little attitude because she was in my business.

"I know. He called me too, but I ain't answer my phone," she said.

"Just like ya ass to leave me to have to hear the bullshit," I replied.

"Of course. That's what little sisters are for. Let's get outta here," she said with a smile.

I paid the little sister comment no mind and grabbed my keys as we exited my house. We decided to ride in my Lexus coupe to the meeting. Her ass was gonna drive because that was her punishment for being late. I had the car washed the day before and it looked as fresh as new money.

As we rode down the road, these two clowns pulled up next to us at the light. They were in a Dodge Neon with tinted windows, trying to get our attention. They had the nerve to have chrome rims on the car. The music coming from the speakers in their ride sounded like nothing but pure distortion. I had to put my head down to prevent from laughing in their faces.

"Hey, sexy, why don't you pull over for minute so we can holla at y'all?" the driver asked enthusiastically. He had on a knock-off Iverson jersey and New York Yankees cap that looked three sizes too small. I couldn't even see the passenger's face because he was so dark that he blended in with the black seats in the car. All I saw were a set of stained yellow teeth gleaming from the passenger's side of the car.

"A'ight, that'll work. Get in front of us and pull over at the gas station in the next block," I said in a sexy manner.

"What the hell—?" Tamara started to ask curiously before I cut her off.

"Just play along with me, silly," I said.

They pulled in front of us and turned into the gas station as I instructed them to do. However, when they pulled over, we kept on going and left them i looking stupid. I looked back to see the driver standing in the middle of the street with his arms flailing in the air. The nerve of them fools to think they ever had a chance to pull two fine females like us. The joke was truly on them as we went about our way.

"Girl, you are crazy," Tamara said. She laughed so hard that she swerved in her lane as she drove.

"I was just having some fun," I replied. I had to laugh as well because it was too funny.

"I know them assholes feel ten carat stupid for playing themselves like that," she said. We both had to laugh because it was funny as hell.

It took us about twenty minutes before we reached Heavy's spot on Fairmount Avenue. He held his meetings in a pool hall he owned in the neighborhood, called The 8 Ball Lounge.

We parked our car in front of the lounge and went inside to meet with Heavy. We were greeted at the door by his boy Binky. He frisked us to make sure we weren't packing any heat. We left our pistols under the front seats of the car. Binky's perverted ass got a thrill outta frisking us. This was probably the first time in a good while he got a chance to touch an ass as soft as mine with his ugly, reptile-like hands and big, alien-shaped head.

"Right this way, ladies. The boss is waiting for you," he said. He pointed us to a small office in the back of the lounge, not too far from the restrooms. He shot us a sly grin. The thought of his hands on my flesh made me wanna puke.

We entered the office to see Heavy seated in a leather chair with half of his big, moon-sized ass hanging outta the sides. He had two of his young female fans seated on top of his desk. Neither one of them looked to be older than fifteen. Somebody needed to lock his butt up for a statutory rape charge.

"Run along and play, girls. Daddy Heavy has some business to take care of right now," he said. The two young concubines were escorted outta the office by Binky.

"It's about time y'all got here. You're lucky that both of y'all are so fine that I didn't mind waiting to get another glimpse of your pretty smiles. I must say that I am truly impressed by what I see."

"Nigga, whatever plans you have of hittin' this, you might as well cancel. It just ain't gonna happen. We're here for business and nothing more," Tamara said.

"Well, I know I ain't your type because I'm not of the female persuasion, but your sister on the other hand, might be more amenable to the personal services that I have to offer," Heavy said.

"Heavy, please stop playing. I ain't one of them lil' chicken heads like those two that just left outta here. This here ain't for you. Now let's get down to business. Let us hear what you got to say," I said.

"Not a problem. Heavy understands. We can talk about that at a later date. I called this meeting because I was presented with a business opportunity recently that I wanted to share with y'all because you seem like you love gettin' money just like I do," he said.

"No doubt. Keep going," I said.

"Well, I met this dude from Trinidad that can get me some keys for ten grand a pop if I can buy at least fifty each time I re-up. To make moves that big, I need some help. That's where you two come in. That's a lotta work to move and money for me to put up all alone. I need some peoples in this with me that think like I think and that ain't scared to take the risks that come along with gettin' that Escobar-level money. I've been peeping how y'all handle ya business over East, and I like what I see. I can tell that Timmy Barnes taught y'all well," he said.

"True. So, where do we fit into ya plans?" Tamara asked.

"I'm suggesting that we become 50/50 partners in this venture. I wanna put y'all brains together with my muscle and we can put the whole city on pause. I'm proposing that I take over the West Side and I help y'all take over all of the East Side. Whoever don't wanna bow down and give up them drug strips peacefully, their asses is gonna have to get laid the fuck down by this artillery that I got stocked up for just that purpose. With the amount of money I'm trying to make, going to war is not only an option, it's the only option," he said.

"I'm feeling you," I said.

"So do we have a deal?" Heavy asked.

"Does a bear shit in the woods and wipe his ass with a rabbit? Hell yeah we got a deal!" Tamara said.

"Now, that's what I'm talking about. Tell your soldiers to get ready to do battle. We can set up a meeting between them and my boys to strategize how we're gonna go hard at these lames out here," Heavy said.

"That's a done deal," I said.

My eyes lit up when I thought about how much money we could make if we got down with his business proposition. We had no problem at all going to war to expand our territories on the East Side. Our soldiers were ready for combat. If somebody had to die for me to get my snaps, then call me the motherfucking undertaker. Let the body count begin.

Tamara
3

The game was about to change for us in a major way. Heavy put some shit on the table that only a fool would turn down. You had to be built for this lifestyle because only the strong survived out in the streets. Everybody ain't cut out to be a boss in this game. It was situations like this that separated the real Gs from the fake ones. Anybody could put work out on the block and make a few ends, but it took a genius mind to build an organization. Niggas got knocked off every day in the game, and if they were lucky enough to come home from jail, they had nothing left to show for all of that hard work because the Feds took all of their shit just like they did my pops. We didn't plan to go out like that. This thing we were about to build with Heavy would definitely make my pops proud of how he raised us. After we were done, he would see the fruits of the seeds he planted in us come full circle. Twenty years from now, we planned to still be sitting fat off of the money we made today whether we went to jail or not.

"Yo, you know once we set this war off ain't no turning back, right?" Tamia asked.

"What, are you scared?" I asked her.

"Hell no, I ain't scared. You know me better than that. I'm just thinking about who we gotta knock off first to set this shit off. The first motherfucker that comes to mind is D-Bo and his clique. Them niggas is gonna be some shit to deal with, fa sho. He's got a lotta soldiers over there. After him, there's Derek's boys that we gotta deal with over on Old Harford Road. Once we take care of them, the rest of these crews will be a piece of cake," she said confidently.

"True, D-Bo does have a lot of soldiers, but from what I'm hearing on the streets, them niggas ain't eating right. D-Bo and his brothers got them niggas working for pennies while they're living high on the hog. I say we plant some seeds amongst his crew to see who wanna come get money with us. What you think about that?" I asked.

"I think we need to get with Marky so he can round up the troops. Let me take care of D-Bo. I know just how to get him right where I want him. Once we're done with him, we can let Marky and the youngstas take care of Derek and his crew," she said.

"Sounds like a plan to me. I just hope you know what you're doing," I said. She shot me an evil stare and rolled her eyes, but I was dead serious about what I said. If she was gonna handle D-Bo, she had to be sure that she made no mistakes. One wrong move and this whole thing could blow up in our faces.

"I know what I'm doing. You just sit back and watch a master at work," she replied to reassure me.

D-Bo was our major competition on the East Side. His government name was Delbert James, and he went to high school with me and Tamia. Our paths had crossed on numerous occasions in the streets since high school, and there was a mutual respect between us in the hustling game. D-Bo's spots pumped major weight off of Biddle Street. He and his two younger brothers, Jabo and Preston, came up in the game just like us. They were taught the family business by their father, Lionel James. He was locked down in the federal pen, doing football numbers for drug and murder charges.

Lionel and my pops used to hustle together back in the day before they went their separate ways on bad terms. My father never told us exactly what went down between them, but we knew it had to be some shit just by the intense look of anger that came over his face whenever he spoke about him. All he would tell us when he mentioned his old partner was that Lionel was no good and not to be trusted. If my pops didn't fuck with him, then we didn't fuck with him or his seeds either. His enemies were our enemies down through the generations.

As we pulled up on the corner of Barclay Street, we saw Marky putting his mack game down on some young thing. We looked at Marky as the little brother we never had. His mom was a stone cold base head, and his father was AWOL since he was born. He was all alone in this world. He started working for us when he was nine, and we became the closest thing to real parents that he ever knew.

He was homeless and looked raggedy when we took him under our wings. He lived between my crib and Tamia's house up until about six months ago when he had saved up enough money to get his own place. He looked like a totally different person now after we schooled him on the finer things in life. All of his gear was brand name and he drove a money green colored Acura RL that we bought for him for his sixteenth birthday.

Marky had game for a young cat. I observed him on many occasions as he said some slick shit outta his mouth to make one of these young hot ass B'more tramps drop her drawers. He had more bitches than he had fingers and toes. He was a cutie with his clean-cut baby face and cornrows that were always neat and tight. His young ass had two kids already even though he was only eighteen. One of them was by this older chick named Charlene who was twenty-five. The other one was by his main girl, Twiggy. We told him umpteen times to use rubbers, but he wouldn't listen. Now he had to suffer the consequences. Shit, he had to hustle just to take care of his kids because there were no jobs out here that would pay a nigga his age enough to be able to provide the kinda life that this drug money afforded him to live.

All of our young troops were out there on the job like they were supposed to be. We sat back and observed the scenery as we appreciated their hard work. I could smell the scent of money when I rolled the window down on the coupe. I saw the fiends lined up to get served some of that bombin' Prime Time crack rock. I saw the hand to hand exchange of money for goods and got a rush from that shit. I loved the hustle and bustle of the street life. No matter how big a nigga got in this game, a true hustler got an adrenaline rush just being in the midst of all the action.

On the right day, you could get a flat screen TV or chinchilla fur for next to nothing if you found the right ambitious fiend wanting to trade his shit for a blast. You could see a motherfucker get his ass whipped if he ain't share that last rock with his walking buddy. We saw women come through, wanting to sell their kids just to get a hit. Of course, their trifling, smoked-outta-their-mind asses were sent on their way without as much as a dime of rock. Buying a child was a low that not even two money-hungry hustlers like us would sink to. We also wouldn't serve a broad if she was pregnant. If you ever saw a crack baby, you would understand why. That's a gross sight to see. We had some standards to live by, although they were few and far between.

"Hey, Marky, come here, yo. We need to holla at you for a second," I yelled out the window. Marky stopped what he was doing and ran across the street to see what we wanted.

"What up, big sis? You see I got things on point out here. These fools are on their jobs, earning their keep. The money is flowing nonstop. You know how I do. What's good with y'all?" he asked.

"I hear you talking, Mr. Smooth. Don't think I didn't see you over there trying to put a bug in that young thing's ear. You better learn to keep ya dick in ya pants before you wind up catching something that you can't get rid of, boy. On the real tip, we need to holla at you about some things. Hop in so we can go get something to eat and talk business," Tamia said.

"Nah, I'm straight with the broads. That's just Shay, my new flavor of the week. If it's about getting money, then I'm all in. Let me go leave instructions for these young niggas until I come back, and I'll be ready to bounce," he said eagerly.

"Hurry up, man. Time is money. Remember that," I said with emphasis to let him know how serious this business.

Marky left his orders with Joey, one of our other young Gs in training. About a half hour later, we pulled up at Applebee's on Reisterstown Road. The hostess seated us in the bar area. It took almost twenty minutes before a waiter came to take our orders. Bad service pissed me the fuck off. After what seemed like forever, we ordered our food and drinks. Now it was time to talk about business as we waited for her to return.

"So, what's up? What do we have to talk about?" Marky asked.

"We've got big plans coming up, lil' bro, and we want you to be a major part of what we've got going down. You remember that nigga Heavy from over West, right?" I asked. He nodded his head as he responded.

"Yeah, I remember that fat, cupcake-eating motherfucker. I used to fuck one of his girls, Brittany. What about him? You want me to knock his ass off so we can take over his spot?" Marky asked with the bluntness of a cold blooded killer. He was a straight soldier like that. If we gave the order, I knew that he would 187 Heavy's fat butt in a heartbeat.

"Nah, it's just the opposite. We're talking about hooking up with his crew and building a team so strong that we run this whole city," I responded.

"Linking up with his team? I thought we were doing just fine on our own. I'm confused right now. What do we need his ass for?" Marky asked in a hostile pitch.

"Slow ya roll, Marky. Sometimes you gotta make partnerships in this business if you wanna go to the next level. He's got the connections to get coke dirt cheap, and he wants us to hook up with him to take over the whole city. Would you rather keep making what you make now or would like to get a larger piece of the pie like what we plan to give you if you down to ride with us?" I asked in an attempt to reason with him.

"Shit, Tamara, if it makes dollars, it makes sense to me. You know which one I'ma choose. Count me in," Marky said. I was glad that he saw the logic in our thinking.

"Cool. Now what we need you to do is get the meanest lil' niggas that we got in our clique together and hook up with Heavy's peoples because we're about to go to war. They have the artillery, but we need you to be our field general and make sure our interests are represented properly," Tamia said anxiously. I could tell from her body language that she was ready to put in work.

"That's not a problem. What do I get in return?" Marky asked boldly.

"Once we have everything in place, we'll make sure you get your own spot to run as you see fit. That's gonna mean a shitload more money and responsibility for you, but we know that you can handle it. All we want in return is a nice kickback for you renting out a piece of our territory," I said calmly. I knew that if we wanted him to go along with us then I had to make it worth his while.

"I'm with that. Let's make this happen. I love doing business with the two baddest bitches in these here streets," Marky said jokingly. Tamia smacked him playfully on the arm. Marky crouched down in a defensive position to guard himself from the light blows that Tamia threw at him.

"You better watch your mouth, lil' bro because you're in the presence of two ladies here and we ain't those lil' skanks you be fucking out in the streets. Show us some respect," Tamia said.

"I'm sorry, sis. I ain't mean nothing by what I said. I was just playing," Marky said with an innocent look on his face. His baby-making, freak behind might be young, but he was hardly innocent.

"Yeah, you better be. Here comes the waitress with our food. It's been almost forty minutes. It's about damn time," I said. The waitress heard my comment as she placed the food on the table.

"Here goes your order," the waitress said as she threw the food down on the table. She rolled her eyes at me in disapproval of my statement as if I gave a fuck.

"Is there a problem?" I asked her angrily. The look on my face dared her to say something sarcastic. I hadn't had a fight in a good while and didn't mind getting some wreck in on her. She was kinda cute, though, with that nice round ass of hers. I might have to get her number instead.

"There's no problem. Can I get you anything else?" she said.

"I thought so. I ain't think you wanted no problems with me. We're straight for now, but don't go too far because we might need ya services soon," I replied.

"Not a problem, miss," she said. She walked away with her head down, mumbling under her breath. I saw her outta the corner of my eye, standing by the bar. She took my words to heart and did what she was told in not straying too far away from our table. I planned to excuse myself from the table before we left so that I could slide my number to her on the low.

"Tamara, you are crazy as shit. You've got that poor girl scared to death. You are too gangsta for me," Marky said.

"And you know this, man!" I said. We shared a few jokes and acted a fool as we ate our food. It was good to be able to have fun now because pretty soon it was gonna be time to get serious—no smiles or laughs.

Tamia
4

Niggas like D-Bo came a dime a dozen and were so predictable. The one thing that most men had in common was a weakness for pussy. That is usually their downfall in this business. Most of them ran their damn mouths too much to their girls about their dealing in the streets. Then they wondered why, when they got knocked off, them same bitches were the ones they saw on the witness stand, testifying about everything from where their stash house was to where to find the secret bank accounts where they laundered their money. All the Feds had to do was to put pressure on them bitches to give up the info or offer them immunity, and they would run their mouths non-stop, like water flowing from a faucet. Most of them broads wanted to get back at their dudes anyhow for all of the lying and cheating they did with other chicks while they played the wifey role. I planned to use this weakness against D-Bo, to have him like putty in my hands.

Even though our fathers had beef, D-Bo had tried on several occasions to get with me when we were in school and even recently. Of course, I brushed his ass off every time because I never went against my family for no nigga. Whenever he saw me out at the club, he would try to get my attention, no matter how many times I rejected him. Some niggas just don't know how to take no for an answer. Well, tonight he would be in for the shock of his life—he was gonna finally get his wish. I planned to give him a chance to get to know me a little better.

I knew that he would be at Sista's Place tonight because he and his boys went there every Friday night. If anybody ever wanted to knock him off, he was an easy mark because they would know just where to find him. My Pops taught us to always change up our daily routines and never to take the same way home two nights in a row because you never knew if the Feds were tailing you or if some nigga might be trying to set you up for a jack move. Being unpredictable was the best way to survive in this business. I made sure I stayed alert to everything that went on in my surroundings.

I pulled into the parking lot of the club in my bright red CLK Benz and parked my ride. I got out of my car and before the heel of my shoe could even hit the ground firmly and I was able to stand up, all eyes were on me. My skin tight dress had niggas' tongues hanging outta their mouths as I sashayed through the parking lot to the front door. A few of them tried to get my attention, but I kept a stone face as I made my way past the line into the club. The security guard knew who I was and always let me in for free. I didn't have to say a word because my ass did all the talking for me. I was one bad, dangerous bitch on a mission.

I made my way over to the bar ordered a glass of Grand Marnier on the rocks. The music was pumping loud as Lloyd Banks' *On Fire* blasted through the speakers. The place was packed as usual with a professional-looking 25 and older crowd. Normally, this would've been the perfect crowd for me to get my party on with, but tonight I had business to handle.

I saw D-Bo and his boys, Pop and Lenny, standing at the other end of the bar. I grabbed my drink off of the bar and proceeded to the dance floor to get my groove on. I usually danced by myself when I went to the club because I couldn't stand when some fool tried to dry-hump my ass on the dance floor. When I went to a club, it was just to enjoy the music and to soak up the atmosphere. If I wanted to feel a nigga's dick on my ass, I would've hooked up with him outside of the club so that we could handle that business the right way and in the right place– the bedroom.

As I danced to the music, I made sure that I was in plain view for D-Bo to see me as my body gyrated to the beat of the music. Once we made eye contact, I turned up the heat and began to dance more enticing to lure him into my trap. I shot him a big smile to further whet his appetite. He couldn't take his eyes off me as he watched my hips move from side to side with a motion that was as wicked as could be. His hormones got the best of him because he left his boys at the bar and proceeded to the dance floor to check me out up close and personal. He fell right into my trap.

D-Bo was a cutie with his Hill Harper-like good looks and chiseled body. He wore his hair tapered slightly around the edges with a thin mustache. He was dressed in a cream colored linen set that hung from his frame just right. Under different circumstances, he might've had a chance with me, but unfortunately for him, he was just a pawn in my sick little game.

"Damn, Tamia, that dress was made for ya body. You are wearing the shit outta that motherfucker!" he whispered into my ear playfully.

"Thank you, sexy. You ain't looking too bad ya self," I said in response. I pulled his head down toward my mouth with both hands so that he could hear me. I made sure that I accidentally brushed my tongue up against his ear when I spoke. He smiled, and I could tell that he was turned on.

"So, are you gonna just stand there and talk all night or are you gonna join me?" I asked him invitingly.

His smile spoke volumes as he pulled me closer to him. We began to dance, our bodies colliding in rhythm. I couldn't front because D-Bo had some skills on the dance floor. When he pressed his body up against mine, I could feel his nature rising. He was packing some serious heat down there. I would say that he had about eight and a half inches judging by the bulge that I felt in his pants when I grabbed his crotch as he danced behind me. I saw his eyes almost roll into the back of his head when I looked over my shoulder to make sure that he was being enticed by my charm. I pushed my ass up against him with more vigor when the DJ played my joint *Candy Shop* by 50 Cent. He wrapped his arms around my waist and I grabbed a hold of his neck. We danced for about two more songs before we made it over to the back of the club to talk.

"Damn, you tried to put it on a brother out there, didn't you? So, what's up, Tamia? How come you done shot me down so many times and now all of sudden you're acting like you feelin' a nigga?" he asked.

"I don't know. I guess it might've had something to do with the beef between our fathers. I never said you weren't fine, though. I guess I finally decided to let the past be the past. Plus, I had to make you sweat a little bit to get a chance to get with me. Timing is everything, and when we were in school, the time just wasn't right. However, now I think that it is.

Don't ask so many questions. Just be man enough to step up and take advantage of this opportunity that I'm giving you," I said.

"Oh, I'm more than man enough for you, baby," he shot back cockily.

"We'll see. Let's get outta here so we can go somewhere more private and talk," I said with a frankness that made him think he had hit the jackpot. His eyes lit up like all of his fantasies were about to be fulfilled.

"Where did you have in mind, my place or yours?" he asked.

Damn, this nigga was dumb. He was like a poor lamb leading himself to the slaughterhouse. Let's see, our fathers were rivals, I never gave him the time of day before tonight, and outta the blue I'm giving him some play. One would think that he would suspect something was up. A smart hustler should know that something was up. However, he was too caught up in the moment, with the idea of getting some ass, that he let the head in his pants guide the one on his shoulders.

"We can go to your place, but what about ya boys over there?" I asked.

"I'ma holla at them real quick and then we can be out. You can follow me back to my crib," he said.

"Cool. Go handle ya business and I'll be outside waiting for you in my car," I said.

I made a call while I walked to the front door to wait for him. I had to return Devin's missed call. He didn't answer, and after four rings, I left him a voice mail. My message stated that I was hanging out with Tamara and would be out late. That would buy me enough time to do what I needed to do without him suspecting a thing.

About ten minutes later, D-Bo appeared in the parking lot, and we were on our way to his place. He lived not too far away from the club, off of Liberty Heights. I had Marky follow him for the past week to find out where this nigga laid his head down every night.

When we turned down his block, he parked his Acura truck in front of his house and I parked up the block, near the corner, because all of the other spaces were taken. That was cool for me because it just made it easier for me to slide once I took care of business.

We walked into his house and I was surprised at how whack his crib was. With all the money this nigga made, you would think he would at least have a laid-out home. Instead, this nigga had a beat-up-ass sofa and love seat set in his living room that looked like he got it from a second-hand store. The only other thing in the room was a big screen TV. He probably got that for cheap from some crack head, because it looked like it had been through a war with all of the dings and scratches on the sides. There was no artwork hanging on his walls or any kinda style to his place. He must have eaten on the floor because he didn't have any dining room furniture. He drove a truck that cost over 40 grand, but lived in a home that was worth half that much. This nigga was a straight Bama and any sex appeal I thought he had was dead and stinking at this point.

"You want something to drink?" he asked.

"Yeah, let me get a glass of wine," I said. I looked around to make sure there were no roaches before I took a seat on his couch. He came back in the room and handed me a glass of Boone's wine. This nigga was straight low budget. I drank the wine and smiled like I was really feeling him.

"Tamia, let's go upstairs and get more comfortable. My bedroom is a lot more cozy than it is down here," he said.

"After you," I responded as I hid my utter shock at how jacked-up his place looked.

I followed him up the squeaky stairs. After I saw the downstairs, I could only imagine what his bedroom looked like. When he opened the bedroom door, I was speechless. This clown had a king-sized waterbed with a bearskin comforter laid across some red silk sheets. His bedroom set was so small that it looked like the same one he must've had when he was a kid.

He flipped the light switch and a neon red disco light lit up in the middle of the ceiling. He turned on the stereo and *Smooth Sailin' Tonight* by the Isley Brothers played outta the speakers. This dude must've thought that he was Shaft or some shit.

"So, do you like the layout? I know that it looks old school, but you gotta admit that it's fly, right?" he asked me with a dead serious look on his face. He obviously thought he had it going on. In reality, his style was as stale as ten day old bread.

"Yeah, you definitely have your own style, man. Nobody can take that away from you. Enough of the small talk. Let's get down to business. I wanna see if you move as good in the bed as you do on the dance floor," I said.

"Damn, you get right to the point, don't you?" he asked.

I pushed him down onto the bed and got on top of him to straddle his already hard penis. He kicked off his shoes while I unbuttoned his pants. My estimate was right. His manhood was just as big as I thought it was. He pulled me toward him and attempted to kiss me on the lips. I put my hand over my mouth to block his tongue from entering.

"Damn, baby, why you teasing a nigga? You know I how long I've wanted to get with you," he said.

"Slow down. We have all night. I'm running this show. Remember that," I said. He was like a little kid in a candy store, with the big grin he had on his face. I could do whatever I wanted to him at this point.

I ripped his shirt open to reveal his bare chest. I ran my tongue across his nipples and he raised up off of the bed outta sheer excitement. I stroked his hardness swiftly. His thighs tensed up, and I sensed that he was about to cum. That's when I released my grip and lifted up my dress to reveal my pink thong. I turned around so that he could see my ass up in the air. I slapped it real hard to make him go wild.

"That's that shit right there! Give me that ass, girl! I wanna hit that thing from the back!" he yelled.

"You can have it however you want it, daddy, but first you have to let me tie you up. This is my game, and we have to play it my way," I said.

"Tie me up? I ain't never had a broad do that before," he said

I unzipped my dress from the back and let if fall to the floor. I stood in front of him with nothing on except my bra and thong set from Victoria's Secret. I sensed that he was a little hesitant, so I had to dig a little deeper into my bag of tricks.

I crawled up onto the bed and put my secret place up against his face so that he could smell the sweet scent emanating from my crotch up close and personal. He tongue wagged outta his mouth like a dog in heat. That was all I needed to do to make him fully submit.

"Fuck it, I'm down for whatever!" he said.

I retrieved my purse off of the floor and pulled out the handcuffs I had purchased the other day from Spencer's. I had also bought some metal chains to tie around his ankles. I walked back over to the bed towards him as he laid there like a lil' bitch, curled up in the fetal position. I put the chains around his ankles first. Next, I sat on top of him and took his right arm and cuffed it to the right bedpost. I did the same thing with his left arm. His body jerked a little, and I sensed that he might've had a second thought. To calm him down, I grinded my hips on his manhood, and he relaxed his nerves. I crawled off of the bed and stood in front of him.

"So, what's next?" he asked. His inhibitions about being bound up were gone. He was down to do whatever was necessary to get a taste of me.

"Well let's see. I think I might have a little fun torturing you before I kill ya stupid ass," I said. He tried to jump up, but his level of movement was restrained by the handcuffs and metal chains. I think it finally started to sink in that he let himself be set up. I lit up a cigarette as I contemplated how I wanted to toy with this idiot.

"What the hell is going on? Bitch, you better untie me. I should've known that something wasn't right with you. All these years you ain't give a nigga no play, and now you was actin' like a slut up in the club tonight," he said frantically. His ass was petrified and powerless.

"Hindsight is always 20/20. Yeah, you should've suspected that something was up, but that's what you get for thinking with ya dick and not ya brain," I said as I laughed. I got my switchblade from my purse and sliced an X across his chest. He got that mark for calling me a slut. He yelled in excruciating pain as his blood dripped down his chest.

"Tell me what the fuck you want. Shit, is it money? If it is, we can work something out. Untie me and let's talk shop," he said. I took my lit cigarette and pressed it up against the side of his face. The scalding heat left a lasting impression on his left cheek. I could see that he wanted to cry. It was funny to see a so-called thug reduced to a pathetic, whimpering shell of a man.

"Oh, there ain't shit to work out. Yeah, this is about money, but not in the way that you think. You see, we plan to take over your territory once I get rid of you and ya stupid-ass brothers. Heavy made us an offer that we couldn't refuse," I said.

"Come on, baby. This ain't even got to go down like this. You can't trust that nigga Heavy. He's a snake. He'll sell you out as soon as you do his dirty work. Trust me. I know him a lot better than you do," he said.

"Well, it's a shame for you that you won't be around to worry about that, now, will you?" I asked.

"My brothers ain't gonna let you get away with this. My boys saw me leave with you, and once they find out something happened to me, they are gonna put two and two together and know that you had something to do with it," he said.

"Oh, are you talking about Lenny and Pop? They already know what's going down. I hooked up with them last week. They helped me set you up. I told them to make sure you were at the club tonight so that my plan worked to perfection. You see, you shoulda paid ya people properly and then they wouldn't be so eager to off ya ass for exploiting them. As for ya brothers, they'll be joining you in hell once this is all over," I said.

After we had our sit-down with Heavy, I put Marky on the case to find out whatever dirt he could on D-Bo's crew. It turned out that Lenny and Pop were two young, hungry niggas that were eager to knock off their bosses if the money was right. D-Bo and his brothers had shorted them on their cut of the profits of a package on more than enough occasions. Once we offered to make them lieutenants in our organization, they were dying to help us rid the East Side of the James Boys. They put together their own little crew that would take care of Jabo and Preston tonight. Lenny and Pop had respect among the lower level workers in the James crew, so it would be easy for them to assume a leadership role over them in the new regime we were about to build.

"This is fucked up. I ain't never did shit to you. Why the fuck you gotta do me like this? It's enough money out here in the streets that we ain't gotta go this route," he begged and pleaded.

"That might be true, but I guess you could say that we're greedy like you are. We want all of the money. Do you have any last words before we bring this thing to a close? I need to be home so that I can watch *Nip/Tuck*," I said nonchalantly to his cries for mercy.

"Yeah, I got some last words. Fuck you and your dike ass sista. You both are gonna get yours one day. Fuck your pops, and I hope he rots in jail like the weak ass man he is. He shoulda killed my father when he had the chance, but he was too soft. Fuck that ho of a mother of yours, too, for spittin' you outta her funky snatch. My father said the pussy wasn't that good anyway," he said.

He continued his ranting and raving until I pulled out the .22 that was in my purse and put three fatal shots to his dome. He died instantly from his wounds.

I gathered my clothes off of the floor and put them on. I made my exit outta the back door of his funky, tore-down shack so that none of his neighbors had a chance to see me leave. I walked around the block through the alley to get to my car.

My mind was a little messed up by the things that D-Bo said about my parents. This motherfucker just insulted my whole family. If I could bring him back to life and kill him again, I would, just to make him relive the pain. Nobody ever talked bad about my family and lived. He called my pops soft and said my mother was a ho. He said that his father fucked my Moms. I knew that couldn't be true because she was always faithful to Daddy to my knowledge. I knew that she wouldn't go out like that, especially not with one of Daddy's friends. Nonetheless, the possibility that what D-Bo said could be true weighed on me heavily as I drove off. I planned to talk my mother to get to the bottom of this issue. I had to know the truth for my own peace of mind.

Tamara
5

"That's it right there, baby. You're hittin' my spot. Oooh, yeah. I love that shit. Make this pussy cum. I wanna shoot my juices all over your face," I said to Latoya. She was on her job tonight.

Latoya ate me out like my coochie was a sour apple-flavored Blow Pop. She teased me with her tongue until she reached the sweet treat in the middle that was my throbbing clit. She took it in her mouth and then proceeded to give me immeasurable pleasure for the umpteenth time that night. She knew all of the right spots to hit to make me release every bit of my fruity-tasting juices on her chin.

"Whose pussy is this?" she asked as if she didn't know already.

"It's yours, baby. It's yours. You can have me any time and in any way you want me," I replied.

Like on cue with what I just said, Latoya flipped me over on the bed so that my ass was up in the air. She strapped on her dildo and entered me from behind. I buried my face in the pillow to muffle my screams of passion. She spanked my ass in rhythm with her every stroke. I grabbed onto the bedposts to keep my balance while she made love to me so intensely from behind.

Throughout our relationship we'd had sex more times than I could count, but each time it just seemed to get better and better. I released my fluids all over the ten-inch strap on she wore.

"Damn, that shit was good. Now I wanna return the favor," I said without a hint of doubt in my voice that she had fully satisfied my needs.

"You'll get no arguments from me," she said submissively.

Latoya lay back onto the bed and braced herself for what came next. I bent down and kissed her on the mouth. Our tongues danced together intimately for about two minutes while my hands fondled her beautiful 34C breasts. I maneuvered my tongue down her chest and took her left, then right, nipple into my steaming hot mouth. I could tell that Latoya loved every minute of it when she began to play in my hair.

After we enjoyed the warm vibes of the heat that our bodies generated from being rubbed up against each other for a while, I reached under the bed and pulled out my trusty Bullet. I parted her smoothly brown toned thighs and placed one of each on my shoulders. I switched the power on for the Bullet and placed it up against her clit. The vibrations of the Bullet made her body raise up off the bed. When I added my tongue into the mix, it was all she wrote.

"Ummm, T. You make me feel so good. I love your ass so damn much. I ain't never gonna leave ya ass or let you leave me! Oh, shit, I'm cummin'! Don't stop! I'm cummin'!" Latoya yelled.

I felt the same way about her as she did about me. We would be together for ever. No other bitch could make me feel the way she did. We fell asleep in each others arms. I awoke in the morning about nine o'clock to the sound of the Keisha Cole ring tone on my cell phone. It was Tamia.

"What's up, sis? What's good with you?" I asked.

"Everything is going according to schedule. However, we need to talk. We might have a situation to handle. It's family business. I'm on my way over to your crib. I'll be there in like fifteen minutes," she said. I noticed a bit of nervousness in her speech that had me concerned.

"A'ight. I'ma see you when you get here," I said.

"Baby, what did your sister want?" Latoya asked.

"I'm not sure. She didn't sound like herself. She said that she had some family business to discuss," I replied.

"I hope everything is OK. Tamara, I meant what I said about us being together forever. I love ya ass to death. I also want you to think about getting outta the game. The streets are starting to be more and more dangerous every day. Every time I turn on the news, I hear about somebody getting shot in a drug-related incident. I hope and pray all the time that you weren't involved in any way because if you were, I would just go crazy," she said.

"You ain't got anything to worry about. I'm careful about how I handle my business. Besides, you knew what I was into when you get involved with me. I'm a gangster bitch now and plan to stay that way until I die. You can either accept me how I am or roll out," I said.

"You ain't gotta be so mean. I hate it when you act like that," she replied.

I tried to hug her, but she pulled away and curled up in the bed. I left her there and went into the living room to wait for my sister. My mouth was writing a check that my ass couldn't cash because I would be lost without Latoya in my life. I loved her much more than I let it show.

Latoya worked as a receptionist for a company that sold aluminum siding. She also went to 'school part-time at Baltimore City Community College. She came from a two parent family. Her mother was a sales associate at Hecht's department store and her father was a janitor for the Baltimore City school system. She never got into any kind of trouble with the law. She represented my good side with all of the bad things that I did being in the game. She kept some sort of balance in my world so that I wouldn't totally go off the deep end in my dangerous lifestyle.

I was in the kitchen getting myself a glass of orange juice when I heard Tamia walk in the front door with a pissed off look on her face. She was in a bad mood. I knew what she had planned for D-Bo last night, and I hoped that nothing went wrong. If it did, then we were fucked.

"So, what's up, lil' sis? What's on ya mind? Did something go wrong last night?" I asked.

"Hell no. I played that nigga D-Bo just like I said I would. Lenny and Pop took care of his two brothers as well," she said. She ran down the whole scenario of how she offed D-Bo. I felt a sense of relief. My lil' sis had come through big time. I was relieved.

"Well, then what is the problem?" I asked. She had me utterly confused at this point.

"When I was with that D-Bo, he said some shit about our mother that has me thinking," she replied emptily. Her incomplete statement added to my confusion, and I started to get a little upset at her vagueness.

"He said something about our mother? He doesn't know her. What did he say?" I asked with a hint of anger in my voice.

"He said something to the effect that his pops had messed around with Mommy behind Daddy's back," she replied.

"That's bullshit. Mommy ain't never fool around on Daddy. That's probably some bullshit his father made up and told him," I said.

"Maybe so, but I think that we should ask Mommy about it just to be sure. If you think about it, something had to happen that was serious between him and Pops for them to have such a serious beef," she said. That point never occurred to me until she brought it up at that moment.

"You might be right. We'll just have to ask Mommy and get to the bottom of this whole nonsense," I said. When I turned around, Latoya stood in the doorway. She had to catch the tail end of our conversation.

"Hey, Tamia. What's up?" Latoya asked.

"What's up, Toya? I'm chillin'," Tamia said.

"Never mind how she's doing. Can't you see that we're having a private conversation? Why you gotta be sneaking up on us like that?" I asked.

"Well, excuse me. I wasn't sneaking around. I was coming to get something to eat. I do live here too. I'm sorry, Tamia. I didn't mean to interrupt y'all conversation. I guess I'll go back in the bedroom. Some people are just so rude," she replied. She shot me an evil stare as she exited. I would deal with her ass later.

"You better stop being so mean to that girl. She's gonna leave ya ass one day," Tamia said.

"She ain't going anywhere. She'll be a'ight. Moving on to more important things, we can settle this whole situation with Mommy when she comes back from her vacation next week," I said.

"You're right. Besides, we've got bigger fish to fry. Now that D-Bo is outta the way, we gotta move onto our next target. We need to get with Marky and make our move on Derek's crew," she said.

"I spoke with Heavy yesterday, and he's on point with his team. Once this is all over, we're gonna be sitting fatter than a mother," I said.

"That is without a doubt. I'm outta here. I got a lunch date with Devin," she said.

"Cool. Tell him I said what's up. Holla at me later," I said. We hugged and she was on our way, but she left me with something to think about. My mother was cheating on my father? No way, no how. It just couldn't be, especially not with one of his boys. However, the truth of the matter would have to wait. I had to block that shit outta my head. I placed a call to Marky to give him the green light on Derek. It was time to move to the second phase of our plan.

Marky
6

"Hell yeah, this some good-ass weed, son. Pass that Henny over here so I can hit that real quick," I said to Joey.

I passed him the blunt and he passed me the bottle of liquor. I put the bottle to my mouth and took a shot straight to the head. I damn near finished off the whole bottle. There was nothing like getting twisted right before you had to go push some nigga's shit back. This was how a real G was supposed to get down before he had to put in some work. It was best for me to be high as a motherfucker so that there was no way for me to be second guessing what I had to do or to get caught slippin'. When the weed took its effect, any subconscious thoughts of guilt that I might've had about laying somebody down was blocked totally outta my mind, and the euphoria from the high had me alert and ready to bring my "A" game to this mission.

"Damn, nigga, I thought you said you wanted a sip of the Henny. You done damn near drank the whole bottle. That's exactly why you can't share your shit with black folks," Joey said jokingly.

"Yeah, whatever, fool. I got you on the next go around. While you over there running ya mouth, you're lettin' the blunt burn out. Pass that shit back over here. Let me show you how a real man hits that shit," I said. I took a deep toke of the blunt and damn near crashed the beat-up hooptie I was driving into a light pole. I was high enough to touch the sky. The other members of our crew that were in the two cars behind us had to slam on the brakes to avoid rear-ending us.

Joey was my right hand man, and I chose him to ride shotgun with me to take care of Derek and his crew. He was just the typa nigga that I needed to ride with me because he was fearless and money-hungry just like I was. We hustled together out on the strip all day long until the sun came up.

We both came from the same kinda fucked-up, broken family life. His pops was missing in action and his moms used to love to use his face for a punching bag whenever she came in the house amped up on liquor and heroin. We were like brothers. He was older than me by like two months, and he had me by about two inches in height. Nonetheless, he respected my position as lieutenant in the crew and never questioned my authority. He knew that I would never ask one of my niggas to do something that I wasn't down to do myself. That was just how I rolled.

Joey and I had scoped out Derek's crew on the low for the past two weeks. We monitored their operation so that we could figure out the best time to catch Derek in his hood with his guard down. He usually came through every night around ten to do a money pickup and to shoot the shit with his crew.

Derek only had one bodyguard with him when he came through the strip. I noticed that he had two niggas out on the strip at each end of the block as lookouts, and ten niggas out on the block doing hand to hand sales. There was no telling how many of them niggas had a burner on them, so we needed to come strapped with some serious firepower. I had my trusty .38 in my dip and Joey packed a .45 revolver. All of my other niggas had their heat locked and loaded for action as well.

Joey and I rode together while Tommy, Marcell, Slim, and Iggy rode behind us in a beat up Malibu. In the whip behind them, a couple of Heavy's boys, Skip and Deuce, pulled up the rear. I felt that we really didn't need them outside niggas to do the job, but since Heavy was supposed to be a part of our team now, I had to go along with whatever the twins wanted. I didn't know any of them niggas like that and I just hoped they didn't do anything to fuck up my plans. I had a lot to lose and a lot to gain from this situation. I had been a team player for a good minute, but now it was time for me to get my weight up and make some major moves. This was the opportunity of a lifetime and I didn't plan to blow it for anything.

We weaved through traffic en route to Derek's dope strip off of Harford Road. I cruised through the strip to observe the scene before we made a move, and there was Derek, out on the corner, holding court with his bodyguard and some other dude that I didn't know. He was dressed in green army fatigues flossing enough platinum and ice around his neck to make Jacob the jeweler stop and stare for a minute. I was definitely gonna have to get them jewels up off of him after I merked his ass.

I hit a left at the next light and parked my whip at the end of the block. The rest of my team did the same.

I sent Tommy around the corner to creep up on the far end of the block, where one of the lookout dudes was located. Slim and Iggy hid behind a car on the next block and sat tight, waiting for my signal. Marcell went into the corner store and acted like he was in there to buy something. Skip and Deuce were posted up at a phone booth while Deuce acted like he was making a phone call.

Joey and I planned to come straight at Derek and his niggas on some slick shit. All we needed for the rest of our team to do was have our backs in case any of Derek's boys went for their heat. I had on a pair of dusty jeans, a dingy hooded sweatshirt, and a beat-up Orioles hat. Joey had on a black Russell sweat suit filled with holes and a pair of run-over Air Force Ones. We looked like two down-on-our luck junkies on the hunt for our next fix. We had the perfect disguise. These niggas wouldn't suspect that we were up to shit.

As we approached the corner where Derek and his boys were posted up, I saw his black Hummer parked with the passenger door open and the stereo blasting at full volume. He sat on the hood of the truck talking shit to his bodyguard and the other dude as they passed a blunt back and forth. They were so caught up in conversation, they didn't see us coming. Before I knew it, we were right up on them. It was show time.

"Excuse me, homey. Do one of y'all got a light?" I asked, holding a cigarette butt in my hand.

"Hell, no, we ain't got a light. You better take your dusty ass up the block somewhere, fool. Don't you see me talking over here? You dirty junkie motherfucker, you better show some respect," Derek yelled at me. This nigga was putting on a show for his boys. That was cool because I had something for that ass real soon.

"My bad, big man. We didn't mean any disrespect," Joey said timidly.

"Nigga, was I talking to you? Hell no, so keep ya fucking mouth shut!" Derek yelled at Joey. Derek's boys ate that shit up as they all laughed at his antics.

"You da man. We don't won't no trouble, boss," I replied humbly.

"Good, now walk ya ass up the block and buy a coupla of them chunky crack rocks we got for sale. If you ain't out here to cop, then you ain't got no business out here on my strip," Derek said.

I said nothing and put my head down to make it appear as though I was walking away. When Derek turned his head back around toward his audience, I reached into my dip for my pistol and had it at the back of his dome so fast that none of his boys had time to react. Joey reached for his shit just as quick and held Derek's partners at bay.

"Now, what was that shit that you were talking, fool? Run them jewels that you got around ya neck," I said. I stepped back some with the pistol still pointed at his head so that he could take off his jewels. I snatched the chain outta his hand and put it in the pocket of my sweatshirt.

"Nigga, you don't know who you fucking with out here. You got that pistol pointed at my head, you better be sure you ready to use that motherfucker," Derek said defiantly.

"You ain't in no position to talk shit, Derek. Get ya ass down on ya knees. I wanna make you beg for ya life before I kill ya ass," I said with venom.

Derek got down on his knees with his hands behind his back. His bodyguard stood silently with a stupid look on his face. There was nothing he could do. We had the drop on them.

Some of Derek's other workers at the other end of the strip noticed the commotion and came toward us with their pistols drawn. Little did they know that we had them surrounded and were ready to let them hammers go.

Derek's crew let off a coupla shots in our direction, but none of them hit us. Tommy and the rest of my team returned fire from all directions and caught them off guard. Joey squeezed off a slew of shots that found their mark in Derek's bodyguard and the other sap that was with them. They both slumped over onto the ground as their blood ran out onto the sidewalk.

Derek tried to whip around and reach for my gun, but he was too slow. I put three slugs at point blank range into his chest. I knew his ass was dead when I saw his eyes roll into the back of his head and his eyelids shut.

Derek's boys tried to run for cover, but they were too slow. I know that a few of them, if not all of them, were hit because I saw them laid out on the sidewalk. It was time to get the fuck outta dodge.

We all broke camp and headed back to our cars. With all of these bodies laid out on the streets, we were sure to make the 11 o'clock news. I could see the headline in the morning paper *A Blood Bath on Harford Road. Another drug deal/robbery gone bad. Several victims were dead, while several others were seriously wounded. No witnesses were found or suspects arrested.*

Our mission was accomplished. It was time to celebrate. I was about to be a rich nigga. Even though Tamara and Tamia said they would promote me in the new organization, I wanted more than that. I wanted to be the boss. I had it laid out in my mind how I planned to make that come true. They were my girls and all and they had looked out for me through the years, but I had my own dreams and ambitions that didn't include them in the mix. It was a dog eat dog world out here in the streets, and I was a pit bull ready to lockjaw on the whole game, regardless of who I had to step on.

Tamia
7

Mommy had just returned from her Caribbean cruise with her girlfriend, Melissa. They had been gone for almost two weeks. Tamara and I paid for the trip and all of their expenses. My mother never had to want for anything because we took care all of her bills and all of her shopping needs. She lived a life fit for queen because to us, that's exactly what she was. She didn't care if we all survived off of this dirty street money because as far as she was concerned, drug money spent the same as money earned from working a 9 to 5 job. It was all green and came from the same source, the United States government. She worked part-time as a teacher's assistant, or paraprofessional as they were called, at an elementary school because she loved kids, and it was something for her to do to pass her days away.

Our mother was in her early 40's, but she didn't look a day over twenty-five. Whenever our mother went out to the mall with me and Tamara, everybody swore that all three of us were sisters. More than enough dudes our age tried to push up on her. She kept her figure in shape by working out at the gym three times a week—and courtesy of the good lipo job we treated her to for her birthday last year. She had plans to get a boob job done next fall. Shit, there wasn't anything wrong with using plastic surgery to hold onto your youth. When I got older, I planned to do the same thing.

Mommy had no problem playing the Stella role since Daddy had been locked down because she had a thing for young men. She said they made her feel like she was still in her twenties. It also boosted her self-esteem that she was able to hold her own in the bed with a younger man. The last coupla dudes she dated were barely pushing thirty, but she had every single one of them wrapped around her finger.

I didn't mind her dating younger guys because if it made her happy then I was all for her gettin' her groove back as long as them cats showed her respect as a lady. Shit, Daddy wasn't gonna be home anytime soon, and as a woman, she had the right to sow her oats any way that she pleased. He sure sowed his oats enough with other women throughout the years. No matter who she messed with, the bottom line was that both of them were my parents and I loved them equally.

This situation involving Lionel James was something that had been eating away at me. I had to know if what D-Bo said about them messing around had any truth to it. That was why I was on my way over to Mommy's house to meet her and Tamara so that we could all talk. If what he said had any truth to it, I would be mad as hell. Shit, it was one thing for her to mess around on him, but to do it with one of his friends was a level of betrayal that was almost unforgivable. You just don't violate the ones you love that way. If I ever thought that Tamara would mess around with a nigga that I was in love with behind my back, I would kill her and that nigga without a second thought. In my eyes, one couldn't do anything more cruddy to family or a close friend. I would definitely look at her in a different light. Mommy had no idea what we wanted to talk to her about, but she would find out soon enough.

I pulled up into the driveway of the cozy four bedroom house we purchased for Mommy out in the quiet suburban Reisterstown, Maryland area. I saw her Lincoln Navigator parked out in the driveway, and Tamara's Benz was parked right behind her. I felt a little nervous as I walked towards the front door, but I knew that we had to have this conversation if I wanted to know the truth. My palms were sweaty and I had butterflies in my stomach.

God, I hope this nigga told me a lie, was all I kept saying to myself. As I got closer to the porch, I noticed that the door was ajar and there was a loud commotion going on inside. When I opened the door, I couldn't believe my eyes. Mommy had Tamara pinned down on the living room floor and was whaling away on her with both hands like it was nobody's business. Their clothes were ripped up and their hair looked a mess. There were spots of blood on the carpet and broken furniture everywhere.

"You lil' bitch, don't you ever raise your hand up against me. I don't give a fuck what you think about something that I did. I brought your ass into this world and I can take you the fuck out of it just as quickly," Mommy said in a tone I had never heard before.

Tamara somehow gathered the strength to flip Mommy over. "Fuck you. You ain't nothing but a tramp. You ain't no mother of mine," Tamara yelled. She landed several sharp blows to Mommy's face. I pushed her off of Mommy and stood between them.

"What the hell are you two doing? That's your daughter, Ma. Tamara, that's your mother you were hitting on. Are you both crazy?" I screamed as loud as I could. They both tried to charge at each other, but I refused to let either one of them get to the other one. I felt like a matador fighting off two charging bulls.

"She ain't no daughter of mine. When she's grown enough to raise her hands up to swing on her mother, then she better be woman enough to take this ass whoopin' that I got waiting for her," Mommy said eagerly. She was ready to get back to battle, but I wouldn't allow it to go down.

"Whatever. I ain't scared of you. You ain't nothing. Tell her what you just told me. See if she don't wanna help me beat ya ass for what you did to us. I hate you for what you did to our family," Tamara said with fire in her eyes. As those words came outta her mouth, all of the rage that Mommy displayed turned into tears as she sat on the couch in an obvious state of turmoil.

"Somebody please tell me what's going on" I said, totally taken a back by the whole situation.

"I'll tell you what's going on. When I asked your mother here about her messing around on Daddy with Lionel, she admitted that it was true. She fucked around on Daddy with his best friend. However, that ain't all she admitted went down. She told me that nigga Lionel James was our *real* father. She said that they had a blood test done years ago and found this to be true, but that Daddy didn't know anything about it. It's been a secret for all of these years. Our father ain't really our father. Can you believe this shit? She deceived him and us all of these years. That's why I hauled off and slapped her ass. That woman ain't no mother of mine," Tamara said.

"Mommy, tell me she got shit confused. Tell me what she just said was a lie. It is a lie, isn't it?" I asked. I was hoping that she would deny it all, but she didn't. My heart wasn't prepared for what came next.

"No, Tamia, it's true. Lionel James is really your biological father. It only happened one time. It was a mistake. I swear. I just lost it when I found your father in bed with another woman in our house. I had caught him cheating so much that I accepted his womanizing ways, because I just loved that man that much. However, for him to fuck another woman in our bed, that was a violation. I had to get back at him for disrespecting me like that. I figured that the best way to do that was to sleep with his best friend.

I saw the way that Lionel used to look at me, and I knew that he would be down for it if I made the first move. It happened, and I regretted it right after it was over. I wish that I could take that night back, but I can't.

Your father found out and wanted to kill Lionel, but he gave him a pass because he loved him like a brother. If it were anybody else, he would've killed that person on the spot. This was why they stopped speaking to each other. It was over me.

When I found out that Lionel was your father, I made the choice not to tell Timmy. I know that I was wrong, but you're both still my daughters. Please forgive me! Tell me that you forgive me!" she pleaded. She reached out to hug me, but I pushed her arms away.

"Mommy how could you? Our whole lives have been one big lie. You want us to forgive you for hiding our real identity from us all of these years? I wanna see how Daddy feels about this when I tell him the truth. He's gonna be crushed. It's good for you that he's behind bars," I said. I was confused and hurt at the same time.

"Baby, please don't tell him. Let me be the one to break it to him. At least give me that much of a courtesy," she pleaded.

"The only courtesy that you get from me is that I'm gonna give you one week to pack your shit and get outta this house that our money paid for. As far as I'm concerned, I no longer have a mother. You're dead to me," Tamara said coldly. The words dropped like a ton of steel on my mother's head as she balled up on the couch.

"Mommy, I really don't know what the fuck to say right now. My head is so jacked up. I need to get away to clear my thoughts. I can't believe you did this to me. I can't believe you did this to us," I said repeatedly. I tried to be as calm as I could in the face of the madness that my life had become in such a short time. My head started to pound with such intensity that it felt like somebody was grinding my brain between two cinder blocks. I sensed that a migraine headache was about to come on.

"Tell me what I have to do to make this right. I swear I will do anything to make this right!" Mommy said. I wanted to believe that we could make this all go away, but I knew that wasn't reality.

"Drop dead. That would be a huge favor to us all," Tamara interjected with nothing but hatred in voice.

"The Barnes family ain't shit. We have no loyalty between us at all. Everything that Daddy—or the man that I thought all of these years was my father—taught me about honor was just one big lie. Where do I go from here? What the hell am I doing here? Who the hell am I? Is my last name Barnes or James?" I blurted out in agreement. I felt like my spirit had left my body and I was just a being suspended in nothingness with no aim or purpose in life anymore.

"You're Tamia and Tamara Barnes, the daughters of Timmy Barnes. Just because he's not your biological father doesn't mean anything. He is still the only father that you both have ever known. Let's not let this mistake of mine tear us all apart," Mommy said as she tried to be a voice of reason.

"This ain't no family anymore. I'm done talking about this. I'll be back through next week to pick up the keys to the house. I'll expect for you to have ya shit outta here by then. T, are you ready to bounce?" Tamara asked.

"Tamia, baby, please don't leave like this. We all need to calm down and come to our senses," Mommy said.

"I can't handle this right now. I need to get outta here. I just need to be free so I can make some sense outta this mess. I gotta go! I just have to leave now!" I yelled. I ran past both of them outta the house. I started my car and raced off.

As I drove, tears started to stream down my face. I tried to calm down and see this whole situation as rationally as I could, but I just found myself getting more enraged. I was mad at my mother. I was mad at my sister for bringing up the situation to her before I got there. She had no right to do that because she promised me that she would wait until I got to Mommy's house before she brought up the issue. It was just like her to do what she wanted when she wanted. I felt that I couldn't trust her either. I was mad that the man that I looked up to all of my life and called Daddy wasn't really my father. I tried to see the situation through my mother's eyes and imagined how hard it was for her to carry around this lie all of these years. However, I just couldn't muster up any sympathy for her. All that I felt was hatred and contempt.

To top it all off, D-Bo was my brother and I killed him. How could I live the rest of my life knowing that I killed my own brother? I not only killed him, but I was also responsible for the deaths of my other two brothers as well. I actually kissed D-Bo like a woman kisses her man. His mouth had brushed up against my private parts. I felt so filthy. How could I not know that he was my brother? We had to resemble each other in some way. Was I crazy or was it just that I was born into a crazy world? My life was one big blur at the moment.

My cell phone rang several times. It was Tamara. I didn't answer it because I didn't want to deal with her right now either. I didn't even care about this thing that we had going on with Heavy. It was the last thing that I had on my mind. I needed to pay a visit to Timmy Barnes to try and get some clarity in my life. I needed to see him in person so I could look into his eyes. I wanted him to hold like he did when I was a little girl and give me the secure feeling that he could make whatever was wrong be all right.

I placed a call to Devin because I needed to be with my man right now for some comfort and support. I just wanted to get away from this city and my whole family.

Tamara
8

"Damn, T., where the hell is you at? You're not home. You're not answering the phone. I've called you a thousand times. All I get is your goddamn answering machine. We need to talk girl. I need you right now for real! Stop acting like a shit head. I need to talk to my other half. Pick up the damn phone and call me when you get this message!"

This was the last in a long line of messages I left for my sister and she had yet to return my calls. It had been five days since the incident we had with the woman who gave birth to us, and I had no clue where she was. It wasn't like her to not reach out to me for this long. I sensed that something wasn't right. I tried to call Devin, but his cell phone went straight to voice mail. I went past his barber shop and his barbers told me that hadn't been in for a couple of days. That led me to believe that they must be together somewhere. However, she could have at least hit me up to let me know that she was all right after the way she stormed out of that woman's house. I knew that the bombshell that was just dropped on us weighed heavily on her, but we needed each other to get through this. We were two sides of the same coin, and without her here to be my support system, I felt empty. Latoya tried to be as supportive as she could, but it just wasn't the same.

That woman, Priscilla Barnes, had called me several times in an attempt to make amends, but I cursed her out every time I answered the phone. I guess she must have gotten the message that I was serious about not wanting to have anything to do with her, because she hadn't called me in a day or so. I was also serious about her ass moving outta that house that we bought for her. I planned to send some niggas over there to make sure that her shit was outta that house as I commanded her to do. There was no way in hell that I was gonna be kicking out no money to pay for her to live in a phat-ass crib after the way she deceived us. I would burn in hell before I let that happen.

I heard it said somewhere once that you should never hate your mother or father no matter what they did wrong because they were the ones who gave you life, but I felt differently. That was some bullshit said by some motherfucker who didn't have his whole world ripped to shreds by somebody who claimed to love him. After what my mother did, I just couldn't see myself trusting her ever again.

In the midst of all this family drama, I managed to keep a pulse on what was going down in the streets. I had got at Marky, and everything was going as planned. With our competition out of the way, it was open season for us to set up shop. All we had to do was lay low for a few more weeks to let the police heat die down from them murders and it was on and poppin'.

Heavy had the West Side on lockdown exactly the way that he said he would. The little fat motherfucker was true to his word, because the coke that we got from his connect was some top grade shit. The crack zombies around Barclay Street started spending more and more money with us after we put out a test run on the streets. Our profits doubled in no time. Once we opened our new spots, all the money would be enough to make this drama worth it in the long run.

I cruised down Loch Raven Boulevard on my way to pick up Latoya from her mother's house. She went over there to attend her little sister's tenth birthday party. The Dirty South sounds of the rapper TI pumped outta the two Infinity Basslink subwoofers I had installed in the new Lexus truck that I copped yesterday. I wished my sister was here to see my new whip. I knew that she would be jealous once she saw the custom made navigation system I had installed in the dash. She would definitely have to go out and scoop up something to outdo me because that was just her style.

I turned down the volume on the radio when I pulled up in front of Latoya's family's house. All I needed was for her judgmental mother to start in on me about my loud music and me driving this balla ass whip that cost more than the house she lived in. She didn't like the fact that her daughter was a lesbian, but over time she grew to accept her lifestyle. However, she hated the fact that Latoya messed around with the likes of me. She always told her that I was no good and would only wind up in jail one day.

However, my boo paid her no mind. She knew who that pussy belonged to, and that I was the only who could treat it right. Her Pops was cool with our relationship and had no problems with his daughter's sexual preference. On the low, I think he was an old freak who had fantasies about his daughter hooking him up with one of her bisexual girlfriends. I just sensed that vibe about him for some reason.

I parked the truck and got out to walk up to the front door of the Iverson home.

"How are you doing, Mrs. Iverson? Is Latoya ready?" I said. She eyed me up and down with a dirty stare. She stood in the doorway to block me from entering the house.

"Toya, your friend, Toni or Tammy or whatever is here for you. Hurry up and come to the door," she yelled up the stairs.

"It's Tamara, Mrs. Iverson. My name is Tamara," I shot back.

"Whatever," she said brushing me off. She was lucky that she was Toya's mother, because if this was anybody else in the streets, I woulda rearranged her front teeth with a sharp right hand to the mouth.

"Here I come," Latoya yelled down the stairs. When she appeared at the front door a few minutes later, I was relieved. Mrs. Iverson stepped aside to let her pass and we were on our way. When we reached the truck, I looked back toward the house and noticed that she was still in the doorway. I opened the door for Latoya to get in the truck and leaned down to kiss her on the lips. I turned toward her mother and flashed a smile. She slammed the front door in disgust. I was glad to have pissed her off.

"You know you need to stop playing like that. My mother is gonna kick ya ass one day," Latoya said jokingly.

"Kick my ass in what lifetime? Ya moms don't even want it with me," I said.

"A'ight, gangster. I was just playing, honey. Have you heard from ya sister yet?" she asked.

"Nah, I don't know what's up with her. She's probably just kicking back with Devin, trying to clear her head. She'll call me when she's ready," I said.

"Baby, I know you don't wanna hear this, but I think you really should talk to your mother. Right or wrong, she's human and knows that she made a bad mistake," Toya said. I pulled the car off the road and slammed on the brakes.

"I told you before to stay the fuck outta my family business," I said. With my right hand I delivered an open-hand smack to her mouth. I knew that I was wrong to hit her, but it felt good to let off some steam that I really wanted to release on Priscilla Barnes. Latoya rose up in her seat like she wanted to swing back on me, but she knew that would've been suicide.

"I'm sorry. I was just trying to help," she said.

"When I want ya help, I'll ask for it. Until then, only speak on my shit when you're asked to do so," I said.

The rest of the ride home was silent. I loved Latoya but she had a habit of saying things to me at the wrong time. She should have known me well enough by now to know that I don't like to be questioned about my family business. I hated to have to discipline her for putting her nose in my private business, but sometimes a pimpstress had to do what she had to do to keep her bottom bitch in line.

We pulled up at the house and both got out of the truck. As I got closer to the front door, I was surprised to see my mother sitting on my front steps. She looked a hot mess, dressed in a wrinkled up Baby Phat sweat suit, her hair in a shambles. The bags under her eyes suggested that she must not have slept in a couple of days. That was probably from feeling guilty about what she had done to us. The thought of her suffering gave me a sick sense of joy.

"Why the hell are you on my property? You got one minute to leave before I call the police and have you removed," I said.

"Tamara, please, I don't want to fight with you. I just wanna talk to you. You're my daughter and I love you," she said.

"Well, you had ya chance to talk to me and my sister. At this point, talk is cheap. I want you to leave," I said.

"You have every right to feel that way, and I understand. Have you talked to your sister? I've tried calling her and keep getting no answer," she said.

"No, I haven't heard from her. If I did, I wouldn't tell you. The fact that she hasn't called you should tell you something," I said.

"Well, I see you're stuck on being nasty towards me. You'll get over it in time. When you're ready to talk, I'll be at your grandmother's house. Here are the keys to your house. Having all that money will never make you happy if you don't have family. I want you to remember that right or wrong, I'm your mother and I will always be here for you no matter how much you hate me right now," she said and walked off. I peeped her make a right at the end of the driveway. She hopped into her car and drove off. I must have been so distracted when I pulled up because I didn't notice her car sitting up the street.

Latoya walked with me into the house. She had a look on her face like she wanted to say something, but given what happened in her last attempt to lend her two cents to my business, she chose to keep her mouth closed.

I went into the kitchen to check the caller ID and there were still no calls from my sister. I had to leave back out shortly because I had a meeting with Heavy.

"Baby, I'm about to bounce. I gotta go make a run. I should be back in about two hours. You want me to bring you some food from Southern Blues?" I asked.

"Nah, I'm good. I'll just be in here watching movies. I love you," she said.

"I love you too, sexy. I'ma show you how much when I get back. Why don't you put on that sexy lil' negligee that I bought you the other day," I said. I bent down and kissed her on the lips.

I met Heavy at one of his secret meeting houses in Edmondson Village. I called Marky earlier and he told me that he would meet me at the location. I wished that my sister was here to go with me because she was my partner. The meeting was to discuss how we planned to bring the shipment of drugs into the city and how our crews were to be set up at the different locations. Every part of this thing had to be carried out to perfection. One fatal error and we all would be facing serious Fed time.

When I pulled up to the meeting house, I saw no signs of Marky's car. I felt a little leery that he wasn't here to have my back, but I was confident that he was on his way. He probably got caught up with one of his female fans. I packed my lil .22 in my purse for security just in case things didn't go right. Even though Heavy said we would be partners in this venture, you never knew what could happen.

When there was money and street niggas involved, greed was always a possibility to emerge. When I walked up to the porch, I saw Heavy seated on the steps with Binky by his side.

"What's up, cutie? Where's ya other half at?" Heavy asked.

"She's sick. She doesn't need to be here for this meeting. I can take care of everything for the both of us," I said. I had to lie to cover for Tamia. If Heavy knew there were problems in our camp, he was the kinda nigga that would definitely take advantage of the situation.

"Cool. Let's go inside so we can talk in private," Heavy said.

I followed him into the house. Seated in the living room was a girl about my age with some ghetto-ass home-done braids in her hair. She had a bunch of her home girls in the living room, watching rap videos on the big screen TV. This must have been her house and Heavy paid her to use it for his business purposes.

We walked past them into the basement area to talk. When we got down there, I was thrown off guard to see several of Heavy's goons seated around the room. I had none of my people with me so I was a little nervous.

Marky had better hurry his ass up I thought.

"What you need all of these other niggas down here for if me and you need to talk business?" I asked.

"What's wrong, Tamara? Are you nervous? There's no reason to be. We're all family in here," Heavy said. He took a seat on the couch against the wall.

"Hell nah, I ain't never nervous. However, I would feel more comfortable if we waited until Marky got here before we got down to business," I said.

"Marky is already here. Hey, Marky, come out here. Ya boss lady wants you to be a part of this meeting," Heavy said.

Marky emerged from the back part of the basement with a smirk on his face. Joey was right behind him. My mind was twisted. I started to feel a little nervous. Something shady had to be up.

"What the hell is going on here?" I asked.

"Well, T, there's been a change in our agreement. It seems that you and your sister's services are no longer needed in this organization. The board has decided that your part of the organization would be more suitably run by my boy Marky here. In addition, we're appointing Joey to be his under boss," Heavy said.

"Heavy, what the hell are you talking about? Marky would never sell us out like that. Tell'em Marky," I said. Neither Marky nor Joey would look me in the face. These disloyal motherfuckers had turned on me after all I did for them. I wanted to kill both of them. I felt hurt and betrayed.

"It's nothing personal, Tamara. This is business. You had your time to shine, and now it's my time to do my thing. You always told me that if there was something I wanted outta life, that I couldn't be afraid to go get it, no matter who I had to step on," Marky said. He had the nerve to laugh in my face.

"Fuck this shit. Ain't no way in hell I'ma let this go down without a fight. I worked too hard for my shit to let y'all bump me outta position," I said. I tried to reach for the pistol in my purse, but one of his goons grabbed me and pinned me down.

"I was afraid of that. That was why I knew that we had to deal with you so that things could go along smoothly. Your sister ain't the killer type like you are. We'll get to her later. I want you call her and tell her to meet you here," Heavy said.

"There will be a cold day in hell before I do that, nigga," I said defiantly.

"Have it your way. We'll get to her sooner or later. She can't hide. Marky, take care of this business here. You wanted the job as the boss, well, this is ya initiation into the family," Heavy demanded. Marky did as he was instructed because he knew that if he didn't, he would be dead right along with me.

I kicked and screamed as much as I could, but it was useless. Five against one was no fair fight. My hands and feet were bound with rope and a piece of duct tape was placed over my mouth. I knew that I was trapped. I should've cancelled this meeting until my sister was here with me. I wasn't thinking clearly. Now death had placed a call to me. There was nothing I could do to not answer the call. I just closed my eyes and prepared for the inevitable. I hoped that karma caught with all of these disloyal motherfuckers.

Tamia
9

Devin was so good to me. He was my saving grace at this critical time in my life. After I told him about what my mother did to deceive us, he let me know just how much he had my back. He didn't judge me about how I felt about my mother nor did he try to tell me what I should do. He just gave me unconditional support, and that was what I needed at the moment.

Devin came up with the idea that we should go on a little vacation so that I could clear my head and I was down for the trip. We decided to go to the Bahamas for a five-day getaway. We stayed at a five-star hotel that catered to my every need and desire to be pampered. Every morning, I went to the day spa to receive a full body massage. I got my hair, nails, and feet done. The room service was outstanding, and the sights that we toured on the island were just as magnificent. When it was time to go home, I didn't want to leave, but I knew that I had to come back to the real world.

When I got off the plane, I checked my phone. I had countless messages from both my mother and my sister. All of them pretty much said the same thing so I erased most of them. They wanted to know where I was and why I hadn't returned their calls. Shit, I was grown and I just didn't feel like it at the time. Hearing their voices made me almost forget about the good time that I just had with Devin on the island. All of the feelings of betrayal and hurt that I thought were gone came rushing back to me at once. But I couldn't run from reality forever, so this was the day that I finally decided to face my demons.

"Are you sure that you're ready to do this, baby?" Devin asked me.

"Yeah, I'm sure. I might as well deal with this now as opposed to later," I replied.

"A'ight, I'll be right here waiting for you. You know I got your back always, no matter what," he said.

"Without a doubt," I replied. I leaned over to kiss him on his mouth and exited my vehicle.

Devin drove with me to Pennsylvania from BWI airport so that I could visit my father at the Lewisburg Federal Penitentiary. We stayed at a local hotel that night so that I could get a good night's rest before I faced my father. I hadn't been to see him in about two months, due to what we had going on with Heavy. However, I spoke with him several times over the phone, so I knew that he was all right. I was kinda nervous as I approached the steel gates of the jail. I had butterflies in my stomach. I didn't know what to expect. I was about to tell him some news that would definitely shock him and I wasn't sure how he would react.

I didn't know whether he would still accept me as his daughter or if he would disown me because we didn't share the same bloodline. To me, genetics didn't matter. Timmy Barnes was my father because he was the one who raised me, and he was the only man that I ever looked up to. I loved him like a girl should love her father, and I hoped that he felt the same way about me after I dropped this bomb on him.

As for my mother, I wasn't too sure how I felt about her. I tried to see things from her point of view. I imagined that it must have been a great burden to keep this secret for so long. I knew that she loved my father and that he had to have hurt her pretty bad for her to resort to sleeping with his best friend. However, her pain didn't excuse her actions. Right or wrong, she would always be my mother, and I would have to find some kinda way to forgive her over time. I just needed some time and space away from her to process my feelings.

"Timmy Barnes. Inmate Timmy Barnes," the CO called out from the desk positioned in the front of the visiting room. I was in a daydream, thinking about what was about to take place.

Timmy Barnes strolled into the visiting room, looking handsome as ever. I could tell that he was working out regularly because his tall, medium-sized frame was muscular. His salt-and-pepper hair showed that he had aged some, but he still looked distinguished to me.

When our eyes met, he flashed a big smile as though he was happy to see me. He walked toward me with his familiar gangster bop that I remembered so well. Timmy Barnes epitomized a true OG in the game. Even though he was in jail, he still had that shine about him that would let anybody know that his name still carried weight out in the streets.

He reached across the table to give me a big hug. Even though we were twins, he was always able to tell me and my sister apart. I guess you could call that a father's intuition. There was no way in hell that I could see any other man as being my father.

"What's going on, Tamia? It's so good to see you. What are you doing here by yourself? Where's your sister? How come she didn't come with you?" he asked.

"It's good to see you too, Pops. I see that you've been working out. Which one of these female COs out here are you messing with?" I asked. He flashed me a sly grin to indicate that I was right on point with my assumption. His grin soon turned to a look of seriousness.

"Never mind what your old man is doing. Answer my other question. Where is your sister?" he asked. He must have sensed that something wasn't right because he knew that we always came to visit him together.

"Have you spoken to Mommy in the past week?" I asked. Even though they were divorced, they still kept in touch, and my mother would come to see him from time to time. She also sent him money whenever he needed it. It didn't matter who she messed with because Timmy Barnes would always be her first love. Any man she dealt with would just have to accept their relationship.

"No, I haven't. Now, do you want to tell me what's going on? I'm not gonna ask you again. I see that you're trying to avoid my question. You should know that I know you better than you know yourself. I've heard about this thing y'all got going on in the streets. Just because I'm in here, it doesn't mean that I don't know what's going on out there in the world. These walls have ears as big as satellite dishes," he replied.

"I don't know how to say what I'm about to say to you. I guess I might as well just spit it out," I said. I proceeded to run down the whole story exactly the way that it was told to me. I also told him about D-Bo and how I killed him. I told him about what we had going down with Heavy in detail. I told him how furious I was with my mother. I also told him why I hadn't spoken to my sister.

He just sat silently with a pensive look on his face. I had never seen him look so calm. I expected him to explode, but he just kept his cool. A tear formed in the corner of his right eye. He shook his head from side to side before he spoke.

"I had a feeling that one day the whole situation between me, your mother, and that bastard Lionel would come to a head. In the back of my mind, I've always had a hidden fear that he might be your father because of the timing of when he slept with your mother. I just hoped and prayed that it wasn't true. I never shared my suspicions with your mother," he said.

"So, even though you had those suspicions, how could you still look at us as your daughters?" I asked.

"How could I not? When the two of you were born, I wanted with everything in my being for you to be my daughters. From the first time that I held both of you in my arms, I knew that you were my seeds, regardless of what any blood test would ever say. That was why I never asked your mother to have a blood test done. I don't need any doctor to tell me who my real family is," he said.

"I love you, Daddy," I said. All of my insecurities and doubts were erased. I was Tamia Barnes, not Tamia James.

"I love you, too. Don't be mad at your mother, because this is mostly my fault. If I hadn't cheated on her so much with other women and abused her love, then maybe she wouldn't have had a desire to get back at me. Being behind bars, a man is given an opportunity to see things a little different than when he's out in the streets," he said.

"Okay, Daddy, whatever you say. If that's what you want, I'll do it. If you can forgive my mother for what she did, then I guess I can too. As for Tamara, that's a totally different story. She hates Mommy, and I don't think she will ever get over this," I said.

"Yeah, she always was the most stubborn one. Just keep talking to her. She'll come around. As for this thing you got going on with this dude Heavy, you better be careful, baby girl. A coupla cats in here tell me that he's a shady character and not to be trusted. I thought I taught you both to be a better judge of character than this. It seems that since I've been locked down, your thirst for money guides your actions as opposed to respecting the rules of the game that I taught you," he said.

"That's not the case at all, Daddy. You told us to never let a good opportunity pass us by," I said.

"True, I did tell you that. However, I also told you that you always investigate who you do business with thoroughly because they could have some shit waiting around the corner for you that will bite you on the ass. All of these bodies y'all got on the streets are gonna come back to haunt you one day," he said.

"You're right. I never looked at it that way," I said.

"I wish that I had never turned you both onto the game. If I could take back anything that I've done in my life, that would be at the top of my list. This life ain't nothing but a dead end road. No matter how rich, slick, and cool I thought I was, I wasn't smart enough to avoid the heap of time that they gave me. All of the power I thought I had to control people's lives has been taken away from me. In here, I'm just another nigga with a DOC number. That's the cold, hard truth. I miss being with you girls whenever I want to and not when this damn system says that I can see you. I lost my marriage because of my selfish greed for money. I don't want this kinda life for you two. Take whatever money that you have now and walk away from the game. Just walk away," he said.

"Okay, Daddy. Once we tie up a few loose ends, I will get with Tamara and we will do exactly what you want us to do," I said.

I never in a million years thought I would hear Timmy Barnes talk in this manner. He put something on my mind for me to think about. What he said made some sense. We should have thought this thing through a little better before we started a war on the streets. However, it was too late for second-guessing at this point. Whatever was to be would be at this point.

We talked for another half-hour about other things. I told him about Devin. He gave our relationship his blessing and said that he wanted to meet him one day. I told him about my book project, and he was impressed. He encouraged me to keep writing because he saw a number of dudes in jail with him that loved to read street fiction books and was amazed at how popular they had become. He even told me that he thought about writing a book based on his life.

When it was time for our visit to be over, I embraced him once again and we both expressed our love as I exited the visiting room.

As I approached my car, I saw that Devin was in the driver's seat with the seat leaned back. He had fallen asleep while he waited for me. I tapped on the glass and startled him damn near to death. He awoke with a dazed look on his face.

"So, how did it go?" he asked.

"A lot better than I expected. My father surprised me. He's not the same man that he was when he went to jail. Hell, he seems different from when I saw him the last time. He seems much wiser and looks at things in a different light than the way he used to," I said. I ran down the specifics of our conversation to Devin as he drove down the road. It was time for me to get back to B'more. I retrieved my phone to call Tamara at home. I had made her suffer for long enough.

"Tamia, where have you been? Something awful has happened. You've got to get here now! Tamara is dead! My baby is dead!" Latoya yelled into the phone.

"What the fuck are you talking about?" I asked. I knew that she had to be mistaken.

"The police found her body last night. She was shot five times and brutally tortured," Latoya said.

I hung up the phone on her as her last words resonated in my ear.

"We've gotta get back to B'more now! My sister is dead! My sister is dead!" I said frantically to Devin.

He drove like a bat outta hell down the road. I had to find out who the hell killed my sister. Nobody was gonna be safe on the streets of B'more until I found her killer.

Tamara's funeral
10

The heavy rainfall and cloudy skies were a reflection of the dreary mood that engulfed the inside of March's Funeral Home on the day that Tamara Barnes was laid to rest. Family and friends gathered to pay their last respects for another young black life lost senselessly in the streets of Baltimore as a result of drug related violence. Emotions ran thick throughout the funeral hall as tears swelled in the eyes of the multitudes who came to mourn. Some of the city's biggest and most infamous drug dealers, from the past and the present, came to pay their respects to a fallen soldier in the game. Even though they were her competitors in the drug game, there was a great deal of respect attached to the Barnes name in the streets of Baltimore.

Obviously absent from the funeral was Marky and the rest of the crew from Barclay Street. Heavy didn't show up to pay his respects. This didn't go unnoticed by Tamia. She knew without any investigation that they had to be involved in her sister's death. Her father's words about watching who you did business with flashed in her head repeatedly. She only wished she had heard them sooner rather than later.

Tamia sat with her mother in the front row of the funeral parlor throughout the service. They had talked since she returned home and reconciled their differences. They both realized that they were all the other had left in this world and that they needed each other for support through this rough time. Devin sat with Tamia to console her as she cried endlessly throughout the service. Latoya was also there and sat with the family. Both of Tamara's maternal and paternal grandparents were also in attendance.

Timmy Barnes was not allowed to attend the funeral due to the restrictions placed upon him by the warden at the jail. It turned out that he wound up getting one of the female COs at the jail pregnant, and this caused a scandal at the institution. The CO got fired from her job and aborted the love child. Timmy Barnes faced more legal drama in the wake of his indiscretions. He would have to mourn for his child while locked up in solitary confinement.

It was a closed casket service due to Tamara having suffered so much physical damage to her face and the rest of her body from the gunshot wounds and tactics of mutilation that were inflicted upon her body. She had taken five point blank range blasts to the face from a .38 that made her face look disfigured. Her body had been so severely burned and beaten that she would have been unrecognizable to anyone. The only way that the coroner was able to identify her body was by her dental records. It was clear that her brutal death was to serve as a message to Tamia that she was next on the killer's list.

Reverend Christopher Holland performed the service for the family. He was the minister of Holiness Temple Baptist Church, the church that Priscilla attended and where the twins were baptized as infants. His eulogy to the audience was a stirring and powerful message that resonated throughout the hall and appealed to the conscience off all in attendance.

"Brothers and sisters, we have gathered here today to put to rest our young sister, Tamara Barnes. It pains me deeply to have to say goodbye to this young lady who was a victim of such a heinous crime.

I remember her and her sister from when they were little children when they used to come to my church with their mother. Over the years, they strayed away from the church and chose to take another path in life. While we are not to judge another, I must hasten to say to you all that we should not let sister Tamara's death be in vain.

Let us take from her death that the senseless killing of one another in the streets over drugs, money, and fast cars must cease. We must begin to respect human life and love one another. Our streets are becoming like a cemetery where we kill each other in the multitudes over inanimate objects and the pursuit of riches. I appeal to all of this young lady's friends and loved ones to stay close to one another in the most troubling time and to look to each other, as well as God, to see you through this chapter in your life. It was hate that took this young lady's life away and only love can make a bond out of this insanity that our inhumane behavior has created."

Reverend Holland's words hit home with many in attendance. Loud chants of "Amen" and "Praise the Lord" were heard as he continued with his closing words. However, Tamia turned a blind ear to his call for peace, because she still had revenge in her heart. There was no way in hell that she could let her sister's death ride with no retribution. Her mind was made up, and nothing that was said or done by anyone could change this. As Reverend Holland concluded the service, he gave everyone an opportunity to greet the family and to pay their last respects to the family. When the pall bearers were called to carry the casket out of the funeral parlor to the hearse, Tamia lost it all and ran toward the casket. She flailed her body across the casket. All of the hurt she felt inside couldn't be contained any longer. Her other half was gone, and she would never see her again.

"No, please don't take my sister! God, please bring her back to me! Tamara, please don't be dead! Don't leave me!" Tamia yelled.

Devin ran up to the podium in an attempt to calm her down. She fell into Devin's arms as he carried her deflated body back to her seat. He stroked her hair and rubbed her back while he cradled her in his firm, reassuring arms.

There was nothing t she could do to bring her sister back. That was a reality she would have to live with for the rest of her life. She pulled herself together enough to make it through the trip out to the cemetery to bury Tamara. She planned to return to her gravesite every year on their birthday and hold her own private memorial service. Without her sister around, her life would never be the same. Somebody had to pay for every ounce of pain she would endure.

Marky—The New East Side King
11

Marky enjoyed his new position as the boss of his own crew. He struggled for a while with his conscience about killing Tamara, but that feeling faded away when he started to see the increase in his cash flow. He was successfully in turning all of the workers that used to report to the twins against Tamia once he upped their pay. In the streets, if the money was right, then almost anybody had a price for their loyalty.

He treated himself to a few new trinkets to announce to the world that he had arrived. He bought himself a Bentley, a Porsche and a half million dollar house in the Owings Mills section of Baltimore County. He threw wild parties at his crib for him and his crew to celebrate with some of the finest strippers in Baltimore City.

His flashy lifestyle was sure to attract the attention of the Feds soon enough due to the fact that he was so young and had no legitimate income to justify all of his assets. However, Tamia had a plan to get to him before the Feds got a chance.

On this particular day, Marky had just returned from a weekend gambling in Atlantic City. He played the Blackjack and poker tables and had lost close to thirty grand over the weekend. That money was nothing to him because he would have that back in a day's time.

He parked his Porsche in the four car garage of his estate. He had Rainy, one of his latest conquests, with him. She was a petite cutie, with her hair down to her lower back and an ass fit for a king to feast on. She was just his type—a woman with a bangin' body and no brains in her head. Her elevator never made it up to the top floor. He could tell her that the sky was pink and she would believe it was true. He told her that he was a rap video director and she believed his story. He planned to sex her crazy for a few hours before he sent her home.

Rainy leaned across the seat and grabbed his crotch firmly. "Damn, Marky, your crib is tight. I see you done really came up in the world," she said.

"Yeah, I'm doing my thing, shorty. You're in the presence of royalty right now. Ain't nobody out here ballin' like me. When you see the inside of my crib, you might just cum on ya self before I let you get a taste of this dick," Marky replied. He placed his hand inside her shirt to fondle her breasts. She closed her eyes and groaned like she was having an orgasm. Marky was getting cockier and more arrogant with each passing day in his abuse of his newfound power. That was always a hustler's first downfall in the game.

The pair entered the house through the garage. Marky flipped the light switch in the kitchen. When he looked down, he was shocked at what he saw in front of him. Rainy let out a loud scream of terror. His two pit bulls, Murder and Mayhem, were both dead, with their throats slit. He left them in the house for extra security whenever he went outta town. Somebody obviously had gotten past his high tech security system and his second line of defense with no problems.

"What the fuck is going on here?" he asked rhetorically.

He knew that somebody might still be in the house, so he played it safe. He instructed Rainy to go back outside and wait in the car. He opened up the cabinet under the kitchen sink to retrieve his .357 revolver, but it was missing.

He carefully crept through the house to see if he saw any signs of an intruder, but there was no one there. Marky made his way up to his bedroom where he had a safe secretly concealed under his bed. He kept another pistol in there in case of an emergency.

When he reached his bedroom, he noticed that it was in shambles. His bed was turned over and his safe was wide open. All of the money and his pistol were gone. He had over 300 grand in the safe. This was his getaway money, just in case he ever had to go on the lam. It was all the cash that he had saved up, and now it was gone. He was pissed. Somebody had violated his home and jacked him for his stash.

"Shit! How the fuck did this happen? I'ma kill some motherfucking body over this shit! Don't nobody get me for mine and get away with it!" he yelled. In a rage, he took one of the statues on his dresser and threw it up against the plasma TV that hung on the wall. It shattered into a thousand little pieces. As he proceeded to tear the rest of his room to shreds, he didn't hear the door to his room open.

"Damn, Marky, why are you so upset? Are you looking for this?" Tamia asked. She stood in the doorway with a coy look on her face. She held his .357 in her hand. Beside her was a bag which contained the money from his safe. Marky stood frozen. He couldn't say or do anything. As he attempted to speak, he began to stutter.

"T-t-amia, wh-what are you doing here?" he asked.

"Marky, don't play dumb. You didn't think I was gonna go away that easy did you? You thought I was gonna let you kill my sister and get away with it? You thought I was gonna let you just take over my drug strip that we built without a struggle? Little brother, I see you totally underestimated me. I also see that you didn't take pay attention well enough to the lessons that we taught you. If you did, it wouldn't have been so easy for me to get in here," Tamia said.

"Yeah, I killed the bitch. So what? T, you taught me this game. It's kill or be killed out here. Death is a part of the life. You love this money just as much as I do. Your sister is gone and she ain't coming back. You and I are still here. We can work something out. We can split this pie two ways now instead of three. Heavy and I got rid of her because you were always the smarter one of the two.

Put that gun down, hand me that bag of money, and let's sit down and talk business, baby. Marky is open to negotiating with you," he said. Speaking of himself in the third person only showed how drunk with power he had become. He started slowly walking toward her. When she wrapped her finger around the trigger tighter he stopped his stride.

"Marky, you have truly lost ya mind. How could you think that I would fall for that little mind game that you just tried to run on me? I'm a Barnes, fool, and don't you ever forget it. It breaks my heart to have to see you go out like this. I used to look at you like you were my lil' brother. You used to sleep at the foot of my bed. We took care of you when nobody else gave a damn.

Yeah, it's true that I do love money, but I loved my sister more than any of this shit here. You took that away from me, and now ya ass has got to pay," Tamia said with tears in her eyes.

"Come on, T. Let's not get all sentimental and shit. I'm trying to get this money. Come get it with me," he said.

He threw his arms in the air in a windmill-like motion and this distracted Tamia. In that split second, Marky lunged toward her and knocked the gun outta her hand. He jumped on top of her and knocked Tamia to the floor. He punched her in the face and blood splattered from her nose.

Tamia dug her nails into his face and left a set of scars that would be permanent. They struggled back and forth in an attempt to get to the gun. Tamia was soldier and could hold her own with any female, but she was no match for Marky's strength.

He overpowered her eventually and retrieved the pistol that had slid across the floor. He rose to his feet and stood over her with the pistol in hand. He walked over to retrieve his bag of money. When he leaned down to get the bag, Tamia reached for the .22 in the holster attached to her ankle. She hid it in her hand behind her back as Marky turned around to face her.

"You are a stupid bitch. You should've shot me when you had the chance. Now I get to say that I killed both of the Barnes girls. I'll be a legend in these streets forever," Marky said.

"Fuck you, Marky. Pull the fucking trigger and get this shit over with. Ya ass is gonna burn in hell, you disloyal faggot," Tamia said, defiant even in the face of death. She was determined to be a soldier to the end.

Marky kicked her in the head as she lay helpless on the ground. He pointed the gun at Tamia's head. Just as he was about to pull the trigger, Tamia's arm swung around and she squeezed off three shots that landed in his chest. Marky was able to get off two rounds before he fell to the ground, and one of them hit Tamia. As they both lay unconscious on the floor, the sound of a cavalry of feet stampeded into the room.

"Police, nobody move!" one of the officers yelled.

Once the officers got a chance to look around, they noticed that they had two gunshot victims in front of them and no one to arrest.

"Somebody call for an ambulance. We've got a woman bleeding from the shoulder up in here. We think she'll be all right. We also have a young, black male with multiple gunshot wounds. It doesn't look like he's gonna make it," the officer said to his fellow officers in the room.

Rainy stood in the doorway behind the officers. She screamed when she saw Marky laid out in a pool of blood.

"Officer, this woman must have been the one that broke into my friend's house and killed his dogs. He told me to stay in the car while he checked out the house. I figured that since he was in the entertainment business, some crazy stalker must have broken into his house. I didn't know what to do, so I called you guys," Rainy said.

"You did the right thing, young lady. The officer here has some questions for you. Follow her downstairs and she'll be able to get your statement," the officer said. When he looked across the room, he noticed the bag full of money and his eyes lit up. The money certainly wouldn't make it into the evidence room of the police department.

The ambulances came and the paramedics attempted to revive Marky, but were unsuccessful. He was dead at the young age of eighteen, another victim of homicide in Baltimore City.

Tamia in the hospital
12

The doctors performed surgery on Tamia to remove the bullet that was lodged in her shoulder. The surgery was a success. However, she would need a lot of rest to recuperate to return to her normal self. She was on a heavy dose of opiates to help her with the pain for the first few days. She constantly pressed the buzzer by her bedside to release the morphine drip into her veins. She stayed higher than Fat Charles' ass. She spent most of those days in a deep sleep. Her mother was by her side throughout the entire ordeal. Devin had also come by the hospital on several occasions to check on her.

Even though she survived being killed, Tamia still had to answer for Marky's murder. Once the police did an investigation of the crime scene as well as Tamia and Marky, the picture became clear to them that this was a drug related crime. They also uncovered that it was connected to the string of drug related murders that had occurred throughout the city recently. The police had her handcuffed to the bed and waited for her condition to improve so that they could cart her off to jail. Two officers were stationed outside of her hospital room.

Tamia awoke from a long sleep to see her mother seated by her bed. She had no idea how much deep shit she was really in at the moment. She was in for a rude awakening.

"Hey, Mommy, how long have you been sitting there? It seems like I've been sleep for like a month," Tamia said. She attempted to raise herself up, but the handcuffs on her wrists and ankles kept her restrained.

"Lay back and relax. I've been here for a few hours, waiting for you to wake up. The doctors said that you will be fine," Priscilla responded. As she looked at her daughter, she reminisced back to a time when both of her daughters were little girls playing with dolls. She wondered how their lives had become so outta control that one of them was now dead and the other headed to jail for a very long time. She tried to hold back her tears with a smile, but was unsuccessful.

"Why are you crying, Mommy? None of this is your fault. I got myself into this situation and I'm prepared to face the consequences for what I've done. I ain't scared to go to jail," Tamia said.

"You are truly Timmy Barnes' daughter. You sound just like him with that big, bad talk. I know you're not afraid of jail, but I just wish that I had done something to dissuade you girls from living the street life. I should have been a better mother. Your sister is gone, your father is not here, and soon I'm gonna lose you. I feel so alone," Priscilla said.

"Mommy, don't go beating yourself up about any of this. I miss Tamara too. I know that my life will never be the same, but at least you have a chance to be happy for all of us. I have some money stashed away in a secret place and I want you to have it. I want you to move outta this city and start a new life for yourself without all the baggage from our mess. You deserve a better life," Tamia said.

Priscilla got up from the chair and hugged Tamia. She held onto her and cried with her for a few minutes before they were interrupted. Two burly law enforcement officials entered the room.

"Ms. Barnes, I'm Detective Hammonds from the homicide division. We're glad to see that you're awake. I'm here to formally charge you with the murder of Markell Ivory. It also appears as though the DEA has had you and your organization under surveillance for quite some time. The young man you murdered was an informant for them and before he died he implicated you as one of the leaders of the Barclay Street drug gang. Since your sister is dead, all of the weight is gonna fall on you," Detective Hammonds said with a proud look on his face.

"Whatever, you pig. I'm ready for whatever false charges you have to bring my way. You might have me for killing that bastard Marky, but you don't have any evidence of me receiving or selling any drugs. Once my lawyers are done, that case is gonna be reduced to a manslaughter charge. You're just fishing for something, hoping that I take the bait," Tamia said with a grin.

"I'm Agent Marx from the DEA. You're not in the clear like you think because you see, we not only have countless hours of recorded conversations, as well as video footage of you, your sister and Mr. Ivory engaging in drug transaction, but we also have several members of your so called crew that are willing to testify against you.

Mr. Ivory got busted with two kilos of cocaine about a year ago and began working for the DEA in exchange for him staying free. We gave him a license to sell drugs in order to get to you. He proved to be a useful asset for us.

We had already planned to use him to help us bust up Heavy's ring as well. When y'all decided to merge your organizations, it just made our job that much easier. We were able to kill two birds with one stone. We already have Heavy and his gang in custody. In federal cases, you don't have to get caught with your hand in the cookie jar to get convicted. All we need is for somebody that is believable to say that you conspired to commit a crime. So, for all of your tough talk, Ms. Lady, you're royally fucked, unless you wanna offer up some information that the DEA might find useful," Agent Marx stated. Tamia's grin turned to a look of shock.

"Well, you can forget about that. I will never be a rat. I'm just not built like that. I'm true to code of the streets," Tamia said. She was hurt and surprised to find out that Marky was working with Feds for quite some time against them.

"Why can't you people leave my daughter alone? She's been shot. Can't this whole thing wait until she is fully healed?" Priscilla asked.

"I'm afraid not, Mrs. Barnes. The doctor says that your daughter is well enough to be carted out of here to the infirmary at the jail. It looks like you'll have a lot of time to write your father, being that you both will be behind bars for quite some time. The apple truly doesn't fall far from the tree in this case.

Mrs. Barnes, you should have done a better job raising your children, and this could have all been prevented. What a shame, another crime family in the black community that ends up in a twisted tragedy," Officer Hammonds said.

"You are two no-good motherfuckers. Who the hell are you to judge me and question the way that I raised my kids? You have no right to do that. You both can go to hell!" Priscilla yelled.

Priscilla reached for a chair and hurled it at the officers as they stood near the door. They both ducked and just missed being hit. She ran toward them with both arms swinging. She connected with a few of her blows before she was subdued. The commotion caused a stir in the hospital and got the attention of several of the doctors and nurses on the floor.

Tamia flashed a faint grin when she saw her mother wild out on the two officers. She wished that she could've joined in and helped her whip their asses.

When the dust was cleared, Tamia was carted out of the hospital and off to jail, pending the outcome of her cases in court. There was no doubt that she would spend the rest of her days in jail. Her dream of becoming a bestselling author was over.

She accepted her fate like the true soldier that she was with no remorse or an ounce of regret for her choices in life. She was born into the game and enjoyed the fruits of the life until her time was up. There was no room for her to complain about the outcome of it all.

She wished that she had more time to spend with Devin because he had become an important part of her life. She also wished that her sister was still alive to stand trial with her as her codefendant, like they were in everything else in their lives, but fate just wouldn't allow any of that to be. The inner city streets claimed another victory in its strategically planned annihilation of black youth, and eagerly awaited a new crop of young, deaf and dumb ghetto soldiers yet to be born into the game.

URBAN BOOKS PRESENTS

PAT TUCKER

ARMED AND DANGEROUS

Acknowledgements

Thank God almighty first and foremost. I'd like to thank my patient and wonderful mother Deborah Tucker Bodden for teaching her daughters, Denise and me that everything worth having requires hard work. Then, my stepfather Herbert for keeping my mom happy, and Lydell R. Wilson, thanks for loving and supporting me in ways I can not fathom.

I have a list of Sheros I'd like to thank for their constant support in my work and in my life... Monica Hodge, Shanell Cavil of the write Impressions.com, Marilyn Glaizer, LaShawanda Moore, Lee Lee Baines, the most exquisite ladies of Sigma Gamma Rho Sorority Inc.

Reshonda Tate Billingsley, my sister in publishing... I hope these words attempt to express my appreciation for all of your unwavering support. Thanks for the advice, the nod when something worked, and the hmmm, when it just didn't click. I know I've been Changed is a gem!

I'd like to thank my handsome little brother Irvin Kelvin Seguro, my nephews, nieces and the rest of my supportive family.
Finally, how do you thank someone who has taken you from dreams to a world surreal? It is not easy, but I will try...
Roy Glenn mere words can't begin to express my gratitude for your guidance, encouragement and constant support... Thanks to Carl Webber for your vision and the voice it has given so many talented writers.

Pat Tucker

My sweet Payton... your existence mystifies me,
Your smile inspires me
until you...
I never knew I could love so much.

Prologue
1

Alex brought her cupped hands to her mouth and blew into them, hoping to warm up a little. The soft mist had turned into a continuous drizzle nearly an hour ago. Every so often a biting cold wind attacked her legs and traveled up to her thighs, chilling her to the core. On top of the teeth-chattering cold, it had been slow all night.

Alex glanced up at the sky and cursed, knowing the unexpected rain would definitely hurt her cash flow. After spending two hours sashaying up and down Century Boulevard, a few blocks away from LAX on what she considered her little slice of the territory, her feet were killing her and the short skirt kept riding up her bare ass.

She pulled at her denim half jacket and remembered she couldn't button it completely because her titties would be covered. Usually the site of a little tittie showing was enough to make men stop their cars and spend some money. Occasionally, she'd flash a few drivers, but still, she usually made off better than most of the girls who worked the area. And she didn't need anyone to tell her that it was her big titties that did the trick. The twins really had a way of attracting customers. She was five seven, and still showed traces of a voluptuous and curvy frame. At 135 pounds, her time on the streets and smoking that rock hadn't completely taken its toll just yet, but there were signs.

Alex sighed, she was tired of bum rushin' any and every car that slowed and pulled off onto a side street. Many times, by the time she even made it the car, someone else was already seated comfortably in the John's passenger seat.

"Say, Jewels, whatchu doin' over on this side?" Alex asked, as another girl approached. She couldn't help but think of all the money she'd lose once men saw Jewels' skinny ass prancing around in that short jumpsuit. It was cut to show off her cheeks, which jiggled freely from each side. Jewels may have been thin, but she had a nice shape, with a huge ass.

"Girl, just try'n ta make this money, same as you," Jewels said as she flipped her copper colored weave that desperately needed work, and pulled her own clear plastic jacket closed. "Damn it's cold out here. I shoulda wore some jeans," she said.

Alex didn't give a fuck about Jewels being cold or what she shoulda wore, she just wanted her gone. She could handle competition from the other girls on the stroll, they all looked tired, like death warmed over, but Jewels was actually pretty. And something about the gap in her teeth seemed to drive the tricks insane. On a hot and dry LA night, they both walked away with a nice stack of cash. But the weather all but guaranteed nobody would be leaving rich tonight, Alex thought.

Jewels' back was toward the street as they stood in front of a closed storefront. Although she and Jewels made small talk, Alex kept her eye on every vehicle as it slowed or looked as if it wanted to slow. That was her problem, she had convinced herself. She needed to be more like Jewels, easy going, not so desperate and eager to make that money. But shit, she wanted— no, she needed—to get high.

When the minivan pulled along side them and splashed a little water, it all but drenched, Jewels' back.

"Shit!" she screamed. "Fuckin' asshole, didn't he see us standing here!"

Alex used the distraction to rush the passenger's side of the vehicle. "Aeey, Daddy, looking for some action?" she asked, trying not to beg as soon as he lowered the window. The homely looking man wearing a button down shirt and pair of Khakis looked at her and offered a weak smile. Her eyes followed his hand to his crotch; he stroked himself. But to Alex he still appeared nervous. She didn't care, she just wanted his money.

"Ah, Yeah, how much?" His eyes shifted to the rearview mirror. "You a cop?" he asked nervously.

Here we go, Alex thought. She looked in both directions, grateful that the rain had eased up a bit. But she didn't have time for this shit. She wanted to give him whatever he'd pay for, so she could go get hers. "Nah, I ain't no cop," she twitched, and leaned in closer, all but shoving her chest forward. His eyes immediately fell to her titties.

"Bastard!" she heard Jewels snap behind her. Alex didn't want to look away; she was hoping the John was ready for some action, she needed to get paid. If push came to shove, she only really needed ten dollars. Yeah, ten would do just fine. Alex cleared her throat and used a hand to rub her breast. The tricks liked it when they thought they were getting a real freak. She licked her lips.

"I need some head, you like sucking dick?"

"Hmm, nah," she shook her head and licked her lips again. This time slower, "I love suckin' dick, Daddy! And I'm damn good too," Alex said enthusiastically. She fought the urge to scratch an itch. Scratching in front of customers was always a turn off. She just wanted the bastard to hurry up before Jewels was able to finish her hissy-fit and try to move in to close the deal.

"Here, why don't I get in, we can go around the corner, and um, you know, go from there." Alex bargained.

"Okay, but how much first?" he asked. "I ain't got a lot of cash."

Damn, twenty would be good, she thought.

"Twenty," Alex said.

"Ten?" he looked in the rearview mirror again.

"Okay, ten," Alex said and quickly opened the door and climbed in before he could change his mind. Nearly a block up, he turned the first corner and parked.

"Where you want it, Daddy?" Alex cooed.

"Here, let me climb over there and move the seat back, you need to hop out for a sec," he said.

Alex hesitated. She couldn't afford for him to drive off. He was the only customer she'd had in the last three and a half hours. Reluctantly, she got out and watched as he climbed into the passenger seat of the minivan. After he adjusted the seat, he opened the door and looked at Alex.

"Come on," he said motioning to her with his hand.

His pants were already down on his legs. Alex looked over at his limp dick then got in on her knees. Alex felt squeezed into the space, but figured she'd be able to make him cum quick enough, and they'd both be on their way.

She tucked her teeth under her lips and opened wide. Normally she'd start out by licking behind the head and along the shaft, but the truth was she just needed the money so she could go. For ten damn dollars he'd be lucky if she let him cum in her mouth. As she sucked on his head, something was sticking into her knee. She tried adjusting her legs, but couldn't in the cramped space.

"Yeah, that's it, take it all, bitch," he cried. She felt him thrust his hips forward. Once she worked him a bit, he swelled to a pretty decent size.

When her saliva was covering him completely, Alex used her hand to squeeze along the shaft as she sucked the head.

"Ssssss. Oh, yeah," he squealed.

She couldn't concentrate with the pain in her knee. Finally she reached below and pulled at the firm object. She moved her head back to see it was a yellow plastic duck. She flung it into the back where it landed in a child safety seat.

Before she could get herself comfortable, he pulled her head back down into his lap. "Come on, you got more work to do," he said.

Again Alex took him into her mouth, slopping, slurping and sucking his head. She bobbed her head up and down, pulling her jaws tighter as she went down his shaft.

"That's it, now we talking," he encouraged.

A hand-blowjob combo was usually her signature move when she wanted quick results. But the harder she sucked the more he wiggled his hips, pulled at her head and squealed with delight. When her motions still didn't get him off, Alex grabbed for his balls and squeezed them gently at first. That just seemed to get him more excited, but still no nut.

"Oh, yeah, that's it, that's it," he squealed.

Alex didn't usually like when a John held the back of her head in place, but if this was what it would take to make him cum, she didn't mind. The faster he did, the quicker she could get her cash.

"Emm hmm. That's right, bitch, suck it good," he said.

She sucked, then used her teeth to rake up and down his shaft before suckling the head one good time.

"Oh *shit*!" he screamed, grabbing her head tighter.

When she felt his precum, she sucked harder. Just as he was about to explode, Alex tried to pull back, but he shoved her head into his lap and thrust his dick deeper and down her throat.

"Aaaahhh," he cried.

When the warm, salty liquid filled her mouth, she was relieved. She was moments away from heaven. He leaned back in the seat, as Alex moved away and used the back of her hand to wipe her mouth.

"Shit, you're pretty good," he huffed.

Alex watched as he opened the door and reached toward his pants as she waited for him to give her the money. Silently, she hoped his compliment would result in an extra ten, but she knew better.

"Just ah, let me get myself together here," he said.

She pushed herself as far against the dashboard as she could, hoping he'd have the room he needed. Alex didn't want to get out without payment, she knew better. She had had too many bad experiences. This muthafucka was taking his time paying her. She didn't like it one bit, but what could she do, she needed the money, so she'd have to wait.

"Yeah, I'ma have to come back here and look for you again," he said.

When he finally dug into his pocket, she became more optimistic about actually getting paid, she smiled for the first time since she had reeled him in. He pulled his hand out with a few crumpled bills then motioned toward the opened door.

"Here, let's step out," he said.

"Um, no, I think you should pay me first, you know, in here," Alex said.

He looked around as if realizing for the first time that what they were doing was illegal. "Oh, shit, yeah, smart thinkin', okay, well, here," he said and nervously pushed the bill into her hand.

Alex looked at the bill then frowned. Quite surely this was a mistake, considering he clutched nearly a handful of bills.

"Um, this-this is only five," she stuttered.

"Ah, yeah, about that," he cleared his throat. "I really don't believe in going broke over no ho, I mean you're good and shit, but I work too damn hard for my money," he said nonchalantly. "'Sides you did kinda stopped mid-stroke and that threw off my concentration a bit," he shrugged.

Alex's head snapped back, she frowned and struggled to believe what she was hearing. But before she could put up much of a fuss, he shoved her out of the car and pulled off. After tumbling to the wet ground, she stood in the rain, holding half of what she was promised, Alex was pissed. What the fuck could she get with five lousy, fuckin' dollars? She could spend another four hours walking along Century or she could use the five to convince Dre that she was good for the rest.

That's it; that's what she'd do. Dre knew she was good for it. Alex didn't want to think about what would happen if Dre wouldn't cut her some slack. She'd just have to think positive. *Dre will hook me up, he always does.* As she made it back to Century Boulevard, it looked even more deserted than it did twenty minutes ago. Jewels was nowhere in sight, and most of the girls were gone as well. It was a slow and washed-out night.

2

The rain always made Alex think about how she even got to this point. She wasn't supposed to be working the streets like this. Alex had big plans. She wasn't supposed to wind up on the streets in the first damn place. And even though it had been a year since it happened, she remembered it like it was just the other day: The day the argument with her mother went from bad to worse, and she left for what she thought was a life of freedom.

Alex's hands trembled as she stood at the corner, pressing the button to change the light. Her mind went back to her mother's hurtful words.

"*You are a child. You have no say. If you live under this roof, you will follow my rules, or else!*"

"Kim, why you trippin'?" Alex had yelled into the pay phone. "Besides, I thought you said your mama wouldn't care how long I crashed there. I was counting on you. Now I have nowhere to go!" Alex screamed. Her mother's words haunted her every thought.

"*I don't agree with your stupid-ass rules. So I'm out!*"

"Kim!" Alex heard nothing on the other end. "Kim, please don't hang up!" When she heard the dial tone, she slammed the phone against the hook and cried. It was nearly eleven at night, with less than twenty dollars left and her stomach growling, she had no idea what to do.

For the three weeks she had been away from home, she'd stayed with friends here and there, until her favors ran out. Just when she was about to call another friend, a man walked up and stood as if he was waiting to use the phone. Alex wiped the tears from her face and tried to straighten her clothes.

"Are you okay?" He asked in a tone slightly above a whisper.

Alex sniffled. "I'm fine. I'll just be a few minutes," she said to the man.

The man walked closer. "Hey, I'm Iceman. I have a cell phone you can use." His smile exposed a diamond encrusted gold tooth. He looked around. "Besides, you don't need to be out here all by yourself."

For the first time since he stepped up, Alex looked at him. He was handsome and dressed to the nines. When he hit the button to trigger the alarm on his shiny Escalade SUV, she figured he must be all right.

"What's a fine-ass honey like you doin' out here all alone and upset? I overheard your conversation," he said. "I think I can help."

Five days later, Iceman Ivan had taken Alex shopping for sexy new outfits. Most were clothes her mother would never let her wear, but since she was on her own, she could do whatever she wanted. She and Iceman Ivan had eaten at some of the most expensive restaurants in town. He treated her like an adult and he let her to stay in his nice loft apartment in downtown LA.

"The view from up here is that bomb!" Alex squealed.

"Baby girl, you ain't seen nothing yet. Stick with me and I'll always show you the very best. Besides, a woman like you should always have nice things." Iceman eased his arms around her waist.

Alex liked that he referred to her as a woman. "I have . . . err . . . a lot of nice things at home. But none of 'em come close to what you've shown me. Besides, my moms treated like

I was still a child. That's why I had to bounce," she confessed. "I am not a child, and I can make it on my own!"

Iceman turned her around to face him. He touched her chin. The way men did in romantic movies when they cared about a woman. "Well, I can definitely tell you're not a child. You're all woman from where I'm standing. Even a blind man can see that," he chuckled.

"You are so good to me." Alex said, a little uneasy by his closeness. "When I get on my feet, I promise I'll pay you back for all the nice clothes and shoes and stuff."

"Ah, baby girl, don't worry about that. But I tell you what. I know how you can make yourself some real money and buy even more nice things. How would you like that?"

"For real? Sounds cool. What would I have to do?" Alex asked, intrigued by the possibility of making some real paper.

"You may think you're grown, but you're not. You're a child. Nobody will ever love you and care for you the way your family does. I have rules because I love you." There was her mother's nagging voice again.

With no curfew to worry about, or rules that didn't make sense, Alex felt more carefree and alive. Three weeks later, she looked at her outfit in the mirror. The short leather mini was tight. Her fishnet stockings weren't the cheap ones her classmates bought at the mall. And she didn't mind the tube top, because Iceman had bought her a real rabbit fur jacket to wear over it.

At first, being on her own wasn't nearly as hard as her mother had made it sound.

"*Nothing good comes from hanging out in the streets. One day you'll thank me for the rules.*"

When the shiny car pulled up, she sashayed out of the hotel lobby sporting one of her new outfits and a bad pair of platform high-heel boots. She waited for the man to get out and open the door.

"Hi. Alex right?" he asked with a devilish grin.

She smiled, nodded, sat, and then swung her legs into the car. When she flipped down the visor mirror, she noticed two infant seats in the back. That gave her pause, but Alex reminded herself this was just business. Besides, she had to do what she had to do to make it on her own.

"Where are we going?" She asked, as she eased back into the seat.

"I thought we'd go to the park," the man said.

"The park?" In the months she'd been selling her body, her Johns always sprang for a nice room. Iceman had said they knew quality, and were willing to pay well for it. Most nights she worked from ten to four in the morning, and made up to twenty-two hundred dollars. Iceman said it was mainly because she was seventeen, pretty, and he had said class like hers was near priceless.

Four months into her new profession, Alex was tired, lonely, and homesick. Iceman hadn't been attentive like he once was. He held all of the money she had made, meaning she still had to ask for it, just like at home. And lately, she often thought about burning in hell for sleeping with men for money.

Deep down inside, she wanted to call her mother, but she was terrified. She thought about reaching out to her sister Porsha, but after what happened to her, she ran off and joined the Army, and Alex hadn't spoken to her in nearly two years. Alex considered even calling her other sister Paris, who always acted like *she* was really her mother, instead of her sister, but Paris was away at school in Bakersfield, and she didn't think Paris wanted to listen to her problems anyway. In the past Paris always sided with their mom, especially after Porsha moved out. Paris would tell Alex their mom Naomi, was only doing what was best for her girls. In the early days Alex often remembered the nasty words from the fight she had had with her mother before she left. But the words came back to her at the worse times possible. She'd be ready to do her thang, then they'd creep up on her.

"If you can't follow my rules, you need to go!"

Alex knew if her mother, or even her sisters, found out what she had been doing, they'd be upset, embarrassed and disappointed. All of that ran through her mind as she lay on the floor of a Ford Sable. She was no longer excited about the money she'd earn from the tryst.

When she turned her head she noticed a doll lodged beneath the driver's seat. For some reason that made her sick and sad.

"Good for you, baby?" the man asked breathlessly.

"Um, yeah. Real good." She managed weakly.

When he finished, Alex took the money, crumpled it in her hands and sulked back toward the hotel.

By the time she arrived at her room, Keisha, one of the other girls that worked for Iceman, was preparing to go back out.

"Why you back so early?" Keisha asked.

"I'm tired of this." Alex said.

"Tired? Girl, it ain't even midnight. You know Iceman ain't going for that."

Alex sighed. "Keisha. I mean I don't want to do this anymore. I want to leave . . . go back home to my family."

"Hmm. Well, good luck with that one. If Ice heard that, he'd knock your teeth out." Keisha looked around as if Iceman might see or hear her. "He took the last girl who tried to leave, and tied her up. Then he stuffed her into a large cardboard box and put it in the middle of a busy street. He sat in his truck and watched as cars zoomed by, honking and dodging the box. When he finally let her out the box, he beat the shit out of her." Keisha checked her makeup in the mirror. "After all that, he used his cell phone to take pictures and show the rest of us." She shrugged. "He don't play when it comes to his money."

Alex was horrified. What if Iceman tried to beat her too? He certainly wasn't the nice man who helped her out when she needed a place to stay. Just the thought of what he might do made her decide to stay. But still, she couldn't bare the thought of being touched by another man. Many of the men were old enough to be her father. Some were even married and had children themselves. She began to feel filthy—no matter how often she showered.

When Keisha left, Alex counted the money she had earned and decided to stay in for the rest of the night. She prayed Iceman wouldn't decide to drop in on them.

3

The next day her lunch with Iceman was cut short when he had to take an important phone call. "Wait here," he demanded, in the callus tone she'd become accustomed to hearing lately.

"Out here?" Alex asked, as she stood shivering on the sidewalk.

Since he didn't answer, she waited until he got in his truck, then she dashed back into the restaurant. She knew time was essential. At the back of the restaurant Alex dropped coins into the pay phone and quickly dialed her home phone number.

When her mother answered, she covered the phone with her hand and silently reminisced about being back at home.

"Hello?" Naomi said again.

Alex hung up, looked toward the front door then slipped into the ladies' room. Iceman gazed at her suspiciously when she emerged from the bathroom. But he didn't say anything.

Later that night as she worked, she replayed her mother's voice in her head. Alex suddenly burst into tears. She wanted desperately to go home. But her mother's warning was firm and Alex knew she meant it.

"If you walk out that door, don't even think about coming back!"

Alex sighed. The green light brought her back to the corner of Century and Western. She hurried across the street and headed toward the apartments that changed her life. As she walked she thought about how she had fallen to rock bottom. When Iceman was arrested and his house raided, she again found herself alone and back on the streets. It was either that or jail with most of the other girls. Only this time, she was also struggling with a serious addiction to crack. She had started smoking crack to make her forget what she was doing out on the streets. That's how she first met Dre. He was on his way up, he and his boys hanging out at the Normandy Casino. Back in the day she thought he was actually doing her a favor by breaking her off some for free. Alex thought about the irony of it all. There were times she'd actually pass on his sweet treats—but that was then. Now she had to have it. Feeding that monkey was all she lived for. When she approached the old apartment building, Alex could spot the regulars hanging around.

The streets were still as dark and spooky as she remembered from her previous visits. None of the faceless figures mattered; she knew exactly where to find what she wanted.

Alex ran up to the third level of the apartment complex and knocked hard on the door marked 2B. She could hear the music blaring through the door. She took a deep breath and knocked harder.

"Who there?" an angry voice growled.

"Aeey, Dre. It's me, Alex. C'mon let me in. It's cold out here," she tried to sound hard.

The door swung open. But it wasn't Dre who stood in front of her. It was his friend Razor. He stood about six feet five inches tall, and was razor thin, which is where he earned his nickname. He wore baggy jeans and a Khaki shirt that hung open to reveal his wife-beater and his platinum link chain with a diamond encrusted R. His hair stayed in two long braids with blue rubber bands wrapped tightly on the ends.

"Yo, dawg, it's that ho Alex," he said as he stepped aside to let her in.

"Who you callin' a ho?" Alex mumbled as she stepped in. The music was still blasting, and Dre sat reclined in a leather chair with a blunt lodged between his lips. He had a jelly jar filled to the rim with liquor and his eyes were glued to the 62-inch screen. There were two half-naked women gyrating their behinds in perfect sync with the music. Dre was shorter than Razor but stocky. He wore a black skull cap and always wore jeans with a long sleeved white T-shirt.

Alex rolled her eyes at Razor as she moved toward Dre's chair and kneeled to the floor. She waited through two videos, each more explicit than the pervious before she spoke.

"Dre, I really need some. And I got money too," she tossed in.

Razor released a laugh, glanced at her then back at the screen. Dre picked up the remote and pressed the mute button. He looked at Alex for the first time since she squatted next to him.

"You know, you used to be one fine muthafucka," Dre said.

"Yeah, I used to always try and holla at you back in the day, but you wasn't feeling a brotha back then. Wouldn't give a nigga no play," Razor chuckled. "But look atcha now."

Dre looked away and shook his head.

Alex didn't have time for this shit, she knew they knew exactly what she wanted, but she also knew she couldn't rush into it either. Once they found out she only had five dollars, she was sure they'd be ready to kick her ass out; and she wasn't having that.

"You used to be all thick and juicy. Now, shit, I can see your ribs. Titties still tight and shit, but still you look bad, girl," Dre said. He shook his head and frowned. "And damn . . . is that you smelling like that?" Dre fanned his nose and Razor doubled over in laughter.

"So whassup? What you want anyway?" he asked, still struggling to contain his laughter.

"I just need a little something," Alex confessed. She started picking at her nails, not wanting to admit she only had five dollars.

Razor shook his head, and Alex rolled her eyes. She wasn't even talking to him. She wondered why Dre even hung out with him,. He was nothing but a busta; always riding on somebody's coattails, but she didn't dare say anything. She just tried her best to appeal to Dre's weakness.

Soon she glanced at the women dancing on the screen. She figured she'd have to wait for another commercial break before she'd get his attention again.

"I tell you what, Alex. I'll give you what you want If you convince me."

She perked up a bit. She'd give him some ass if that's what he wanted. Alex knew she'd really get her blast on if all she had to do was spread her legs.

"Dre, you name it, tell me what you want me to do. You know I'm down," she said eagerly.

"Okay, okay. Chill for a minute. We 'bout to have a dance contest. You win, you get what you want, that simple," Dre said laughing.

"Oh yeah, dawg," Razor grinned, rubbing his hands together.

"You 'bout to dance against the bitches in the videos. If you win, you get what you want; you lose, I get what I want," Dre chuckled. Again, Razor reached over to give him some dap.

Alex got up and started bouncing her shoulders to the music. She spread her legs, shook her ass and turned to the screen.

"You could probably win if you take off some clothes," Razor screamed. Alex wasn't in the mood to play their game, but she knew it was the only way she was getting high that night.

Alex pealed the wet jacket from her body and flung it to the floor as she twirled to the beat. She leaned over exposing her ass in hopes of wrapping up the little contest.

"Damn this nasty bitch is making my dick hard," Razor admitted.

When Alex released the strings from her bra revealing her breasts, Dre turned off the TV. That's when she knew she had them.

"Are you having a good time, Daddy?" Alex asked, zeroing in on Dre. She licked her lips and squeezed her nipples for him. Dre leaned forward, but quickly frowned and leaned back when she turned to shake herself out of the tight miniskirt.

"Look, why don't you go wash your ass and we'll see if we can work something out when you through," Dre said.

"Yeah, go clean up, stank bitch," Razor said. "Come back, suck my dick and you can smoke as much as you want."

Alex's eyes lit up, she snatched her clothes up from the floor and dashed toward the back to the bathroom. In the shower, she marveled at the sensation of water prickling her skin. For the first time, it dawned on her that she hadn't taken a bath or a shower in weeks. It felt good, but she knew after the shower and after her work, she'd feel even better.

Moments later, she was on her knees sucking Dre's dick. It didn't take him long to fill her mouth, then she sat back on her ass and wiped at her mouth. She was more than ready to get high. She thought after her first hit, she might just give him some ass. She was hyped about getting high for a little bit of work.

"Is that a real Diamond A in your ear?" Razor asked.

Frowning, Alex touched her ear, "Oh, this old thing? No, it ain't real. And it's sapphire; my grandmamma gave it to me."

"I shoulda known it wasn't real. I'm sure you woulda smoked it up by now if it was," Razor said.

Alex ignored him and kept her eyes on Dre. She hoped he wasn't about to renege on his promise. She waited for him to catch his breath, but she was ready to get what was coming to her.

"That was tight," he said. "Yo, why don't you suck my boy off too," Dre said over his shoulder, as he walked to the bathroom. Alex rolled her eyes. She didn't want to suck Razor's dick, but she wanted to get high. She shrugged and scooted toward his lap while still on her knees.

By the time Dre walked back into the room, Alex had Razor yawning and ready to go to sleep. She was more than ready to get high. When Dre didn't move fast enough to give her the drugs he promised, Alex stood and put her hands on her hips.

"C'mon now, Dre. You said you'd hook me up if I sucked y'alls dicks. I did what you wanted, now where it at?"

Dre just looked at her.

"I know you ain't 'bout to do me like that," she pressed.

"You need to chill," Razor said.

She turned toward him, "I don't need to do shit but get what y'all promised. So what's up, Dre?" she asked.

"I'll tell you what's up," he sat back in his chair and looked up at her. "The head was a'ight, but you still gotta pay, 'cause nobody gets high for free."

"But Dre, you said if I sucked your dick you'd hook me up," she snarled. "I sucked you and him, now you try'n ta say that wasn't good enough, you still gon' charge me?" she pleaded.

"I know you didn't roll up in here broke expecting credit or charity, right? You got some money, so what's up?"

Alex sucked her teeth. Ain't no way in the world she was giving up her money after she got carpet burns on both knees suckin' them off.

"You ain't even right, Dre."

"I say we put her ass out and let her get somewhere with that ol' beggin' shit," Razor chimed in.

"Ain't nobody begging, Razor. This business!" Alex snapped. "That head wasn't free, nigga. Y'all the ones who don't wanna pay!"

Dre wasn't moved. He simply eased back and asked, "What's it gonna be? 'Cause you can't hang out here. You bad for business boo."

Alex reluctantly dug into her pocket and slowly pulled out the bill she had carefully folded. She shook her head and sucked her teeth again.

"How much she got, dawg," Razor asked co-signing. She couldn't stand his ass.

Dre snatched the bill before she could unfold it and laughed. "You jokin' right?"

"Wait, Dre. You put that with the head y'all just got, you know, that's good for at least a quarter."

"Bitch, please."

Dre dug into a small bag and pulled the smallest rock he could find, broke off a piece and gave it to her. Alex could barely see the thing in the palm of her hand.

"What the fuck!" she hollered. "Oh I know you besta come correct. This little shit ain't even worth the nickel I gave you. Plus I had to suck your dick, and that one over there with his stank, sweaty balls!" Alex was in rare form. With her arms flapping and her neck twisting. "I'm not leaving here until one of y'all break me off something proper."

Alex lunged toward the bag. "Nah ah, you owe me, you fuckin' bastard!"

In one sweeping movement, Dre hauled off and back handed her. Before she knew what was happening, her body went flying across the room. Her head struck the edge of a nearby table before she tumbled to the floor.

"Oh, hell fucking no!" she screamed. She pulled herself up and started swinging wildly. Before she was able to make contact with Dre, Razor grabbed her by the midsection and tossed her back to the floor. He started plummeting her with punches to the face and head. Dre soon joined in. "You nasty, bitch. Try to steal from me," he said before kicking her in the midsection.

They both started kicking her about the face and body until she started coughing up blood. When she stopped protecting herself, they noticed she was no longer breathing. Dre looked down at her still body.

"Hold up, dawg," he said using his arm to stop Razor from kicking Alex again.

"The bitch ain't moving," Dre said.

CHAPTER 1

Naomi McCain's knees buckled beneath her weight as she clutched the kitchen counter. Her eyes were fixated on the small TV screen attached to the bottom of the cabinet. She knew this day was coming, had dreamt about it often—at times while she was wide awake.

The news reporter's voice still rang in her ear, even though they'd gone to commercial break nearly two minutes ago.

. . . The body of a young, black female found . . .

Those words gave Naomi pause. She had been at the sink washing dishes.

. . . dumped in the abandoned row houses on Figaroua.

Could it be? She removed the rubber gloves and listened closely.

. . . Police are trying to identify . . .

"No! She shrieked.

. . . five feet seven inches . . . a birthmark on her neck...

That's when she knew. Naomi found strength in her legs just in time to make it to the bathroom. She fell to her knees and hugged the toilet, throwing up until her insides felt raw. She began to dry heave and cry at the same time. Later, with trembling fingers she dialed her twin sister's number and waited for her voice to ring through the phone.

"Hello?"

"Naomi? Is that you?" Natasha asked. "Are you crying? What's the matter?"

"I think they found Alex," Naomi managed. She burst into tears again.

"Naomi . . . Oh-my-God! I'm on my way over," Natasha cried.

"Alexandria . . ." Naomi sobbed. "Oh God, my baby is goooone," she hollered.

Naomi didn't know how much time had passed since she dialed her sister's number. She wanted the entire day to start over. She didn't need to wake up and discover that her child's body had been found in some abandoned house in a slimy part of town.

Since the day Alex walked out, Naomi had regretted ever allowing her child to leave. They should've been able to work out their differences. The knock at her door brought her grim situation to the forefront again.

Natasha was a medium-built woman with wide hips and a trendy pageboy haircut. Except for the beauty mark prominently beneath her left eye, she and her sister Naomi were identical twins. Their lives mirrored each other so much at times. Natasha had buried a son only three years earlier and lost the other one to the streets. She and her sister were both mothers of twins. Naomi, twin girls and a younger daughter Alexandria. Natasha had twin boys. Now this sick twist of fate had left both sisters mourning the loss of a child. Natasha sat and held her sister's quivering body in her arms.

"Did you call Paris?" Natasha asked.

"She's on her way. She told me to wait before I go down there."

Naomi wanted to ask; the words sat at the very tip of her tongue. Before she had to, her sister quickly said, "I haven't heard from Porsha yet. But I did leave word for her." Natasha closed her eyes and inhaled; she looked at her sister and said, "You—you ain't been down there yet?"

Naomi knew exactly what her sister was thinking. She could feel the hope seeping through her eyes. She herself had gone through the exact same false sense of maybes and what ifs. But deep down inside, she already knew that that was her child they described on the news. She had no doubt that had been her baby's body they found.

"I wanna wait for Paris," Naomi sobbed onto her sister's shoulder.

Around four that evening, Paris came busting through the front door. She was frantic, upset and her eyes were swollen. From the moment she got her mother's tearful phone call, she had been a nervous wreck. So much so that a classmate agreed to make the two hour drive from her college in Bakersfield for her.

When Paris witnessed her mother all wrapped up in her Aunt Natasha's arms, she knew then for sure that her baby sister was gone.

It had been two days since Paris and her mother went to the Medical Examiner's office to identify Alex's body. But still each time she closed her eyes or even blinked, Paris was haunted by the picture of her dead sister lying on that cold concrete slab. And the fact that her own twin Porsha, still had not arrived, helped to reinforce every bad thing their mother ever thought about Porsha. Paris stopped at the kitchen entrance and listened to her mother talking on the phone.

"Yeah. My baby was beaten so badly her face was purple and blue. Emh hmm, chile," Paris heard her mother say.

For some reason she didn't want to move. She stood just out of sight and listened to her mother's crackling voice.

"Just a shame. Could barely tell that was my child I birthed. And you know them cops ain't even try;n'ta find out who did this to my child."

Paris closed her eyes when the wailing started. Since she'd been home, late at night, she'd hear her mother trying to sob quietly. She hadn't had a good night sleep since she saw that picture of her sister. Paris clutched her chest and quietly cried too.

On the day of Alex's funeral, a parking spot near the small Baptist church on the corner of 61st and Western Avenue was hard to come by. Every pew in the church was full. One of Naomi's co-workers had just finished a tear jerking rendition of "Take Me Home, Sweet Lord." Just as everyone had gathered their composure and prepared for the eulogy, the doors of the church creaked open and nearly every head turned to the back. A quiet hush fell over the small church, but soon whispers floated from the front to the back then up to the front again.

All eyes flocked toward the middle of the aisle. No one spoke until the woman wearing a Navy pantsuit found a seat near the back. At the end of the service, everyone followed the progression toward the front of the church and viewed Alex's body for a final time.

Natasha released a loud gasp at the sight of her niece. She felt a sense of relief now that Porsha was there. Natasha extended her arms and Porsha collapsed into her aunt's embrace. She barely even looked her mother's way. No one had seen Porsha in nearly two years. After leaving her mother's for her aunt's house, she suddenly ran off and joined the Army. She never called or wrote home, and no one ever knew why. At that moment, Natasha, Naomi and Paris, didn't care why she had left; they were just glad she had made her way back home.

Once again, the church was filled with sounds of sobs and shrieking cries.

Back at the house, Paris and her sister Porsha sat hold up in an upstairs bedroom.

"What happened to her?" Porsha asked.

Paris shook her head and turned up her drink. The Remy Martin burned her throat, but warmed her insides.

"I'm still try'n ta find out. I been askin' some questions, you know, just try'n ta see what really happened." Paris shrugged. "But ain't nobody talkin'. That's what's fuckin' wit me. How the hell nobody know what happened to her," Paris started crying.

Porsha wanted to take her into her arms, but she couldn't bring herself to do it. As she watched her sister break down, she couldn't help but wonder whether Alex had taken her secret to the grave. As she looked at Paris, she made a silent promise to herself. She got up from the chair and walked to the bed where Paris sat. "You know what we gotta do, right?"

Paris looked up at her through swollen eyes. "What you talkin' 'bout?"

"Look, we can't let these muthafuckas get away with this."

"But the police said . . ."

"I know what the fuck they said. Shit, I remember what *your* mother said the detective told her when she asked if they caught the person who did it," Porsha pressed.

"She's your mother too, you need to put that shit behind you," Paris snapped.

Paris couldn't believe her mother and sister were still tripping over their disagreement. For years, Porsha had accused their mother of favoring Paris, it finally blew over when she stormed out and moved in with their Aunt Natasha. The two hadn't spoken since.

She shook her head then said, "The cop—he said they'd probably never find who did it, and that we should just be glad we got some closure," Paris admitted.

"Closure!" Porsha snapped, "Who the fuck cares about some goddamn closure? I want revenge. I don't give a fuck what Alex got into, she didn't deserve to die like that. She didn't deserve to be beaten to death. You know the cops lookin' at Alex like just another junkie, but we know better. After all we been through together?" Porsha shook her head trying to fight back her own burning tears. She bit down on her lip. "Nah, it ain't even goin' down like this. We gon' fix this ourselves."

"How?" Paris shrugged.

“I say we find the muthafucka that did this and hang him by his balls until he dies a slow and excruciating death.”

For the first time since she broke down, Paris looked up at her sister with hope instead of sorrow. “Are you serious?” she sniffled.

Porsha gave Paris a cold stare. “Serious as I’ve ever been in all my twenty-four years,” she hissed. Porsha shook her head. “It’s the only way we’ll ever have peace.” Porsha exclaimed. “The only way,” she vowed.

CHAPTER 2

". . . Find me in the club . . ." Porsha was rockin' to a 50 Cent jam, snappin' her fingers with one eye shut as smoke from the cigarette danglin' between her lips, trailed upward. Paris was right next to her, silently jammin' as she sipped her Remy Martin. The dance floor was packed at the Century Club, in Century City.

It had been two days since Alex's funeral, and they were still no closer to finding her killer. They had been riding and talking to everyone they knew who was usually up on everything that went on around the way, but nobody knew shit, and it was starting to get depressing. Porsha suggested they go out, relax a little, hang out like they used to.

". . . go, shorty, it's your birthday," they sang in unison. A waitress came by the table again.

"Aeey," Porsha screamed before she passed. "I need another one. I'm drinkin' Grey Goose and cranberry juice; she's drinkin' Remy straight up," she bobbed her head to the music.

"Damn it's packed up in this bitch tonight," Paris said looking around the crowded club. The dance floor had been stacked since they walked in nearly two hours ago. The deejay had the house rockin'. It didn't seem like he was gonna let up on them anytime soon.

"Yeah, I miss this shit, for real," Porsha admitted. She took one long drag of her cigarette before putting in out in an astray and turning up her glass. "So you give any more thought to what we discussed a few days back?"

Paris scrunched up her face.

Porsha said, "What are you over there thinking about? I asked you a question."

"Just thinking about back in the day," she said.

"Shit, we had some fun, smokin' that weed, drinkin' gin and juice because we thought that's what real gangsta girls did." Porsha said.

"*We*?" Paris giggled.

"Yeah, we," Porsha responded.

"I remember *you* hangin' out with them Crips for more than a minute," Paris said, taking the real trip down memory lane.

Porsha shook her head at the memory. "Yeah, that shit was deep. Shit, I had been hangin' with Wanda and them for months, doin' all kinds of dumb shit, I didn't know nothin' about being no damn Cripett. Then that fool Coltfrog came up talkin' that shit 'bout I gotta get in the way everybody else did. Fuck that, wasn't no way in hell I was 'bout to let all them niggas fuck me."

"That ended your gang career," Paris said and they both laughed.

Porsha wondered just how she made it. Hell, how they all did, because they had done a lot of dangerous shit back in the day. They just didn't know any better. Their mother and her sister were holding down two jobs, and they didn't have any other family, so the girls were forced to be on their own a lot sooner than they needed to be. But they made it out. No teenage pregnancies or deadly diseases. Now it was just those two left. They sat silently listening to the newest Snoop Dogg song and drinking liquor. The dance floor was still packed.

"Oh, hell nah!" a familiar voice screamed. Paris and Porsha looked toward a group of women, who looked like they just slid off a pole at the strip club. The leader of the pack was wearing what looked like a bikini under a fishnet body suit, with a pair of stacked heels tied up to her knees.

"I know this ain't double trouble, Porsha and Paris McCain!" Trina Blackwell screamed.

"Trina! Girl . . . get over here! I ain't seen you since, shit, I don't even know when," Paris yelled. She jumped up to hug her friend.

"Shit, I know I need to go play some numbers. It's one thing runnin' into one of you, but both of y'all, and then here in Club Century! Shit, what's really goin' on?"

"Girl, not a damn thing, just try'n ta chill for a bit, get our party on like we used to," Porsha said.

"Oh, y'all not try'n ta hang like that, 'cause ain't no niggas around. You know niggas would've been lined up from here to the next block over try'n ta get next to us. Okay, maybe really just y'all, but you know what I mean."

Trina was brown skinned with short hair, a pretty face and a body that was nothing like it was before she had them four bad-ass kids. She had always been known for squeezing herself into clothes that were either too small or just too skimpy.

"Girl," she squeezed herself next to Paris, "I heard about what happened to Alex. I couldn't believe it. I mean who the hell would want to do anything to Alex?" She looked at the glasses on the table. "Y'all done with these?" Before Porsha or Paris could answer, Trina picked them up and drained them both. "Shoot, these niggas be so cheap up in the club. Won't even buy you a drink, but expect to be grinding all up on you on the dance floor, working up a sweat and shit," she complained. "Oh, I'm so thirsty."

Porsha waved the waitress over. "We need more drinks, what you havin'?" she asked Trina.

Trina hesitated. Her eyebrows elevated making her oval shaped eyes appear wider. "I ain't buying no drink up in here. Shoot, they too high. 'Sides, I left my wallet in the car."

"Don't worry about it, we gotcha'," Paris added.

Trina sat up a little straighter. "Oh, okay then. What y'all havin'?" she asked.

"My girl is drinking Remy straight up, and get me another Grey Goose and cranberry juice."

Trina's eyes lit up, "I'll take a double shot of Tequila; um, Jose Quervo 1800," she tossed in. "No ice!" she shouted at the waitress' back.

By the third round of drinks, Trina was grinding to whatever song the Deejay played that she swore was "my song." Porsha leaned over to her a bit closer. "You know, Trina, we try'n ta figure out what happened to Alex. I mean somebody really fucked her up."

"I heard," Trina said and dropped her head. "You know, I'm sorry I couldn't make it to the funeral. I didn't have nobody to watch my kids, but let's just say after y'all left, things changed around here."

"What you mean?" Paris asked.

Trina looked between Paris and Porsha with uneasiness across her face.

"Come on, Trina, you can talk to us. You know we ain't even try'n ta put your business out in the streets. We just wanna know what happened to Alex."

"I don't believe I'm about to do this," Trina said. She sighed, her shoulders fell and she closed her eyes and shook her head. "All I know is she hooked up with this pimp, calls himself Iceman. But y'all didn't hear this from me!"

Porsha eased back. "Iceman? Who the fuck is he?"

"He's a real nasty nigga. I mean, he'd put his own mama on the streets if he thought she could make a nickel. Well, here's what I heard," Trina leaned in. "Shit, I'ma need another drink," she hissed. Again, Porsha waved the waitress over. She had their orders memorized by the time she went for another round. "Paris, you was already gone away to school. You remember, Porsha, it was the weekend we went to that party at Catalina Island. Anyways, when we got back and the cops started askin' questions about that nigga Nelson and how he died."

Porsha remembered Nelson well. Her eyes shifted at the mention of his name and thoughts of the night she'd been running from.

"Mrs. McCain found out Alex had gone, they got into it and she bounced." Trina took a gulp of her Tequila. "Next thing you know she's down with Iceman, and he moved her out to the valley. They were trickin' out there for nearly a year, then there was this huge sting operation. It was all over the news. The *Wave* had like this week-long story about it. Anyway, they picked up Iceman and a bunch of his girls."

Paris and Porsha sat hanging on Trina's every word.

"From what I heard, Alex and about four others didn't get picked up, but the Feds took everything, right? They didn't have anywhere to go. So anyway while this nigga is locked down, he made some deal with that baller Jimmy Fly."

"Wait, the same Jimmy Fly I'm thinkin' 'bout?" Porsha asked.

"Yup, the same one, except he big time now. He ain't out hustlin' on no corners these days. I knew I shoulda got with that nigga after my second baby daddy bounced," Trina reflected. "But shit, I had mouths to feed. I wasn't trying to get with no nigga on the rise. I needed somebody who was already doing big things. But imagine where I'd be if I'da got with that nigga back then?"

"Okay, Tee, what happened with Alex?" Paris interrupted.

"Oh, yeah, well anyway, Iceman owed Jimmy Fly, right? And he needed some cash to fight his case. So he basically sold the girls he had left to Jimmy Fly, and Alex was one of 'em," she shrugged, and finished off her drink. "Here's where the shit gets flipped. Jimmy Fly ain't no pimp, but being the hustler he is, the shit just fell into his lap, so he put them to work. But problems started when he goes from baller to smoker. Next thing you know, him and the girls are all strung out. Alex and the rest of them out there hustlin' to get high. After that, I lost track. I know one day we was on our way to the airport . . ."

Trina stopped talking, and dramatically closed her eyes and put a pudgy hand over her chest as if she had to catch her breath. Porsha took that to mean she needed another drink. When the waitress returned with fresh drinks, Trina looked and said, "Oooh, thank you." She sipped, shook her head and started talking again.

"Anyway, like I said, we was on our way to the airport, when lo' and behold, I see Alex switching up and down Century Boulevard with her titties and ass all hanging out—clear as day." Trina polished off the drink. "On my way back, I tried to look for her, but I didn't see her before the light changed, so I just went on home. But I said a prayer for her that night. When I heard what happened to her," she shook her head and drained the empty glass. "Well, I couldn't help but feel like, you know, like there might've been something I could do to help her. I just hated to see her out there like that."

"So Iceman sold her to Jimmy Fly, huh?" Porsha clarified.

CHAPTER 3

It wasn't hard to return to life on the streets. Paris and Porsha just revisited a few old spots on South Central's east side in LA. They showed up at old familiar places in the Bottom, and soon they were back in the swing of things. One Saturday, Paris came rushing up out of a hair salon on the east side.

They agreed Porsha would wait in the car, since Paris had a friendlier disposition. They may have shared the same face, but they were as different as sugar and salt, Porsha never felt anyone's pain. They had finally come up after a full day of running around, trying to find a lead on Jimmy Fly.

"Okay, what's up?" Porsha asked an excited Paris as soon as she slammed the car door shut.

"Well, Mookey just told me that she heard Jimmy Fly's ex-girl Quin-Quin, works at Woody's. Apparently she can't stand the nigga either; something about his kids. Anyway, Mookey said if we go over there and tell her that Mookey sent us, she'll not only tell us whatever we wanna know, but she'll break us off some of them slamming hot links."

"Damn, which Woody's? The one over there in Hyde Park off Crenshaw?"

"Yup, that's the one. We can take Slauson straight there. It's right past the Van Ness Playground."

"Oooh, girl, why you mention that? You know what we used to do in that park," Porsha smiled as she turned the car around and headed west toward Slauson.

"You don't want to hop on the freeway?" Paris offered.

"Nah, let's cruise down Slauson. Bring back some ol' memories."

"Okay, but I ain't hanging out in no damn park just so you could have an orgasm thinking about the good ol' days," Paris teased.

"Girl, that's what we 'bout to do at Woody's. Cum all over ourselves when that barbeque beef sandwich hit our tongues. Oooh, the way it just melts and that tangy sauce. Hell yeah. Let's go right on over to Woody's. They still in that little run-down strip mall?"

"Yup, west of Crenshaw, you remember the place?" Paris asked as she turned up the radio and listened to Jamie Foxx's new hit.

Woody's was a hole in the wall that was just as famous for its barbeque as it was for its long wait. But very few customers complained.

At Woody's you walked up. placed your order, waited, then you left to eat someplace else. Parking was good because they were in a strip mall. So when a waitress yelled, "Who's next?" Porsha quickly stepped forward.

"I'm looking for Quin-Quin," she said.

"Quin?" The woman called over her shoulder.

Another woman walked up as the waitress again yelled. "Who's next?"

"I'm Quin-Quin," she said, eyeing Porsha and Paris suspiciously. Quin-Quin was a healthy woman, thick gone out of control with beefy arms. She wore a pair of dingy-white jeans, an apron and a matching white button down shirt with short sleeves. She had shoulder length, wavy hair that was wrapped up tightly in a hairnet and a rough looking face. She didn't smile once.

"Uh, Mookey sent us," Paris offered.

Quin-Quin looked at Paris then back at Porsha, she snickered. "I keep telling that chil' don't be sending folks up here for no damn free food!" Quin-Quin snapped, turning several heads. "Shit, everybody gots to pay up in here. I ain't 'bout to lose my job over no people I don't even know," she reasoned.

Porsha started shaking her head frantically. But Paris spoke up, "We ain't here to beg for no damn free food. We got money, shit!" she snapped.

"Oh, my bad," Quin-Quin offered. "What's up? What y'all want then?" It wasn't a smile, but her face broke into a friendlier appearance.

"We're looking for Jimmy Fly, and Mookey told us you'd be able to help us find him."

Quin-Quin threw up her big arms. "Jimmy Fly? That fucking sewer rat . . . What? That muthafucka owe you money too? I hope you ain't got no kids by him 'cause if you do, you can forget ever getting a dime. I knew I shoulda had that nigga set up back in the day when he was ballin', now his sorry ass ain't got nothing and ain't good for nothing. Last time I saw his beggin'-for-change ass was over in Lemert Park, hustling women who walked out of that hair shop over there. You know that place where all them drug dealers' girlfriends go?" Quin-Quin started snapping her fingers as if that might help her remember the name of the salon.

"Y'all know he still on that shit, right? I know ain't neither one of y'all fucking him. Shit, 'cause I can tell you this now, as God is my witness, his peter ain't but—" She held up a shriveled up pinky. "—that big. Makes you kinda wonder how he could have all them damn kids planted all over the city. Huh?"

Paris held up a hand to try and silence Quin-Quin, "You can't remember the name of the salon?"

"Oh, chil', Cuttin' Up. Yeah, that's it." Quin-Quin shook her head. "A damn shame how he fell from grace like that. You know back in the day he used to have serious money. He was running hoes and selling that stuff; now look at his stupid ass."

"Look, we need to head on over there," Porsha said.

"Y'all don't want nothing to eat? I mean, damn! Don't nobody come up into Woody's without getting at least a link or something. Shit, y'all sleeping on the wrong thing over here," Quin-Quin said.

"Actually, we could use a couple of sandwiches, but shit look at that line," Paris tossed in. She pulled out a twenty-dollar bill. Quin-Quin looked at the money, frowned then looked at Porsha before returning her gaze to Paris.

"Now, how you gon' insult me like that? We damn near family, and you expect me to take y'all money. Look, put that away. Anybody who can't stand Jimmy Fly is a friend of mine. Here, I'll be back with a couple of plates for y'all. Hold up just a sec," Quin-Quin said.

"Damn, did you think she'd ever shut the fuck up?" Porsha asked.

CHAPTER 4

There was absolutely nothing fly about Jimmy Fly. He was a frail looking man who was close to six feet tall. He was the color of black coffee with thick, tangled dreadlocks that hung to his waist. He had a matted beard that still held traces of his lunch, and maybe even his breakfast if Paris or Porsha had to guess.

He gave Paris the creeps and made Porsha's skin crawl. By the time they walked up, Jimmy Fly was trying to sell body oils to a woman who had just walked out of the hair shop. They stood a few feet away and listened to his pitch.

"My queen—My queen. Your beauty is like the exotic birds of paradise: unique and all your own." Paris snickered. Jimmy Fly used his arm to turn the woman away from Paris and Porsha.

"Please, let me share with you some of my intoxicating body oils. Not only will the fragrance entice, but it's good for your skin. Here, I give free samples. It glides on like silk and holds its scent for hours," he said. Jimmy glanced over his shoulder at Paris and Porsha standing there watching him. When his customer walked off without buying anything, he turned his attention to Paris and Porsha.

"My Nubian sistahs," he greeted.

Paris frowned. Porsha rolled her eyes.

"Drop the act," Porsha said.

Jimmy Fly glanced around nervously. "I know y'all?" he asked.

Porsha stepped over to his makeshift table.

"Look, I don't give refunds, if that's what this is about. Besides, I just lost out on a customer because of y'all. So what y'all want?"

He started pulling tubes of oil from the table and began to stuff them into a bag. Just as he finished packing up the table, another man walked up.

"I think we should follow them and see what's going on," Porsha said.

Paris was wondering why they hadn't confronted him about Alex's death. Truthfully, she didn't know for sure if Porsha was serious about her threat, but Paris had to admit a part of her wanted revenge too.

When they fell back and rushed to the car, Porsha said this was a good thing. Paris waited until they were buckled in before she asked what she meant by that.

"Here's the plan. We follow them to wherever, lay in the cut until we can get Jimmy alone, then we step up and smoke his ass." Porsha said easily.

"Shouldn't we find out if he actually had something to do with her murder?" Paris asked.

Porsha turned and looked at her, "Oh, yeah, we'll do that, then we'll smoke him!"

They stayed a few cars behind the men. Along the way Porsha continued to make her case for killing Jimmy Fly. "See this one's gonna be easy, think of all the people who want this muthafucka dead," Porsha said as she stopped at a red light.

Three hours into their stakeout, Paris was getting antsy. Their trail led them to a gay club in west Hollywood. The parking lot was packed and they could hear the music from the club blasting from their car. Their luck paid off when Jimmy Fly came stumbling out of the club with another man close behind.

They were laughing and talking with each other, as they eased around the back of the club. “Okay, let’s go,” Porsha said. She and Paris got out of the car and crept around the side of the building. When Porsha and Paris made their way behind the building, they saw Jimmy Fly on his knees with his head buried between the other man’s legs—they nearly gagged.

“I cannot believe this shit,” Paris whispered.

“Ssshhh,” Porsha warned.

They watched as the man pulled up his pants and tossed a bill at Jimmy Fly. That’s when Porsha moved in. Jimmy Fly was sitting on the garbage can with his legs spread and bent at the knees.

“So you like to party in alleys, huh?”

His eyes widened in horror as he looked up the barrel of Porsha’s gun.

“Oh-my-God! Where’d you get a gun!” Paris snapped.

“Look, don’t worry about that, I need you to walk over there,” she motioned with her chin, “-and make sure there’s not a line waiting for lover boy here.”

Jimmy Fly raised his hands in surrender. “Look sistah, you can have the money. It’s fifty dollars. I ain’t even trippin’.” Jimmy Fly looked up at Porsha with pleading eyes. “I don’t know what this is about, but shit, we could work it out,” he cried. “I can get more money, I swear; just don’t shoot.”

“We don’t want your fucking money!” Porsha snapped.

“What do you want?” he offered.

“You remember Alex?” Porsha asked.

Jimmy Fly shook his head, “I don’t know no Alex. Who is he?”

“*She*, you fucking bastard!” Paris screamed. “She was one of the girls you turned the fuck out!”

“Aaalex!” Recognition settled on his face.

“Yeah, Aaalex,” Porsha said, mocking him with her finger still on the trigger.

Jimmy Fly shrugged his shoulders. “I haven’t seen her in damn . . . at least a year. I heard she was strung out, strollin’ up and down Century Boulevard. We had a fight ’cause she was smokin' up all my shit," Jimmy Fly said, with his hands still up near his ears. "She came at me first, shit, that bitch fought me like a man. Alex left after that and I swear-'fo'-God, I ain't laid eyes on that bitch since that night," he said.

"That *bitch* was our sister!" Paris screamed at him. Porsha took a step closer and the barrel of her gun was pressed against Jimmy Fly's head.

"Please, don't kill me. I didn't hurt her!" Jimmy fly pleaded. "She tell you I owe her money or something?"

"Where did she go after she left you?" Porsha demanded.

Jimmy Fly shook his head. "I don't know. Last I heard she was gettin' her shit from this nigga named Zeke."

"Where is he?"

"I don't know. All I know is Zeke is down with some dudes in a low-rider club from Fifth Avenue. I swear to you!" Jimmy Fly dropped to his knees and tears started rolling down his cheeks.

"My sister is dead because of you!" Porsha snickered.

"Ddd-dead?" He shook his head as if to deny what Porsha was saying.

"Alex is dead?" Paris screamed as Porsha fired two shots in Jimmy Fly's chest.

"Yeah, muthafucka, and now. . . ." Porsha pulled the trigger again and put one in his head. "So are you!"

CHAPTER 5

Porsha was breathless as she and Paris ran to the car, jumped inside and sped out of the parking lot. Looking back in the rearview and the side mirrors, Porsha finally calmed herself enough to drive the speed limit. The last thing she wanted was to be pulled over for speeding and get caught with the gun. Paris sat gripping the door as if she might jump out any minute.

"I can't believe you shot him. You just killed a man," Paris screamed. Porsha looked over at her in astonishment. "You just killed him, like it wasn't shit," Paris yelled again.

She jumped on the 101 Freeway and switched to the Harbor Freeway. By the time Porsha pulled into the driveway, she decided it wasn't a good idea for them to be at the house. She backed out of the driveway and hopped back on the freeway and drove out toward Redondo Beach. Porsha decided it was best that they stayed away from crowds, so she found a deserted area of the parking lot and got out of the car. She looked at Paris and noticed the tears pouring from her eyes. In addition to the tears, she was still breathing heavily.

"You okay?" Porsha asked.

"What do you think?" Paris spit out. "I just watched you kill somebody!"

"I thought you wanted to find the muthafuckas who killed Alex!" Porsha snapped. "Do you remember what she looked like, all bruised, beaten and swollen, we could hardly even recognize her. And that was after they fixed her up."

Paris cried a little louder and harder.

"Look, don't flake on me now. We've gotta do this—you and me!" Porsha shouted. "Think about it. What are the cops gonna do? I'll tell you what. They're not gonna do a damn thing. Alex's file is probably already on the pile of unsolved cases they give less than a fuck about. You know cops don't give a fuck about us. Especially someone they saw as nothing more than a two-dollar ho!"

Paris shook her head, she was shaking, but her sobs had started to subside a bit. "I'm okay. I just wasn't ready for it, that's all. I thought we were just gonna talk to him, find out if he knew anything."

"Is that all? Didn't you hear him say he beat her? He got her hooked on that shit, beat her ass and put her onto the streets," Porsha frowned. "Am I the only one who wants someone to pay for our sister's murder?"

"No!" Paris finally answered.

Porsha sat on the hood. Out of the side of her eye she could see Paris still crying. Then she remembered why she and Alex always kept things from Paris. Paris wasn't strong like her and Alex. Sure, she used to give Alex a hard time playing the role of second mother, but they both knew Paris was really soft at heart.

Just seeing Paris fall apart like that confirmed that Alex never told her about Porsha's secret. For that reason and so many others, Porsha felt an everlasting loyalty to Alex. She knew she had to avenge her sister's death—no manner what. Even if it meant she'd have to single handedly kill every baller, drug dealer, or wanna-be hustler in the neighborhood.

When Porsha looked up, she was shocked to see Paris standing in front of her. Her tear-streaked face had an intense look on it, and her chest was heaving up and down.

"Who's next?" Paris asked. "I'm ready!" she declared.

CHAPTER 6

Paris slipped into the skintight, black minidress and stepped into her stiletto slippers. Once she checked her reflection in the full-length mirror, she was satisfied with what she saw. Before she could slip into the bathroom, she nearly bumped into her mother in the hall. She had spent the day thinking about what happened the night before. Paris remembered the shock she went through when Porsha pulled the trigger. She remembered the rush of adrenaline she felt running to the car and speeding away. At first she was confused, then she was excited; then Paris was scared. She thought about what Porsha said.

"*Do you remember what she looked like all bruised, beaten, and swollen? We could hardly recognize her.*" Paris could never forget seeing Alexis' body. How could anyone do that to her? What could Paris have done to deserve a beating like that? She'd have to keep that image in mind; she'd use it to strengthen her resolve.

"*We gotta do this, Paris. You and me.*"

Paris felt her mother's cold stare run up the length of her body. "Hmm, where you think you goin' dressed like that?" Naomi's hands flew to her hips.

"I'm going out with Porsha," Paris said as she tried to squeeze by her mother. Paris was not in the mood to fight with her mother, she quickly stormed out of the house.

As she walked to the car she remembered the heated discussion she'd had with her mother. Again Naomi had started in on Porsha.

"As God is my witness, Paris, I will not sit by and lose another child to Porsha's foolishness. Now, I don't have any proof, but I'm almost sure she had something to do with what happened to Alex."

Paris tried to shake the traitorous words from her head as she approached the car, but they stuck with her.

"I just want you to go back to school. You don't need to be here running the streets with Porsha. I don't care what anyone says, I'm telling you, Alex changed when they came back from that damn island. She had no business going anyway."

Porsha smiled when Paris opened the car door.

Porsha put on 50 Cent and eased back for the ride to the club. She looked over at Paris. "I'm glad you brought out the big guns for tonight. This tells me you mean business." Porsha nodded.

"I'm so glad I decided to wear a dress that's equally sluttish," she tossed in.

Two songs into the CD, Porsha lowered the volume on the radio.

Paris closed her eyes and swallowed. She kept thinking about their mother's words. "C'mon, let's roll," she said.

Porsha looked over at her sister and said, "You do remember why we're doin' this, right? You know why we're here."

Porsha grabbed her by the arm, but Paris finished her sentence. "For Alex."

CHAPTER 7

"Damn the club is poppin' tonight," Paris said as they pushed their way through the thick throng of people. Every where they looked, the ladies were dressed and the men were suited. Paris immediately got into the invigorating atmosphere. The music was tantalizing. After jamming to the music for a few seconds, they found a table that sat between the bar and the VIP room. They were upstairs at the Normandy Casino where the ballers went to get their groove on in between expensive rounds of Blackjack.

The deejay was mixing old school Pac and the dance floor was full. Porsha was wiggling in her seat, when suddenly, something made her stop and turn toward the glass divider that separated the VIP section from the rest of the club. As they bounced to the music, they closely watched everything going on in the VIP section. A few guys slipped by their table asking her and Porsha to dance, but they turned them down.

"Don't look now, but to your right, Delbert 'Shake 'n Bake' Baker just strolled into the VIP room." He earned the name Shake 'n Bake playing basketball. He might have gone pro if he had any interest at all in going to school, but Baker was all thug—all the time. He raised up through the ranks, slangin' sacks on the corner while building his rep as a no-nonsense hustler—who wasn't takin' any shit—from anybody. It wasn't long before he put together a team of his own and went from hustler to neighborhood kingpin.

Paris smiled easily and sipped her drink. She didn't glance over in that direction, instead she got up from the table and sashayed toward the ladies' room, where she quickly shed her fishnet stockings and her panties. When she returned she took the seat facing the VIP's massive glass window. Her job was simple, to make eye contact with Baker.

Porsha waved the waitress over and when she arrived, she said, "What are you ladies drinking this evening?" Porsha ordered the usual for them both and the waitress went away.

When the waitress returned with their drinks, Porsha tried to pay, but she refused her money. "Compliments of the gentlemen over there," she said.

"Sweet," Paris smiled as she and Porsha turned and glanced at the table a few feet away. Two guys tipped their glasses when they looked over. Porsha mouthed 'thanks' and they turned their attention back toward the VIP.

When Paris looked into the room she stared right into Baker's dark and alluring eyes. The scar on his cheek was sexy to her. She held his stare then smiled. He looked away quickly, but didn't return her smile. Even though her gesture went ignored, the contact was long enough for him to notice her. The game had begun.

Paris watched as a couple of women pranced over to him and his boys. The ladies were animated; laughing, talking using their hands and drinking up everything in sight. This time when Baker looked at her, Paris shrugged and smiled and then she shook her head. When Baker looked surprized by her gesture, she pointed toward the woman sitting next to him and shrugged again.

When he frowned and took a sip of his drink. Paris smiled and looked away. A couple of times, she caught him staring at her. When she looked back, he'd quickly glance the other way. She thought it was funny.

For the next thirty minutes a crowd prevented her from seeing Baker, so she and Porsha sat enjoying the music and drinking. Paris didn't want to get too wasted, so she sipped her Henny slowly. When the deejay started playing Busta Rhymes, the crowd thinned a bit in VIP. Baker sat in the exact same spot. This time when he looked her way, Paris kicked one leg up on a nearby barstool, and flashed him.

With his eyes glued to the space between her legs, he smiled and she knew she had him. Nearly ten minutes later, she looked up and saw Baker motioning with his head, toward their table. Ten minutes after that, a stocky man dressed in black approached their table.

"Bake wants y'all to hang out in VIP," he said.

When Paris looked back into the room she shrugged and smiled. Baker simply tilted his head back beaconing her to come.

"We'd love to," Paris said, hopping off her seat. Paris ignored the strange look Porsha flashed her way. As far as Paris was concerned, she was doing exactly what they had come to do.

She and Porsha followed the man into the VIP section. Once they arrived at Baker's little area, the same man made the introductions.

"Bake, this is Paris, and, as you can see her twin Porsha," the man said.

Baker's eyes never left Paris, even though he said, "Pleasure to meet you ladies. I'm glad you could join us." Up close she stole a glance at the thick keloid scar across his cheek. Paris thought it gave his face character. He had thick eyebrows and matching eyelashes that framed those dark, but dreamy, eyes.

Paris felt moisture gathered between her thighs and wished she kept her panties on. She knew her dress would be soaked before the night was over. Baker was solid with a square head and matching square shoulders. His lips were pink-perfect for sucking the lips between her legs and or kissing, she determined.

He wore one-carat diamond studs in each ear, and a platinum Rolex chain with a matching watch. He dripped power;

the kind Paris hadn't been around in quite a while. She gave Porsha a knowing look and turned her full attention to Baker.

"Come closer, I don't bite," he said.

"Well in that case, I'll just wait until you will, I like it a little rough at times," Paris flirted.

Baker looked at Paris for a second then he laughed.

When she tried to sit next to him on the sofa, he patted his lap. "Don't act shy now," he said. "I've seen what you got to offer."

"And I take it you're interested," Paris teased.

"What's your name again?" he asked.

"I'm Paris," she cooed. "And I should warn you, most men wouldn't get a second play after forgetting my name."

"Here, whisper in my ear. I love when women whisper in my ear. Especially fine, sexy ones like you." He eased a hand around her small waist. "And by the way, I'm not most men. But you'll learn that soon," he said.

"Ah, Paris, can I talk to you for a moment?"

"Yeah, what's up?" Paris asked Porsha.

Porsha looked at Baker, then at her sister. She frowned. "I meant in private for a quick sec."

Paris giggled, then drained her glass. "Oh, girl, I'm sorry. What was I thinkin'?" She turned to whisper in Baker's ear.

Porsha sighed.

"Boo, I'll be right back. Keep my seat warm," she warned.

Baker smirked.

As they walked out of the VIP section and back through the thick crowd, Paris was all giggly and feeling good. She snapped her fingers and bobbed to the music. She could sense a little animosity from Porsha, but wasn't sure what it was all about.

The moment they arrived in the bathroom, Porsha started fuming. She looked at the attendant who tried not to glance directly their way.

"What the fuck are you doin'?" Porsha lit into Paris.

"What are you talkin' about?" Paris started fingering her hair. She dug into her purse for lipstick and started to remove the top from the tube.

Porsha snatched it from her, "Don't fuck with me, Paris. This is business. You sittin' up here gettin'' all cozy with this nigga, we don't need any distractions here, you understand?"

Paris blinked back tears. The truth was she had forgotten all about the freedom she used to feel in clubs: the crowds, the music, the floating sensation from the liquor. She'd long resisted her attraction to thugs like Baker, but this little rendezvous had awakened something in her. But after listening to her sister rant, she realized Porsha was right, this was business. And when they returned to the VIP section, she'd behave in a way that said as much.

She hoped.

CHAPTER 8

Porsha stood by as Baker tried to get Paris' number. It was closing time and everyone was clearing out.

"I tell you what, why don't you give me the number to your celly. I'll call, we'll talk and go from there."

Baker looked at her all stone faced. He hesitated for a second then a smirk appeared on his face.

"So lemme get this straight. You ain't handin' over your digits, but you'll take mine, and you'll call *me*," he pointed at his chest. "I shouldn't call *you*, right?"

Paris stood her ground. "That's how it's gotta go, boo," she said.

"Well, ah, boo . . . most women would write their number on their wet panties for me. You turned me down for the after party, and now you holdin' out on the digits?" He chuckled.

Porsha was about to be sick. If he wasn't surrounded by his posse, she'd blast his ass right then and there. She rolled her eyes, shifted her weight to one side and continued to watch the drama before her.

"Boo," Paris began. "I'm not most women," she said. "So what's it gonna be? My sister is gettin' tired of waiting."

"You better be glad you fine," Baker shook his head. "You just better be glad you a fine-ass muthafucka."

Paris shrugged easily.

"You got a pen?"

"Nah, boo."

One of Baker's boys produced a pen and a piece of paper. He grabbed Paris by the arm and pulled her close. Again.

Porsha sighed. *I can't wait to put a bullet into this muthafucka.*

When Baker scribbled his number on Paris' breast, she looked like she was about to cum. Porsha shook her head in disgust and hissed, "Are you ready yet?"

Baker put the cap back on the pen and looked at Paris.

"Don't make me wait too long," he warned. As they walked away, Paris stood, using her finger to trace over the number he had written across her left breast.

In the car and on their way home, Porsha wasn't sure if she should say something else to her sister about the way she dealt with Baker. She decided it was best to leave it alone.

When they pulled up in front of Paris' house, Porsha turned off the car and sat for a moment.

"We still cool, right?"

"Yeah, why you trippin'?" Paris said. "We're right on track. It may not have been the way you wanted, but you wanted me to hook the nigga—I hooked him. Now let's work on doin' what we gotta do." Before she opened the car door, she looked at Porsha.

"We don't have any problems, right?"

"Nah, we straight," Porsha confirmed.

"Okay then, I'm about to lay down. We'll hook back up tomorrow. Drive safely," Paris said before leaving and walking into the house.

After dropping Paris off, Porsha decided she wasn't quite ready to call it a night. She figured a good drive would help clear her mind. She wanted their plans to go off the way it was supposed to, so she had to admit a few things to herself.

First off, deep down inside, she was a bit envious of her own sister. She knew it wasn't anything that would really surface to cause friction, but she did have to admit it existed. Actually, it had always been there really. It was why she gravitated more to Alex than Paris. The truth was, even though they were the exact image of one another, Paris had always carried herself in a way that implied she was better. Paris was overly concerned with what others thought and how she was perceived. And in the past, Porsha felt like she wasn't really good enough to measure up to Paris. And their mother didn't help with the way she was constantly putting Paris on a pedestal. But when girls wanted to beat the shit out of Paris, well, at that point, Porsha was who she turned to. A part of her wondered what Paris might think if she knew what happened on that island that night.

Before long, Porsha turned onto Century Boulevard, a few blocks away from LAX. Her intentions were to go somewhere and park, but she felt drawn to the busy street when she saw various chocolate legs rushing vehicles as they slowed.

Porsha turned the next corner and quickly jumped out of her car. The street was lit up with large billboards, neon signs and vehicles whizzing by in the center lanes. Everywhere she looked for about a two block stretch, was bustling with activity. She watched as cars slowed, then pulled to the curb. In many cases, hordes of scantly dressed women would rush over in their stilettos and platform heels.

They were clawing at each other for a prime position at the open passenger window. Once the chosen one was seated in the vehicle, the other women would sulk away from the car. Occasionally, a few cars would drive by honking their horns. That usually got a middle finger salute from the women.

After watching this scenario a few times, Porsha walked over to a pack of four rejected women. She heard them suck their teeth, as they eyed her up and down and tossed her cold stares.

"Just what we need; more competition on a slow-ass night," a woman wearing a thong and a wife-beater mumbled as she lit a cigarette.

Porsha tried to appear friendly. She started smiling, hoping they'd realize she wasn't there to work.

"Hey. What's up, ladies?" Se smiled.

No one responded.

"Um, I was wondering if any of y'all know—knew this girl named Alex."

Nobody paid any attention to her, regardless of how sweetly she asked. Finally, she dug into her purse and pulled out her .22. She fired a shot into the air and everyone froze where they stood.

"Okay, I see you, bitches, wanna do this the hard way. I tried to be nice, but I guess you only understand one language." As she slowly waved the gun between the four women, they ducked or dodged with their hands raised in surrender.

"I asked if anyone knew Alex. And I don't have all fuckin' night to be out here with y'all," she snapped.

"Alex . . . Ah, is she about yea tall?" one asked, using her hand to signal a height above her head.

"Wait. It's that young chick; kinda thick. You remember her. Used to wear that little black leather skirt riding up her ass," someone else tossed in.

"That's her, she was cool, but stuck to herself mostly. Wait, she used to hang with that bitch," another woman snapped her finger, "You know the one who always smelled like fish, with the gap, drove the tricks wild," she stomped and tossed her hands to her hips. "Now I know y'all, bitches, remember her. She's skinny, but got a big ol' butt; always got it hangin' out too . . . matter of fact, I think I saw her down the street about an hour ago."

"And you say she used to hang with Alex?" Porsha asked.

"Well, I don't know how much they hung, but they worked that corner together," she confirmed, pointing across the street.

Porsha looked in the direction she pointed. "Y'all hear what happened to her?"

"Oh shit, wait. Was she the girl they found near those row houses on Figuaroa? Yeah, I remember hearin' about that. She was beat to death, right?" Wife-beater said. "I remember her. And yeah, she used to work right over there with Jewels."

Satisfied with the information, Porsha lowered her gun. "I wasn't try'n ta hurt nobody, but shit, I wasn't gettin' nowhere," she said tucking the gun back into her purse. "Now you saw Jewels out here tonight?" she asked the woman who reported seeing her earlier.

The woman nodded. "She's wearing a sheer stocking body-suit with tassels taped to her nipples and some thigh-high boots."

"Damn, how she workin' that?" Wife-beater asked.

"Girl, the nasty ho got a big ol' hole in the crotch. I saw it when she tried to kick her leg up on trick's car window. You know I had to let her have that one, 'cause the smell alone was enough to make my eyes water. I was like, damn, if he still want her after getting a whiff of that, he deserve whatever he picks up from her stank ass."

CHAPTER 9

Nearly an hour later, Porsha got lucky. Jewels rounded the corner and nearly bumped right into her.

"Oh, excuse me," she said.

"Watch where the fuck you goin' next time," Jewels snapped, popping her gum.

"You Jewels?" Porsha asked.

Jewels' eyes lit up.

"You been lookin' for me?" Jewels asked sweetly. "Whatchu want, a little lickey-lickey?" Jewels stuck her tongue out. "I'ma let you know now, I charge extra for girls. I ain't taking less than fifty!" she said.

"I don't roll like that," Porsha corrected.

"Hmm, that's what you say now. You lucky you not my type. . . . Shit, I'd turn you out. I got mad skillz," Jewels rolled her eyes and flipped her weave over her shoulder.

"I'll bet."

Porsha noticed no matter what they discussed, Jewels kept an eye on every passing vehicle. At times she'd blow kisses or rub her titties at drivers.

"Look, I need some information. That's all I want from you," Porsha clarified.

"Well, you can get just about anything you want for the right price," Jewels said.

"So you try'n ta say you're chargin' me?"

"Aeey, you think I wanna spend time out here talkin' to you? I'm missing out on serious duckets right now." Jewels eyed another vehicle. Porsha wasn't sure if she'd run to it or just stare at the driver longingly.

"I'll give you ten now, I tell you what I wanna know. And after you tell me what I wanna know, I'll give you the other ten."

"You must think I'ma a cheap ho . . . if you wasn't here I'da already cleared at least a C-note," Jewels said.

"Bitch, please, I smell you from here. Ain't no nigga that damn desperate!"

Jewels sniffed as if she was trying to smell herself. She frowned then looked at Porsha. "Are you serious? You can smell me?" she whispered.

"Yeah, but that's none of my business. I'm try'n ta find the nigga who killed my sister. Her name is Alex. You remember her, don't you?"

Porsha noticed the far away look that appeared on Jewels' face.

"I know you knew her," Porsha pressed.

A few cars slowed and drivers yelled, but Jewels ignored them. That's when Porsha knew for sure something was wrong.

"You know who killed her, don't you?"

Suddenly, Jewels walked off. "Look, I need to get back to work, if you ain't buyin' nothin', you need to get to steppin'. I don't want these tricks to think we're a package deal."

Porsha jogged to catch up with her. "Wait, Jewels, I really need your help. I mean, I know you know what happened to Alex. The other girls told me you two used to hang out, I know all of 'em ain't lying. So why don't you just tell me what you know."

Jewels stopped, but only because Porsha was blocking her path.

"I don't know shit!" she spat. She spun away from Porsha and took off in the opposite direction. This time she walked to the edge of the curb, turned around and tried to flag down a car. After a couple whizzed by without stopping, she sucked her teeth and looked at Porsha.

"You gon' stand out here all night? I ain't gon' make no money if you do!" Jewels pleaded.

"Tell me what I wanna know and I'm out. Shit, I even offered you some cash."

"You think your little twenty-dollar bill is some cash? Shit, I could make five times that amount in less than thirty minutes."

Porsha frowned and looked at her. "Get real, Jewels. The way you look might turn a few heads, but girl, I don't see how you get anybody to pay for what you got with that odor you blasting. I can smell you before I see you!"

Again Jewels frowned. "I can't believe this shit! Maybe that's why it's been so slow tonight. Shit!" She stomped her foot and sighed.

"Okay, what do you wanna know? But my price has gone up, it's gonna cost fifty dollars now," Jewels said uneasily.

She looked shocked when Porsha nodded.

"I mean sixty," Jewels snapped.

"Bitch, please, you oughta be glad I'ma give you fifty."

"C'mon," Jewels took Porsha by the arm. "Let's talk around the corner. These some nosey hoes out here."

They found a dark stairwell and sat on the bottom steps. Jewels pulled a crumpled cigarette out of her pocket and offered it to Porsha, who declined.

"Okay," she looked around in the dark, "You didn't hear this from me, 'cause from what I hear this nigga ain't no joke." Jewels sucked on the cigarette. She glanced around at nothing again. "You got two twenties and a ten?"

"Jewels, I ain't got all night," Porsha threatened.

"Okay, okay . . . well, It was a rainy night, real fuckin' nasty and cold. You don't make shit when it's like that out here, so you can imagine me and Alex was really fienin' for a hit. You know we got high once in a while. So anyways, here we are like lookin' for a John. Shit, anything, you know. Well after like three hours of nothing, we agreed the next trick who pulled up, we'd share him," Jewels shrugged her shoulders. "So anyway, this dude pulls up in ah, um, he was driving a Monte Carlo. Alex spotted him first. She taps me on the shoulder and says, 'Let's offer this nigga a threesome.' "

"Okay, then what?"

"Well, I had seen dude before, and I don't know what it was, but there was somethin' about him that made the hairs on my arm stand up. I don't know why. Anyway, he pulls up, and we rush him. Alex is flashing her titties and I'm popping my ass. You know, just giving him a real freak show. That nigga was like, what y'all want? C'mon both of you. Alex was like a hundred a piece. At first I was like, she 'bout to fuck off our money, but dude was like hop in!"

Porsha seriously doubted anyone in their right mind would pay more than ten dollars for any of the girls she saw walking up and down Century, but she let Jewels finish.

"So anyways, this nigga took us over to some apartments on 52nd and Hoover, you know the ones behind that house, and it was like all gravy. Shit, he had all kinds of dope and liquor all up in that bitch. Me and Alex was like, this is heaven!" Jewels puffed her cigarette, then took a long drag. "So we at the apartment chillin' and he said he wanted me to sit on his face, and Alex to suck him off at the same time, then we could get high. Well, we did all that, then when it was time to get high, the nigga started hoggin' the pipe."

Jewels shrugged, took the near butt that was left of her cigarette and examined it closely as if she wondered where it had gone. "Anyways, I was like, enough of this shit. C'mon, Alex, let's bounce. But she was like, 'Nah, you go 'head. I'ma catch up with you later.' " Jewels smashed the butt into a stair then turned back to Porsha. Before I got out the door good, I heard him and Alex arguing over the pipe. Next thing you know, two days later, this other hoe tells me they found Alex's body. Said she was all beat up. I knew right away who did that shit. I told you, I just didn't have a good feeling about him."

Porsha sighed. "So who is this nigga?" she asked.

Jewels eyes widened. She looked around again, then back to Porsha. "I think you should pay me first, 'cause I don't want no shit. I don't play when it comes to my money. 'Sides, if this nigga find out it was me who told you. Shit, I'm just as good as dead. He ain't no joke. I be seeing him pass through, lookin' at me like, yeah, ho, tell somebody and I'ma kill you."

Porsha pulled the money from her bag. She acted like she was giving it to Jewels, but snatched it back when Jewels reached for it. "Tell me his name," Porsha said in a firm voice.

Jewels eyed the bills. It was as if her mouth was salivating.

"Okay, but, I swear you ain't talked to me. Y you ain't heard shit from me—that nigga is mean."

"You let me handle him. What's his fuckin' name?"

"Threat. They call him Threat. He always be comin' by here terrorizin' the hoes and shit. I didn't even wanna go, but I wasn't about to let Alex go by herself." Jewels shook her head. "I knew I shoulda stayed with her, but I had to get back out on the streets."

Porsha paid Jewels then left and headed back to her car. She finally had a name. And soon, he'd pay for what he did to Alex. Now all she had to do was wait for sun up, so she could go tell Paris what she'd found out and they could find that nigga.

Thoughts of watching Threat die a slow and painful death filled her mind, as she drove home with a sense of renewed energy, at four in the morning.

CHAPTER 10

Porsha replayed her evening with Jewels for Paris.

"You did all of this after you dropped me off?" Paris asked, astonished.

"Yeah, girl. I couldn't sleep no way. I wasn't tired. And I'm glad I went over there. I can't wait to find this nigga."

"Where we goin' now?" Paris asked.

"I wanted to swing by Century to see what it's lookin' like in daylight. If Jewels is over there, I'ma make her to take us to this nigga's apartment. If not, we'll roll and try to find him ourselves . . . it's off Figorura."

Paris wasn't sure how she felt about finally being able to confront the man who killed their baby sister. She knew for sure that she was grateful to Porsha for staying on task. She swallowed hard, then leaned back in the seat as Porsha drove.

Paris' mouth hung wide open when she watched several young black women dressed in provocative outfits strolling up and down the busy street. "I can not believe this shit." She turned to Porsha who seemed to be taking it all in stride. "And they not the least bit shamed? I mean, look at that one over there. She's really pretty; walking around here damn near naked. How come ain't no body doin' anything about this?"

Just as she said that, one of LA's finest zoomed by. The officer never even looked toward the women, Paris was astonished.

"I know he saw them!" she screamed.

When Porsha brought the car to a slow crawl, several girls rushed the window on the passenger side. Paris jumped back before Porsha could lower the window.

"Shit, they serious, huh?" she said.

Porsha lowered the window.

"Aeey, baby, what y'all looking for?" one of them asked.

Paris flinched and frowned.

"I'd do delicious things with you." Another girl flirted, stroking Paris' arm. Paris looked at Porsha with pleading eyes.

"We're looking for Jewels," Porsha said.

"Jewels? What you want with that smelly skank? I can suck you better," the girl answered.

"Nah, it ain't like that. We're doing business with her. Y'all seen her?"

Two of the girls walked away. The one talking to Porsha seemed determined to prove she could be better than Jewels.

"What's the matter, you only like skinny girls? I ain't fat, I'm just big boned, baby. When your eyes closed we all the same size," she offered.

"Look, we don't get down like that. We just need to talk to her," Paris said.

The girl looked at Porsha then back at Paris, as if she was trying to determine whether she spoke the truth.

"Oh, shit. So y'all really ain't lookin' for no date?"

"Nah, we're looking for Jewels for some information." Paris confirmed.

"Well, shit then, I don't even know that ho." She sucked her teeth. "Y'all need to move on. We try'n ta make some money out here dammit!" she snapped and sauntered away.

"Okay, well, we can find this nigga on our own," Porsha said as she pulled away from the curb and headed east toward Figorura.

"I just can't believe that!"

"Well, it was a fluke, but I was hoping Jewels would be hanging out today. Maybe she only works at night," Porsha said.

"I'm not talking about her. I'm talking about all of them," Paris pointed toward the back. "I can't believe they're allowed to just prance around like that. I mean, with all the people coming in and out of LAX, ain't the city shamed? I don't believe they would have them on the stroll right here, for all the visitors to see, that's all."

Porsha didn't respond. Paris could be so bourgeois at times. She just kept driving. After a while, she turned onto Figuora and found a place to park.

"Now, how do we find this nigga Threat?"

Paris looked up at a little mom and pop shop on the corner. "Here. Why don't you pull over there. I'll go inside and buy something and ask if they know him."

When Porsha pulled into the parking lot, Paris jumped out. She was back in less than ten minutes.

"You drive around this block and go behind the third house on the left, you'll see the complex. He's on the first floor, the unit on the far right end."

Porsha looked at Paris. "Damn, you work fast."

As they pulled away, she blew a kiss at a guy who stepped out of the store wearing sagging jeans and a wave cap.

Porsha turned the car in the direction they were told and went to find Threat.

CHAPTER 11

By the time they arrived at the apartment complex, it was close to five in the evening. There were few people on the street and even fewer hanging outside. Porsha considered this was their lucky day. Usually, she figured a place like this would be crawling with folks. Instead of pulling to the back in the parking lot, she looked at Paris and said, "I think we should park here and walk to the back. I don't want anyone to see the car near the complex."

"Good idea," Paris said.

When they got out of the car, Porsha glanced around. Satisfied no one was paying attention, she and Paris walked to the back of the house and to the apartment complex.

There were at least four broken-down cars: two sitting on cement blocks, one with the hood held up by a block of wood, and trash was everywhere. The two nearby dumpsters smelled like they hadn't been emptied in weeks.

Paris grabbed her stomach. "Jesus, does anybody smell this?"

Porsha thought it smelled like a dead body was rotting nearby, but she had smelled worse. They stepped carefully and knocked on the last door on the right.

"Damn, who you want?" a growling voice asked.

"I'm looking for Threat," Porsha answered.

The door crept open far enough for them to see two blood-shot eyes starting back at them.

"Who is you looking for banging on this door like you done lost your rabbit-fucking mind?" he yawned.

"Aeey, Daddy," Paris cooed.

He looked at Paris, then back at Porsha. "Man, what the fuck y'all want, a nigga was sleeping good," he said.

"Jewels said we should come find you, for um . . . some work," Porsha smiled.

The sleepy eyes lit up. They flashed to Paris, rolled down her body, then up it again and back at Porsha. "She told y'all that?" he asked.

Porsha could see his entire demeanor changing. He stood straighter and opened the door a bit wider.

"Y'all looking for work, huh?"

"Yeah, we need to make some fast money, and Jewels told us you're the man who can make that happen. Big Bank Hank said the same thing," Paris tossed in.

"You been talkin' to that street-level nigga? Well, they told y'all right," He opened the door completely and Porsha wished he hadn't.

It wasn't just the stench that nearly made her lose her breath, but the room was a wreck. Porsha pulled her purse close to her body and stepped carefully into the littered room.

There was trash all over the floor, old pizza boxes piled up in one corner, and beer cans stacked in the other. Paris hadn't said a word since they entered the darkened room. There was only one chair, and Threat was quick to plop down on it. The big screen TV was on mute. It was the cleanest thing in the room.

Threat was a short and stocky light-skinned man. He wore a dingy wave cap that matched the dingy wife-beater he had on. He was very buff, and didn't try to adjust his boxers when he sat down.

"So y'all wanna be down with my crew?" he asked, sizing them up again. "This ain't my normal spot, I mean, this just a crib for the girls to hang out between shifts and shit. You know, I sometimes crash here to check up on 'em and shit, but my other place is the tilt. So basically, this where y'all would chill too." He waved his arms like he was showing off the Taj Mahal. "I knew my shit was gon' take off, I'm 'bout to blow up for real," he boasted. He nodded a couple of times as if to confirm his assessment.

"Yeah, y'all gon' make a real nice addition to the stable. Plus y'all twins? Hmm, let's get down to business," he said.

Paris walked closer to Porsha. They both looked down on Threat sitting in his chair.

"You said Jewels told y'all about me?" he frowned.

"Yeah, she was tight with our sister Alex," Paris said.

Porsha looked for a sign of recognition when Threat heard Alex's name, but he didn't even flinch.

"So Jewels' ass musta got over that little misunderstanding we had a coupla weeks ago. I can't have no hoes disrespecting me . . ." He had a look that said he caught himself. "I mean, we family and shit."

"So you remember Alex?" Porsha asked getting straight to the point.

"Alex? Who that? What she look like?"

Paris described their sister and waited for Threat to break in and say he remembered her, but he didn't. Porsha felt herself getting heated. "You trying to say you don't remember her?"

"I dunno no damn Alex, but shit, you can send her over too, 'cause I'm 'bout to blow up—believe that," he said.

Porsha looked at him. She didn't say anything. Then she asked again, "Do you know Alex or not?"

"Why? That make a difference whether y'all wanna be down with me or what? I ain't met no damn Alex, but if y'all want me to say I knew her, then I knew her," he snapped.

"Aeey," Paris reached toward Porsha, "Why don't we all just calm down. Remember, we're here for a job."

"Yeah, remember that," Threat said. He gave Porsha the evil eye.

She flashed a lame smile. "Can I use the bathroom?" she asked sweetly.

"Um, the toilet is broken, but you can still use it, just don't flush," he said matter-of-factly.

"Oh, well, I gotta go. Where is it, in there?" she pointed at a nearby door.

"Nah, it's back there in the bedroom," he pointed over his shoulder. "You straight, just gon' back there. When you're done we can talk about getting y'all a change of clothes, 'cause I wanna take y'all out to meet the other girls. It's almost dark so everybody oughta be out or getting ready to hit the streets," he said.

The stinch intensified as Porsha walked back toward the bedroom. Once there, it wasn't much bigger than the living room, there was a cot in the middle of the floor, with four dingy pillows. Porsha walked over and picked up the fluffiest of the four. Slowly, she crept back into the room and walked up behind Threat. He was in mid-sentence talking to Paris about how he ran his operation. Just as he turned, Porsha held the pillow up and fired one shot to the back of his head.

CHAPTER 12

Soaked in blood, shivering and crying, Paris thought she was going to loose her mind. "What the fuck! What the fuck!" she screamed.

She looked at Threat's body which had slumped onto its side, and held her hands out. Porsha looked at her. "Okay, okay, I need you to calm down. Let's get outta here, go burn those clothes and go somewhere so we can talk."

Paris looked down at Threat's body again, when he twitched, she jumped. "Oh my God, he ain't dead."

Porsha calmly bent down, held the pillow to his head and fired another shot. "C'mon, let's get outta here before somebody calls the law," she said.

Paris wasn't sure why she was tripping. She knew she wanted Threat dead too, but she just didn't like the way Porsha caught her off guard. Paris felt like murder had come too easy for Porsha, she did it like she blinked an eye. Paris kept wondering if it would've been better had she known exactly how he was gonna die. She decided it wouldn't have made a difference. She threw her head back, closed her eyes and eased her body into the seat.

She felt Porsha staring at her, but she didn't really care. It was dark by the time they pulled up to the Wal-Mart Supercenter at the Baldwin Hills Mall.

"I'm gonna go get some stuff for us to take care of those clothes with; you just sit here and rest yourself," Porsha said.

The few moments alone did her some good. Paris calmed herself and took deep breaths. She was glad it was dark outside, so people walking by wouldn't notice the blood still on her clothes.

About twenty minutes later, Porsha walked out, like she had no care in the world. Paris thought about her carefree stroll as she watched her sister approach. She opened the trunk then slid into the driver's seat.

"You okay?" she asked Paris.

Paris nodded. "Yeah, I'm fine."

"Okay, I brought you another outfit and some flip flops."

"Cool. Why don't you find a dark corner so I can get out of these clothes," Paris said.

Paris was glad Porsha had the forethought to buy some wet wipes and alcohol. She scrubbed the splatters of blood from her skin and gladly changed clothes.

Once refreshed and calm, she stuffed her bloody clothes into the Wal-Mart bags and climbed back into the car.

"You ready?" Porsha asked.

"Yeah, I'm straight."

"Okay, let's go get rid of the clothes. I got everything we need," Porsha confirmed.

Paris offered a weak smile. Something about them killing Threat bothered her. She wasn't sure what, but something just didn't feel right about this one. She kept seeing the image of his brain being blown all over the place, but she didn't want Porsha to think she was weak.

She jumped when Porsha touched her arm. "Damn, you okay?" Porsha asked.

"Oh, yeah, I'm good. I'm good."

By the time they were ready to call it a night. Threat's murder no longer took center stage in Paris' mind. She just wanted to go home, take a long, hot shower and lay it down for the night.

"So why don't we hook up tomorrow evening. Maybe we can go out," Porsha shrugged. "I don't know, to celebrate maybe. We could visit Alex's grave and tell her we got the job done."

"I'd like that," Paris said. "But first, I wanna sleep till at least noon."

Paris was so glad the house was dark when they pulled up.

After a long shower, Paris wrapped herself in satin pajamas and took the phone to bed with her. She called Baker again, and again got his voicemail. She remembered the second that she hung up that she didn't block her number. "Oh well," she shrugged.

The next morning, she woke to the glorious aroma of bacon as it was sizzling on her mother's grill. When she made her way downstairs, there were pancakes topped with blueberries and whipped cream, and grits with butter and sugar. Once again, Paris felt her mother had tipped the scales. She fixed enough food to feed an army, and Paris knew she'd try to eat enough for a battalion, despite knowing she didn't need to.

"Almost ready?" Naomi asked over her shoulder.

Paris sat at the table. What caught her eye was a headline on the front page of the Wave newspaper. It was one of LA's oldest black newspapers. And Naomi was a faithful subscriber.

MAN FOUND SHOT TO DEATH INSIDE APARTMENT. Paris picked up the paper and quickly read the article. The paper showed an old mug-shot of Theodore 'Threat' Robinson. As her eyes ate up the words, Paris could feel herself beginning to get hot. According to the paper, Theodore had been recently released from the county jail after being held for nine months for a crime that DNA evidence, proved he didn't commit.

Her heart started racing. The paper said he had only been out for seven days. She thought she was going to be sick. Paris read the short story over and over again. If Threat had only been out a week, there was no way he could've killed Alex.

When Naomi put Paris' plate down in front of her, she got up and ran upstairs to her bedroom. Her hands were shaking as she dialed Porsha's number.

She didn't even say hello when she heard Porsha's voice. Paris said, "We need to talk. It's important. How long will it take you to get over here?"

"Um, what's this about?" Porsha asked.

"Can't talk now. I need to see you right away."

"Okay, I'll get dressed and be there in about thirty." Porsha said.

The only reason Paris and Porsha were spared Naomi's sharp tongue was because Porsha came over with her aunt in tow. They didn't spend long together; as soon as Paris walked into the living room, Porsha jumped up.

"Are you ready to go?" she asked, looking directly at Porsha. The minute they closed the front door, Paris pulled the paper out.

"Threat did not kill Alex. You know what that means, Porsha? We killed an innocent man!" Paris spat. She shoved the paper toward her sister who seemed unmoved by the revelation.

Porsha stared at the paper, but she didn't take it.

"What are you saying?"

"I'm saying whoever you talked to, lied. Threat was in jail when Alex was killed, there was no fucking way he could've done it!"

"Okay, okay. I think you should lower your voice. Let's get in the car. I don't want *your* mama to come out here and ask what we're arguing about."

Paris knew something felt wrong about Threat, but she had no idea. She didn't even consider the possibility that he may have been the wrong man. The truth was, a part of her was glad Threat was identified as the killer, because she didn't know how she would allow Porsha to kill Baker.

Despite the fact that she hadn't spent any real time with him, something about him turned her the fuck on. Labeling Threat the killer meant she might've had a chance with Baker. Now the reality had settled in. Was she developing feelings for the man who killed her baby sister?

CHAPTER 13

Porsha's head was spinning and throbbing at the same damn time. She wanted to find Jewels and ring her fuckin' neck with her bare hands. She couldn't believe that dirty ho lied.

She didn't even have the heart to say anything to Paris. But they both agreed they needed to go somewhere and chill for a few hours. Porsha knew they wouldn't find Jewels until it was dark.

Porsha was hitting corners so fast, she noticed Paris clutching the door handle and forced herself to slow down.

When they arrived on Century Boulevard, Porsha spotted Jewels stumbling up to a car. She didn't have to worry about whether the John would choose Jewels, because there were at least four other females jockin' for position at the passenger window.

By the time they parked and walked around to where the girls worked, Jewels and another female were the only two left. When Jewels saw Porsha she broke into a bright smile.

"Aeey, there are two of you now . . . or am I seeing double, either way, whassup? You two ready for some girl on girl action yet?"

The other girl looked at Paris. "I'll take you, if that's whassup," she said.

Paris shot her the evil eye.

"We need to talk to you in private," Paris said to Jewels.

They didn't have to wait long when a car pulled up and slowed. Jewels' friend bolted toward it.

Porsha took Jewels by the arm and walked her around the corner.

"Why you gotta be so rough?" Jewels whined.

Once they were in the dark stairwell, Porsha jumped on her.

"You fuckin', bitch. Why you tell me Threat killed my sister when you knew damn well he didn't."

Jewels sat there shaking. "I dunno . . . what you're talking about," she cried.

"Oh, you know exactly what the fuck I'm talking about. That nigga Threat was in jail when my sister died. You fucking lied. Now I want to know why?"

Jewels blinked quickly and swallowed hard. She was shaking. "You fuckin' up my high with all this shit," she mumbled.

Porsha slapped her once, then immediately followed up with a backhand. "Bitch, you ain't seen nothing yet. Now you better tell me why the fuck you lied or I swear-'fo'-God, I'll kill your stankin' ass right here!" When Porsha put the barrel of her gun to Jewels' cheek, she started crying.

"Www-what's the big deal? I mean, what difference do it make anyway?"

Smack!

"What difference do it make? Bitch, I killed a man 'cause you lied!" Porsha spat.

Jewels eyes widened. She tried to look to Paris, but she just stood there watching.

"I didn't know y'all was gonna kill him. I thought you'd tell the law," Jewels sobbed.

"Why'd you do it?"

"He—when he got out, he came back—he came and just started try'n ta run things. He'd take our money, he even beat me a few times. I was just desperate. I just wanted him gone that's all," she offered.

"So you lied just like that?" Paris spoke for the first time.

"I'm so sorry," Jewels cried. Snot and tears melted on her cheeks.

"I oughta put a bullet in your brain," Porsha said through gritted teeth.

Paris tugged on Porsha's arm.

"Please don't shoot me. I ain't gon' tell nobody. I ain't saying shit. You did us a favor. I swear I won't tell anybody."

"Let's just go," Paris pressed.

"You think we should just let her go?" Porsha asked, shocked.

"Yeah. Let's just get outta here," Paris said. "Think about it, who's she gonna tell?"

"Ah, five-0, maybe?" Porsha snapped.

"Shit, I ain't talking to no law!" she cried.

Porsha let Jewels go. Once released, she quickly crawled down into the bottom of the stairwell, pulled her legs under her body and wrapped her arms around them. When Porsha and Paris walked away, they could still her crying.

When they arrived at the car, Porsha unlocked the doors and climbed in. She turned the key then smacked her steering wheel. "Damn, I got one more thing I wanna ask her. I'll be right back," she said.

Paris looked at her, "You wanna drive around there?"

"Nah," she reached over and turned the radio up. "I'll be right back. Just relax."

Jewels jumped at the sight of the barrel. She put her hands up, but it did little to block the bullet that caught her between the eyes.

CHAPTER 14

The moment Paris woke after a restless night, she looked up at the ceiling and decided she needed a break. She needed a break from the killings, the guilt, and mostly her sister. When she walked down to join her mother for breakfast, she had made up her mind. She was going to take a day to herself—plain and simple. The guilt she felt wasn't as much about the killings as it was about the tug of war going on in her heart.

She was very interested in Baker, wanted to get to know more about him and get closer, but not to kill him. It was a huge disappointment when she discovered Threat wasn't the villain they thought. She was saddened when Porsha verbalized the sad truth. They had made a pact . . . they agreed, they'd find the bastard responsible for Alex's death and see that he pay with his life.

Paris had called him the moment she got home last night. She even called before she came for breakfast. She knew this was so juvenile, but his ignoring her made her even more eager for the hunt.

The phone rang. She looked at the caller ID. When she saw her aunts' name, she knew it was Porsha, so she ignored it.

It stopped, then started again. This time the name on the caller ID was different.

Before she even heard his voice, her face broke into a wide grin. "Ah, hello?"

"Ah, hello yourself, sexy," Baker said. "What's up, Ma?"

"It's all you," Paris responded.

"Did I call at a bad time?" Baker asked.

"Nah," she cooed. "So what's up with you, Daddy?"

"You, Ma, I'm all about you. What's up with you? That's what I'm try'n ta find out."

"You ain't been tryin' too hard. I've been calling since we met and nothing, you don't even answer the phone."

"Well, you been calling from a blocked number. I don't know who you are if I can't recognize the number. Why you blocking your calls anyway? What you got to hide?"

"Nothing, it's just, I don't know you," she answered.

"Well, I'm tryin' ta change that. Say, why don't we hook up tonight at the club, then see where the night takes us, how that sound?"

"That sounds like it might be a plan."

"So you want me to pick you up or send a car? Whassup? How you wanna roll tonight?"

"I'll just meet you there. How about we roll like that?"

"You kinda sassy, Ma," Baker said. "But I like that. I'll meet you at the club tonight, boo."

"Cool."

Later that evening, she walked down the stairs dressed and all made up.

The blue wrap dress she wore was elegant but sassy. It hugged her curves and covered her breasts just enough to show a healthy amount of cleavage.

As she slid behind the wheel, Paris told herself she was just going out with him, so that she could get a better handle on whether he had anything to do with Alex's death. She denied all the way to the club that she really did have feelings for him, and wanted nothing more than to be his girl.

She knew she couldn't betray Porsha, and falling in love with the man they were planning to kill would defiantly be traitorous.

"This is business," she said as she pulled up in the club's parking lot.

CHAPTER 15

When Paris arrived at the Normandy Casino and pulled up to valet, she couldn't help but wonder if she was making a mistake by coming alone. Yeah, she needed a break from Porsha and the craziness that had become their lives, but she knew the plan included killing Baker, and getting close to him may hinder that.

All of her fears about being alone were reinforced the moment she looked into the VIP lounge. Baker was surrounded by two women who made it clear he could have anything he wanted.

One was on his lap, like she had been only a few nights before. She was vexed. Since she couldn't get into the lounge without being invited, she stood and gazed at the threesome waiting to happen and frowned. Paris sucked her teeth and turned to leave. Instead of calling it a night, she decided to go to the bar and have a few drinks.

She said, "Um . . . let's see, I'd like a Clit Stimulator."

"Shit, I'd like to stimulate it for you," a deep voice said from behind.

Parish blushed and turned to see Tyson Beckford, the supermodel turned actor standing behind her. "I'm Reggie," he said.

The bartender looked at her. "Daaayyum, I've only had one person ask for that since I've been working here."

He grabbed a glass. "That's with Lemon Gin, Vodka, Tequila and cream, right?"

"With a cherry on top," Paris smiled. Reggie closed in on her.

"You want sugar on the rim?"

"Is there any other way to have it?"

When the bartender returned, Reggie said, "I'm paying for her Clit Stimulator and my drink," he smiled.

"Thank you," Paris blushed.

"Don't worry about it, dawg, I got her," another voice said. Paris turned to her right to see Baker peeling a twenty off his thick wad of cash.

Tyson's twin looked confused. He looked at Paris then at Baker, as if he was hoping she'd confirm it wasn't so.

"Oh, my bad. Y'all together or something?"

"Yeah, nigga, whassup? What? You harda hearing or something?"

Paris was torn between confusion and embarrassment. The way Baker spoke up on her behalf was an instant turn on. But she was embarrassed by the way he was handling her in front of Reggie. Still, the shit made her hot; she couldn't deny, she really liked the way he carried it. She decided then that she'd have to fuck him, at least once.

The Tyson look alike grabbed his drink, tossed Paris one last look and walked away. She didn't miss the swagger in his stroll.

Baker stood in front of Paris.

"Whassup, Ma? I told you to meet me in VIP," he said sternly. "Then I come out here to find you getting your flirt on, you try'n ta get these niggas laid out up in here or what?"

Paris studied him closely, but she didn't respond.

"I don't like fools messing with what's mine," he said.

She lifted an eyebrow at that last comment, but still didn't speak. Paris looked him up and down, then sipped from her drink.

"C'mon let's go," he commanded, taking her by the hand.

She loved everything about him; the way he just spoke up for his. Even though she was mad by his behavior earlier in VIP, she couldn't stay angry.

Strolling through the crowd at the club, she knew for sure what she felt for him would have to be reckoned with. At that moment, she didn't want him dead no more than she wanted to leave his side.

CHAPTER 16

Porsha spent the rest of her evening hold up in her room at her aunt's. She told her aunt she wasn't feeling well, and she wasn't. It had nothing to do with the fact that she'd just killed someone; she'd killed before and she knew she'd kill again. She felt no remorse for those losers.

She justified her actions by saying she was doing her part to rid society of pimps and drug dealers, who were only ruining lives. She always hated men like that, and although she felt avenging her sister's death gave her a legitimate reason for killing, a part of her knew this was a path she was destined to take.

Showered, relaxed and resting, she eased back on her pillow and thought about the first time she killed somebody. It wasn't supposed to go down like that, not at all, but once it happened, there was really no looking back.

Porsha closed her eyes and was immediately transported to nearly two years ago. She and Alex were relaxing on the Catalina Flyer, the Yacht that made the daily runs to Catalina Island. They were in one of the cocktail lounges having drinks.

Alex had been using her fake ID to get into clubs and buy drinks for months. She and Porsha had grown even closer once Paris left for college. It was Alex who had heard about the event being held at the Best Western on the island. It was toted as a real player's ball. Alex and Porsha had both been excited.

"Who told you about this?" Porsha asked as she looked at the other women in the lounge. Everyone was dressed to the nines and appeared just as eager for the hour long trip to wrap up.

"Girl, I just came up, that's all. I was at the shop and this dude hands me a flyer. I was like yes, this is gonna be crunk, you know I had to make it happen." Alex said.

When they arrived at the hotel it wasn't hard to tell there was an event going on there. Porsha had doubted the place had ever seen that many black and brown people. It was about seven in the evening. Alex and Porsha weren't planning on spending the night, they were going to take the last boat back, but wanted to make sure they had enough time to get their eat and drink on.

"Man, look at this place. This is really tight," Alex squealed.

Porsha agreed, looking around the lobby. Despite being filled with people, it was a nice atmosphere. She and Alex weren't sure what to do since most of the people were checking into rooms.

The hotel was right at the foothills overlooking the Avalon Bay. The hotels' grounds were like a massive garden. They learned the party was being held in a ballroom that had a patio. Porsha was struggling to suppress her own excitement.

As the night wore on and the party started, she was a bit disappointed at the way she and Alex hadn't really mingled with the others. They kind of stood off to the side, nursing a drink and holding up the wall. The party was nice with a 70's dance contest to boot. Then when it was time for the pimp and baller of the year, things started looking up a bit.

Someone had come to pull Alex away to dance. Porsha stood alone for almost an hour, feeling invisible, but still she was having a good time. She walked over to the bar and bumped into a guy she knew from the neighborhood. He wasn't a bad looking man, but he had acne scars all over his face that made his stock plummet. He was average height and had a light brown complexion. His hair was short and curly and his grill was messed up. Tonight though, he was dress to the tee, just like the rest of them. He was wearing a Khaki suit, heavily starched with a pearl colored fedora and matching walking cane. He had a huge diamond ring on his pinky with a small sapphire A on his lapel.

"Nelson?" she called.

He turned, looked at the bartender, then back at Porsha. "Aeey, what are *you* doing here?"

It was the way he said *you*, like she didn't belong that made her fume. All night long, Porsha had watched as these men and their women pranced around in designer clothes, and big truck jewelry laced with ice. She wondered how they were able to live as well as it appeared. She knew she didn't fit in. And the fact that no one had approached her all night, only made matters worse.

"What are *you* doing here?" she asked, serving up much attitude.

"Oh, nah, I didn't mean it like that. I just meant that usually these things are hard to get into unless you know somebody, that's all I'm saying."

Porsha nodded. To her surprise she and Nelson were sort of hitting it off. The music was pumping loudly and it was difficult to hear, but he seemed cool.

After a few drinks, Alex still hadn't returned, so she was kept talking to Nelson. Suddenly, he looked at her. "Hey, why don't we bounce up outta here?"

She shrugged. "Well, I'm here with my sister," Porsha held up Alex's purse. "I don't wanna just leave her hanging," she said.

A part of her was excited about getting some attention after the way the evening had played out. She looked and didn't see Alex.

"Okay, suit yourself." Nelson shrugged. "But I thought we could step out for a few. We'd come right back," he assured her.

"What the hell, whassup?"

"Well, I got a blunt. Thought you'd wanna hit it. We could go out to that garden," he pointed toward one of the large picture windows.

It was dark out there, with greenery everywhere. Nelson managed to find an even darker corner where the music was still thumping just as loud, but a bit muffled. He cleared out an area behind some bushes and sat down.

Porsha wasn't sure if that was such a good idea, but thought, *what's the worse that could happen?* She sat next to him and he passed the blunt. Once they finished it, Nelson attacked her.

She could barely keep up with his tongue and his hands. Both were all over her body. At one point something kept jabbing her in the belly as he forced himself on top of her. Porsha pushed him off, "Ouch," She rubbed her belly.

"Oh, my bad," he said. Nelson reached under his shirt and removed a small handgun. He placed it next to Porsha and began attacking her with the same vigor as before.

After a little while, she tried to push him off again; this time he wouldn't stop.

"Aeey, raise up," Porsha managed.

Nelson eased up a bit, but he was pissed. He raised his head, but not much else and said to her, "You can't just tease a man and expect me to turn it off like a switch. If I wanted this type of shit, I'da stayed with my girl. Now, you know what you came out here for," he said before shoving his tongue down her throat.

"Wait," Porsha screamed after pushing him off again. "I didn't come out here for nothing but the blunt."

"Oh, so you expect to smoke up my shit and not give me none?" He shoved her back down. He ripped off her panties.

"I'ma show you why you don't play with a nigga like me," he said. When he eased up on his knees to unbuckle his pants, Porsha grabbed the gun and fired once to his chest.

He fell back clutching his chest. She scrambled to her feet, and looked around trying to see if anyone heard the shot. When no one came, she pulled his body completely behind the bushes and was about to toss the gun away. But she thought better of it. She stuffed it into Alex's purse, brushed herself off and scrambled away from the area.

As she turned the corner, she ran right into Alex.

"Hey!" I was just looking for you.

Porsha couldn't control her heartbeat. She glanced around again to make sure no one would stop her to ask questions.

"What's wrong?" Alex asked. "Oh, are you okay?"

Porsha didn't want to break down; she just needed to get as far away from there as possible.

"We need to go," she warned.

"Why, did something happen?" Alex pressed.

"We need to get the fuck out of here. C'mon, I'll tell you at the docks."

They rushed out of the hotel, into a cab and back to the docks. When they were seated comfortably on the boat, Porsha took a deep breath and spilled her story to her sister.

She wasn't sure what Alex's reaction was going to be when she was done, but the open arms she fell into assured her that Alex was not passing judgment. Alex held her body close and rubbed her back.

"I can't believe that bastard tried to do that to you. He deserved that and more. We should go back and burn his fucking body," she hissed.

Porsha closed her eyes and released a huge sigh of relief. When their embrace broke, Alex was still shaken by the entire incident.

"You're talking about Nelson from around the block, right? Got all that acne on his face, got a brother; I forget what they call him. Real, real skinny?"

"Yeah, that's why I didn't mind going out there with him. How many times have we seen him and his brother and that other guy they hang with?"

Alex shook her head. "Don't even worry about it. We'll take this to our grave. He got what he deserved," she assured Porsha.

It was moments like that that sealed the bond between Porsha and Alex. She was mature far beyond her age, and Porsha was glad they got along a lot better than she and Paris. Instead of going home that night, they hung out and partied at a few spots in downtown LA.

They picked up a couple of guys and hooked up with them. It wasn't until late Sunday morning when they both returned home. Porsha would later learn that Alex and their mother had fought over the weekend of partying. Next thing she knew, Alex left. Porsha was so guilt-ridden over the murder, she found it hard to sleep at night. She was also paranoid about the law coming after her. That one day while she was at a shopping center, she walked right into a Army recruiting office and walked out a soldier. A week later, she was gone to basic training.

She flashed back to the present and wondered why she hadn't heard from Paris all day and all night. Convinced she was far too tired to worry about that, Porsha made herself comfortable in bed and was sleeping good by the time her head hit the pillow again.

CHAPTER 17

Paris woke with a huge grin on her face. She was spending the day with Baker and she couldn't wait. Their night could've easily extended into breakfast, lunch and dinner. But Paris knew it wasn't time to give it up just yet.

She smelled bacon before she could make it to the shower. Paris rushed into the bathroom and quickly changed. She didn't want to change her mind about eating because she wanted to have a healthy appetite for her breakfast date with Baker.

They were going to M & Ms for breakfast then wherever she wanted. That's what Baker told her.

When she called to tell him she was on her way, he simply said, "I'll be waiting for you."

By the time Paris arrived at the restaurant, Baker's Hummer was surrounded by a few men and women. She wondered what was going on, but she wasn't about to melt in with the crowd. She sat back and watched as women smiled all in his face. Paris could read their body language and tell they were flirting with her man. After having seen enough, Paris got out of the car and casually strolled over to the passenger's side of his truck.

He immediately unlocked the door and she climbed on in.

"Who does she think she is?" she heard a woman say.

"That's my woman," Baker defended. Amid the teeth sucking and comments mumbled under breaths, Paris was smiling inward.

Baker rolled up the windows and leaned back in the driver's seat. "So whassup, boo?"

"I'm just not hungry," she admitted.

"Well, that's cool, no worries. Why don't we run up to the Beverly Center real quick. I gotta go pick up a couple of things."

Paris nodded, "I've never turned down a trip to a mall, and I don't plan to start now," she said.

To Paris' amazement, once they hit the mall, they only went into women's stores, where Baker sat back patiently as she tried on various outfits, and he paid for everything he liked. This was repeated again in numerous shoe stores. And if that wasn't enough, he took her to a place he called his favorite jewelry store and bought her a pair of diamond stud earrings, a matching tennis bracelet and anklet. In there alone he spent close to fifty-five hundred dollars.

Paris could hardly believe her day. By mid-afternoon, she had nearly worked up an entirely new appetite. They went by Hotdog on a Stick and she ordered two corndogs with two large cherry lemonades.

Baker confessed he loved their lemonade and they strolled through the mall with arms full of shopping bags. Paris felt like a princess. It reminded her of her days back in high school. She used to look on at the drug dealers' girlfriends with envy. She wondered how they were able to get their hair and nails done, new clothes, cars and jewelry all from men just like Baker.

Once again, she felt herself getting all caught up in his lifestyle and she was nearly defenseless to do anything about it. Coming out of Victoria's Secrets while he was in Footlocker, she nearly bumped into a woman.

"Oooh, excuse me," Paris said.

The girl looked her up and down. "You wit' Baker?"

Paris' eyebrows shot up. "Yeah, why?"

At first the woman didn't say anything. She didn't even move. She looked a few years older than Paris. She was dark-skinned with light brown eyes. Her hair was in micro individual braids and hung down her back in a ponytail. She was wearing a pair of Baby Phat denim shorts and a matching denim tank top. She had big thighs and a small waist.

"So I guess you're supposed to be his new woman, huh?" She looked Paris up and down.

"Excuse me?" Paris didn't try and control her building attitude.

"I'm Destiny," she huffed.

"Okay, I'm Paris."

"You don't know who I am, huh?"

Paris shrugged. "Should I?"

At that moment Baker ran up to them. "Say Destiny, don't start no shit in here today," he snapped. Baker stood between Paris and Destiny.

"You ain't nothing but a fuckin' dog, Baker, that's all you are—a fuckin' dog!" she screamed.

"Okay, you've said that before. You need to move on," he warned.

"Or what?" The woman screamed. "What you gonna do to me that you ain't already done, Baker?"

He started trying to move Paris toward the car.

"You know what Paris, you a fool. I know it's all good now, he probably showerin' you with gifts and shit, takin' you out clubbin', eatin' at nice restaurants and shit, but you ain't seen his mean side yet."

"You better go on with that shit, Dee."

"Don't Dee me," she shoved him.

Baker and Paris stopped walking. He turned to her.

"Whatchu gon' do? Beat my ass again? C'mon, Baker, show your new girl how you really get down," she yelled.

"Bitch, you just mad 'cause I caught yo' ass in my shit. I told you, I ain't try'n ta kick it with no damn crackhead," Baker said.

"I ain't no fuckin' crackhead," she sobbed.

"No, not yet, but still, where you think you headed? Yeah, I don't even roll like that." Before he turned, his arm flew up and he intercepted her hand just as she was about to slap him.

"Get the fuck on, before you regret this little scene you creatin' in here." He took her arm, twisted it until she dropped to the ground. She yelped out in pain.

"Sssstop, Baker!" He finally released her. "I give you three months, and I'll bet you'll be smoked out, just like your nasty-ass mama." Baker stepped over her and took Paris by the arm. "C'mon, let's bounce," he said.

Before they got to the parking lot, Paris turned to see Destiny brushing herself off. She looked at Paris.

"One day he's gonna do you the same fuckin' way, believe that. You better leave him now before it's too late," she screamed.

CHAPTER 18

Porsha 's thoughts shifted to Paris. She wondered what her sister was up to and why she was flaking out on their plans.

As she turned down her old street, she wondered what excuse she would get this time. That's why she figured she'd get up and out early, so she could head Paris off before she even thought about going MIA again.

Porsha watched her sister bounce down the stairs. She was wearing a pair of hip hugging low-rider jeans and a sequenced tank top. Porsha didn't miss the look of sheer shock across her sister's face at the sight of her standing there. It appeared as if Paris nearly fell down the steps when she saw Porsha there.

"Oh, hey," Paris said.

"I was just about to knock. " Porsha shrugged. "Where you headed?

"Um." Porsha could tell Paris wasn't sure what to say.

"I was about to pass by your place and see what's up for later," Paris said.

"Well, I guess I saved you a trip then, huh? You hungry? I was thinking we could go to Roscoe's. I'll drive."

In the car Porsha turned the radio down and glanced at her sister. "I think we need to talk."

Paris nodded. "Okay, whassup?"

"Well, I haven't seen or heard from you in what, two days now?" Porsha waited for Paris to say something, but she didn't.

"When I call or come by, I just missed you. I mean, what's going on, Paris?"

"What do you mean, what's going on? I'm with you now, right?"

"Yeah, but that's only because I came looking for you early today. A few minutes later, and you would've been gone again. I thought we were working on a plan here," Porsha said.

"We are," Paris stressed.

"Well, shit, I can't tell. I mean, I don't know what you've been doing for the past two days, not to mention who you've been doing it with."

"I didn't know I had to check in with you daily!" Paris snapped.

"That's not what I'm saying."

"Hmm, sure sounds a lot like it. I mean, so we didn't hook up for a couple of days. Did it ever cross your mind that I might be out working things my way? I mean, let's face it, we—you and me—we do things differently. We said we wanted to find out who killed Alex, but I ain't into killing first then asking questions later. I mean, we've already killed the wrong person once, I just wanna make sure that Baker is the one. That's all I'm try'n ta say."

Porsha nodded her head. She listened as Paris raged on. And she knew Paris had a good point, but something told her that Paris was doing more than just making sure Baker really was responsible for Alex's death.

"So what have you found out about Baker?"

"Huh?" Paris responded.

"I said, what have you found out about Baker so far. I mean, you say we do things differently, so what have you found out during the last two days you guys have been kicking it?"

"Well, I haven't found out too much yet, but the point is he's trusting me," Paris said.

They pulled up into the parking lot of Roscoe's Chicken and Waffles on Manchester. Before they got out of the car, Porsha looked at Paris. "I just need to know that you are still committed to this."

"I am, but I just need to know that the next person we knock off actually had something to do with Alex's death. It's not our mission to rid the world of pimps, wanna-be hustlers and drug dealers. I just want to see the bastards responsible for killing our sister pay. That's all."

"Well, I don't want to get to a point where I feel like you're gonna have to choose between Baker and me, or our mission," Porsha admitted.

"Not a chance. Not a chance. Blood is always thicker than water."

Over their meal, Porsha again told Paris about the importance of staying on course. "You've gotta hurry and figure out who is supplying him. Because ain't no use in us getting him out the way if the nigga will still keep on doing his thang once B is gone, you feel me?"

Porsha couldn't help but notice the new jewelry sparkling from Paris' ears and arm. But she didn't say anything. She was just glad they were still working toward their original plan.

"You know, my leave is only thirty days long, we really need to wrap this up," Porsha said.

"Yeah, I've gotta be making my way back to school too. Don't worry, we'll do what we gotta do, and by the time we're through, B, and whoever his boy is, will both pay," Paris said.

They waited in awkward silence for the waitress to bring back change.

"So what are you up to tonight?" Porsha felt funny asking Paris that, but with the way things were going, she couldn't take anything for granted.

"Well, I probably really need to catch up with Baker. I don't want him to start tripping and shit. I mean, I've already invested a lot of time if you ask me, so I want to keep things cool."

Porsha nodded her approval. Paris had a point, the last thing they needed was for Baker to start getting suspicious. That could throw their plan all off. She couldn't wait to see him begging for his life. Paris had no idea, but if it were up to Porsha, she'd kill each one of those no good bastards—one at a time. Porsha found it strange how the police couldn't find anyone responsible for any murders that happened in South Central LA, it was like these niggas were in a constant state of lawlessness. They sold their drugs, did what they wanted and answered to no one.

As she drove Paris back home, she thought about the fact that if the cops were on their job, both she and Paris might be locked under the jail by now. In a sense, she was glad they didn't care about black-on-black crime.

CHAPTER 19

After an entire day of shopping with her mother, Paris was tired and ready to rest her feet. She bought a few small items here and there, but nothing major because Baker had already hooked her up a few days ago. The shopping trip was mainly to spend time with her mother. Lately, Naomi had been complaining about Paris spending more time with Porsha and this new Baker, than her.

Of course every time she could, she got in a word or two about Paris needing to go back and finish her education. It was about four o clock. Paris figured she had enough time for a quick nap before she was to meet with Baker.

Since Naomi had a plans of her own, Paris had arranged for Baker to pick her up at the house. She didn't want to run the risk of him having to meet her mother because she knew Naomi would be full of embarrassing questions. Before going upstairs, Paris yelled back down at her mother. "Ma, I won't be here when you get back, so have a good time tonight."

Paris woke to a light knock on the door. Her mother stuck her head in, "I'm about to leave. I'm meeting your aunt and her new boyfriend there. So I'll see you later?"

Rubbing her eyes, Paris pulled herself up from the pillow. She yawned. I won't be here, I'm meeting Baker. I think we're going to some new club tonight. So I'll see you in the morning."

"Okay, well, be careful and have fun," Noami said.

"Oh, Ma, where are you guys going anyway?"

"It's a surprise. This is all your aunt's doing. I'm just meeting them at the house and we're going from there. I'll tell you all about it in the morning."

Later, when Baker arrived at the house, Paris was purposely dressed in nothing but her robe and sexy underwear. She even had on the furry stiletto slippers he had bought her from the mall.

"Whoa!" she screamed and jumped back when she opened the front door.

Baker stood in front of her wearing a Chocolate colored pinstripped suit, with a butterscotch shirt.

"Damn, you look good enough to eat," she said.

"I was hoping I looked good enough for you to want to tag along with me tonight," he said. "I have a business meeting, you coming?"

"Well, I want to, but I don't think I have anything to wear; nothing that would have me looking as good as you," she teased.

"I thought you might say that. C'mon we've got time to stop by the mall to pick up an evening dress for you." Paris took his hand and put it at her chest. She stared into his eyes.

"Don't worry, we'll get to that later too. Business before pleasure though, okay," Baker promised.

Paris was a bit disappointed; she couldn't help but wonder what he was like in bed. That little voice in her head reminded her that this was not a part of the plan, but still she was curious.

At the mall they quickly bought her a brown laced dress with a pair of shoes to match. The sales lady allowed her to wear it out, and soon they were on their way.

They pulled up at 555 East on Ocean Boulevard in Long Beach. The restaurant was famous for its variety of fine steak cuts. Paris and Baker were having cocktails at the bar because the restaurant didn't seat incomplete parties. As they waited for Baker's friend to arrive, Paris felt herself drawn to him.

She didn't want to go back to school, she just wanted to be his girl. Maybe they could get a place together and she could find something to do without having to leave him.

As Baker got up to go to the bathroom, she started thinking about how she could prove he wasn't involved with Alex's death. She wanted so badly for that to be true.

The way he walked with his sexy swagger made her even more determined to get in his pants. She wondered about his skilled in bed.

When Baker walked back to the bar, he looked at Paris and said, "Our table is ready."

She slid off the barstool and followed as he led the way to their table. Once there, she was surprised to see the older man staring back at her. He looked very distinguished. He was graying at the temples, his fingernails were well-manicured and his teeth were the whitest she'd seen on anyone—especially someone his age. He stood as Paris arrived.

"Perry, this is Paris," Baker said.

"Good to meet you," Perry's voice was deep. It reminded Paris of the late Barry White. "This is Candace," he said pointing to the woman sitting next to him.

"Everybody calls me Candy," she said.

The waiter came and placed water on their table, he stood ready to take their orders. "Mr. Watson, are you having your usual?" he asked Perry.

"Yes, for the ladies the rib eye, and I believe Baker is having the New York strip. A bottle of Moët too," he said.

Paris wondered if she should try and make small talk with Candy, but decided not to. Soon their meals arrived and it didn't matter. They sat silently as the men talked. From what Paris could tell, they weren't discussing anything too heavy or important. One thing she noticed was the way Baker had changed around Perry. He wasn't as thuggish as he normally was. She was glad to see that he could play the role if needed.

Candy looked like she was bored. So Paris smiled at her and said, “Oh, I love your earrings.”

Candy tugged at them. “Oh, these old things? They’re fake,” she shrugged. “Now yours look real nice. They real?”

Paris blushed. “Yeah, Baker got them for me the other day. He’s so sweet.” Candy’s eyebrows went up, she smiled and looked at Baker. Paris hoped she wasn’t getting any ideas. She leaned toward Baker as if to say, he’s mine.

Just as she did, Baker eased her away gently. “Excuse us for a minute,” he said.

When Baker and Perry left the table, Paris looked over her shoulder to make sure they were gone before she started to question Candy.

Before she could get her first question out, Candy leaned in. “Your boobs real?”

Paris looked down at her chest, “Ah, yeah, why? Aren’t yours?”

Candy chuckled, “Girl, nah, I’ve had mine done for wha,t four years now. And I’m telling you, I stay busy too. They were definitely worth the investment,” she admitted.

“So how long have you known Perry?” Paris asked.

“Oh, Perry? He’s cool, I’ve known him for a little while,” she said.

“What does he do? He looks real nice,” Paris said.

“Girl, I have no idea and I don’t even ask. He’s one of my best clients, so when he calls, I come running.” She leaned in to Paris. “Besides, girl, he tips really well.”

Paris frowned. “What are you talking about.”

“Oh, I’m sorry, sweetie, I’m an escort, so Perry pays for the pleasure of my services.” Candy smiled. “With those jugs you got, you’d make out real nice,” she said motioning toward Paris’ bosom.

Paris was beyond speechless. “So you have no idea what he does?

“Darling, I don’t even care what he does. He’s reliable and he spends well,” she leaned in again. “Between you and me though, if I had to guess, I’d put my money on pharmaceutical sales. But he doesn't strike me as the kind who gets his hands dirty, so I'm not really sure. But that's what I'd have to say. We go to a few of these . . ." She used her fingers to do air quotes. ". . . dinner meetings each month. I'm paid to be pretty and quiet. If I'm lucky, he wants me to spend the night," She shrugged. "Now that's the real big bucks."

Paris was glad when she turned her head. She saw Baker and Perry headed back for their table. She cleared her throat to try and shut Candy up.

"I just assumed you were in the biz too, sweetie. I'm sorry."

Paris smiled for fear that saying another word would keep the woman talking. Just then, she felt Baker's hand on her bare back. She jumped at his touch.

"We're done here if you're ready," he said.

"Oh, yeah, I am a bit tired," Paris admitted. She rose from her chair and smiled at Candy. "It was nice meeting you," she said.

"Emmm, me too," Candy offered. "I think you should give some thought to what I suggested," she smiled and looked directly at Paris' chest.

"I'll keep that in mind," Paris lied.

In Baker's truck, Paris wondered what the hell she was doing. Here she was falling for a man who could've very well killed her baby sister. Even if he didn't do it directly, he may be the man responsible for the people who did. It was a constant battle brewing in her mind. Paris knew she was falling for him, and still she tried her best to fight it all the way.

"Where are we going?" she asked.

"I thought we'd go back to my place," he said. "But we don't have to."

"I think that steak is messing with my stomach. All of a sudden, I'm not feeling too well," Paris said.

Baker looked at her.

"I can make it up to you tomorrow night," she promised.

"How you plan on doing that?" He asked.

"Why don't you plan a romantic evening for us, 'cause I can show you way better than I can tell you."

Baker turned to head toward her mother's house. When he walked her to the door, he took her face into his hand. Paris prepared herself for a kiss, but Baker wasn't offering his lips.

"Tomorrow," he said. "I'm not the kind of man who's used to waiting for what he wants."

Paris fought off the chill that was creeping up her spine. "I can assure you I'll be worth the wait." She teased. It took some time, but he did finally break into a smile.

"Well, get some rest tonight, 'cause I like it rough, rugged and raw," he said.

"Is there any other way?" Paris asked.

He chuckled again and moved away so she could go inside.

"Tomorrow night, I promise," Paris said.

CHAPTER 20

Some Crips were having a party at Avalon Park in the bottom on the east side. Porsha had nothing against gang bangers, and something told her if she hung around a bit, she might just be able to find out who killed her sister. Back in the day she used to hang out with the Hoovers, the east coast Crips, the Avalons and even some of the Rolling Sixties Crips gang members. With them, she always had a good time. The liquor stayed flowing and the weed was nonstop.

The thing about them, especially on the east side, was it didn't matter how long you were gone, when you came back, there was always someone who remembered how cool you were back in the day—as long as you *were* cool. And Porsha was always cool because women never saw her as a real threat, and the dudes always looked at her as one of them at times. So that meant her ghetto pass was never revoked.

Mimi was the one who recognized her this time. Back in the day Mimi had been one of the hot girls. She was pretty, with long wavy hair and a nice tight little body. The years had not been good to her at all, but she was still hanging tough with the crowd.

Now Mimi's thin body was a far distant memory, only for those who remembered her back in the day. Her hair was still long and wavy, but her face looked as if it had been run over a few times, and she had a few scars to prove her life had been rough.

"Now I know you ain't been gone that fuckin' long that you don't remember me!" Mimi hollered. She jumped up, nearly jiggling out of her too-small, too-tight outfit.

"Mimi, I could never forget your ass, girl. How you been?"

"Just chillin' with these youngsters," she said, looking around the packed park. "We here celebrating Pookey's birthday. You know how we do it. Oh, girl, I heard what happened to your little sister, but how's um, what is her name? Your twin," Mimi said.

"Paris, yeah she still around, went off to college, but she still keeping it jiggy," Porsha said as Mimi passed her the blunt.

"Girl, I heard you went off to the Army, you still there?"

Porsha nodded. "Yeah, I'm on a 30-day leave, you know after Alex was killed I just needed some time. That shit is fucking with me."

"Girl, I know what you mean. Folks around here dropping like flies though. Shoot, we just buried Junebug last weekend. I know you remember him, don't you?"

"Junebug is dead?" Porsha asked. She wasn't really sure she remembered him, but Mimi seemed so broken up about his death she couldn't disappoint her.

After a while, Porsha was thriving in her old environment. They had the music blasting, and somebody was always passing the forty or a blunt. She felt right at home. When these dudes got up and started Crip walking, Porsha started to join them, but she decided not to.

"Girl, things ain't nothing like they were when we were out here," Mimi told her. "Now, all these young thugs ain't no joke. I mean, they'll kill you for looking at them wrong. Shit, they're slanging more than rocks. Shoot, girl, they selling pussy like they invented the shit, and they're making boocoo money too."

"I was wondering about that. You know somebody turned Alex out and had her strolling Century Boulevard," Porsha said.

Mimi acted like she was shocked. "Girl, no, your little baby sister?"

"Yes, girl, I'm just sick over it too. I just wish I knew who did that shit."

Mimi cut her eyes and cast her stare downward. She pulled Porsha to the side. "Girl, you didn't hear nothing from me. You tell anybody where you heard it, I'll deny I told you that shit. But all I know was I had to hold on tight to my oldest girl. Chil' these fools was trying to pull my baby out on them streets."

Porsha frowned. "How old is your oldest, Mimi?"

"Michelle just made thirteen, but you know she look like she twenty, so I gotta watch her like a hawk. You know these niggas don't care nothing about age," Mimi said.

"But 13, damn that's so young," Porsha frowned.

"Girl, how old you think them girls are, you see walking along Figoura or Century? Chil' them ain't nothing but babies. They found the body of a 12-year-old a few weeks before they found your sister. Girl, these niggas on a whole different level these days."

Porsha didn't know if she was getting more sick or disgusted. Mimi pulled her close.

"Anyway, I don't know if you remember Razor and his brother Nelson. Well, Nelson dead now, but that damn Razor." Mimi looked around the park. "I'm surprised he ain't here. Anyway, chil', him and that brother of his, they the ones who started doing that shit."

"Razor?" Porsha said. She shook her head and struggled to remember him, but couldn't. Porsha went cold for a moment at the mention of Nelson's name, but for the life of her, she couldn't remember his brother Razor.

"He got that nickname 'cause he so damn skinny. Like I said, I'm surprised he ain't here. I'll bet if you hang around a bit he'll show up." Mimi said. "He don't miss no party."

"So you think he had something to do with what happened to my sister?"

Mimi shook her head, "But I'm not sure."

After about an hour, Porsha's patience finally paid off. It was as if Porsha had a sign on her forehead announcing she was the new booty in the park. She had more attention there than she had had in years. But it was attention from a tall, skinny man she cherished most.

Razor was already a bit drunk, but still he looked at her and said, "Where I know you from? You look familiar. I know you, don't I?"

She said, "Nah, I don't think so, but we can get to know each other."

When he suggested they take the party to a bar around the corner, Porsha thought they were finally getting somewhere.

At the little hole in the wall, Porsha started to baby-sit her drink as Razor downed shot after shot. Not long after they arrived, Razor was on the verge of being falling down drunk. Porsha wasn't stupid. She needed to find out more about him, and she had to remain as sober as possible. She never wanted to have to face Paris and say 'ooops, I think we've killed the wrong person again.'

"Aeey, why don't we get on up outta here?" Razor slurred. When she got up, he slapped her on the ass. Porsha jumped.

"I'ma get all up between those thighs," he promised.

The moment Porsha opened the car door and let him in, she wondered whether she should put a bullet in his head. It was a struggle for her, but she decided against it. He pounced on her the moment she climbed behind the wheel.

"I want some pussy," he slurred.

Porsha struggled to push him away. "Look, I gotta get you home or wherever you want me to drop you," she said.

"Look, bitch, a nigga want some pussy. I don't play that teasing shit," he insisted.

She was really struggling to keep her patience with him.

"I once killed me a bitch when she wouldn't act right," he boasted.

That caught Porsha's attention.

"I'm not that nigga to be fucked with," he warned. "I'm serious about mines." Razor started pointing a finger at his own chest. "I wants what I want, you don't believe me?" He looked at her. "It was me and my boy, we had to let this crackhead know. See, you bitches be dangling the pussy then you don't wanna give it up when it comes down to it. I ain't having that shit, and neither is my boy," he said.

"So you and your boy killed a crackhead over some ass? Yeah, whatever," Porsha said, like she didn't believe what he was saying. As she turned the key she looked at him and said, "When was this, back in the day? Nigga, please, you ain't hurting a fly."

"You don't believe me? Shiiit, I'm telling you, I don't play. I'm serious about mines," he grabbed his crotch and shook.

Porsha felt her trigger finger itching. But again she told herself she needed to wait. She wanted to get a line on his boy and she wanted to prove to Paris that they could get it done.

"Where you want me to take you?"

"Let's go to the motel," Razor said.

"Nah, I don't do motels, let's go to your place; a real important nigga like you, I know you got a spot, right?"

Razor shook his head. "Hell yeah, I got me a spot. Take Vernon to Figoura and make a right," he instructed. Razor laid back as Porsha drove.

"You sound real important. That's the kind of nigga I like, all thugged out and shit," Porsha said.

Razor lifted his head and looked at her. "You gon' give me some pussy?"

"May even suck your dick," Porsha said.

"Damn! That's what I'm talking 'bout, boo," he said, before easing back into the seat. He looked out of the window. "Okay, make a right, right here. You gotta park on the street, ain't no parking in the back."

The moment they arrived inside the apartment, Porsha helped Razor onto the sofa. She turned on the big screen TV and a few minutes later he was snoring. The only reason he was still alive was because she wanted to get him and his boy together. She knew his busta ass didn't kill Alex alone.

Porsha walked over to the kitchen, there was nothing in there, not even dishes. She shuffled through a couple of drawers and found useless mail. The cabinets were empty too, she wasn't even curious about the refrigerator.

She looked in on Razor before she went into the bathroom. He was still snoring. She opened the medicine cabinets; nothing in there but a tube of toothpaste, no toothbrushes, but there was an old rusted razor on a shelf.

On her way to the bedroom, she opened a closet door where there was what looked like pieces of a vacuum cleaner. She flipped through a few towels that appeared to be dirty. There were several pairs of old tennis shoes on the floor. When she closed the door, she thought it might wake Razor, but he never even stirred.

She was about to turn and go to the bedroom, when something sparkled and caught her eye. At the right leg of the couch she noticed it again. She crept over quietly and stooped down to get a better look.

When she grabbed at it, it wouldn't move. Porsha got on her knees and pulled at the earring. After closer inspection, she noticed it was the Sapphire A; the very one she had given to Alex herself. Porsha knew what it was, because it was the same one she had stripped from Nelson's dying body.

She stepped back and for the very first time, she knew that her sister had been in that apartment. With her pistol pointed right at Razor's sleeping head, she had to tell herself not to kill him just yet. But oh how she definitely wanted to.

Porsha had to take that to Paris. She had finally found a piece to the puzzle. She wanted to have her ducks all lined up when she went to Paris. No, she wouldn't kill Razor just yet, but his days were definitely numbered there was no doubt.

As she watched his chest rise and fall, she marveled at the fact that he had no idea just how close he had come to dying. Porsha tucked her gun away and walked out, determined to put the entire puzzle together. She was sure by the time it was all over, there would be at least three more dead men in the city of LA.

Just who the walking dead were, depended quite a bit on how they were connected to Razor.

CHAPTER 21

The next day, Paris couldn't wait to get to Porsha. She was hoping that maybe Perry would be enough to satisfy her sister. She had already started visualizing Baker coming to visit her at school. Imagine her having a baller drive all the way out to Bakersfied just to see her. Paris thought she might even try to transfer to Northridge or Long Beach State to be closer to him, depending on how their relationship flourished.

Before Paris could finish brushing her teeth, her mother was at the bathroom door. "Porsha is holding on the line," she hissed.

"Well, I think I may have found the guys who actually killed her, so . . ." Porsha said.

"Oh-my-God, what'd you do? Did you kill 'em?"

"No! I wanted to wait for you. Now, I just have to figure how they're connected to Baker," Porsha said.

"Well, I was just relieved to find out about this guy Perry, that's who's supplying Baker. I'm thinking we should just handle him first, you know that cuts off Baker's supply. Then if we get the other two you're talking about, that's even better."

"Are you okay with the plan still?"

Paris didn't answer right away. Deep inside, she was hoping that by serving up Perry she could spare Baker, and they could live happily ever after. She knew she was living in a fairytale world if she suspected for one second that her sister would allow Baker to live. Porsha made no fuss about the fact that she wanted them all dead.

Paris finally nodded her answer. "I'm good, as a matter of fact, that's why I'm hooking up with Baker tonight. I want to find out as much information as I can," she told Porsha.

"Good, we're doing the right thing here," Porsha said. "All we gotta do is stick to the plan. We need to make absolutely sure this Perry is the man, then we take him out. . . . We get Baker and then these two fools and we're done. It's that simple, just stick to the plan," Porsha reinforced. "If we stick to the plan, we're gonna be just fine."

"Oh trust, I feel you. I feel you," Paris said.

"Good, and don't worry about Baker and his supplier, I have a plan," Porsha assured her.

After spending most of the day and part of her evening with her mother, aunt and sister, Paris was more than ready for some sexual release. She had packed an overnight bag and was ready for Baker to come and pick her up. She didn't want to think about anything but the nice, big dick that would soon be lodged deep inside her. And she was hoping that Baker would know how to lay it down.

The way Destiny had acted up in the mall that day, Paris was sure he had to be working with something special. She recognized Destiny's behavior as being that of a woman who was simply dick-whipped. Paris herself had been there before, and recognized the symptoms.

In the Hummer with Baker, she was a new woman; the seductress had been released. As he drove, she used her fingernails to playfully claw at his chest.

"A real tiger, huh?" He said.

Paris chuckled.

"I thought we'd get a room somewhere, but changed my mind. Let's go back to my place," Baker said.

"We can go wherever you want baby, this is your night. Remember I asked you to plan a romantic night for us? I don't care where we go, as long as we're together," she purred.

When Baker pulled up the street leading up to Baldwin Hills, Paris started getting a bit nervous. Could she really be close to a good fuck? She was hoping so. She started wondering how she'd face Baker on the night they planned to kill him. Then she wondered if she really should've been getting so close to him.

As he pulled into a driveway leading to a gated set of condos, she grew even more excited.

The truth was, she wanted to get fucked, if only for one good time. She was just certain Baker would do right by her, and if nothing else, this would be her way of saying sorry to him before she helped send him six feet under.

Paris didn't know what to expect when Baker opened the front door to his house. Rose petals greeted them at the deep-colored cherry wood entryway. The floor was beautiful. She gasped, then walked down three steps onto the thickest, softest leather shag carpet she had ever seen or felt. Baker stood next to the front door. Paris looked up at the tall, flat fish tank that extended up to the second floor.

"How do you feed the fish in that thing?" she asked in awe.

"Come here, let me show you," he guided her up the cascading staircase onto the second floor landing. Next to the railing was a custom made shelf that stored an array of fish food. "You stand up here, and toss the food right in there. Wait, you can see them swim to the top when they see the food."

"This is nice," Paris said as she watched him toss food into the tank.

She could get used to living living lovely like this; there was no doubt in her mind. The second floor to his condo was just as nice as the first. He had a massive game area with a pool table and a plasma screen TV. His bedroom had a balcony and a bathroom twice the size of her bedroom. Again, rose petals were scattered all over the place.

"I can't believe you live in such luxury," she said.

"Why? You think 'cause I'm all thugged-out I don't know about nice things?"

Paris smiled. "Nah, that's not what I'm saying; it's just . . ." she shrugged as she looked around the room. "From the satin sheets to the rose petals, the ice bucket next to the bed, this looks like something you'd see in a magazine," she said. Paris also knew he probably had a parade of women in and out of there too. But she was determined to become the main one.

Baker placed her bag on the footstool which sat at the foot of his massive California king-sized bed.

Paris jumped when she heard sounds downstairs. "Oh my goodness, did you hear that?"

"*No*, what?" Baker asked.

"There again, you didn't hear that? Sounds like someone's in the kitchen."

"What?" He faked concern. He grabbed Paris by the arm. "We better go see what's going on."

When they arrived downstairs, Paris thought she was gonna die. In the kitchen was a man standing over a massive pot on the stove. He was dressed in a chef's outfit, and a woman was cutting up vegetables on the breakfast island.

"Dinner should be ready in thirty minutes. Have a drink while you wait?" the woman offered.

The minute Baker and Paris walked back to the living room, she leaned over to him and whispered. "Who are those people?"

"Oh, they work at Harold & Belle's," he said easily.

"What?" Paris turned to look back in the kitchen. "You mean at that bomb-ass Creole restaurant on Jefferson, *the* Harold and Belle's?" she asked.

"The only one I know of," he confirmed.

Now Paris was impressed.

After serving dinner the chefs left, Paris and Baker eased onto the sofa and finished their drinks. She was stuffed. Paris was ready to get liquored up and fucked.

"I'd like to go take a shower and change," she whispered in his ear.

"Okay, I need to make a call anyway. But I'll grab the bottle and meet you upstairs. I'll be done by the time you get out. Let me know if you need help washing your back," Baker said.

Upstairs, Paris looked around the bedroom and wondered just how she'd be able to find anything in the meticulous room. Everything was neatly in its place. She quickly stripped naked and rushed into the bathroom. She turned on the shower, but instead of getting in, she crept back into the bedroom and cracked its door. She tiptoed over and began with the dresser drawers.

She opened each one as quietly as possible and shuffled through the neatly folded clothes, using her flat palm to feel her way around the edges of the clothes. After finding nothing in them, she went over to the nightstand near the balcony and did the same.

When she found a leather date book in the nightstand closest to the bedroom door, she flipped through it quickly and glanced toward the cracked door. Confident she found something that might lead her and Porsha to Perry, she made her way back into the bathroom. She stashed the date book in the bottom of her bag and climbed into the shower. Paris closed her eyes and allowed the water to soak her skin.

When she opened her eyes, her heart nearly stopped. Baker was standing there watching her. For a moment she wasn't sure if he had seen her searching through his things. But suddenly he smiled, then moved toward the shower door. The way he washed her body was seductively X-rated. When turned off the shower, she stood for a moment waiting for her body to drip dry a bit.

"It's time to come out," he said, barely able to catch his breath.

When she got out of the shower her pussy was so wet she thought it was water from the shower trapped between her thighs. But she knew better. It was time to get her kitty stroked.

"Okay, but I need you to give me a moment. I want to put on something nice for you," Paris smiled as she stood before him in her moist skin. She could feel his eyes burning through her. She wanted him more than she had wanted anyone else.

His dick was massive and it tilted a little to the side. She couldn't wait for him to tickle her spot.

When he left the bathroom, she dug into her bag and felt around for the book. It was still there. She pulled out a skimpy negligee and slipped into it, along with a pair of stiletto slippers.

When Paris walked into the bedroom the lights were dimmed and soft music played in the background. Baker was lying on the bed, his upper torso propped up by pillows. Paris sashayed over to his dresser, climbed on top and spread her legs. She began to stroke between her legs.

After a few minutes of stroking the wetness, she used the same fingers to suck her own juices.

Baker's eyes hadn't moved.

She squeezed her breasts and released a moan. He tilted his head to the side, as if he was trying to get a better look.

"Ssssss, oooh, Baker," she cooed.

"Damn you a freak to the core," he said.

Paris closed her eyes and spread her legs wider. She was starting to get hotter by the minute. Her fingers moved faster and her breathing was heavy.

Soon, Baker got up from the bed, walked over to the dresser and took her legs into his hands. He stretched them upward, grabbing them at the ankles and without any preparation rammed himself into her.

"Aaaahhhh, you are so fucking sexy," he moaned.

Paris swore she could feel him in the pit of her belly. His dick was bigger than she imagined. She had never had anyone as big, but she was determined to handle it. When he thrust himself deeper into her, she wiggled her hips and pushed back.

CHAPTER 22

The next afternoon Porsha thought about how she just wanted to see Baker dead. She wanted him dead because of his connection to Razor and his road dawg. But mainly because she didn't like the way her sister was losing sight of the mission.

When she turned into the driveway, she waited before getting out of the car. On the drive over, she decided the best way to handle it was to jump into the plan to get to Razor and Dre. If they were all caught up in those two, Paris wouldn't have time to think about Baker, and the bottom line was, she was going to see him dead, even if she had to handle it alone.

Once Paris was in the car, Porsha looked over at her. She looked tired, like she hadn't gotten enough sleep.

"What'd you do last night?"

Paris shrugged. "Didn't sleep much, that's for sure." She eased back into the seat and closed her eyes. When she released a yawn, Porsha decided against talking anymore about the night before. She just had a feeling that Paris was fucking Baker, and the thought didn't make her happy.

It wasn't as much the fact that her sister was getting hers and Porsha wasn't, but she just felt like once dick got involved, alliances were formed. If the dick was good, and by the way Paris looked, Porsha assumed it was, that meant Paris would land on the side of the dick, leaving Porsha to fin for herself.

"You know that this won't last forever, right?"

Paris opened her eyes. "I know. Soon we'll get everybody involved in Alex's murder, then we can go on with our lives. Oh, speaking of which, I need to go back to school next week."

"Oh?" Porsha asked.

"Yeah, moms keeps riding me. Besides, I didn't want to take the entire semester off. If I get back by the end of the month, most of my professors will let me take a makeup mid-terms and I'll be good to go. Anyway, isn't your leave almost up?"

"Girl, I got two more weeks to go, but I feel you. We need to finish this job and get on with our lives like you said."

Porsha turned on to Figoura.

"Okay, I want you to check this fool out. I told you I found Alex's earring here, so I know for a fact she was here. I'm almost certain him and his boy killed her. All we gotta do is somehow get him to lead us to dude and then we do what we gotta do."

Porsha knocked on the door as Paris looked around. It didn't take long for a voice to yell out from behind the door.

"Come on in," it said.

Porsha and Paris walked into the apartment.

When Paris turned around, Razor stumbled backwards. He nearly fell from his chair. Dre, who had just walked into the living room, nearly stumbled himself.

Dre walked forward. "Who the fuck are ya'll?" he shouted at Paris and Porsha.

"I'm Paris," she turned to Porsha. "Is this the dude you were telling me about? Why he tripping like this?"

"Oh, it ain't nothing," Razor said. He pulled Dre back. "It's just you look just like this strawberry we used to know."

Paris shrugged it off. Porsha gave her a knowing look and said, "Well, look, we 'bout to run to the liquor store, what's up?" she gestured.

"Oh, yeah, we down with that," Razor said. "I know last time we hooked up, we didn't really get a chance to you know—

handle our business, but yeah, why don't y'all come back through and we can chill here at the crib." He looked at Dre, "What you think about that, dawg?"

Dre was still staring between Paris and Porsha. "Yeah, that's cool," he said.

CHAPTER 23

About an hour later, Paris wasn't sure how she felt about finally getting the men responsible for their baby sister's senseless murder. She and Porsha had to go regroup. This was their moment. When Porsha said they needed to run to the liquor store, Paris wasn't sure what was going on. But once in the car, and Porsha admitted she wasn't strapped, Paris was glad she thought quickly on her feet.

"So this is it, huh?" she asked her sister.

"Yeah, we're almost there. I want these niggas so bad, I'm creaming just thinking about pulling the trigger," Porsha admitted.

"Damn, like that?"

"Yes, for real," Porsha confirmed.

"Look, why don't you let me off these two?" Paris asked with all seriousness.

"Nah, let me handle that part. I just need you there for back up." Porsha pulled into the Tam's burger stand parking lot.

"Wait, I think I should blast these fools. I mean, you've done it all up to now, let me in on some of the action," Paris all but begged.

"Let's not deviate from the plan," Porsha began. "I pull the trigger, you watch out and back me up just in case something pops off."

Paris got out of the car and ordered her pastrami sandwich as Porsha ordered a burger. They ate at the little stand then hopped back in the car. First, they stopped at a nearby liquor store and stocked up on Remy and Grey Goose.

"You ready for this?"

She was ready, but she wanted in on the action. It wasn't enough that she was just there, she wanted to look those fools in the eyes just before they took their very last breath. Paris wanted them to know that they were dying because they killed her sister. As if she was reading her mind, Porsha looked over at Paris and said, "I just think it's best this way. If I handle the hardware, I'd be the only one held accountable," Porsha said.

"So you think I'd roll over on you if it came down to it?" Paris wanted to know.

"That's not what I'm sayin'. I'm just sayin' that it's best this way. Besides, I'm trained to shoot, you probably don't even know how to fire a weapon. Let's just leave that to me? Cool?"

Paris reluctantly agreed.

This time when they returned to the apartments, they parked around the corner and walked the rest of the way. Back inside the small apartment, Porsha could tell the guys were more relaxed. Or at least they didn't appear as nervous.

"So what's up, y'all, wanna get buck-naked or something?" Razor asked.

Porsha raised the large, brown paper bag she was clutching. "We got some drinks. Why don't somebody hit the music, I like it loud," she said.

"Damn! That's what the fuck I'm talking 'bout. Let's get this party started!" Razor yelled.

Dre turned the TV to BET videos and turned up the volume. Porsha went into the kitchen to mix the drinks. She returned, handed Paris her cup and gave the guys theirs.

The moment Paris took a sip she understood the game plan. Her drink was more water than liquor, and she knew that meant Porsha wanted to make sure they'd stay on point.

Nearly another hour passed, and Porsha and Paris were just wrapping up watered-down drink number one. The guys were starting drinks number three. Signs of them losing their faculties were already present.

Paris knew they were pissy drunk when she challenged them to a drinking contest. The music was loud, and things were getting a little rowdy. Razor had said he wanted them all to fuck in the same room. Dre mentioned he liked a good blow-job. By the time it was over, they were both stumbling all over themselves.

When Razor grabbed at Paris' breast and they both broke out laughing like Dave Chappell was performing an original skit, Porsha stood in front of the TV.

"I have an idea," she said.

"Whassup?" Razor looked at her.

"You guys like handcuffs?" She dangled them in front of her.

Dre looked at Razor and the two busted out in laughter. Porsha didn't wait for an answer. She walked over and clamped the cuffs on Razor's right hand and Dre's left hand. When she was done, Paris walked over and refilled their drinks.

"Oh shit, it's about to be on and popping up in this bitch tonight," he said excitedly.

Dre was slouched down in the chair after the last drink. Razor tumbled next to his chair. They were drunk.

Paris looked at them. "You think they're ready?" she asked Porsha.

"Yeah, I think they're ready," she said, digging into her purse.

When Porsha pulled the gun from her purse, Dre and Razor barely even looked up at her. Paris finally walked over and held Dre's head up so that he could see.

"Wwhaat's—what the hell?" he questioned before slouching.

"You remember Alex, don't you?"

"Fuck yeah, I remember her," Razor answered. "But what about that bitch?" He shrugged..

"Well, she was our sister," Paris spat.

"What?" Dre questioned.

Razor looked over at Dre and confusion settled on his face.

"Yeah, that's right, our sister, my sister—and you fuck-ups picked the wrong person to fuck with. The way you beat her, well, let's just say this is judgment day for you," she pointed the gun first at Razor.

Horror took over his face. He looked back at Dre then at Porsha holding the gun.

"Whoa, hold up a sec here. That was nothing but a misunderstanding with Alex. We didn't mean to kill her ass, shit!"

Dre never said a word. He stared at Paris the whole time Porsha spoke.

"Well, the point is, you killed her, and now, you're gonna pay."

"Well, bitch, don't just talk about it, be about it," Dre said. "Do what you gotta do," he taunted and grabbed his crotch.

Porsha fired one shot to his chest. Before Razor could react, she planted one bullet in the right side of his temple.

"What the fuck is going on here?"

Paris turned and her heart nearly stopped. The gun directed at her went from her to Porsha. "I said what the fuck is going on here?"

"Oh-my-God! Baker!" Paris cried.

When she looked back at her, Porsha had her gun pointed at Baker. "I guess ain't nobody gonna make it out of this bitch alive then, huh?"

"Www-ait, let's chill," Paris said, looking from her sister to her man.

He pointed the gun at her. "I said what the fuck is going on here?" When she didn't answer right away, he pulled the trigger, and lowered his weapon.

Porsha dropped the gun and slumped. Paris lunged for it, grabbed it and fired a shot before Baker knew what was happening.

EPILOGUE

Paris barely avoided jumping the curb and crashing into the pole as she skidded away from the apartments. She couldn't believe Porsha had been shot. After weeks of killing and being so close to death, it had finally come too close to home for her.

"You cannot die on me," she screamed at her sister. "You just cannot die on me! This isn't supposed to be happening like this!" Paris sped down Vernon Avenue and raced toward the Harbor Freeway. She was headed to the hospital.

"I'ma be fine," Porsha whispered.

"You damn right you're gonna be fine. I won't let you die on me, not like this, this ain't how it's supposed to end for us. I need you to hold on!" Paris reached over and offered her sister her hand. "Take my hand and squeeze it. I know you're in pain, but hold on for me," Paris begged.

Her own eyes started filling with tears. They had had their differences, but she couldn't handle losing Porsha now. She didn't want to think about her mother having to bury another child, and she didn't think she could handle knowing this was partially her own fault.

"I'm so sorry, Porsha. I'm so sorry, I should've stuck to the plan. It's all my fault," Paris cried. She pressed the pedal even harder. "Damn, where's the fucking freeway, I've gotta get you to the hospital."

"No!" Porsha screamed. "I can't go to the hospital. How will you explain me being shot? You know they're gonna call the law," she said.

"Ain't no fuckin' way I'm about to let you die. I don't give a fuck what they ask me. I'm not just gonna let you die on me," Paris said. "Shit, we just buried our sister two weeks ago, we're not about to bury you now! You fuckin' hang in there," Paris screamed back.

When she finally found the freeway entrance ramp, she barely slowed to make the curve and drove even faster. No matter how fast she drove, she still felt like she was going nowhere fast.

Paris could hear her sister whimpering. On one hand, she wanted to pull over and comfort her, but on the other, she felt like she could make it downtown to the county hospital. It was the only place she knew to go.

When she saw the signs for downtown, she started to get excited. Paris tried to calm herself a bit. When she saw the exit for Hill Street, she started thinking about her story.

She'd say they were leaving a club, and shots were fired. They were at Mister Jay's downtown; she and Porsha were getting into the car when the shots rang out. They didn't realize she had been shot until they were on their way home.

"You just hang on, we're almost there," Paris sang.

Paris had taken her hand back from Porsha a couple of times and gave it back. This time she noticed the grip wasn't quite as tight.

"I think we should take some time to chill," Porsha said.

"Huh?" Paris kept driving. She could see the building, but with all the one way streets downtown, she didn't want to get too overwhelmed and waste time getting lost. Her sister was getting delirious.

"I've always loved you, Paris. I know we didn't always see eye-to-eye on how to work this plan, but we got it done. And if

I die tonight, I'm happy knowing that we avenged Alex's death."

"Don't start talking about dying, girl. I need you to hang in there. You are way too strong to go out like this. You gotta go back to the Army, I'm going back to school—we did this shit! Come on now, hang in there for me."

"It ain't happening for me. You tell moms I've always loved her, I hate we wasted so much time at war, but let her know I loved her.. Tell my auntie the same. You know the first time I shot a man, I wondered what death would be like, and I gotta tell you . . ." Porsha coughed and Paris cringed. "I don't think it's gonna be that bad. I'm tired. I'm tired and I want to go to sleep. I never wanted you to pull the trigger, because I kinda knew my luck would run out. And I never wanted to put you in a position where you'd face jail time. If they ever ask you about it, you tell them all it was my idea, you tell them how you tried to talk me out of it. Let them know I was really the devil," Porsha said.

Paris didn't respond, she pulled into the hospital's parking lot but she still had a ways to go. She followed the signs leading to emergency and listened to her sister at the same time.

"I killed a man on Catalina Island because he raped me. Alex never told a soul, she never shared my secret and now I just want you to know that what we did here will go to the grave with me. I love you, gir—"

Paris came to a screeching stop at the ambulance entrance for the emergency room. But she was no longer in a hurry. She didn't need the doctors to confirm that her sister was dead. Paris dropped her head to the steering wheel and cried.